SPECIFIC GRAVITY

A Novel by

J. Matthew Neal

Published in the USA by Dunn Avenue Press, Muncie, IN. ISBN 978-0-6151-4137-4

What reviewers are saying about Specific Gravity:

Specific Gravity deserves to be held within the canon of Cook's and Crichton's best . . . Neal has written a first-class techno-medical thriller that readers will find themselves unable to put down. The combination of his experience as a physician and researcher, his natural abilities to create unforgettable characters, and a great sense of plot and pace add authenticity and accomplishment rarely achieved in a first novel.

—*Lee Gooden, Foreword Clarion Reviews*

He's Mensa-smart, as are his male and female protagonists out to solve the riddle of a pharmaceutical company executive's mysterious death. What a pleasure it is to be in intelligent hands. Every explanation—from an escape artist's techniques, to voiceprints, to the workings of antique fountain pens--is unusually engaging . . . when danger finally catches up to her (Mendoza) and her Hardy Boy-like physician partner, your blood pressure rises and your heart starts pounding.

—*John Lehman, Bookreview.com*

"The world is burning in the fire of desire, in greed, arrogance, and excessive ego."

--Sri Guru Granth Sahib

Prologue

Ninety–three million miles away, the glowing yellow orb burned at a temperature of fifteen million degrees Kelvin as it appeared on the horizon of the trendy San Diego suburb at six AM. This sight, paired with the fragrant aroma of morning dew this beautiful April morning, would elicit eagerness to meet the new day from most people. However, John Markham didn't feel particularly appreciative of the weather as he rose from another sleepless night. The complex thermonuclear reactions that allowed the star to provide light and warmth held no significance as he peered eastward from the window of his lavish bedroom suite. But the dying man had far more in common with the giant fusion reactor than he would ever know.

The humiliating nausea and vomiting, which required him to frequently take a handful of disgusting pills, had worsened dramatically over the past several weeks. Ironically, his own company was the manufacturer of some of the hated drugs. He then looked at the empty half of the king-sized bed next to him, remembered how things used to be, and what they had become. A robust giant of industry now reduced to a shriveled medical cripple. He carried only 110 pounds on his meatless five–ten stick of a frame, and had long ago lost his once thick head of salt-and-pepper hair.

The sixty–eight-year old chief executive officer of Clystarr Pharmaceuticals called for his nurse and butler to help prepare him for his appointment, and quietly wished his wife was still there to help care for him. If he had treated her better, maybe she wouldn't have left. But those were the consequences of the things he had done. It was difficult for him to be optimistic as he prepared for his regular appointment with his oncologist, Dr. William Underwood, and he reflected on the privileged life he had led up until now.

Other than problems with his wife Anne, things had been going fairly well for him until nine months ago, when one of his young bedmates noticed a lump in his neck. Not one to go to his physician regularly, he ignored it until three months later, when it had tripled in size. By that time, several other lumps had appeared, and a visit to his physician confirmed his worst fears: cancer—specifically, a high-grade lymphoma. Fortunately, he had been told by Underwood this type of lymphoma usually responded well to chemotherapy and radiation. But he appeared to be one of those "other" cases, and the famous Markham luck had finally run out. The brain scans showed continued infiltration of his nervous system, and his bone marrow was full of tumor cells.

After dressing, he ate a small fraction of the breakfast prepared by one of the servants and was helped to his chauffeured car. His younger daughter Kristin had now arrived to travel with him to his appointment. The driver made his way from the large circular drive of the estate as he pondered the solemn fact he could no longer drive, as his visual and coordination problems had worsened. The brief ten-minute ride to the medical pavilion seemed to take forever.

The chauffeur parked the Mercedes sedan in the handicapped parking lot of the Parkwood Medical Center building on outskirts of the city. He was helped by Kristin and the driver into a wheelchair, which they pushed into the building on the way to the familiar elevator leading to the second floor.

They arrived at Parkwood Oncology Associates to see Underwood, where he also routinely saw the radiation oncologist, Dr. Bhavin Agarwal. They were greeted by the receptionist and escorted immediately to Underwood's private office, since there was no waiting for the CEO of Clystarr Pharmaceuticals. Five minutes later, a tall, thin man in his late fifties entered, wearing a wrinkled white coat whose pockets were filled with cheap pens advertising various Clystarr products.

"Hi John . . . Kris," Dr. William Underwood said cheerfully.

"Hello, Bill," he replied.

"How are things?"

"Cut the bullshit—tell us the news."

"John—I want you to know we've tried everything. The chemo, radiation, nothing seems to be working." Underwood pulled up his CT (computed tomography) scan on the large computer monitor at his desk for their perusal. Film X-rays were a thing of the past; everything was now digital, available at the touch of a button.

He stared blankly at the screen for two minutes. "Things look pretty bad, don't they?"

Underwood looked down at his desk. "Yeah. Your latest CT shows definite signs of progression. The lumbar puncture fluid also demonstrates persistent lymphoma cells consistent with the original cell type. This is despite having received thirty Gray—the maximum radiation dose—and multiple courses of aggressive multi-drug chemotherapy."

"I want more radiation and chemo, then. Can't Agarwal just give me more radiation, dammit?"

"No, he can't, because you'd lose significant higher brain function. We tried that experimental platinum drug, and we also have some monoclonal antibody products to try, but it's still palliative at best."

He scowled in disbelief. *"Higher brain function?* If I'm dead, who gives a shit about my goddamned brain?"

"You'd be a vegetable, not aware of your surroundings, or with any meaningful cognitive function as you know it. You don't want to live like that."

"What about a bone marrow transplant?" Kristin asked. "I've called around, and that should be our next step."

"I've thought about that, Kris. But we can't use his marrow because it's too infiltrated with tumor cells. I know M.D. Anderson Cancer Center told you the same thing—I talked to the chief of hematology there."

"Stephanie or I can be donors. We're both compatible."

"The problem is—he'd never survive it, Kris." Underwood turned to him. "We'd have to completely eradicate your existing marrow with what essentially amounts to lethal doses of radiation and chemotherapy. It would kill you in your current state."

He knocked a year's worth of unread medical journals off the desk. "A Hobson's choice, then—either the treatment kills me, or the lymphoma does. I'm not going to live at all, am I?" he asked angrily, realizing his physician was brutally honest with his patients. "Bill? Answer me, goddamn it."

Underwood paused for a moment. "No, you're not. You're going to die within the next couple of months. I don't know how else to say it—I'm sorry."

"You said at the beginning there was an eighty–five percent remission rate," Kristin said loudly, pointing her finger at the physician. "What the hell went wrong?"

"I know, but that also means a fifteen percent failure rate. I don't know what we could have done differently. We've been through all this."

Markham continued to feel numb over what was essentially a death sentence. He'd never taken very good care of himself; like many highly driven executives coming up in the 70's and 80's, he drank too much, smoked too much, and didn't get enough sleep. He also felt like he might be dying alone. M.D. Anderson Cancer Center in Houston and Cleveland Clinic had given him the same grim prognosis.

"None of this is a surprise to me, Bill. I knew it was coming, I just had better hopes."

"We can keep you comfortable. I know you don't want to be in the hospital, with all the company visitors and such. I'll be there for you."

"I'm sorry I got mad at you," Kristin said. "It's just hard."

"I know you probably want some time alone. Stay here as long as you want. I'll be back to check on you in a little bit."

He cried while his daughter checked her personal digital assistant to review her appointments for the day. Recently he'd separated from Anne, whom he had neglected for many years. He had participated in several extramarital affairs during the last twenty years, but became angry when Anne finally cheated on him. Many associates thought he was now getting what he deserved. He had hopes they might be able to get back together;

now, he only saw her on rare occasions when she needed to get something from the house. She had filed for divorce and was in the process of appraising the estate.

Although Kristin often went with him to physician visits, he felt closer to his older daughter Stephanie Farren, who lived in San Francisco and came up every other weekend. Stephanie was divorced and dabbled as an artist and sculptor, and had little to do with the operations of Clystarr. He knew Kristin wanted it that way.

After the diagnosis, he became optimistic and decided to go on a health kick. He began consuming expensive health food supplements and drank only expensive, ultra-purified bottled water (made by one of Clystarr's food subsidiaries, of course). Since about seventy–five percent of the body's fat-free mass was water, it seemed like a wise investment at the time. Unlike most of the investments in his storied career, however, this one didn't pay off any dividends.

His only comfort was that Kristin would continue managing Clystarr with the same vision he had when it was in its heyday. His greatest fear was a quick sale to another company, but Kristin had promised never to do that. As cold and distant as she often seemed, she had never lied to him.

Before leaving, he was to give a routine urine sample. The left-handed Underwood wrote out the order on a prescription pad with a hefty vintage Rettermann fountain pen his wealthy patient had given him as a gift. He had also had given Underwood bottles of ink he had recently mixed himself. The ink flowed like no other, as it seemed more viscous than usual ink and smeared less with their left-handed writing. He knew Underwood put the cheap pharmaceutical pens in his white coat to humor him, and never actually wrote with the pathetically inferior styli.

He pulled out his bottle of expensive water and took a sip. The label read, "Quattra Super Premium Drinking Water—Arsenic Free, Chlorine Free, Chemical Free." One wouldn't think regular water would contain arsenic, but you could never be too careful. He took a few more sips, left the bottle on the table in the office, and forgot about it as he and Kristin left.

Chapter One

Dr. Alexander Dirk Darkkin woke up on the humid morning with the familiar sensation of a jackhammer breaking his head open. The temperature was already eighty–five degrees on the Saturday morning in Nashville. On the bedside table lay several empty beer bottles, tumblers that once contained Tennessee bourbon whiskey, and an ashtray filled with cigarette butts.

Next to him was another staple of his existence: an attractive twenty–something redhead he had met the night before at a bar. The hangovers made him again vow to quit drinking and smoking so much, but he obviously needed to try a new approach. The irony of smoking brought a twisted grin to his face. He was a radiation oncologist—a physician who treated cancer patients by using radiation—inhaling thousands of different carcinogenic chemicals. Cigarette smoke also contained trace amounts of polonium-210, one of your more toxic radionuclides.

About the other problem, a colleague recommended he start going to Alcoholics Anonymous meetings again. He'd always denied he had an addiction, but the growing body of evidence was becoming difficult to ignore.

He caressed his female companion, who was still asleep, and eventually rolled out of bed and got ready for the shower after cleaning up the bedroom. He was usually tidy but had slipped in the fog of the last few weeks.

The young woman woke up. "Hi, Alex. You were really great last night."

"It was good for me too, Angie," he drawled as he patted her on the bottom. An extensive discussion of Tolstoy, Renaissance art, or quantum mechanics seemed unlikely to occur. But he hadn't chosen her with those activities in mind.

"Jeez—my name's Alicia. That's the third time you called me the wrong name." Her manner turned suddenly from happy to sour.

"Sorry." He didn't remember the names of many of his lady friends in the morning. Names just seemed to complicate things. "I'll fix us some breakfast."

"No, that's all right—I have to get to work at Super-Mart by ten, anyway." She picked up her purse, obviously peeved he'd forgotten her name. "Well, I'll see you."

"Yeah, right—later." At least the machinery worked properly last night—something that had been an intermittent problem the previous few months. Things usually didn't go well when that happened; most of his bedmates left if there was a failure to launch. But such was life in the superficial lane. His psychologist said intimacy and commitment issues were the cause of his periodic difficulties. Shrinks—what the hell did they know, anyway? They were probably crazier than he was.

Alicia left while he got up and went into the shower, where he reflected on his life during the last few weeks. The hot water stung the red welts on his neck and chest from where he had come in contact with her cheap jewelry. Stupid nickel allergy—he was unable to wear or come in contact with any nickel-containing alloys because of this problem.

He took three ibuprofen tablets for the headache and put on a pot of coffee to help him think about what he was going to accomplish today in his tiring, monotonous routine. Was there purpose for his existence on Earth? Blessed by affluence, health, and intellect, he was envied by many, although viewed by others as arrogant and self-centered. That meant he had nobody to blame for his problems but himself. The quest for perfection apparently had fallen short.

• • •

Alex's phone rang at seven-fifteen that evening. He spied the 865 area code, which usually meant an incoming call from Oak Ridge, 150 miles away. The number was unfamiliar, but his paranoid caller changed it all the time. He didn't get many calls from his birthplace any longer. Didn't want to.

"What's up, Dad?" he said in a tepid tone.

"Hey," the deep, raspy voice said. "What's going on, Dirk? Where the hell you been?"

His father always called him that, but he'd always preferred his first name. His sister went by her middle name, and one of them with an alliterative moniker was enough. "Busy. I'm getting ready to go somewhere."

"Where are you, heh, going? On vacation again? Seems like your whole life's a goddamned holiday."

"San Diego."

"Visiting Wendy? Hell, you're as different as night and day."

"Not visiting. I'm doing a *locum tenens* for a friend of hers for a few months. Part time. Pay's pretty good, and I need some breathing room." A *locum tenens* physician was one who filled in for another physician for a period of time when no other coverage was available.

"Next thing I know, you'll be out there for good."

"Don't think so, Dad. Just another path on my journey."

"Yeah. Your journey to nowhere, just like always."

The dysfunction—his father was always trying to start a fight, to draw the attention away from himself. "Was there something you needed?"

"No, not like you give a crap about how I am. And say hello to my grandson I've never seen when you get there."

"Whose fault is that? You alienated her, so what the heck do you expect?"

"Nothing from anybody. I wish I was dead, anyway. This year will be my last Christmas."

"This is going to be your twentieth straight 'last Christmas', isn't it? How are you going to kill yourself this year?" He recalled the wonderful childhood memories of high drama at holiday time.

"Shit—what do you, heh, think you'll find out there? You think your saintly sister can solve all your problems?"

"In case you didn't know, I'm really not seeking your sage advice."

"Yeah, you sure know it all. I hope you can quit drinking, though. You know I couldn't. But we're the same, you and I—you've got my genes."

"Only half of them, fortunately, thanks to meiosis. I view it as a glass half full rather than half empty."

"You can't run from who you are, son. Just, heh, remember that I'm always here for you if you're in trouble."

"That's always great to know. Nice talking to you too, Dad." He slammed down the phone. Why did he let his father get him so angry? He wished he could simply ignore the needling. There had been good times in the past, but that was long ago. But, despite his father's problems, Alex knew he'd do anything he could to help his children. Could Alex change his life, though? Or had his DNA programmed him to become another Rad Darkkin?

The tall, light brown-haired physician needed to burn off some energy and decided to straighten up his apartment. The cleaning girl who came every two weeks always seemed to leave a few things dusty, including the few framed photos on his living room shelf. Jenny's picture was still there. He had recently broken up with his girlfriend of two years, Jenny Mortensen, a financial advisor in Nashville. Jenny was gorgeous and had a brief career as a model in her early twenties. But he had ignored her more and more in his failed pursuit to become one of the "players" in the Nashville scene.

Jenny had hoped for a commitment, a word that meant little to him. After several tries to alter his mind proved fruitless, she broke the relationship off, as he obviously had little interest in altering his dysfunctional state. As usual, he wanted what was best for him.

He made coffee, continued dusting his few photos, and picked up the framed 8x10 of his sister's wedding party. God, that seemed so long ago—ten years, wasn't it? She was only twenty-four then, and he twenty-six. He tried to remember the other people in the wedding party. Stan, her husband, was someone he never got along with. The maid of honor was some friend from her medical school class. Stan's two sisters were bridesmaids, as well as Wendy's young deaf friend, whose name he couldn't remember, since he'd been pretty loaded that night. His father also had been so drunk he was about to fall over. Wendy had lots of friends, it seemed. Where had all his gone?

He looked at his mother's photo and observed how he had her features—his sister looked more like their father. But that was the end of Wendy's resemblance to Dr. Conrad Darkkin—*he was his father's child*, his mother Marianne had told him emphatically years ago after an argument. Like a stereotyped, self-fulfilling prophecy, he was slowly morphing into the old man—a troubled person gifted by high intellect, yet cursed by personal problems.

Where was he headed ten years ago? He had just graduated from medical school and was preparing to begin his four-year residency in radiation oncology, an option he pursued partly due to an interest in nuclear physics inspired by his father. The other reason had been that it was lucrative with ample time off for other pursuits; he certainly didn't want to take care of whiny sick kids like his sister. The practice in Nashville had been profitable, but he had gone to half-time two years ago to further develop the software firm that he started five years ago. DarTech provided sophisticated radiographic imaging and dosimetry solutions for radiology centers, and was one of the leading firms of its kind in a small niche market. Maybe he had done a few things right, after all. But they didn't make him happy.

The morning sadness that had enveloped him for the last several months was worsening exponentially each day. He knew his dependence on alcohol was partially responsible, and that he was probably clinically depressed. One of his colleagues even tried to turn him on to religion, but he didn't believe in any omnipotent "higher power." His mom had a strong religious upbringing and had tried to infuse faith into the family. Some of it took on his sister, but it failed miserably on the Y chromosome-possessing members of the family.

Wendy had been bugging him for months to come fill in for her radiation oncologist friend for six months, and San Diego was a nice place all year. Southern California would be a blast for a while, and then he'd move on again. He didn't like to commit himself too far into the future—that just wasn't for him.

Chapter Two

The cinnamon-colored woman's thick hair shimmered in the morning sunlight like polished obsidian as she was led into the jail by the San Diego County sheriff, a man in his fifties, and a deputy, a woman in her mid-thirties. They were accompanied also by a TV reporter and camera crew, while a large crowd formed outside. A number were children holding action figures that resembled the woman. Her father bid her goodbye as she went in, although the officers made sure he didn't touch her.

"Hey, Carlos," a man in the crowd yelled to the woman's father. "Your kid in the pokey again? She can't stay out, can she?"

"No, it's almost as if she likes it," the trim sixty-year old man laughed as she was led in. "We try to make it a big family outing. But, anyway, is the hot dog stand still open? I'm hungry."

The five–nine woman, in her late twenties, was clad in a well-fitting pressed orange cotton jumpsuit and matching sneakers, with her hair tied behind in braids. She wasn't allowed hair clasps, pins, or metal devices of any kind, because of their concern she would turn them into some type of weapon or escape device. She was not unusual in appearance, except for the two quarter-sized buttons on the sides of her head that were connected to small devices that went behind each ear. She had worn a cochlear implant since she was thirteen, a result of the devastating illness that took away her hearing and most of her memory two years before that.

"What a beautiful day outside. A fine way to spend a nice Saturday morning in May," the speech-impaired yet oddly verbose woman said in her typical slow, lispy, high-pitched voice. "It is a shame I am spending it in here. But, do you like my new jumpsuit, officer?"

The deputy looked at her name embroidered in gold letters on the back of the velvety garment. "Oh, yes, it's the nicest I've ever seen. About this morning, you're the one who chose to be here," the female officer in the room laughed as she fastened the prisoner's ankle chains with a padlock to an eyebolt in the middle of the room. "We drew lots for this assignment and I got lucky. I wanted to see for myself—they say you're really something."

"Yes, something that is very dangerous," she said in her characteristically stilted speech as she squinted down menacingly at the woman officer. "Were I not so encumbered, you and your colleague would be in big trouble. I am like a container of nitroglycerin—stable when calm, but extremely hazardous when agitated."

The average-sized female officer laughed after a pause, no doubt to decipher what she had said, but the orange-clad woman was used to that from new acquaintances. "Have fun," she said as the closed the door to the old jail cell.

"I shall—I always enjoy this," she said happily, glancing down at the waist chain with handcuffs, attached to leg shackles separated by a fourteen-inch chain. "I'll see you soon, as I'll be walking out right before your eyes. There is nothing that can be done to stop me."

"You're loco, just like you've always been," the sheriff said, shaking his head. "There isn't any way you're going to get out of here."

"You pitiful minions of the law are mistaken, and overconfidence shall again be your undoing," she declared dramatically, not entirely certain if they understood her proud boast or not.

It was common for very dangerous criminals—murderers, bank robbers, and kidnappers—to be locked up in such a fashion. However, the woman wearing makeup, tailored orange jumpsuit, and fifteen pounds of steel had never even had a traffic ticket. And, despite her campy trash-talking and build, she'd never appeared terribly dangerous, although she sure didn't look like the kind of gal you'd want to pick a fight with.

Bonita ("Bonnie") Mendoza was a singular individual with a peculiar hobby—master escape artist. The twenty–nine-year old scientist had become a minor local celebrity because of her adeptness at breaking out of jails and other confinements. She also wanted to set good examples for young girls and boys—to be the best you can be despite whatever obstacles life puts in your way. She was, at first glance, an unusual-looking role model, though.

Although female magicians were fairly common, female escapologists were distinctly unusual; there were perhaps a handful of good ones across the country. Part of the reason for their rarity was that the more difficult escapes required a great deal of upper body strength in addition to flexibility. Escape from a regulation straitjacket, for example, required pulling and contortion that would leave even the most skilled performer sore for days. Curious spectators wanted a peek at *Mendoza the Miraculous,* a strange amalgam of flexibility, strength, speed, and intellect, who used her knowledge of science to aid in her unusual escapes.

The deaf conjurer was conned into this stunt by her best friend to raise $10,000 for children's cancer research. If she succeeded, the money would be donated by Clystarr Pharmaceuticals. The media were always interested in her capers because she was an amateur who never performed for her own gain, but exclusively for children's charities or other worthy causes. Besides, she was better and more entertaining than many professionals. Her only stipulation was that no one be allowed to monitor her with cameras while in the cell. Today, she had a maximum of thirty minutes to escape and be free of all constrainments.

She had been allowed to examine the cell several days earlier, but was searched to ensure that she did not plant any escape devices there. The old jail was mainly used as a museum, maintenance center and warehouse, and was no longer used to house real prisoners.

A squad car had earlier brought her to the jail, to add dramatic effect. The female officer had patted her down earlier, and ran a portable metal detector over her from head to toe; it was sensitive enough to detect a small key or other small piece of metal hidden on her person. The officer also examined inside her mouth, but nothing was found. The officers were perplexed by how she was going to pull this off. That was her secret.

Many wondered how someone became indoctrinated into the secret society of the escapologist, and why anyone would do that. There was no single path for the education of a magician, and no textbooks, Web sites, or video courses on how to be an escape artist. Most magicians learned their craft from others, and had some competency in all areas of specialization, but many would emphasize one area.

Membership in magicians' societies also required taking an oath that the secret of an illusion never be revealed to a non-magician. Most magic required the use of sleight of hand and trickery, and audiences typically were aware of this; however, revealing the "secrets" of magic would simply reduce the illusions to mere intellectual puzzles and riddles. This rule also preserved the secrets of professional magicians who performed for money.

Escapes weren't really mystical, and this one would be difficult. Proper execution required preparation and demanding attention to details. She would need a key to open the jail door, if she even freed herself from her shackles. She had been allowed earlier in the week to open the door with the key. Hidden on her person had been a piece of clay to imprint both sides and the edge of the key, to ensure proper thickness. The clay had then been used to make a short, stubby key. And, most importantly—any decent escape artist needed an equally talented assistant; hers had that makeshift key as well as any others she would need.

The contraption she was placed into was almost impossible to escape from. A metal chain was placed tightly around her waist. Her handcuffs were "sandwiched" inside an aluminum alloy box, attached to the waist chain, and locked with a padlock. As well as restricting movement, the box prevented any access to the keyholes, even if in the wearer were in possession of a key. Her ankles were encased in larger versions of the handcuffs—"leg irons"—connected together by a fourteen-inch chain.

Everything was going according to plan, assuming her partner showed up on time. But there were food vendors outside, and her assistant sure liked to eat.

• • •

The six-one, disheveled, and bearded worker walked up to the side gate of the old jail while carrying a set of plumbing tools. He had long, greasy dark hair and wore dirty, oily overalls, and his name tag identified him as a plumber.

The overweight officer at the door stopped him. "Hey, chief—where you think you're going? Can't go in there today—there's some special event going on."

"Gotta fix a leak in the old soil pipes, officer," the plumber said in a hearty Southern drawl. "Boss man said to shut the toilets down today. Whole place will stink like crap if it ain't done."

"I didn't hear anything about it, buddy."

"You wanna get us both fired? My ass sure ain't gonna be responsible!"

The officer looked at the name tag and paused for a few seconds. "Bud Raleigh, huh?" He looked through Bud's toolbox, which contained typical plumbers' tools, as well as a long black tubelike device. He then looked at Bud's hands, which were oily, rough, and callused. "What's that?" the officer said, pointing to the long black device.

Bud laughed and scratched his scraggly beard. "Ain't you never seen a snake before?"

"Snake?"

"To ream out the old pipes where they're clogged."

"Huh. Well, okay, Bud, I guess you can go through. But get finished as soon as you can."

"Yessir, and thanks for givin' the workin' man a break." Bud took out the dog-eared men's magazine that was rolled up in his overalls. "Hey, you wanna read my girlie mag? I don't need it no more—I done read all the articles," he said as he winked.

"Sure thing—kinda boring here. Thanks, man!" the officer said as he eagerly grabbed the pulpy periodical and excitedly perused the many pictures of scantily-clad, busty young ladies. The articles would have to wait.

Bud went in the side door and turned on a radio attached to a small earphone, where he heard a transmission from a second man. "Doc—the handcuffs are Smith & Wesson 94's, the soda machine key type. The leg irons look standard. Padlock on the belly chain is a pin tumbler Trinity."

"Great. Got it," Bud replied in a somewhat higher-pitched voice than he used a few minutes earlier. He had, in his tool box, almost a hundred different catalogued keys, one of which would match the description of what his confederate had observed earlier with binoculars. He looked like a typical workman, albeit with longer hair than most, but otherwise not unusual. A bit of careful observation, however, would've revealed the plumber had a very small thyroid cartilage, or Adam's apple. Dutiful inspection of his hands would have also exposed latex calluses on the back of the hands that peeled off. But the calluses on the palms were real—earned from years of lifting Olympic barbells.

Dr. Mary Gwendolyn Williams wasn't just *Mendoza the Miraculous'* best friend and magic assistant—she was an amateur theater enthusiast who took pride in her ability to disguise herself as various unusual personalities. The mezzo-soprano's three-octave vocal range coupled with her stature also allowed her to easily pass for the opposite gender.

Most people didn't know most handcuffs opened with a standard key, but there were dozens of oddball exceptions that always seemed to surface at escape challenges—assistants needed to have a working knowledge of keys and have them on hand. The cylindrical key for the handcuffs would be the most difficult. There were sixteen different key combinations for that model, Bonnie had told her. Luckily, she had a master cylinder key that could open all the different sets, and Bonnie could open most other standard tumbler locks with a set of picks.

The large woman poured water from a bottle of "Quattra" drinking water into a small ice cube tray into which the required keys had been placed. A small cryogenic cylinder of liquid nitrogen was then removed from the toolbox and attached to a nozzle. After donning a set of safety glasses and gloves, she sprayed the water with the liquefied gas, freezing the keys instantly at a temperature of -235 degrees Fahrenheit. Then she removed the ice cubes from the tray.

She went to a large plastic drain pipe whose diameter was four inches. "I don't get how this works, Wendy," the shorter Miguel ("Mike") Mendoza said as he joined her on the third floor under the guise of another worker. He was dressed in similar greasy overalls, and sported a fake mustache and black wig to augment his closely cropped hair; he was present as a "backup" in case she didn't get into the jail. "How is all this paraphernalia going to help my sister bust out of here?"

"You should never doubt the scientific ingenuity of M-Square." She removed a PVC plastic tee fitting from the toolbox and set it on the floor. It was a "vampire tap" fitting, used to tap into an existing drainpipe.

"If anybody flushes while we're doing this, you'll be glad you have those overalls on."

"Don't worry about it—there's no one else in the building. It's all administrative offices and a museum, and it's Saturday." She affixed the fitting and used an Allen wrench to pierce the drain pipe. She then introduced a small plastic balloon into the pipe and inflated it. Any flushing above her would be stopped by the balloon, made of water-soluble plastic that would degrade in about thirty minutes. A second balloon was then introduced, which would require placement with greater care. It was attached to a weight and was inserted exactly twenty feet and six inches, and a tube inflated the balloon at its destination. She then used a special long Olympus fiberoptic endoscope to verify its placement. For the next thirty minutes, the drain was now sealed for approximately twenty feet. She finally flushed the "special" ice cubes into the drain pipe with a gallon of drinking water.

"I still don't understand. I'm no Bonnie, but I'm no dunce, either—the ice will float on the water, not sink. How will she get the cubes? The water won't go *up* through the cleanout."

"Without the water, there'll be insufficient force to take them to her cell level. But these particular ice cubes will sink—trust me on this."

• • •

A few minutes later, Bonnie kicked her shoes off. She needed to use her feet, as her hands weren't very useful in their current position. She had tried flexing her ample abdominal muscles when they applied the belly chain, hoping to get some slack to slide it off. Unfortunately, her waist was too thin and pelvis too wide for that to make any difference. She could usually count on getting some slack at magic shows where lay people predominated, but not with police officers, who understood such tricks. But there was always a backup plan.

She knocked off the access panel to the drain pipe. The cleanout plug had earlier been removed and greased, making it easier for her to remove it with her feet. Although no easy task, she had practiced it to perfection a dozen times on a replica. After a few tries, the plug popped out. The cleanout drain was at forty–five degrees to the floor, and therefore the water couldn't come out. The lower balloon was expertly placed about a half inch below the cleanout plug.

She looked inside and spied Wendy's ice cubes at the bottom. Inside her bra had been hidden a plastic goldfish scoop, and no one had noticed the small-breasted woman's extra "padding." She was barely able to unzip her orange jumpsuit in front and twist the bra open enough to get it out. Once out, she was able to, with her nimble feet, fish the cubes out and flip them onto the floor.

The cubes thawed quickly, releasing the keys. One was a standard handcuff key that would work on the leg irons, but not the high security handcuffs, which used a different key. The second cube had contained the cylindrical tool as well as the standard lock pick. Finally, the third cube contained the makeshift cell door key.

The handcuff key was useless right now as she had no access to the keyholes that were covered by the security box. She used the lock picks to remove the standard four-pin padlock, which took four minutes to defeat. This allowed her to remove the box encasing the handcuffs. The cylindrical lock pick was rotated to any one of sixteen different combinations until she found the correct one to remove them. The makeshift cell door key was a little rough, and it took her almost five minutes to get that door open. After the cell door was opened, she put the keys into the cleanout plug and closed the access door. In five more minutes the balloons would disintegrate, and no evidence would be found.

She went out into the hallway and entered a restroom with several lockers. She opened one that had a combination lock and retrieved the designer skirted suit, white blouse, pumps, and sunglasses that she'd placed there previously.

Bonnie strolled out the side door and thrust her hands into the air, as she had escaped with seven minutes to spare. A crowd of about eighty people let out a cheer, and a local TV reporter thrust a microphone into her face for comments. Another reporter and the police officers went back to the cell, where they found nothing except for the empty shackles, and appeared truly dumbfounded. They asked how she did it, of course, but she would never tell. Such a revelation would violate the sacred "magicians' code."

The plumber with oil on her face had cleaned up and removed her overalls, wig, makeup, and faux beard to reveal her natural shoulder-length blonde hair, casual top, and shorts. The liquid nitrogen, key assortment, endoscope, and other tools were carefully placed within the hidden compartment of the toolbox and left in a storage bin for later retrieval.

"You owe me big time," she said to Wendy while pointing a finger. "When you win this award for having raised the most money, you'd better mention me."

"Of course—we're partners," Wendy said, as a mid-level Clystarr executive presented Bonnie with the check for $10,000. Bonnie knew her friend wanted to be the number one fund-raiser for pediatric cancer research in San Diego, and also had potential political ambitions for her medical society. After all, it was all for charity.

Chapter Three

The family members of John William Markham stood in vigil on May twenty–third in the bedroom of his estate in suburban San Diego. He and the family had decided long ago that he would die there, rather than in an undignified fashion in the hospital. The grim fate seemed certain to Dr. William Underwood, given his patient's total lack of response to the best of medical care.

At his bedside were his estranged wife Anne, plus daughters Kristin Markham and Stephanie Farren. A nurse was with Underwood by the bedside, and they waited patiently as Markham took his last breath. He had been unable to eat or drink for days, and was only being sustained by intravenous fluids and nutritional supplements. The family had decided, per his wishes, that no heroic measures would be taken to sustain his cachectic, tumor-infiltrated body.

"I'm sorry. He's gone. We've done all we can." Underwood shook the hands of all the family members, while Anne and Stephanie gave him a hug.

"Bill, you've been a good friend to John. I don't know what else you could've done," Anne said without affect. Underwood knew that she was quite weary of the whole ordeal and was glad that it was over so she could start liquidating the estate.

He put his hand on Anne's shoulder. "There was nothing anyone could do. He went down faster than anyone I could remember. You don't have anything to feel guilty about."

Stephanie was almost hysterical, in tears. The late-thirtyish, five–five redhead had flown down from San Francisco and had been there for the last two weeks, although prior to that she hadn't seen him daily as Kristin had. Kristin was her usual emotionless self and was busy returning calls on her cell phone.

The doctor excused himself into another room while the family grieved. The funeral home attendants would be by to pick up the body soon, and he waited to sign the death certificate. He made certain to dispose of the urine catheter bag after noticing how clear and dilute it looked. He sure didn't want *that* lying around when they came.

• • •

Several hundred Clystarr employees, friends, media representatives, and family members were present at Markham's funeral three days later. The service was held at the Presbyterian church where he was a member of the parish council. Various clergy and community members gave eloquent eulogies about the wonderful corporate magnate's life and the people his company's products touched. There was no mention of the billions of dollars' profit that he had made, and of his multimillion dollar estate. This was at a time when many Americans were unable to afford prescription medicines. No one begrudged the man making a good living, but the multiple estates on several continents, corporate jets, and dozens of luxury automobiles were a bit tough for the average American to swallow. Also, no one wanted to talk about his many extramarital affairs, womanizing behavior, and people he'd stepped on to get there.

The family disagreed over the body's disposition. Anne and Kristin confidently argued that he wanted to be cremated. Stephanie said otherwise, stating that she didn't know of any prior intent on his part about cremation. However, Anne still had the final say on the body's disposition. Many thought it odd how quickly Anne wanted to dispose of the body. At least Anne and Kristin agreed with Stephanie to bury the ashes rather than scatter the cremains, which was legal in California.

Stephanie approached Kristin at the cemetery afterwards, and gave her younger sister a token hug. "Well, I bet you're glad this is over, Kris."

"What do you mean?"

"I just meant that it must've been hard for you the last few weeks with your schedule, being with him every day."

"At least I was there, Steph. You could have spent more time here, you know."

"I'm sorry, it was just hard to see him like that. It's easier for you—you just live a few miles away. I was here as much as I could."

"I know, I didn't mean to say that. We will all miss Dad."

"Right. So, when do you get to be CEO—tomorrow? You're the big president, after all."

"I haven't thought about that, for God's sake. The Board will make that decision when the time comes."

"Of course you have. There's no reporters here—just you and me, two sisters sharing the truth. It's what you always wanted, you know. You've been waiting for this day for a long time."

"What are you trying to start? This isn't the time for you to bitch at me."

"I'm not trying to start something, just being honest. Don't lie to me."

"So, because I worked hard to be company president, that means I'm glad he's dead? God, you're nuts."

"I didn't say you wanted him dead. But it's true, isn't it? You and Mom both hated him. Neither of you gave a shit about what he wanted."

"Like you did—I know better." Kristin laughed.

"You know *lots* of things, don't you? Sisters have no secrets."

"I know that this conversation's over, Steph. Please have something else to talk about the next time we talk. Leave me alone." The younger sister stormed off angrily.

"Sorry, Kris," she yelled at her shorter sibling as she walked away. "I know you're all broken up, so I'll go talk to Mom. She's probably relieved, too." Her mother and sister complained bitterly about him when he was alive, and now he was gone. They would probably go out dancing now. She went back to the group and spoke to some other relatives that she hadn't seen in a long time. Kristin likely had e-mails and phone calls to answer. The corporation had to go on, after all.

Chapter Four

The horrid screech of the alarm buzzer woke Dr. Gwendolyn Williams from deep, stage four sleep at six-thirty AM on Monday. To most people, she was a limitless powerhouse of energy who juggled a career in medicine, family, and dozens of other activities—but they didn't see her in the mornings. The thought of destroying yet another alarm clock entered her groggy mind, but she had promised Stan to cut back on that. She instead arose and went to her fifteen-month old son Jacob's room, where he was still asleep. The torpid pediatrician decided to get into the shower and clean up before waking him and getting ready for work.

Stan was already up and had taken his shower. An early riser, the rangy six-footer got up, ran on the treadmill, and read the paper before going over his lecture notes for the classes he would be teaching that day as a finance instructor at San Diego State University.

She finished showering and dressed. By that time her son was awake and it was time to get him ready for the day. She examined the body that she secretly wished was five–eight and 140 pounds, and remembered that it was once like that—when she was eleven. She brought their son into the kitchen, where Stan had prepared a simple breakfast. He had become quite good at cooking during his wife's medical school and residency years.

"Are you working out tonight?" Stan asked.

"I shouldn't be too late. I know we have the party to go to tonight." She thought about her life while she strategically waited for the right moment to break the news to Stan about Alex coming to town. The thirty–four-year old wasn't as academically gifted as her brother, but also lacked his addictions and selfish behavior. In high school and college, she discovered an outstanding gift for oration, leading her to become a skilled amateur thespian, stand-up comedienne, and student body officer. Those talents helped her to become a physician leader whose star was rising.

Pediatric physical medicine and rehabilitation was her chosen field, as she had completed training in a residency program that provided dual certification in pediatrics and pediatric physiatry. Her primary interest was helping people, and she had always enjoyed children. Her gifts for speaking and organizing also compelled her to develop political aspirations, and fund-raising was one means to achieve that.

Stan moved a box off the kitchen table. It contained dozens of keys, each identified with an identifier tag, with some other items, such as a liquid nitrogen cylinder.

"Do you need to leave all this bizarre stuff out? Liquid nitrogen? What the heck is that for?"

"Sorry, it's a mess. Stuff left over a couple of weeks ago," she said in her native Appalachian dialect. She had lived in California since she entered college, but still was easily identifiable as being from the South.

"But it's really weird. Can't you raise money with a different hobby?"

"I tried doing stand-up comedy and other things, but nobody wants to see me, Stan. They want something odd and exotic—like a superhero of science. And Clystarr gave us $10,000 for the new cancer pavilion last time."

"An image you created. I guess it's a worthwhile thing," he grumbled. "I don't want to derail your important political career. Just make sure it's really about that and not about you."

"What does that mean? Bonnie and I went on that mission trip to Guatemala a few months ago to help sick and injured children—I don't see how that's about me."

"But you got a bunch of publicity for that, too."

"It helps a lot of people, and also helps me. So what? There's nothing wrong with that." She paused a moment before taking a deep breath into her big lungs. "I know you'll be mad at me, but

Alex is coming up here for a few months."

Stan stared at her for several seconds. *"What* did you say?"

"Bhavin's going to take six months off for a sabbatical to go back and visit family in India, and Alex will be a *locum tenens* till he gets back." Dr. Bhavin Agarwal was a medical school classmate and friend of Wendy's who worked in the same medical plaza.

He scowled. *"Six months?* Oh, great! I get along so well with my best buddy. You're inviting a bunch of trouble, asking him up here."

"My brother isn't that bad, and you resent him."

"You're used to him. Maybe I'm too sensitive, but sometimes he's a pompous ass who can't relate to normal people. Always thinking he's better than everyone else."

"No, he doesn't. Alex is, at his core, a good person. Living up to the expectations our dad had for him has got to be tough. He's really trying to quit drinking, too."

"How wonderful for him—he deserves a medal for all he's done for humanity."

"Give him a break. The thing with Jenny really hit him hard. But maybe he'll reflect on things after this and see what's really important. You never realize sometimes what you have to lose until you've lost it all."

Stan shook his head in amazement. "Why do you care so much about him, anyway? He hardly ever calls and shows little interest in you."

"Whatever he's done, he's still my brother—I care about him no matter what. It's not like he'd feel that welcome around here anyway, with your constant criticisms."

"You want to save everyone, don't you? Why not start at the source with Rad? Man, talk about screwed up."

"That's different," she yelled, shaking her hand. "I'll never forgive him for the way he treated Mom." She hadn't spoken to her father for almost two years, and had little desire to in the future. "Alex had a lot of hard feelings at me, the way I left and never came back after high school. We're trying to mend fences and have a better relationship."

"You did what you had to. And he needs to start thinking about people other than himself. He had it all—and he blew it."

"Go ahead, say what you really think. He's not perfect like you," she sighed. "I wish I had a friend I could fix up with him."

"Boy, if you do that to friends, I'd really hate to be one of your enemies."

"That's not funny." She finished breakfast, played with her son for a few minutes, removed a bottle of Quattra Super Purified Arsenic Free Water from the refrigerator, and left for work.

Chapter Five

Kristin Markham drove to the large complex at One Clystarr Circle in her red BMW convertible and thought excitedly about the legacy she would likely now inherit. The Board loved her, and would certainly vote her in as Chairman and CEO. And things would be run differently when that happened.

Clystarr Pharmaceuticals began life in 1911 as a chemical supply plant and later progressed into the pharmaceutical industry by entering the antiparasitic market. Clystarr's background as a chemical supplier was vital during the Great Depression, as chemical suppliers continued to prosper despite many companies succumbing to financial woes. Clystarr later diversified into antibiotics after the major impact penicillin made during World War II, and began expanding rapidly.

With his bachelor's degree from Columbia and MBA from Harvard in hand, Markham joined the company in 1963 and worked his way up to vice president by 1974, President in 1985, and became CEO in 1990. During his tenure, Clystarr had its peaks and nadirs. In the 70s and 80s the flamboyant wonder boy could do no wrong, with Clystarr being consistently #1 or #2 in total pharmaceutical revenue worldwide. It had slipped slightly to #3 in pharmaceutical sales during most of the 1990s, but recently had dived below #10 after several profitable drugs had gone off patent. Most recently, it had diversified and become heavily involved in exotic new biotechnology drugs, a departure in ideology for the conservative executive. But the Darwinian environment of drug companies required evolution to survive;

those that didn't became extinct, like the dinosaurs.

Kristin had followed in his footsteps and had worked for the company for most of her career. A stellar financial analyst with a background in basic science and pharmacy, she had laid out new plans for research and development that would hopefully put the beleaguered company back on track. She lamented the poor productivity of the "old baggage," as she hatefully called them — many younger board members agreed that her father's tolerance of mediocrity had led to Clystarr's dismal earnings the last few years.

That was all going to change, she thought as she roared down the freeway. Like sister Stephanie had predicted, she wasted little time in her endeavor to take over the company. Despite improving Clystarr's profitability, she knew there were many obstacles remaining if the company was to remain in the black. Competition in the pharmaceutical industry was fierce these days; it wasn't like "old times" when two or three new drugs could sustain a company's bottom line for years. The average American had no concept of how difficult it was to develop new drugs; in recent years, the pharmaceutical industry had been labeled by patient advocate groups as being nearly as evil and avaricious as the tobacco industry, despite the millions of lives saved by their products.

The popular view of the pharmaceutical company was that it was a license to print money. But the harsh reality was that only a small fraction of promising medicinal compounds made it into human studies. It cost nearly $800 million to bring a new drug to market, and many of those weren't profitable — a huge financial risk. And biotechnology drugs, due to their gargantuan development cost, were even riskier — although the payoffs could be enormous if successful.

Drug patents had a twenty–year patent life from the date of the first filing of the patent application. However, the effective patent term was often far less than twenty years because patents were often obtained before products were even marketed; research studies (clinical trials) took up half of that time, leaving only ten years for a drug to be profitable. After that, it would be grabbed up, manufactured, and sold by generic pharmaceutical manufacturers. So the days of a single company being a dominant force for decades were long over.

It was, therefore, very common for two companies to join forces and merge to form a stronger, more efficient company. The question was—which was the stronger company, Clystarr or one of its competitors? Recently, Clystarr's board had entertained an offer from Pyrco Pharmaceuticals for a buyout. Pyrco had many new products in the pipeline and would benefit from Clystarr's long-term credibility and patents. Clystarr would, in turn, profit from the new, younger administration present at Pyrco.

Although Kristin was a darling of the Board of Directors, the middle managers who did the *real* work knew what she was really all about. The five–one, dark-haired barracuda affectionately known as "Hell On Heels" wasn't above decimating anyone who got in her way. But no one had *ever* accused her of being dishonest. She was unpopular, perhaps—but not inherently evil. Many of the younger Board members were impressed by her aggressiveness and her willingness to "cut the fat" to get the company down to fighting weight. John Markham, on the other hand, was felt to have too much loyalty—he kept long-term employees on the payroll, for example. If you started at Clystarr, there was always a place for you until you retired, John Markham always said. Things sure as hell wouldn't be that way now.

Of course, as with any merger, there would be a downside. Many employees would lose their stock options, jobs, and pensions. The fortunate ones would get a "golden parachute" worth tens of millions of dollars or more. She was one of those individuals. It didn't seem that she cared very much about the people who would lose their life savings in the deal. As per usual, she didn't care about much except herself.

She would surely keep a high-ranking position in the new company formed by the Clystarr-Pyrco merger. Anne and Stephanie reminded her that she had promised him she wouldn't sell the company. But the old bastard was dead, and who the hell cared about him now?

She walked into the executive suite and looked at the large portrait of her father that would soon be taken down and relegated to some dingy back room. Such was the nature of the pharmaceutical industry in the twenty–first century. Corporations founded by a family didn't stay around long—they were re-shaped and re-tooled to meet the financial needs of today, employees be damned. And now she'd get a huge buyout. Thank God he didn't last very long after his diagnosis. Dad was gone, and no one would worry any more about his cancer.

Of that, she was certain.

Chapter Six

Dr. Alexander Darkkin took his bags and left for the airport to catch his flight to San Diego to begin his temporary position. The five other physicians in the Nashville practice were able to take care of his part-time workload until he returned, and the DarTech software company was essentially on autopilot. Any small issues that arose could be managed from San Diego. He already had his California medical license, since he had done his residency training in the San Francisco Bay area, and his provisional hospital privileges had been approved.

After arrival at San Diego International Airport, he picked up his leased Lincoln Navigator SUV and drove to the two-bedroom condominium he had rented, conveniently located about ten minutes from the hospital. He brought his laptop, two suitcases of clothes, and briefcase into the furnished apartment. Anything else, he could buy. He would possibly get a larger apartment or even a home should he decide to stay, but it would take something extraordinary for that to happen.

He went to the hospital on the first Monday morning in June to complete his paperwork, obtain his ID badge, and undergo his drug screening test. All employees were required to undergo drug testing these days. High concentrations of caffeine and nicotine were likely to be found, as usual, but he hadn't taken a drink in several weeks. The morning sadness was still there every day, although he tried to forget about it.

The first morning was spent meeting several of the staff, including Dr. Agarwal, whose practice he was assuming for the

next six months. The hope of the group was also been to potential-
ly recruit another partner into the practice; in all likelihood, that
person wouldn't be him, however. That would require making a
commitment, an activity he never excelled at.

● ● ●

After moving into a vacant office the next day, Alex looked
through several of the patient files available to him on the electronic medical record system. He soon discovered the files of John
W. Markham, who was a patient of Agarwal. He had heard of the
demise of the pharmaceutical kingpin and was vaguely aware that
he had been a patient in the practice. It seemed permissible for
him to review the records, since Agarwal had been Markham's
radiation oncologist; he didn't want to violate HIPAA (Health
Information Portability and Accountability Act) regulations. Not
that he always followed the rules anyway, but he wanted to make
a good impression, at least his first week on the job.

He examined the records and the CT images using image
management software from his DarTech product. Markham's
high-grade lymphoma was diagnosed only six months before his
death, and he initially had been given a good prognosis. Paradoxically, the aggressive or high-grade tumors often had a better
prognosis than slow-growing cancers. The reasoning was that
rapidly dividing cells were more sensitive to chemotherapy and
radiation, which worked by disrupting the cells' reproductive
cycle. Markham had received the standard chemotherapy protocol
that was eighty–five percent effective in inducing remission, and
had received the maximum dose of radiation to the brain, where
the metastases occurred.

It appeared no one thought much about his poor response;
Markham would be simply another depressing statistic to be
reported in the tumor registry. According to the media, he and his
wife had separated due to his extramarital affairs, and his daughter was taking over the company, so no one was complaining that
he was dead.

The images certainly supported the rapid progression of his
cancer. After looking at the last two scans, he was actually amazed

Markham had lived as long as he did. He then noticed the image file sizes were moderately smaller than for the other patients' CT images; he dismissed this as an idiosyncrasy in his competitor's software compression engine.

Magnetic resonance imaging (MRI) images were curiously absent. MRI provided more imaging angles and thus more information than CT. He found his answer to their absence in Markham's past medical history, which revealed that he underwent a metallic right hip replacement ten years ago due to severe arthritis. MRI couldn't be performed on any patient with a ferromagnetic implant; the magnet's Tesla field strength would be sufficient to pull the implant out of a patient's body.

After Markham began deteriorating, he received home health care provided by private nurses. Alex reasoned that the CEO and his family didn't want a constant parade of well-meaning but somewhat intrusive employees—some who genuinely cared, others who wanted to simply make an appearance to gain favor with the family members.

He finally reviewed numerous laboratory reports. Markham's electrolytes (sodium, potassium, chloride) had been very abnormal during his last few weeks. The sodium and chloride values were very low, indicating excess water in the system. His urine specific gravity remained low at 1.005, consistent with excess water burden. Specific gravity was a dimensionless quantity relating the density of a material relative to water. Pure water had a specific gravity of 1.0, by definition.

The experience was eerie—the life of a dead man unraveling in front of him. Who was John Markham? Why had he died so quickly, when the original report showed such a good prognosis? He tried to forget it, but the thoughts continued to disturb him.

He settled into a routine and saw several new consultations during the first few days. He rediscovered the joy of working with patients again, and thoughts of his failed relationships seemed far away. He had even discovered several promising female prospects during the first week. His regenerated social life consisted of the usual fare: superficial relationships with heavy emphasis on sex, although he continued to experience some failures in that department. He still didn't know what to do about that.

Chapter Seven

Alex had tried to find an attractive female companion for lunch his eighth day on the job, but had struck out. He had to settle for going out to lunch with Wendy, who was wearing a tan blouse with slacks, a white coat, and a stethoscope about which was wrapped a small furry bear. He wore his typical black pants, gray golf shirt, and black blazer, as he didn't like to wear white coats or ties—traditional articles of attire that represented conformity to the disliked "establishment." They went to a delicatessen across the street and discussed the latest hospital gossip.

After lunch, Wendy asked him to go with her to the children's pavilion. The time was one PM, and he had no patients to see for ninety minutes.

"Come down to the kids' activity area with me," she said, motioning him to come with her. "There's going to be a magic show."

"Magic? That's just some stinking clown showing kids stupid tricks. Why would I want to watch that?" he said in a loud tone as they walked to the main building.

"I get sick of your attitude," she said harshly. "Why do you make fun of everything? And it's no clown, but an attractive young lady who's volunteering her time to entertain sick kids."

He laughed. "She's doing it for free? That's even dumber."

"You might try doing something nice for people sometime. I know it's against your character."

"Hey, I do lots of good things for people." He stopped and pointed at her.

"You're paid very well to take care of your patients. I don't get paid for this or the other things I do."

"No, you just want to be president of the medical society. You don't fool me—there has to be something in it for your benefit. And if she's one of your friends I'm sure we won't have a lot in common. I don't need to meet any young ladies, I do just fine, thanks."

"Is that right? But don't get too excited—this person is *way* out of your league. You remember Bonnie, don't you?"

He thought for a minute. "Your bridesmaid? Yeah, that was a long time ago. She was kind of cute, I guess."

They walked into the large activity room in the children's pavilion, where about thirty children and staff were in attendance. He had a seat toward the front and noticed Bonnie on a small stage, wearing a navy pantsuit and powder blue blouse. She was perhaps a little heavier than when she was nineteen, but didn't look all that different. He also knew very expensive clothing when he saw it, and wondered how she afforded it.

"Kids," Wendy said, "Some of you remember Miss Bonnie Mendoza from the San Diego Police Department, also known as '*Mendoza Milagroso*' from my television science show. She's going to show you some magic tricks."

Bonnie took the stage. "Thanks, Dr. Wendy. I remember some of you from the last time I was here. I hope you will learn something—this show is to be educational as well as entertaining."

She did various magic tricks for the children, some with a comic angle. She did several card tricks, some of which she botched on purpose, to be funny. Another trick involved dropping ice cubes into a glass of water. She said a "magic word" and dropped different ice cubes into a second tumbler of water. The ice cubes in the second glass sank, while those in the first floated.

"Do you observe anything peculiar about my second glass of ice water?" Bonnie asked them. "Be observant."

"The ice should be floating, but it sank!" a boy, perhaps ten or eleven, said.

"Yes. Why does ice normally float? Can you give me an explanation?"

"I think ice is less dense than water, so it floats."

"That's correct! For almost all other forms of matter, the solid form is denser than the liquid phase. But water ice is *less* dense in its solid phase than liquid. How did I perform this trick, then?"

"Maybe it's not water, but alcohol or something," another boy said.

"Good answer. But if it's alcohol, it should be flammable." She took a small butane torch and attempted to ignite the liquid, but it wouldn't burn. She then took a sip of the water, swallowed an ice cube, and allowed a spectator to come up and feel the ice cubes to corroborate their authenticity.

"How did you do that, then?" another child asked.

"There can only be one answer—Mendoza the Miraculous can manipulate matter in its molecular modes. Ha—say *that* real fast."

He was becoming bored, since he was too intellectual to be interested in pedestrian pursuits such as dumb magic tricks. He yawned and hoped the act would become more exciting.

"Before we do math tricks, I have a joke. How do they give the lectures at a deaf scientists' conference?"

"We don't know," several children said.

"They use sine language," Bonnie said, drawing a sine wave with her hands. The children groaned.

"You are all good at arithmetic, I am sure. I will race you to do calculations with numbers in my head. Give me three numbers, add them up yourself to make sure I'm correct, and then give them to me."

A thirteen-year old girl in a wheelchair wrote down three numbers and added them herself. "32,456 . . . 5,634 . . . 29,825," she said.

"No, you must show the numbers to me. My powers only work if I see them."

The girl showed her the written numbers. "67,915," Bonnie said instantly.

"I'm sorry, that's wrong!" the girl exclaimed. "It's 66,815."

Bonnie laughed. "That is *quite* improbable. Check your computations again."

She checked it again and found she had made two errors. "Wow," the girl exclaimed.

"The product is 5,453,713,126,800, if you wish to verify that. I need Dr. Wendy to assist me with my final trick." The extroverted pediatrician, a favorite of the children, went up to the front of the room. "I will use my vast mental powers to guess any card you choose."

"You can't do that," one of the children exclaimed. "That's not possible."

"But I can do the impossible." Bonnie took a deck of cards from Wendy. "I just purchased these from the gift shop, so there can be no question as to their authenticity." She shuffled the deck and spread the entire fifty-two cards on the table in a row, and looked at them for a few seconds. She collapsed it back into a stack again and handed it back to Wendy.

"I will now be blindfolded in the chair over here." She sat in a chair in the center of the room, and Wendy placed a blindfold mask over her eyes. She also turned around so her back was to the audience, in case anyone thought she could see through the blindfold. Wendy would deal the cards onto another stack until the person told her to stop, but neither she nor anyone else could actually see the cards. Wendy asked the girl who had doubted Bonnie's mental powers to come down and pick the cards. She was perhaps twelve years old and wearing a leg cast.

Wendy dealt the cards down and the girl told her to stop at the ninth card. "I want you to visualize in your mind the card I'm holding," Wendy said.

"Jack of clubs."

The girl turned the card over—jack of clubs. Wendy dealt several more cards and was told to stop. "Quite challenging to Mendoza the Miraculous, isn't it? Can she guess this one?"

"Four of hearts."

The girl turned the card over, and, as Bonnie had said, it was the four of hearts. "No way!" she said. "Do one more."

Wendy dealt several cards until the girl told her to stop. "Mendoza, use your great powers one more time."

"It is difficult to see . . . it must be . . . ace of diamonds."

"That's right," the girl said as she turned it over. "I don't understand how you did it. Dr. Wendy didn't even see the card until it was turned over. Even if it's a sort of code, I can't see how it was done."

"The secrets of magic can never be revealed," Wendy said. "Mendoza's vast mentalist powers are beyond our mortal comprehension."

Several of the children and staff came up to talk to her and ask questions, as he and Wendy went up to the front. "Alex, you remember Bonnie," she said.

"Of course. How are you doing? It's been a while," he said as he shook her hand.

"I'm doing well. Your sibling keeps me informed of your activities and describes you vividly in our many conversations."

"She does? Not all of it bad, I hope."

"Just some of it is bad." She stared at him blankly for a few seconds, then grinned. "Most of it, actually."

"We can all go out and have lunch sometime," Wendy said. "Alex wants to join a gym. Maybe we can go to Morry's."

"Yes, that sounds enjoyable. Well, I must get back, as I'm certain there is some matter that needs my attention. It was nice to see you again, Alex," she said as she walked off.

"Your friend's intriguing. What's she doing now?"

"She's a forensic scientist for the city police. Deputy director of the lab."

"Forensic scientist? Sounds exciting."

"Like your job is real exciting? She's actually a pretty interesting individual."

"No, I meant it—that sounds like a cool job. Anyway, her math tricks were pretty good. She must have used 'complement of nines' or something." Complement of nines was a commonly used method of factoring for mentalists to seemingly perform large number calculations.

"Those aren't tricks. Her mathematical powers are real."

"What? No way."

"She's an exceptionally gifted individual."

"Like a savant? I thought savants were, like, autistic or something."

"Not a savant, but a synesthete—a very strong one.

"A *what*?"

"She has synesthesia—a literal 'union of the senses.' It's pretty rare, but she sees numbers and letters as colors, for example. I wrote a paper on her in med school. To her, numbers and words have smells and sounds. It allows her to process some things much more efficiently than the average person. And some things, not so well."

"Yeah, I've heard of that, I think. But, anyway, gotta get back to work. Thanks for the show," he said as he walked off towards his office building.

"Okay. If you'd like to go to the gym sometime, we can do that. Just let me know," Wendy said as she walked back to her clinic. "And please don't forget the medical staff meeting tonight, Doctor."

He stopped in his tracks. *"Excuse me?* Medical staff meeting? Sorry, I don't do those, sis."

She pointed a finger at him. "Oh, yes, you will—it's required of all physicians, and you need to take some ownership in your new hospital. If we all don't play a role in medical staff leadership, where will we be in twenty years?"

"You'll be running this place, or be a senator or something, I'm sure, but I'll be retired on some beach in twenty years. By the time the wheels come off around here, it'll be someone else's problem. I'm just a short-timer."

"What if everyone felt that way?"

"Just looking out for the person I care most about—me."

"Some things will never change," she said, as a heavy-set, fiftyish woman passed her on the sidewalk.

"Hi, Dr. Williams," the woman said.

"Hi, Ruth," she said. "Do you know my brother, Alexander Darkkin? Alex, this is Ruth Forrester, the director of our charitable foundation."

The woman stopped and smiled at him. "Oh, yes, I've met this handsome young man, but I didn't know he was your brother."

She stopped and put her hand on her chin. "How do you know Alex? He's only been here a little over a week."

"He came in a few days ago and made a large donation."

She pointed at him. *"Him?* Are you sure you don't have him confused with someone else?"

"He gave us a very generous check to help with our pet therapy program—to bring in animals to help lonely hospitalized patients on the rehab unit, many of whom have cancer."

"You're . . . kidding."

"Yes, he's very nice, just like you. Well, thank you again, Dr. Darkkin. I have to go now."

Wendy looked stunned. "Alexander Dirk Darkkin! I thought you only cared about yourself."

"I do. It's a tax write-off."

"Oh, sure. Giving money to help bring animals into a pet therapy program. I'm going to tell everybody."

"Hey, don't you *dare* ruin my bad reputation—I have very low standards to uphold."

Chapter Eight

Over two hundred physicians were in attendance at the bimonthly medical staff meeting of Parkwood Memorial Hospital at seven PM in the hospital's auditorium. Alex begrudgingly showed up a few minutes late and took a seat in the back. The coffee and sandwiches in the lobby were disgustingly mediocre, but fortunately he had brought his own twenty–four-ounce highly caffeinated beverage from the coffee shop across the street.

He saw his sister at the front. Only four years out of residency training, she was already vice president of the San Diego medical society. From student council president in high school to student body president in college, she always wanted to be a leader. But he didn't share her political aspirations. To him, the only reason someone would want to do those things would be ego satisfaction. To Wendy, it was about serving the greater good.

The meeting began with reports from the chief financial officer regarding the hospital's fiscal health. He had no interest in debits, credits, revenue, current liabilities, accounts receivable, or what Moody ratings the hospital bonds had. As long as he received his paycheck on time, the organization was in sufficiently good financial health for him.

The doctors then groaned as the hospital CEO, Richard Wagner, got up and talked about "length of stay" issues. For certain insurers such as Medicare, the hospital received one lump payment for the stay, regardless of its length. It was therefore in the hospital's best interest to discharge patients as soon as it was medically prudent—spending extra days in the hospital cost money. The doctors countered with the argument the extra days were often necessary for intangible or social issues; medicine was as much art as science. Again, he felt this matter had little significance for him, a radiation oncologist, and he continued doodling on a legal pad.

The main part of the meeting was finally led by Dr. Montgomery Buechler, the elected president of the medical staff. A tall, well-built man in his late forties, he was impeccably dressed in a thousand-dollar suit, and obviously commanded the respect of his colleagues.

"I need to remind everyone we'll probably have a Joint Commission survey later this year. As you know, they show up at random these days, with no advance warning." The Joint Commission on Accreditation of Healthcare Organizations (JCAHO) provided accreditation for hospitals, and a positive review was essential.

An older doctor voiced his displeasure. "Do we *have* to hear about the goddamn Joint Commission at every meeting? It's getting old, Monte. We used to talk about important stuff, not this stupid bullshit."

"I'm sorry if it's getting old to you, Bob," Buechler said loudly. "But we have to address these issues. Without JCAHO accreditation, we can't accept Medicare or Medicaid. We'd be shut down, and you wouldn't have a place to practice. Is that really what you want?"

"To hell with this stinking place, then! Lots of us want to build our own hospital. This is a great facility, but the administration sucks—we all know that."

"Bob, this is neither the time nor the place for unprofessional comments. We all have an obligation to our institution. If you don't feel that way, then maybe you should just leave and go somewhere else." The irate doctor blustered for another minute, but was stared down by those next to him, and eventually took his seat.

Buechler then pulled up a presentation on the computer projector. "We need to talk about something else far more ominous. The medical error rate of this hospital is staggering—higher than any other hospital of our size in the country. It's a disgrace."

He showed them several bar graphs which illustrated his point about Parkwood's high number of hospital fatalities. The deaths were mainly from common conditions such as myocardial infarction, pulmonary embolism, diabetes, and pneumonia. He also described a number of medication errors and aberrant pathological diagnoses.

"As you can see, there's no single system at fault. The problems encompass the entire spectrum of services we provide in our health care system."

"What about the task forces, Monte?" another doctor asked.

"We've formed committees for all the areas—pharmacy, surgery, medical units, radiology—we can't find any problems with the equipment or protocols. And I don't think it's us as doctors. I think it boils down to this, and I'm sorry, Rick, but this has to be said," Buechler said as he turned his head to the hospital CEO, "understaffing of the nursing units, poorly trained personnel, and medical education. The residents in training are inadequately supervised."

The director of medical education, Dr. Steve Kahana, rose to his feet and pointed a finger angrily at Buechler. "I'm sick of you bashing the residency programs, Monte. We've been through this many times. Everybody always blames the residents."

"The data don't lie, Steve," Buechler retorted. "The medical errors committed by our housestaff are too high. Maybe we'd be better off without residency programs at all."

Dr. Kahana stared angrily at the disgusting greenish-brown suspension of *coffea robusta* in his Styrofoam cup and tossed it in the trash. "Hell, I'm fed up with you telling me about medical education," the large Hawaiian-American man said as he left in a huff. At least *one* guy here didn't like the chief of staff, Alex chuckled to himself.

"Look, guys," Buechler said after the angry Kahana left. "We've *got* to fix these things. If JCAHO comes soon, we'll get serious censure for the number of sentinel events. Over twenty RFIs—recommendations for improvement—and we're hosed. Our recent internal survey stinks." A "sentinel event" was any unanticipated or unusual occurrence in a healthcare setting that resulted in death or serious physical injury to a patient. "We might even get shut down. This hospital just doesn't have the commitment we need to do things right, and we have to change that. Anyone else agree with me? Who wants change around here?"

About eighty percent of the heads in the audience nodded, a seeming confirmation of Buechler's assertion. It wasn't difficult to get a group of doctors stirred up about something in a large staff meeting.

"Just look at some of the examples here," Buechler said as he projected a number of sample medical records onto the screen. "Mr. 'W' here had a pulmonary lesion. Biopsy report came back as squamous cell lung cancer, and he would've had a lung resection had he not insisted on a second opinion at another hospital. The second biopsy at St. Joseph's showed a benign lesion that he probably had for years; we don't know how the slides got mixed up. It's all electronic now, so the error rate should be a lot less."

"How's that possible?" another physician asked.

"We're not sure, since there should've been safeguards to prevent this sort of thing. Another bad one here—a five–year old child received an intravenous antibiotic for pneumonia. The archived, handwritten medical record clearly indicated she was allergic to ampicillin, but she received it anyway because the pharmacy had no record of that. She had an anaphylactic reaction and spent two weeks in the ICU. That one made the papers, and our attorneys advised us to settle it out of court."

As the disgruntled doctor had mentioned earlier, there had been talk about several of the doctors breaking off and forming their own for-profit hospital. Parkwood, although in an affluent part of San Diego, was still a non-profit corporation that provided significant care for indigent patients. The area wasn't large enough to sustain two hospitals of that size, though.

Dr. Monte Buechler was trying to patch things up, it seemed, but the quality data were there. Buechler said publicly he would defend Parkwood to the end, and Wendy sang the praises of having someone of his caliber as a leader. Alex was simply glad the boring meeting was over so he could find something more enlightening to do—like dig lint out of his toenails.

Chapter Nine

Two days later, Alex met Wendy at Morry's Gym at about six PM. She'd recommended this establishment highly, since she'd been working out there for years. Morry's wasn't a luxurious facility, but was functional in an industrial way. It was known for its excellent personal trainers and as a hangout for serious enthusiasts, which included some local celebrities.

A wall of the main room displayed a number of autographed photos. Wendy's photo was even there—she was the city's female heavyweight powerlifting champion several years ago. Another was a large motivational poster featuring a dark-haired muscular woman in a USA outfit in midair, hurling a javelin. The title read, simply, "Miracles Can Happen." She was kind of attractive, although he'd never been much into female jocks.

"Hey," Wendy said, dressed in green sweats. "You're welcome to work out with Bonnie and me." They met Bonnie, who was wearing baggy light blue sweats with vertical stripes. "So, Alex, why are you coming with us? Won't we cramp your style?"

"I wanted to join a gym, and thought I should show you ladies how it's done." He remembered her as being very thin in her bridesmaid's dress at Wendy's wedding. She probably wore the baggy sweats in an effort not to accentuate that.

"How it's done?" Wendy looked puzzled. "You could always run faster than me, but that's nothing to brag about." She went over to the free weights and did some bench presses.

Bonnie greeted him with a smile. "So, Alex, you are a very skilled athlete, as I understand." He had to listen carefully to make sure he understood what she said. She had the kind of "deaf speech" that wasn't easily understood at first, but became much easier to comprehend after knowing her for a while.

"That's true," he said smugly. "I played basketball and football in high school. Forward and tight end." He didn't tell her he actually had spent much of the time on the bench because of goofing off during practices.

She walked over to the wall next to a large wooden vertical ruler, and he noticed she came up to the sixty–five inch mark. She somehow seemed taller than five–five, but perhaps that was because she seemed thin.

He walked over to the height ruler, put his hand on top of his head, and noticed where it was positioned. Seventy–four and a half inches—his correct height in shoes. It *was* right, after all.

"Do you think you are still growing?" Bonnie asked curiously.

"No," he laughed. "But, for a minute . . . it didn't look right. You seem taller than that."

She went back to the ruler and stood up straight. Sixty–five inches. "Thank you for the compliment, but it's the stripes on my sweats which make me look taller. It is a common error."

He then decided to display his military- and bench-pressing abilities. "These are called Olympic barbells," he said as he demonstrated them to her.

"My, those are far too dangerous for me. I should use the little pink ones over here." She picked up a pink ten–pound dumbbell, struggling to curl it. "These are better."

"If you want, I'll show you good running technique on the treadmill. I'll race you for fun, but I promise to take it easy."

"You would do that for me? How magnanimous of you." He peered at her feet and noticed a pair of rather expensive footwear. He had known some runners while in Nashville, and those shoes went for $250 a pair. So what? Anybody could buy those. He once purchased a $3,000 guitar to impress people, which he could play with all the dexterity of a drunken gibbon.

"Is a mile too much?" He noticed she also had to pay attention to him very carefully, as she apparently didn't discriminate speech very well in noisy environments.

"It's a long distance—I know it will be an embarrassment."

Bonnie got up on the digital weight scale, which read 135.1 pounds. "Yay—it looks like I have gained a whole pound." She clapped several times and smiled excitedly. "You get on and allow me to observe how massive you are."

He got on the scale. 224.7 pounds, approximately what he expected his six–two frame to weigh.

"I cannot believe it—you must be powerful beyond imagination," she said as she felt his biceps. "They are *so* big."

"Oh, not really. But I'm flattered anyway."

They looked at Wendy, who returned from the free weight area. "Don't you even think about it—my weight is protected by federal privacy laws." She walked over to the water cooler to get a drink. A few minutes later, she came back, and saw them now standing on adjacent treadmill units. "What do you think you're doing?" Wendy asked her friend.

"Your testosterone-saturated brother wishes to instruct me in running, and I'm humbly obliging him in a contest."

"Do you want to look like a fool in front of all these people?" After being ignored, Wendy threw up her hands and went to another part of the room as, like an avalanche, the events had now passed the threshold of reversibility. Several people had now gathered around them, including two male athletes, perhaps twenty, who were now laughing and pointing at him.

"What are you—a bozo or something, Mister?" one of the young men asked him.

Smart-ass kid. "I just happen to be a doctor, son. Why?"

The young man howled with laughter. "Just checkin', Dr. Jethro. Don't you know who that is? Everybody around here knows M-Square."

"Who?"

"Check it out, country dude!" the youngster said as he pointed to her. "Who wants to take some bets? Ten-to-one on M-Square against Dr. Hillbilly here."

He watched as the raven-haired woman removed her baggy sweat top and pants and threw them on the bench, leaving her in shorts and a running top that left most of her abdomen exposed. As her tawny skin glistened with sweat beneath the lights, the look on his face changed to an expression he had made perhaps three or four times in his life. The look he got when he realized he had made a terrible error in judgment.

He stared at her powerful physique and wondered how he could have been so gullible. Her sinewy, mesomorphic frame reminded him of the toy airplanes he played with as a child, which used a tightly wound rubber band to supply energy.

This rubber band was about to unwind and kick his butt.

"It's time to go, *mi amigo!* Make sure you monitor your heart rate. You don't want to have a heart attack."

They each attached finger pulse monitoring devices and started running one mile. He started out at five, then advanced to six, and finally to 7.8 miles per hour—about a seven minute mile. Not too shabby. Maybe he could still save face.

The Latina started out at six mph, and over about a minute, increased her rate to over ten mph—less than a six-minute mile. She hit her stride, and finally increased to a peak of eleven mph, and wasn't even breathing hard. Maybe not.

He was gasping for dear life as he increased to 8.2 mph, and saw his pulse was 148—his maximum heart rate. He then noticed hers was 176—about ninety–five percent of the maximum possible heart rate for a thirty year old, the graph on the wall said.

She got off her treadmill three minutes later as the mile ended and again stood next to the height scale, which revealed she had grown four and a half inches in the last twelve minutes. Bonnie had told the kids at the magic show she could manipulate matter—her powers also seemed to include altering gravity as well as shrinking and growing at will.

"Good race! I thank you for showing me how to run. I'll do it this way next time to be fair." She sprung onto her hands like a Slinky toy and walked a few feet, upside down.

He was furious as he again looked at the wall of various celebrities who had worked out there. For some reason, he stared again at the poster of the female javelin thrower. After closer inspection of the autograph, there was no mistaking her identity.

"No, it can't be," he screamed, pointing a finger at Wendy. "Five–five, 135 pounds, my ass. You set me up, dammit!" he said as he tore into the locker room. "Thanks for embarrassing me. I'm sorry I even came here."

• • •

Wendy shook her head in frustration at the paradoxical behavior of her best friend. Most of the time, Bonnie was a gentle and caring individual who enjoyed volunteerism and giving to others, especially children. Rarely, though, she could be almost viciously aggressive.

"I know Alex is pretty arrogant, but did you really have to do that?"

"What did *I* do?" Bonnie said, with an innocent expression on her face.

"Beat him like that—he thinks I set him up."

"What, is he disabled or something? He was the one coming in here to show me 'how it's done.' Why should I have held back?" She was now talking too fast to be understood well.

"We could've just had fun, but you took advantage of the fact his cerebral cortex is in his pants. And what did you do to the scales?" Covertly dialing back the weight scale thirty pounds and resetting it was easily within her magician friend's sleight-of-hand repertoire. She hadn't yet figured out how she did the height scale trick.

Bonnie put her hands over her face and broke out into faux tears. "Oh, no, what have I done to your poor weak brother? Such a defeat by a tiny girl will scar him for life, I'm sure."

"Grow up—you're *so* immature. A little horsing around is funny, but you were over the top." The two were shouting at each other now and had attracted a small crowd.

"Ooooh! I see now—this is a poor reflection on you, that's what this is really all about. We cannot taint your pristine public image in the least!"

"You know me better than that. And you've done this before to guys. When will you figure out they don't like it?"

"I really don't care. It's not as if I will see him again, which is good—because he is intolerable." Bonnie stormed off into the locker room, Wendy following her just in time to see her throw down her towel. She was always patient with her volatile friend, as she couldn't begin to understand the things she'd overcome, but there was a limit to behaviors she could excuse.

"Hey, peewee—you have your own issues to deal with," Wendy said as she peered down at her flustered friend.

"Don't call me that," Bonnie signed. *"You are the one with a problem. Perhaps if you worked harder and ate less you wouldn't have such a big fat ass!"* Bonnie could communicate in American Sign Language several times faster than she could talk, and occasionally reverted to her "first" language when frustrated.

Wendy's rear wasn't really that fat; it was just very muscular because of the tremendous lower body strength necessary to squat heavy barbells. *"You'd be a skinny distance runner if it wasn't for me, but this isn't about my weight. I'm glad I'm experienced at dealing with children throwing tantrums, because I'm dealing with one right now,"* she signed back.

"Don't boss me around. I've been weak and ridiculed. You have no idea."

"But when you misuse your strength to show off, then you're the bully. Is that what you've become? Stooping to the level of people who used to make fun of you?"

"I'm not the best I can be, that's obvious." Bonnie resumed speech and slammed her locker shut. "I'm sorry and didn't mean what I said about you. Tell your stupendous sibling I apologize."

"Oh, trust me, he'll get over it. I'm sure women have done far worse things to him," she said as Bonnie took her sweat top and left. "And I'm not worried about him, anyway. My comments are for your benefit. I do care about you, you know."

She knew Alex sometimes engaged in self-destructive behavior. And it was apparent her friend sometimes did the same thing. Bonnie was the seemingly perfect woman who hid behind her mask of insecurity and gaping flaws. Wendy knew how adept magicians were at concealing things.

• • •

Alex was seething by the time he reached his vehicle. He was used to getting what he wanted—not being set up to be a fool. It wouldn't have been so bad if he'd been beaten by another guy, or if the crowd of people hadn't been laughing. He simply deserved more respect than that.

He thought about stopping at the tavern he passed — how easy it would be. He hadn't had a drink for almost a month, but really wanted one now. He could just order coffee or soda, but he knew he would drink if he went in. Damn, it was hard — there wasn't a day he didn't think about the booze. People didn't understand why he couldn't just take one drink; he would instead drink the whole fifth of bourbon. Wendy didn't have the same problem; she could have a drink or two with dinner and then not drink again for a month. But he wasn't going to fall off the wagon over something like this; after some hesitation, he drove on past the tavern.

He pulled up to his apartment and went in. Not much to eat, as usual. He'd hoped to get something after the workout but was too upset, and decided to fire up his black laptop and surf the Web for a while.

Bonnie again entered his mind. She was kind of cute, although not nearly as pretty as Jenny or many of the other women he'd dated. But she was attractive in an intangible way he couldn't quantitate. He'd never been beaten by a girl in an athletic activity before, except for a tennis professional he had dated in Nashville. And the times after his sister got her growth spurt and knocked him around as adolescents didn't count, either. Right now, he was curious to find out more.

His Web surfing took him to a USA Deaf Track and Field page featuring the world record holder of the deaf women's heptathlon. The heptathlon was a grueling contest that included seven different events: 100 meter hurdles, high jump, shot put, 200 meter dash, long jump, javelin throw, and 800 meter run.

Team USA's Bonita Mendoza set that record with 5,505 points at the 2005 Melbourne Deaflympics — the Olympic games for the deaf. She had also earned the bronze medal at the Rome games in 2001. Her record didn't come close to that for the regular event — Jackee Joyner-Kersee held the women's record with 7,291 points. But 5,505 was enough to break records at a number of Division I universities, he learned. So what? Big stinking deal.

No, he didn't want anything to do with his sister's perfect friend, who had the temerity to show him up. Who the hell did she think she was, treating him that way? Despite his fondness of drink and women, he had graduated *summa cum laude* with a degree in computer engineering from Vanderbilt University; he later went on to medical school at Stanford, where he graduated second in a highly competitive medical school class of eighty–six. He didn't need to take anything from a nerdy scientist, and that type of regimented person was wrong for him anyway. The magic stuff was juvenile, too. She could take her gold medal and stick it where the sun didn't shine.

But getting the unusual scientist's image out of his obsessive mind would be easier said than done.

Chapter Ten

Bonita Maria Mendoza Flores looked forward to the monthly Saturday shopping trips with her mother. She loved Horton Plaza, with its seven twisting and turning levels of shops; there was always some new store to explore. While she waited for her to arrive, she looked at the digital watch on her left wrist which showed direction as well as miles from home—those were things she always needed to know. 12:02 PM. She preferred analog watches and clocks, because the colors of the numbers were always the same—digital readouts were irritating because the colors always changed.

The tall scientist doodled the numeral "3," which appeared green, on a napkin; she then filled in the "3" to form an "8," and watched it change color to a deep violet. She always thought that was fun when she was a toddler, people said; but she didn't remember that, or much of anything else before age eleven.

She wore the simple red anodized aluminum bracelet on her right wrist today. Sometimes she wore the plastic or copper one, but she liked the red metal one best. Most people thought it was simply decorative jewelry—but she needed it almost as much as a myope required eyeglasses.

She drank her vanilla latte as she watched the people go by. People always looked at her and smiled. Were they making fun? The two aural processors were much smaller than in years past, but still quite noticeable. Maybe they were just being friendly.

Their colors were pale, like most people she didn't know, and the sounds they made were faint—she had to concentrate to hear them, the wonderfully detailed harmonics, so unlike the artificial sounds produced by the cochlear implants. The two pre-teen girls who had stopped to get autographs were a light yellow. She secretly fantasized they had asked because she was a famous scientist. But she knew it was only because she was a spandex-clad regular guest on the sappy local kids' show *Dr. Wendy's Science Squad*.

The smells were very interesting today. The old woman who passed by had the faint but distinct odor of octyl acetate—the olfactory component of oranges. Words and numbers had a comfortable, orderly exactness, resulting in her compulsion to speak in verbose, stilted sentences. People often thought she was cold and calculating because of that, but she was actually a quite passionate and emotional person. She had tried to speak different-ly, even as a young child, with minimal success.

She was lost in her thoughts when the tall, fiftyish woman tapped her on the shoulder and kissed her on the cheek. She heard the familiar C-major chord and smelled bananas and caramel.

"*Hola.* How are things?" Elisabeth Flores de Mendoza said to her daughter.

"They could be better. I'm in a poor mood." They walked from the plaza's first level to the third, to one of Elisa's favorite restau-rants.

"How come?" Her mother's magenta color was especially vi-vid today.

"I quarreled with Wendy and said several things to her I am not proud of."

"Why did you fight with her?"

"Her obnoxious brother is here. He tried to show off for me and wanted to race me on a treadmill, and I obliged him. The outcome was not to his liking. She called me 'peewee'—she knows how that perturbs me."

"Maybe her comment has a subtle meaning. One may be strong of stature, but small in other ways."

"Are you a philosopher now as well? I thought it was funny, but they did not share my jubilation."

"Well, was that a fair trick to play on Alexander?" Elisa said as they sat down at the outside bistro.

"I suppose not." In some ways, she felt like the small, weak girl who almost died after contracting meningitis at age eleven. She was in a coma for two weeks, they told her—when she woke up, she was completely deaf and had forgotten almost everything she ever knew, including speech and language. How different she appeared now on the outside. But she still felt like the same little girl inside.

"That was rude, no matter if you like him or not. Wendy has done a lot for you."

"I just wanted to show off, but I know it was wrong. It made her feel bad, and I made fun of her weight." She was thirteen when she was mesmerized by the eighteen-year old San Diego State pre-med student who was volunteering at the rehabilitation center. The garrulous blonde was a girls' state champion shot-putter who helped the skinny teen gain something she desperately wanted: sheer physical power. But her therapists felt that was frivolous. Learn basic life skills and live independently, they said. *Bullshit*, she had replied in American Sign Language—she would do what she damn well pleased. Years later, the obsessive, competitive drive was still present.

"Is he just visiting?"

She woke up from her daydreaming. "What? No—he's doing some temporary work at her hospital for a few months."

"He's her brother. You should be nice to him."

"Synthesis of antimatter would be simpler." The waiter came and took their drink orders while they perused their menus.

"Does Alexander have a color?"

"What? Why do you keep speaking of *him*? How unpleasant."

"Just curious."

She sighed. "If you *must* know, he is bright bluish-green, almost an aquamarine. He smells like burnt cinnamon, which I dislike. Are you satisfied?" She knew her math-teacher mother understood about the sounds, colors, and odors—she was a synesthete, too, albeit a much weaker one than her daughter. Synesthesia was the "gift" that allowed her to remember and manipulate words easily and perform complex mathematical computations in her head.

Some gifts, however, had a downside. Many strong synesthetes had perceptual problems that confounded daily activities; in addition to terrible taste in clothes, she had poor direction sense and allochiria (inability to tell left from right). She had coped with the latter problem since childhood by wearing a "reminder" bracelet on her right wrist. Elisa was minimally affected in this fashion, thankfully, since she helped her pick out clothes and decorate her apartment.

"Anyway, I'm coaching the Mathletes team again this year. You should come by again—they ask about you."

"I know. I need to come and give them a pep talk." She and her three teammates were eighth-graders when they won the 1992 California state mathematics championship. She was the captain, even though she had to sign through most of the competition— her implant at that time only allowed her to discriminate crude sounds.

"They like to hear the stories about how my seven-year old daughter found mistakes in the grading of my students' homework. And how Big Jaime paid you to do his algebra homework when he was sixteen."

"I like to hear them, too." Because she only remembered bits and pieces of her childhood before the illness. It was not until several months after she woke up that she possessed enough comprehension of language to learn she was "profoundly gifted"—her IQ was over 160. She could write English and Spanish at a high school level when she was four, they said. But all that disappeared on that day in 1987. She learned to read lips and saw little purpose in going to a "deaf" school, since she would have to function in a hearing world the rest of her life. She went there for one year, learned the necessary survival skills, and started over at the regular middle school she attended when she was eleven. She didn't want any special favors from anyone. But she knew that sometimes family and friends needed to help anyway.

• • •

After lunch, Bonnie and Elisa went shopping at several upscale clothing stores. Most police employees shopped at cheaper places, but they didn't have a brother who had been a Pro Bowl wide receiver for the Green Bay Packers. Jaime Mendoza had invested his money wisely during his playing years and was quite generous to his family, especially to his sister who many thought would never be functional again.

Bonnie also had a special talent that paid off all her debts and put over two hundred thousand dollars in her bank account. But she no longer wished to use that skill, she proudly told the therapist she saw once a year.

Elisa helped her pick out several outfits, choosing simple colors and patterns she could match up later with numbers. Left unsupervised, she would create hideous color combinations that were rumored to provoke seizures in susceptible individuals. But Elisa made her the best-dressed person in the police department.

The tailor would have to alter the blouses and jackets. She wore a forty–two-inch jacket, with most of the mass in her arms and shoulders, not her B-cup breasts. But most women with that chest size were "plus-sized"—her waist was only twenty–six inches. The saleslady took the expensive items away for alteration.

They finally went to a coffee shop at four PM, after they had finished shopping. "So, how are you going to patch things up with Wendy?"

"We all know I have a bad temper. I'll stop by tomorrow and see her. I promised to watch Jake for a couple of hours."

"What happened to the guy you went out with a couple of weeks ago from the science lab?"

"Robert? Kind of like the others, Mom," she said with a half-hearted laugh tinged with sadness. "I guess I wasn't what he expected."

"Well, what about the electrical engineer guy from the TV show? He's cute."

She shook her head. "Todd? Sorry, Mom—*Admiral Ampere* has a boyfriend. Golly."

"Oh," Elisa said with a sheepish grin on her face. "I didn't know *that*."

"And people think *I'm* naïve. Anyway, the smart ones are threatened because I'm an athlete. The athletic ones are intimidated by my intellect."

"Wendy knows about that. Look at her—she's hardly a

supermodel. She has a happy marriage."

"But she has an ebullient personality I can never have. I just don't understand how people think."

"Don't ever put yourself down—you're a wonderful person. If no one sees that, then it's their loss."

"Guys aren't that interested in who I am—I probably come off as weird or something." Despite her athletic and intellectual accomplishments, she felt socially isolated due to her hearing and speech problems and had few interactions with the opposite sex during her younger years.

"You need to find time for yourself, for your own happiness. That's all your dad and I ever wanted for you. You've far surpassed anyone's expectations."

She frowned and clapped her hands. "Oh, goody for pretty little Bonita! She has surpassed everyone's mediocre expectations. I grow weary of hearing that condescending statement for the millionth time."

"Stop it. Back to Alexander—you said he's a bright color. Most new people have pale colors, you said."

"Does annoying me give you pleasure? I had met him before, so he was not new to me. Duh."

"That was ten years ago, and you didn't really know him. I'm just suggesting . . . color intensity to you is usually proportional to emotional response."

"Naturally—I was very perturbed by him. Mom, I hope you're not suggesting—"

"We never know, Bonnie, what the future holds. You, of all people, should know that."

"After my outburst, I doubt there is any future there. And I don't care for him anyway. Please drop it."

She reflected on what her mother had said as they finished their coffee and left. She would go to her parents' house for dinner, just as she did on many Saturday nights, and would make it clear there would be no more discussion of the ill-mannered Alexander Darkkin.

Chapter Eleven

Alex Darkkin continued working at Parkwood with renewed enthusiasm, and felt happy living in his modest condominium. He also had several dates with a young lady he'd met at the office, a first for him recently. At least she wasn't an elite athlete who embarrassed him in the gym.

Intrusive thoughts about John Markham still troubled him, and even kept him up at night. Something just didn't add up with the images. He had encountered similar cases, but was unsure why this one bothered him so. It would be easy to simply dismiss him as one who didn't respond to therapy, and leave it at that. After all, that's what everyone else seemed to think. But obsession was a familiar frontier for him.

He had reviewed the written medical records and laboratory values multiple times. All evidence still supported a rapidly progressive tumor that didn't respond to therapy. He looked at the computerized CT images again, which showed progression of the tumor exactly as described in the reports.

He took the images home on a portable flash drive and downloaded the CT files into his image processor, and compared them to images from other patients. He had at his disposal extremely advanced technical software, as he had been involved in developing imaging software for radiation oncology. The system at Parkwood used a similar program. He studied the JPEG compression algorithm and noticed Markham's had been compressed two or three times, which seemed unusual. This process introduced minimal loss into the picture, but nothing that would be detected by ordinary means. The non-Markham CT images had been compressed only once, however. Different machines used different algorithms, but those from the same machine should've been similar.

He then performed more advanced manipulations using mathematical analysis software. His program performed Fourier transformation analysis (a robust method of detecting alterations in digital images which was relatively immune to artifacts) of several regions in Markham's CT images that showed advanced malignancy. He had no difficulty understanding the complex equations before him, which constructed a probability map created by multiple iterations of mathematical transformations. The probability map would, in turn, generate frequencies of resampling. The non-Markham images revealed relatively normal sampling frequencies. The CEO's images, however, showed moderate changes of the periodic patterns, due to frequent re-sampling. He checked his calculations a dozen times before he lit a cigarette and inhaled deeply. He thought he'd thrown them away, but was glad he found half a pack.

What the hell had he found? Markham's CT images appeared to be forgeries that mathematically did not parallel the underlying regularities found in naturally occurring images. But why would that be the case? Could he be wrong? Although he understood the rudiments of computer hacking, he was no expert at computer crime. He checked them three more times and reached the same conclusion, and knew he couldn't rest until he obtained confirmation. He hurriedly dialed a telephone number at one o'clock in the morning on the balmy July evening.

The half-incoherent voice screaming on the call's receiving end was most unpleasant. "For God's sake—what do you need? I'm exhausted and only got two hours' sleep last night." Wendy had obviously seen the caller ID, and at least knew he wasn't in jail. One good thing.

"How do I contact your friend Bonnie? Maybe she can help me with my problem."

"*Bonnie*? Why in the world would you want to talk to her? I don't think you two hit it off so well."

"I need some professional help with something."

She sighed. "Oh, you need help, that's for dang sure—but I don't believe she's the professional you need. I have several psychiatric colleagues I can recommend. I'm really not in the mood to chat, so what the heck do you want?"

"Markham's CT images—they were forged. I did a mathematical analysis of the resampling of the images and compared them to other patients. They're vastly different."

"Slow down. Markham? CT images? You're drunk, aren't you? I thought you were going to quit."

"No, I haven't been drinking, and have never been more alert. I knew something was wrong. I could sense it."

"Who the hell is Markham? The drug CEO guy? He's been dead a couple of months," she said in a frustrated tone.

"Someone could've killed him. I just have a feeling."

"God, chill out—no one's killed anyone." She paused for a few seconds. "Wait a minute—I may be killing *you* soon, though."

"You haven't seen what I have. It's real, I tell you."

She paused for a few seconds. "All right, doggone it—I'll call her in the morning, and maybe you can meet her at the police lab tomorrow. I'm tired, so let me please get some sleep. I advise the same for you." She hung up the phone.

But the sandman wouldn't visit the highly wired radiation oncologist that night. He chain-smoked the rest of the cigarettes he could find, drank two pots of concentrated Indonesian coffee, and watched sports shows on TV until it was time to shower, gather the electronic images on his flash drive, and go to the police station. He didn't have any appointments until ten AM, thankfully.

• • •

Wendy called the next morning and directed Alex to go to the main offices of the San Diego Police Department on 1401 Broadway Street at eight–thirty AM. He went to the clerk at the front desk at 8:22 and told her he had an appointment with Bonita Mendoza Flores.

The Tennessee native still had trouble understanding a concept more perplexing to him than particle physics—Latino names.

Wendy, who had lived in San Diego for sixteen years, had explained that most Hispanics had two surnames, or *appelidos*; he wondered how one could have two of the "last thing." The first surname typically came from the father, the second from the mother. Some, like Bonnie, also had one or more middle names, which was even more confusing. And, the person always casually went by the first surname, not the second, as one would intuitively think. Her mother's name, Flores, was omitted in most interactions.

Even more bewildering, the child took the first surnames from both parents, meaning the parents had different second surnames than the children. And, the parents' names were different from each other. Typically, the woman kept her *appelido paterno* (father's surname) and took the husband's; her mother's name was therefore the opposite of hers: Flores de Mendoza.

An officer escorted him through a metal detector, gave him a visitor's ID badge, and took him to a meeting room. Bonnie came in a few minutes later, wearing an immaculately tailored Tahari grey-skirted suit. Her body was like an optical illusion—she didn't look all that big at a distance with clothes on.

"Alex, it's good to see you," she said, extending her hand. "Wendy said you have some official business to discuss with me. I hope I may be of aid."

"Yes. I appreciate your meeting with me on such short notice. First, though, I wanted to apologize for the gym a couple of weeks ago. I was a jerk."

She paused for a moment. "No, I'm the one who should be sorry. I become excessively competitive and carried away sometimes. I assure you, Wendy tried to discourage me."

"That's okay, I deserved it."

"I must also confess about my fun trick to underestimate my size. That was unfair."

"Now, I was really impressed by that. I can't figure out how you did it, though."

"The art of magic depends on the power of suggestion. You wanted to think I was smaller, therefore you believed my illusions. There were many clues that suggested otherwise."

"I guess I stepped right into it."

"Let us leave it that we both could have acted more maturely, and forget it. May I get you something to drink? Or doughnuts? This is a police department, after all."

"Coffee would be fine, if you have that, thanks."

"The adjective I use to describe police coffee is not 'fine', but it's your stomach," she said as she poured a cup from the pot and sat down with him in the meeting room. "Our attorney requires you to sign a release of liability waiver before consuming that. So, how may I help?"

"This may sound weird, but I need some professional confirmation and direction. Does the name John Markham ring a bell?"

"The pharmaceutical executive who died approximately two months ago?" He noticed again that, despite her speech impairment, her vocabulary and grammar were extraordinary.

"Right. He was a patient of the doctor I'm covering. I was reviewing his brain CT images, and have reason to believe they were digitally altered."

"Why would you think that?"

"I have a background in software imaging and use Calculab. If you look at the images and do an analysis, you'll see for yourself."

"Mathematical modeling software—I use a similar product. But why do you believe something is amiss?"

"The cancer he had should've responded better to therapy, at least initially. That's what prompted me to look at the records."

She sighed. "Okay, do you have the images with you?"

"Yes, I have them on a flash drive," he said, holding up the small memory stick which contained four gigabytes of high-resolution CT images.

"We can go to my office and peruse them." They went to her well-organized office, where she opened the files. She went through the same mathematical analyses of the CT images in rapid succession. Fifteen minutes later, her calculations were complete.

"That was quick." It had taken him an hour to analyze the images, and he wondered how she did it so quickly.

"I have had much practice. But the resampling frequencies of the Markham files do differ substantially from the others, and I agree they've been digitally altered in some fashion. I have one question, however—a technician would've looked at these images in real time, correct? If they had been changed, the tech should have noticed the difference when the final images came through for storage on the server."

"Yeah, you'd think so. In fact, I asked all the techs about it. Some can't remember, as they do dozens per day. The others, though, remember them being exactly like the ones you see before you—huge brain mets."

"Come on—how can that be possible?"

"The images must've been encoded in an uncompressed or raw format and introduced at the machine language level. It's the only possible way."

"But why would anyone do that? He had cancer, and would have succumbed to his malignancy in time."

"Yeah, but he should've responded better to chemo and radiation."

"Or perhaps he was just an unfortunate patient who did poorly. *Pluralitas non est ponenda sine necessitate.*"

He was still having some trouble understanding her English, let alone other languages. "Sorry. *No habla español.*"

"Latin, not Spanish," she snickered. "Plurality should not be posited without necessity—a heuristic maxim commonly referred to as Occam's razor."

He always thought he was smarter than just about anyone he'd ever met. But he looked at her for a moment and realized even a ten-cylinder Corvette Z06 would be smoked by a twelve-cylinder *Lamborghini Murciélago.* "Sure—all other things being equal, the simplest explanation tends to be the best one. But I don't buy it in this particular case."

"Okay, then, what about his other laboratories and such? Are they compatible with his supposed mechanism of death?"

"Yes, everything fits—it looks exactly like he died of cancer. Except for the images, I wouldn't think anything about it."

"So, you're now proposing other records may also have been changed. Again, why and how would someone do this?"

"Obviously someone wanted him dead. His wife, maybe."

She formed the letter "T" with her hands. "Time out—what seems obvious to you is *not* necessarily true. The mere fact they were altered does not prove another cause of death."

"But you can't just ignore this."

"I'm not suggesting you do, only that this proves nothing by itself. Your intuition, fabulous as it may be, will not win a court case."

"I don't know what to do. If I did, I wouldn't be here."

She shrugged. "Tell you what—I'll take you to one of the detectives, as a favor. But there's not enough to charge anyone, and you don't even have a suspect. There is a possible charge with cyber crime, but healthcare information fraud is within the realm of federal law enforcement."

"How can you think there's no crime here?"

"Alex, what I believe and what I can prove are two different things. I testify in court about scientific evidence for a living. But we need something more, so I will have you talk to Lt. Marc Owens—he's a bit crusty, but a good guy."

• • •

Bonnie and Alex went downstairs to the homicide division, knocked on Detective Lt. Marcus Owens' door, and were told to enter by the loud baritone voice.

"Alex, this is Detective Lt. Owens. Lieutenant, this is Dr. Alexander Darkkin, who has some fascinating information he would like to share with you."

"From past experience, I know our definitions of 'fascinating' differ. What's your involvement in this, Mendoza? Is this an official case?" the tall, rangy, bespectacled African-American detective asked as he stood up and looked down at them.

"No, it's unofficial. Dr. Darkkin is . . . an acquaintance of mine. But I have verified his findings, and you should hear him out. The information he has is very strange."

"Why should I waste time on something that's not even a case? Look at my desk." Owens pointed to the disorganized stacks of papers covering three–fourths of his desktop.

"You've always known me to be level-headed, so please do this as a favor. I've done quite a few for you."

Owens nodded. "Okay, how can I help you, Doctor?"

"Lt. Owens, I'm currently a radiation oncologist at Parkwood Medical Center, where John Markham was a patient. After examination of his radiological data and other medical records, I have reason to dispute Markham actually died of cancer."

"Markham — the drug company guy who croaked? So, you're saying he didn't have cancer?"

"No, he did have lymphatic cancer, but the radiographic images showing progression of his disease don't belong to him at all. They've been digitally altered, which can be confirmed by Fourier mathematical analysis. Ms. Mendoza can verify my findings."

"Why, I ask, would you decide to analyze these images, Doctor? Cancer patients die every day."

"Actually, my consulting company wrote similar imaging and storage software, and the rapid clinical course of his illness made me curious. I assure you that someone hacked into the record system and altered those images, because they show subtle signs of manipulation by sophisticated imaging software."

"Or it could be that you're just wrong, or someone at the hospital made a mistake. I don't want to waste a bunch of time. You're a doctor, not a computer crime expert." Owens sat down in his oversized chair.

"Marc, I concur with him — the images have been manipulated. The specific alterations could've been engineered to simulate the progression of the cancer, but we have neither a motive nor a mechanism how it happened. Were I in court, I would testify they were digital forgeries."

"Can you explain the process a little bit to me? I can barely figure out how to work my own digital camera."

"Pixels of digital photos, like other things in nature, follow a random, unpredictable pattern. These random imperfections, curiously, follow a specific frequency. But Markham's images were mathematically analyzed and don't follow that frequency, leading Dr. Darkkin and I to our astounding conclusion."

"Huh? You lost me." Owens scratched his head in puzzlement. "Tell me in a way I can understand."

"Okay — here is a much simpler analogy. You certainly must remember the old theory that, if you place a monkey in front of a typewriter for billions of years, its random keystrokes will eventually compose the works of Shakespeare."

"Sorry, I seem to have missed that episode of *Mythbusters*."

"Well, the altered images are just like primates generating *Hamlet*. Both are simply unnatural."

Owens stared blankly at her for several seconds. "Thanks *so* much for sharing that with me, Mendoza. All these years I've worried about that, and now I know."

"You are quite welcome." She nodded her head and smiled.

Owens leaned back in his chair and pointed a pencil at Alex. "But what is it you guys want from me? I'm not cyber crimes. You need to talk to the FBI."

"I'm saying it's likely he was killed by some other fashion, say a slow poison or something," he replied.

"Hold on—just because the x-rays were changed doesn't mean the cancer didn't kill him. His records support he died just like a cancer patient would've, right?"

"It seems that way. But why would someone do that, then?"

"I have no idea. Look, Darkkin, if I go to the DA with that, he'll throw me out on my butt. Do you have any lab work which supports your grand conspiracy theory?"

"There was no toxicology screen done, no reason to. No specimens that directly suggest any type of foul play."

"I see. Well, as a favor to your friend Ms. Mendoza, I'll keep on the lookout for anything interesting. Here's my card if you come up with something else. But I can't do much with what you've given me so far." Owens shook hands with him as they left his office.

They walked out of the detectives' area down the hallway as she extended her hand to him. "Alex, thank you for the information. I don't know what will be done with it, but perhaps something more will come up. I'm certain this will be the most interesting thing I'll encounter today."

"Do you think I should talk to the FBI?"

"It isn't much to go on, so I wouldn't right now. Perhaps you will discover something else. Thank you again—our paths may cross again at a later time."

"Wait a minute." He felt like a nervous teenager.

"Yes? Do you require something else?"

"I was wondering, well—if you wanted to go out, sometime?"

"What do you mean, 'go out'? Do you mean a date?"

"Yeah, I guess so."

She stared at him for a few seconds. "I'm not sure about that. What activity did you have in mind?"

"Probably not a workout date. I really do have a better side, though. Would you have dinner with me?"

She paused and stared at him. "I don't know—I am very busy, and I'm also not sure it's a good idea."

"Why?"

"Your sister and I are friends, and you are only here for a few months. What do you think we would have in common?"

"What does she have to do with it? And how do you know what we have in common? I just think you're an interesting person I'd like to know better." He looked at the small imperfections in her soft, round face—the small freckles radiating out from her nose and forehead. And he wanted to further experience the fascinating mind that he knew must reside inside.

"I am trying to be nice, Alex." The woman with the intense dark eyes could probably take anything he dished out and throw it right back at him. He had met his match, and that made the pursuit more interesting.

"We can go anywhere you want. At least we've met—surely you've had blind dates worse than me."

"You don't give up, do you?"

"No." Maybe he needed to alter his tactics for the situation at hand, as he was desperate. "But, let's assume we don't have much in common. Didn't Alessandro Volta create the first battery by discovering that two dissimilar metals placed together produced current?" He really had to reach deep for *that* load of baloney.

"Volta? Battery?" she said as she opened her eyes and took a few steps back. "Let me get this straight—you are saying a similar 'current' could flow between us, two dissimilar individuals?"

"It's possible. He didn't know until he tried. Those electrons sure knew what *they* were doing."

"Count Volta's experiment also required a briny suspension for a conducting medium—I assume that your invitation would utilize equivalent constituents, Doctor?" She crossed her long arms and frowned as she tapped her foot on the carpet. "Well? Is *that* what you were implying?"

"I hadn't thought of it in that way, but maybe—you never know," he said with a smile as he held his palms out wide. "We should use a non-conductive insulator, of course, just to be safe. I'm sure Volta always did."

"*Insulator*? Hmmm." She chewed on her pen for a few seconds and finally burst out laughing. "You are humorous as well as clever and resourceful—that's certainly the most original line I have ever heard. And I am quite fond of romantic Italian physicists, so I suppose that I could be persuaded into a nice Italian meal." She wrote her home phone number, e-mail, and address on the back of her business card. "Anything but Mexican food."

"Really? You're kidding." She had an outstanding "poker face"—it was almost impossible to tell if she was joking or not.

"No, I don't like it," she said, resuming a serious tone. "Had you grown up on my mother's inedible burritos and quesadillas, you would understand." She stared blankly at him for a few seconds, then broke out in laughter again.

Chapter Twelve

Alex went back to the Parkwood office where he had coffee with Wendy later in the afternoon in the hospital coffee shop. They took a seat at a round table next to the skylight, and he pushed the extra scuffed chairs away so no one would join them. It was noisy enough this time of day as it was, he thought as he took a sip of his espresso. They began discussing the events of the previous medical staff meeting.

"A bunch of the doctors are planning on building their own hospital, Alex. The Parkwood sentinel event rate is so far above the national average, their group has polarized most of the medical staff against the hospital." She stirred five packets of raw sugar into her coffee, then added four containers of cream. "Buechler's trying to calm them down, but it'll be an uphill battle."

"This Buechler guy's pretty good, you say?"

"He's a straight shooter. We're so lucky to have him as president of the medical staff," she said as she gobbled the ice cream bar she had bought.

He watched in puzzlement as she licked the ice cream from her fingers. Why did she work out so vigorously, then eat that kind of stuff? "So, what'll happen now?"

"If they build this new, for-profit hospital, the doctors will become shareholders and reap all the profits. Indigent care and medical education will go down the tubes."

He laughed. "And the reason I care about that is—what?"

"The underserved can't all go to the county hospitals. Where are they going to go?"

"Don't know. What's next, world hunger? Global warming?"

She frowned. "It's everyone's problem, including yours."

"I guess you're right, I'm just giving you a hard time. But I'm glad I'm only here for six months, if Parkwood's having all these problems. Why do you stay here, if the hospital sucks?"

"It wasn't that way a year or two ago. That's when things started going downhill."

"What's changed during that time?"

She spread her hands wide, displaying her seventy–four inch wingspan. "Some changes in administration, a lot of turnover in pharmacy and nursing managers. No single thing or person stands out, but as a whole, it's a huge problem."

"Well, I'd be thinking about a new locale."

"You would. But events like these happen everywhere. You can't just abandon things because they don't go your way."

"I can do whatever I want."

"Yeah, I've seen," she said as she finished her coffee. "Anyway, did Bonnie give you the information you wanted?"

"She helped out some. Pretty bright gal."

"That she is. But what's the deal with you? You were really buzzed up last night. It reminded me a little bit of Dad—not a good thing, by the way."

"As I mentioned, I think someone altered Markham's CT images. He shouldn't have died so quickly."

"*Sshhh!*" she scolded, kicking him in the shin. "Be quiet! We're right in the middle of a public area. Rick Wagner, the CEO, is sitting over there with the VP of finance. You should know better than to talk about patients in public."

"Sorry. That HIPPO privacy crap, I know. But Markham's dead, so what's the big deal?"

"HIPAA, you moron—and it doesn't matter if he's dead or not. It's a federal law that you had better learn to understand, or you'll get in trouble." They got up and went to a small meeting room that was unoccupied.

"I think someone did him in."

"That's crazy. He already had cancer."

"Yeah, but he should've had a better response. At least five years' survival."

"Patients don't always have ideal outcomes. You, of all people, should know that."

"There seem to be lots of bad outcomes around here, from what I hear. But, getting back to Markham—what I found isn't speculation, it's real. That's why I wanted to see Bonnie. She confirmed that the images were manipulated."

"That doesn't prove he died of something else."

"Why would someone do it, then? Just for fun?"

"So you gave it to the police—good. Now you can stop calling me in the middle of the night. I was *so* mad at you."

"By the way," he blurted, "I asked your friend out on a date."

A look of amazement as her jaw dropped. "You're kidding. I sure don't view Bonnie as your type."

"What's that supposed to mean?" he asked snidely.

"For one thing, you don't favor ladies with an IQ in the triple digits," she laughed.

"That's insulting—you have no idea what kind of women I go out with."

"I think I have an idea. Anyway, what did she say?"

"She eventually said yes. After many tries, though."

"I don't believe it. Where are you going?"

"Out to eat at an Italian place, I guess. I'm not sure what else. What does she like to do?"

"She likes the outdoors. Games, puzzles, reading, quiet things. She's not much for movies or music. I've tried to get her interested in the theater." They both stood up and threw their trash in the receptacle.

"Thanks. I want to make a good impression."

She put her big right arm on his shoulder. "Alex, despite my renewed confidence in you, I know your reputation in that department. And, if you're anything less than a gentleman, I'll come looking for you myself," she said melodically as she stared nearly eye-to-eye with him. "You don't want that, do you?"

"Uh, no—I guess not." He remembered watching his solidly-built little sister hurl a four-kilogram steel sphere fifty–one feet to set a new Tennessee girls' high school shot put record in 1990. He then imagined her doing the same thing to his head. They weighed about the same, he figured.

Chapter Thirteen

The next morning, Detective Lt. Marcus Owens sat at his desk in the homicide division. The fifty–two-year old had been a detective for ten years, and had made lieutenant two years ago. He, like everyone else in the department, thought highly of Bonnie Mendoza. He'd known her since she was a child, when her father often brought her to the station. He'd never really liked the snobbish, academic Carlos, but had respect for him and knew the obstacles his daughter had overcome. But he felt she might be way off base on this one. He nursed a black cherry soda and sat at his desk to complete some paperwork. The phone rang a few minutes later, and he pushed the button on the speakerphone.

"Lt. Owens, there's a woman on the line who needs to speak to you," the operator said.

"Who is it?" he grumbled, since he was trying to get some work done. "And who forwarded it here?"

"The lab administrative office. It's a lady who claims to have some information about the Markham case. Tina said you were to take it."

"Tina? I didn't know Mendoza's secretary was now in charge of my workload. All right, daggone it—I'll speak to her." He picked up his handset while the call was transferred. "This is Lt. Owens. How may I help you?"

"You're the detective handling the Markham case?"

"Well, Ma'am, there isn't really a 'case' yet. Someone discussed some things with me earlier, but it's my understanding Mr. Markham died of cancer." That was public information which didn't violate any health information privacy laws. "Can I have your name?"

"Pamela Riggins. I'm a good friend of Anne Markham's—you know, John Markham's widow."

"What can I do for you, Ms. Riggins?"

"I have some information you might want about Mrs. Markham, but I don't want to talk about it on the phone. Can someone come to my house to talk about it?"

He sighed. "Give me your address and I'll be right over." He hoped that this wasn't a colossal waste of his time. He had a lot of other work to do.

• • •

Lt. Owens and his partner, Sgt. Paul Bronson, went over to Pamela Riggins' house, a large two-story home three blocks from the Markham's. She opened the door and let them in.

"Do you want some coffee or something to drink?" she asked. She was an attractive brunette, in her late fifties, Owens guessed.

"No, Ma'am," he said as they took a seat in the living room. "You said you had some information you didn't want to discuss on the phone."

"I don't want to get anyone in trouble. Will what I tell you be held in confidentiality?"

"That really depends on what it is, Ms. Riggins. You could be asked to testify in court if it leads anywhere."

She pondered a moment. "This is terrible, but . . . I was friends with Anne Markham. We went to lunch a lot and talked often on the phone. We haven't talked since John died two months ago."

"What is it you want to tell me?"

"In the last couple of years, John and Anne had grown apart. I don't know if you knew this, but, Anne was having an affair on him. On the surface, he appeared to be this wonderful, good-looking executive, but most people didn't know."

"About what?" Bronson asked.

"His womanizing, his partying, his drinking—he treated Anne like dirt. That was long before he got cancer. After he got sick, there wasn't much left in Anne to help care for him. She'd moved out months before the diagnosis."

He frowned and crossed his arms. "Ms. Riggins, we really don't care about the Markhams' marital habits, unless this has to do with a crime. Can you get to the point, please?"

She blurted it out. "All right, then—Anne said she wanted to poison him with arsenic. Said he was a 'son of a bitch bastard' and deserved to die."

"She told this to you in person?" he asked.

"No, on the phone."

"So, there are no witnesses?"

"No witnesses, but," she said, holding out a digital tape recorder. "It's on here, on tape. My husband tapes all phone conversations. He's an insurance executive, you know."

He took the small digital recorder and hit the "play" button. After a few minutes, they verified what Pamela Riggins had just told them.

"Ma'am, was Mrs. Markham aware you were recording this conversation?" he asked in a harsh tone.

"No. I didn't even think about it myself until I hung up."

"You shouldn't tape conversations without the consent of all parties. It's illegal."

"Like I said, my husband has it set up automatically, so I didn't know. Does that mean I'm in trouble?"

"Not from me, but it may mean I can't use this as evidence. I would like to have it, though." She handed him the recorder.

"Detective, I don't want to cause trouble, but I thought the police should have this. What will happen now?"

"We'll investigate this further. I really appreciate your coming forth with this information, Ma'am. Here's my card, and we'll be in touch." They shook hands with her and returned to their car.

"What do you think, Marc?" Sgt. Bronson asked as he got in the passenger front seat. "This is pretty weird stuff."

"Son of a bitch," he replied as he started the engine and drove off. "Maybe that damn doctor's on to something."

"That doctor who's a friend of Bonnie Mendoza's?"

"Yeah—she started in with this crazy story about 'bits being manipulated' in the guy's x-rays, monkeys writing Shakespeare, and shit like that. I don't understand that geek egghead crap.

Mendoza's a real oddball, but pretty sharp."

"I went through academy with her brother Mike—he's real smart, but a regular sort of guy. She's kind of strange, though. Talks weird."

"What, you never heard a deaf person before? They some-times talk like that."

"Not that, Marc—I mean the big words and stuff. I can't understand some of them."

"You gotta start using those vocabulary builder tapes, Bron-son. Get educated if you want to make lieutenant like me."

"But, anyway, the doctor says Markham didn't die of cancer?"

"He can't prove it—he just says the x-rays were altered."

"Yeah, Marc, but that tape doesn't prove anything. It's just a threat. People make threats all the time with no intention of carrying them out."

"I know—it's probably a dead end. But we've got to check it out. Damn."

• • •

Owens and his partner arrived back at the station and went straight to the forensics lab, where Bonnie's assistant greeted them. "Tina, I need to talk to Mendoza right now. Is she here?"

"She's in a meeting with the techs—room 404. She has a deposition at eleven, so you'd better get her out if you need to talk to her."

They went up to the fourth-floor meeting room and motioned through the window for Bonnie to come out. She paused her meeting and came out of the conference room. "What's up, my favorite gumshoe colleagues?"

"We just had an interesting conversation with a woman who has a recording that could mean your doctor buddy is right."

"Let me tell my meeting attendees to come back later," she said as she went back in and dismissed them. They went back into the empty meeting room, and Owens played the recording for her.

"What do you think?" Owens asked.

"It would help immensely if I could understand it." She took a device from her belt that she plugged into the USB (Universal

Serial Bus) connector on the digital recorder, and adjusted the volume. She had difficulty "hearing" electronic devices with tiny speakers, and had a special direct link with one of her aural processors via an auxiliary amplifier. She could, after playing it several times, understand most of the conversation.

"Pretty good timing, that woman coming forth with this now," Owens said. "Almost *too* good."

She crossed her arms and laughed. "Yes, but now who is talking proof? Even if you get it admitted, Marc, it's suspect. I can construct a phonetic spectrograph and determine if it's her voice, but it means little by itself."

"I'd like you to do that, if you can."

"The results will be optimized if you bring in the real Anne Markham to repeat the same words. But even if she volunteers to do that, which I doubt, it's insufficient evidence."

"By itself, of course not. But I can get a court order to exhume the body and test it."

She shook her head. "That will be impossible, because there *is* no body. Markham was cremated."

"Crap, I didn't know that. What kind of toxicology can you do on cremains?"

"Minimal. Organic compounds are vaporized during cremation. A gas-fired cremator is heated by a blowtorch to approximately 2,800 degrees Fahrenheit, at which point the body, which is seventy–five percent water, burns outside to inside in a rapid cycle of layer by layer combustion, and vaporization—"

"I get the idea. It's frickin' hot," he interrupted. "I don't need a treatise on the details of cremation. I have lunch soon."

"But, in summary, all that remain are the solids that don't vaporize. Bone fragments and heavy metals, mostly."

"What kind of heavy metals?"

"Thallium and arsenic would be the primary ones used as a poison. Arsenic is more typical, of course."

"Are his ashes even buried?"

"Yes, they are at Raintree Cemetery."

"I'm going to get a court order to exhume the ashes and have you guys examine them. Do you think there's enough cause for that?"

"They are merely ashes and it doesn't take much to justify that, Marc."

"Great. I'm on my way."

• • •

Two days later, John Markham's ashes were exhumed and returned to the forensic laboratory. The technician tested the cremains after preparing the sample, and gave Bonnie a printout:

NAME: JOHN W. MARKHAM   MASS: 3.2 kg
CHEMICAL ANALYSIS OF CREMAINS

COMPOUND	% COMPOSITION
PHOSPHATE	52.50%
CALCIUM	27.30%
SULFUR	13.20%
SODIUM	1.66%
CHLORIDE	1.52%
SILICA	1.04%
ALUMINUM OXIDE	0.88%
MAGNESIUM	0.58%
ARSENIC	0.56%
PLATINUM	0.10%
OTHER TRACE METALS	0.66%
TOTAL	**100.00%**

She found Owens in his office. "Marc—analysis of the Markham cremains reveals approximately half a percent of elemental arsenic. We don't know the valence state of arsenic in the original compound before cremation, however."

"Is that enough to kill someone?" he said as he pointed his pen at her from behind his desk.

"It depends on what form it existed in when he consumed it. Arsenic is generally administered as the salt, not the metalloid itself. But, yes—that amount could be lethal, especially in his weakened condition."

Owens stood up excitedly. "It looks like your doctor boyfriend was on the right track. Would it have been possible to tell if the arsenic was in the body before cremation, or if it was added later?"

She pointed her right index finger at him. "He is *not* my boyfriend, Marcus Owens! What an improper assumption."

"Sorry, my mistake." The angular detective laughed.

"But, you're suggesting it could've been added to the ashes later? Naturally, it's possible, but unlikely."

"What do you think about this standing up in court?"

"Cremains are technically a broken chain of evidence — someone could have dug them up and replaced them, or tampered with them before burial. It also doesn't prove Anne Markham gave him arsenic. Finally, we cannot conclusively prove the ashes were Markham's."

"But you're sure they're human?"

"The spectral analysis of the remnants is consistent with mammalian origin, but I can't confirm them as human. DNA, like any other organic compound, would be vaporized, so genetic confirmation is impossible. The platinum is interesting. Some jewelry he was cremated with, perhaps."

"Tell Darkkin, who is not your boyfriend, that I apologize. He's pretty smart, after all."

Chapter Fourteen

Lt. Marcus Owens asked Anne Markham to come in and talk to them at the station. The five–four, late-fiftyish, silver-haired woman came willingly, accompanied by her attorney, Tom McDonald. Owens and his partner questioned her in the sparsely furnished conference room.

"We have a lady who spoke with you on the phone, and said this," Owens said as he played the digital recording:

"I wish I could just poison the bastard with some arsenic or something, get rid of him, and put us all out of our misery."

"Do you deny saying that, Mrs. Markham?"

"You don't have to answer that," McDonald said.

She decided to speak anyway. "That sounds like me, but . . . we had that conversation a long time ago, and I don't remember it well, plus I was upset. John and I had just separated. But I never tried to kill him."

"That's not a good thing to say on tape, Ma'am," said the tall detective. "Not good at all."

"I didn't know that Pam was taping our conversation. Do you really think I would've said that if I'd known she was recording?" Anne replied, her voice shaky.

"So, you're saying you would've said it if you knew she *wasn't* taping?" Owens asked. "Mrs. Markham?"

"That's enough," Tom McDonald said. "I assume that you're considering charging my client. You have trace amounts of arsenic in cremains we're not even sure belonged to her husband, since the chain of evidence was broken. You can't use that recording, either, Lieutenant—it was obtained without her consent."

"We're just talking here, counselor. But, as you know, according to California Penal Code 633.5, a person receiving a threat of harm or violence against another person can make a tape recording without telling the other party."

"Nice try, but that won't go—she started recording before there was any threat. I'll have it thrown out."

"But we *do* have evidence someone altered Mr. Markham's medical records. My forensic specialist has confirmed that certain x-ray images are electronic forgeries. If you want, I'll get a search warrant for her home and its contents, unless you want to let us search voluntarily."

"You'll need to do that, Owens. This entire debacle is absurd, and you know it."

"Mrs. Markham, we'd also like to record your voice with the exact words said on this tape to verify it's yours."

McDonald laughed. "You've *got* to be kidding. She refuses to do that, as it could violate her Fifth Amendment right against self-incrimination."

"It's biometric evidence, not testimony—like getting height or weight, and she's not been charged with a crime."

"Well, she's still not doing it. The evidence was obtained illegally, so there's no point."

"Understood. But we can, then, just use her voice samples from the clips recorded during our discussion here."

"Feel free to do that. Are we done?" McDonald said.

"Sure—you and Mrs. Markham can leave. We might want to talk to you in the next few days, however."

• • •

Anne Markham and attorney Tom McDonald left the police station and drove back to her home, where they discussed the matter privately.

"Anne, whatever you say is protected by attorney-client privilege," he said, as they drank coffee in the large kitchen. "But you'd better be honest with me if I'm going to defend you. I need to know if you actually did anything to John."

"Dammit, you sound like those detectives."

"I mean it—I need to know everything."

"God help me," she sobbed. "There were times I really wanted to do it. I thought about how good it would be to be rid of the son of a bitch. But I didn't. Why can't they just let the bastard be dead and let us all live in peace?"

"Could your daughters be involved in this somehow? Would they have a reason to have killed him?"

"Of course not. Kris isn't real warm and fuzzy, and she's pretty selfish, but she was loyal to him. And Steph had no issues with him." Her eyes started twitching nervously.

McDonald studied his client intently. "Are you *sure* you're being honest with me? Most people say Kris is pretty greedy."

"Yes. Why would I lie about that?"

"I make my living learning to read people, and I've known you for years. I think there's something you're not telling me."

"Listen, you work for me, and I'm telling you the truth."

"I hope so, for your sake." McDonald changed the subject. "Anne, would anyone else have it in for you? Try to frame you for John's death?"

"I have no idea why or who. But what do you think will happen? They won't get a search warrant, will they?"

"I won't lie—John was a high-profile person, and they'll probably get their warrant. The good news is, they don't have anything concrete linking you to the death. I would argue that it's possible arsenic was added to the cremains. The bad news is—the publicity will be bad and will cost you with the Clystarr board."

"I don't give a shit about those assholes—they're Kris' problem now. But, about that recording, are you sure it's illegal?"

"It could go either way. He has a point about the threat of violence giving Pam Riggins the right, but I think I'll get it thrown out if they charge you."

She began crying. "Tom, why in God's name would I have had the ashes buried if I was going to kill him with arsenic? If I'd wanted to do that, I would've had them scattered."

"They'll probably argue that you didn't know it could be

found in ashes. As I recall, you and Stephanie had some disa-
greement about cremation, isn't that true?" he said as he pointed
his pen at her.

She paused for a few seconds, remembering. "Kris and I
remember him saying he wanted cremation. Steph, though, was
vehemently opposed to it, but in the end they had to do what I
desired. What, I'm supposed to disregard what he wanted, even
though I hope he burns in hell? I'm that decent, at least."

"There's no signed affidavit to that effect from John before he
died?"

"No. Just his verbal wishes."

"They might bring that up, and your pushing for cremation
could be a factor in this."

"But he had metastatic cancer. Even if I *had* poisoned him—
which I didn't—that wouldn't have changed."

"You're right—proving you killed him will be difficult for
them. I don't see a great case on their side, but this could get ugly
for you personally. Someone dug up some dirt, and they need a
suspect. If there's anything you need to disclose, you'd better do it
now."

• • •

Bonnie came to work the next day and sat at her office desk to
check e-mail, as her assistant, a moderately overweight, fortyish
woman, came in. "Bonnie, Lt. Owens was up here ten minutes ago
and needs to talk to you ASAP. Can I tell him to come back?"

"What is my schedule? Do I have time, Tina?"

"Yes. You're free until nine-thirty, but have to leave for court
then. I'll send the driver for you, as usual."

"All right—he may come up now, I suppose."

Owens came in a few minutes later, with the digital recording
of Anne Markham in hand. "Mendoza, can you analyze this voice
recording of Anne Markham?"

"Do you have identical speech recorded from her for comparison, as I requested?"

"No, her attorney wouldn't allow it. We have a tape of the
conversation when she came in to talk, though." He handed her

the disk with both recordings.

"Okay, Marc. I'll work on it later today and get back to you."

Later that day she rescheduled several meetings so she could analyze the recordings. She was, of course, a board certified forensic audio/video examiner—no small accomplishment for a deaf person. Certification required completion of several courses as well as the analysis of at least one hundred cases under the supervision of a known expert, and, finally, examination before a board of experts.

Fortunately, both recordings were digital, which eliminated the quality loss inherent with analog to digital conversion. The software used for analysis used an algorithm called "hidden Markov models" (HHM) to compare speech patterns. Each digital waveform would be reduced to a set of variables that could be compared to a reference; the software would then examine specific and unique features from an individual's speech, such as cadence, harmonic level, pitch, and tone. Ideally, the recording in question should be compared to the same syllables spoken by the reference source. Per her attorney's advice, however, Anne Markham wouldn't do that.

Voiceprint, or phonetic spectrograph analysis, was once felt to be as infallible as a fingerprint or other biometric data. One of the developers of this technology, Lawrence Kersta, published data that demonstrated voiceprints were reliable methods of identifying voices. In the 80's and 90's, however, the technology came under scrutiny as not being very reliable. Recent computer technology, however, such as introduction of the Markov models, has made it a more useful tool, although not nearly as convincing as fingerprint or DNA evidence.

Her conclusion was that, based on the data, the recording made by Pamela Riggins had a ninety–five percent probability of belonging to Anne Markham. The evidence itself might be excluded if a judge upheld her attorney's claim it was illegally obtained, but it could be used internally to decide on further prosecution. She went to see Owens immediately.

"It's nearly a perfect match, Marc. Even without the same exact words, I had enough to construct a satisfactory model."

"But it's not the best form of evidence. Could the conversation have been digitally pieced together from other words she said? Like we used to do in the old days, splicing audio tape?"

"Doubtful. The specific speech elements, for example, cadence and other idiosyncratic characteristics, would be unnatural. The person on that tape spoke those words exactly. You can't just put random words together with the same qualities. That, I would defend."

"So they couldn't have just rearranged Anne's voice. Was it her voice, though?"

"I would say so, with almost absolute certainty."

"Could the recording have been forged?"

"I doubt it—the exact speech components match, and that's very hard to fake. Digital technology may exist which could accomplish that, but I'm skeptical."

"Thanks, Mendoza. I'll try to get the DA to admit that as evidence. This will be a big help in getting a search warrant. I'll let you know how it goes."

Chapter Fifteen

Alex came to Bonnie's residence, a condominium in an attractive end of town. An unusually nice place for a police scientist, he thought as he walked up the steps. He was certain the immaculately organized scientist's home would be in disgustingly perfect order. She answered the door and invited him inside. "Hello, Alex. Please come in."

She was impeccably dressed, wearing a light three-quarter length pink dress that left her muscular shoulders and arms exposed. But he looked around and was surprised by how cluttered her well-decorated dwelling was.

"Very nice place you have here."

"Thank you. I funded much of it myself. My oldest brother paid for the rest, as well as my parents' and my other brother Mike's home."

"Is your brother rich or something?"

"Yes. He was a professional football player for eight years, and wanted to give us all something as a present."

He knew a lot about football, and thought for a few seconds of the handful of Hispanic players who came to mind. "I don't believe it—Jaime Mendoza is your brother? He won a Super Bowl with the Packers in '97 and went to the Pro Bowl a couple of years. He was on my fantasy team."

"Yes, '96 and '97. But he blew out his knee in '98 and had to retire. He's the head coach at the University of Missouri now, and wants to get back to the pros as a coach someday."

"I didn't know that." He saw many books on the large book-

shelf in her living room. The subject range was quite wide, rang-
ing from science and astronomy to the literary classics, as well as
numerous tomes on magic and puzzle games. Not a lot of music,
he noticed. No television in the living room, either—he wouldn't
be spending Super Bowl Sunday here.

Another shelf was littered with science and athletic awards,
the latter mostly track and field ribbons from high school and
college. He saw a large framed photo of her in midair at the long
jump, and her heptathlon medals from 2001 and 2005.

"When I saw your motivational poster, I sort of flipped out.
I've never known a gold medalist before."

"They were not the genuine Olympics, but the games for the
deaf. I'm not good enough to be in the regular heptathlon."

"You're too modest. That's a fantastic accomplishment."

"If I had given everything else up, perhaps I could have made
it to Sydney or Athens—but you have to be focused on only that. I
am better at sprints than the other events, but I always wanted to
do the heptathlon."

"I guess I would've known that if I'd been closer to Wendy all
those years. We sort of drifted apart."

"I also owe much to my composition of high-quality DNA. My
grandfather was a silver medalist for Mexico in the 400 meters at
the 1952 Olympics in Helsinki, and my dad and brother Mike
were collegiate sprinters. Jaime, you have heard of. My mom is a
four handicap golfer."

He walked around the living room and looked at more photos,
and saw what appeared to be one of her when she was younger.
She was smaller, extremely thin, and wearing a long white gown.
He looked at another picture of her in the dress, standing next to
his sister, who at that time dwarfed her. He had forgotten that
Wendy had known her for that long.

"That was my *quinceañera*, a coming of age party for Latina
girls on their fifteenth birthday. I don't remember any of the
music, as I was not 'hearing' very well then. Excuse me for a
moment. I have to get a couple of things. I apologize, but I didn't
have time to straighten up."

He went over to the sofa and moved several things to the side
so he could sit down. The exacting scientist was a little unkempt

at home, it seemed. Piled on the sofa were several books, a sweater, a discus, a pizza box, a graphing calculator, several stuffed animals, and a heavy wooden box containing keys and several pairs of manacles, the largest weighing about three pounds, with each bracelet measuring two inches thick. Not the type of things he had seen in any other woman's living room.

"Interesting assortment of items here," he said as she walked back into the room. "Something here for everybody."

"I'm embarrassed. Don't tell anyone about this," she said as she picked up the large pizza box. "I shouldn't be eating junk food, but you know how it is."

"Not the tasty-looking Romo's Pizza remnants. This other fun item on your sofa."

"Yes, that powerful calculator has a gigabyte of memory, and can indeed be very fun. Fibronacci number puzzles, for example."

"I'm sure that is entertaining, but I've never seen anything like these giant metal thingies before. Are they a joke or something?"

She turned her head curiously. "*A joke*? No, those devices are quite functional, I assure you. Each bracelet can withstand a tensile force of 10,000 Newtons for over two minutes."

He stared at the polished steel. "These kind of have that retro industrial look. I prefer the pink fuzzy ones myself, though."

"*Fuzzy*? Oh, 'fuzz'—a colloquialism for police." She laughed as she slapped him playfully on the back. "Silly, those are not for official law enforcement use!"

"So I figured. Where did you get something like that?"

Her eyes brightened as she picked them up. "That set is from Germany and constructed from a titanium-molybdenum alloy. You certainly must want to try them, as most visitors do. Dozens more are in the extra bedroom, along with the many other items, if you want to see those."

"Wow. Do you have many of these 'visitors' to the, uh, 'extra bedroom,' is it?"

She nodded. "Naturally—you may be surprised to know that many of the curious are ladies."

He grinned. "This may be a stupid question, but why do you need so many? Won't just a couple of sets do?"

"Not hardly—my hobby requires many varieties."

"Hobby? Cool." Whatever turns you on, as he was open to just about anything that might lead to interesting adventures. He had dated a girl once who was into that, but Bonnie seemed to have a strange naïve quality—like a little girl excitedly wanting to show a playmate her doll collection.

"Here, I'll demonstrate them for you." She handed him the chunky cuffs, but he hesitated. "Oh, come on. You will enjoy the superb craftsmanship."

"I don't think—well, okay." He reluctantly took them as the thought of touching that muscular, lightly perfumed, caramel-colored body made him a little bit dizzy. She then helped him apply one cuff to her left wrist and then put her hands behind her back.

"Put the other one on me, please, so that there can be no doubt they are on correctly."

"Are you *sure* we should be doing this?" he said nervously.

"What? We are not children who require supervision. I do this all the time and know what I'm doing." It was nice one of them knew what was going on.

"Sounds fun, but, don't we, like, need the key or something?" He was normally quite composed, but now noticed his heart rate had increased and he was becoming diaphoretic as he looked at those long, muscular arms and legs.

"Ha! Are you kidding? We will not require it."

"Got it—whatever you say."

He put the other one on and tightened it appropriately, and was impressed by the silky smoothness of the mechanism. He was now feeling even more light-headed. He had a vasovagal faint once when he was eleven, after he discovered his dad's many eight–millimeter "adult" movies in the attic; this felt much like the same thing.

She turned around to him with her hands behind her and smiled. He liked to get down to business, but this was a bit quick, even for him. Given his reputation, he undoubtedly would be blamed for this little scene if it went badly.

For some reason, he then recalled his collegiate readings from General Sun Tzu's ancient classic *The Art of War*, which taught him that severe consequences might await one who neglected to fully evaluate a situation before plunging in. That doe-eyed, sweet-faced, 165-pound body was built for action, and he didn't want to make it angry with yet another colossal blunder. He enjoyed having all his teeth and walking without crutches.

"Uh, aren't those things uncomfortable? You almost look like you enjoy wearing them."

"Oh, I do—these are actually quite ergonomically correct and cause no abrasions because of the smooth edges. The large surface area also distributes the force evenly over the wrists. European engineering, you know."

So much for his worries about carpal tunnel syndrome. "But I'm unfamiliar with the etiquette here in San Diego. What exactly do we, uh, do now?"

"You don't know what we should do next?" she said with a mischievous grin on her face. "Surely you must know."

"I have a good idea, but let's make sure we're both on the same page."

She looked at his groin area and raised her eyebrows. "Yes, I can see you have brought a friend along. Perhaps someday I will meet him. But, right now, you will time me, of course."

He paused. "Huh?"

"Time me with your watch—start now."

He started the chronometer of his Breitling Chronomat and watched her go into a trance-like state of extreme concentration as she pulled and twisted her arms. Half a minute later, she brought her hands to the front and handed him the empty shackles.

"How long?"

"Uh, thirty–two seconds."

"Oh, that's terrible. My best is twenty–one seconds with those. Sorry to disappoint you—I know you expected more."

"In a way, yeah. That was . . . it, then?"

"For now, yes. We can try something more elaborate when we have more time."

"So, what do I do with these things now? Do we save them for later?" He was now dripping with perspiration.

"You look like you're not feeling well," she said as she tilted her head, as if puzzled. "Perhaps you should lie down so you and Alex Jr. can re-equilibrate your blood supply."

He sat down for a few seconds with his hands between his head. "No problem, I'm just a little overheated. I'll be fine in a few minutes. Fresh air might be better."

"Okay, if you're sure."

She grabbed her purse as they walked out to Alex's vehicle a few minutes later. He felt he had just exited from some alternate universe and gotten back to reality.

"Good, you have a GPS," Bonnie said as she entered his SUV. "I'm not wearing my GPS watch."

"Why would we need *that*? I thought you'd know your way around town, having lived here your entire life."

"Yes, but I get lost easily. It's kind of complicated."

That seemed weird, although the evening had certainly been unusual so far. He was looking forward to something unpredictable for a change.

• • •

They went to dinner at a small, out-of-the way Italian restaurant and exchanged life stories. She said that she liked the small restaurant as it was always quiet—he thought it odd for a deaf person to prefer that. He ordered a steak, she an impossibly large dish of pasta with red sauce. She ordered red wine, he iced tea. He wasn't drinking or smoking at all these days, and felt pretty good about that—a big accomplishment for him.

"So, you're a forensic scientist now. I'm not that familiar with forensic police work."

"I was a crime scene investigator first, before I went into administration of the lab. I obtained my bachelor's in physics and mathematics, and a master's degree in forensic science. I'd someday like to get my doctorate and perhaps enter federal law enforcement, or teach at a university like my father."

"It sounds like exciting work."

"It's often interesting, but exciting—most people think it's like television, what with all the CSI shows these days. It's not like that at all, and people expect the impossible, like getting DNA confirmation in an hour. It's like your job. I'm certain that most doctors' lives are not as they are portrayed in the popular media."

"Not really. Radiation oncology isn't one of your more excit-ing medical specialties. I doubt anyone would make a TV series about it."

"Why did you decide to go into that specialty?"

"My father was a nuclear physicist. I'm not really sure what he did—he was pretty secretive. He left the university when I was little and went to work for the government."

"He was brilliant, from what Wendy has said."

"Yeah. He retired a number of years back. His alcoholism got really bad, though, and he developed these paranoid ideations. Thought everyone was out to get him. He never went to get any help, unfortunately."

"Does he still live back in Tennessee, and are you close to him? Wendy seldom mentions him. She says he has many troubles."

"He still lives in Oak Ridge. I talk to him once in a while, but we're not that close any more. Wendy never forgave him for the affairs he had on Mom. She lives in Tucson now."

"*Grazie*," she said in slurred Italian as the waiter brought her a second glass of wine. "*Un po' di acqua per favore?*" The waiter then filled their water glasses from a pitcher. "I only met your father once, at Wendy's wedding. He seemed quite odd."

"You've got that right—one weird dude."

"I'm sorry. I'm lucky to have my family around. My father was a lieutenant on the police force. He obtained his doctorate and now teaches criminology at San Diego State. My mom teaches high school advanced mathematics."

He worked on his meal. "That's great. Did you always want to be in the law enforcement field?"

"Yes," she laughed. "It was pre-destined. My brother Mike is on the force, too. I wanted to be an FBI Special Agent."

"Why didn't you? You have the education, and I'm sure that you would pass the physical tests."

"Yes, but I don't meet the hearing requirements for the FBI. Agents cannot have more than a twenty–five decibel hearing loss, and I am far past that."

"I know you were ill when you were younger, Wendy said."

"I contracted meningitis when I was eleven and nearly died. I was in a coma and on a ventilator for two weeks, and they didn't think I was going to make it. My doctors were unsure if I would walk or talk again. As you have witnessed, I run pretty well. Talking is still a work in progress."

"I'm sorry about that."

"No need to be. Life is great—I'm just thankful to be here. My deafness doesn't cause me much of a problem with everyday life, simply because I can't remember being any other way."

"Losing the memories, though . . . I can't imagine what that would be like. I feel so bad for you." A few tears rolled from his eyes.

"Hey, it's okay," she said, grasping his hand. "I don't grieve losing what can't be changed. I have a few cherished fragmented memories of childhood that I hold onto. Life is about going forward. There's no other way for me to be."

"I don't know if I could've done that."

She stared at him intensely. "If you have no choice, you must. You find inner strengths you did not know you had."

He changed the subject. "I remember just one implant when I met you before. I've never seen anyone with two."

"Binaural implants are unusual, but give me superior sound discrimination in noisy environments. The speech, though, is frustrating. I can only speak so fast, and some people assume I'm slow or something. I have other ways to compensate, so I'm fortunate."

"What do you mean?"

"I perceive things differently than most people. Numbers and letters form bright colors, wonderful sounds, and intense odors. This allows me to remember and quickly process remarkable amounts of information. It's called 'synesthesia.' Have you heard of it?"

"Yeah, my dad's experienced that, smelling colors, seeing sounds and other stuff, and it was a bit disturbing to him."

"Your father is a synesthete? It's uncommon in men."

He laughed. "Sort of. His was, well—chemical-induced."

"Chemical-induced? Substances he was exposed to in the nuclear industry?"

"Uh, no—a different set of 'chemicals.' Dad had a variety of heightened sensory experiences after using LSD and mescaline in the sixties and seventies."

"That sounds unwise. I can't imagine what would happen to my mind if I used drugs. I see enough strange things as it is."

"Dad doesn't have the best judgment. So, you have synesthesia a result of your illness?"

"No. My mom is a grapheme-color synesthete, the most common type—I inherited it from her. She sees numbers as colors, but doesn't have the rare auditory and olfactory variety I do. But she's a high-mathematical synesthete like me. Some are poor at math."

"So that's how you did those mentalist tricks."

"Sure, the card guessing game. I looked at the whole deck for a few seconds and memorized the place of every card. Every number and suit becomes a distinct sound if I concentrate hard enough, and it becomes a melody. By remembering the melody, I can recite the entire order of cards."

"But how did Wendy tell you which card? Neither she nor the girl saw it until the girl turned it over."

"Right, but Wendy knew the order. She starts the sentence off with a word. One started with 'quite.' That's the seventeenth letter, and was matched with the seventeenth card, which I remembered from memory. The alphabet is only twenty–six letters. For the other half of the deck, she would say my name as the first word, indicating the card is in the second half."

"You should try Las Vegas. I'm sure you'd make a fortune."

She paused, frowned, and put her head down. "Yes, well, that's not for me, thanks."

After dinner, he took her back to her condominium and took her to the door. He was much more nervous than usual; although he was usually quite confident with women, tonight he felt more like a teenager on his first date, and didn't know what other interesting things were in store for the remainder of the evening. He was used to a high degree of intimacy on the initial outing, but something told him not to push too hard.

"I had a good time tonight, Alex."

"I did, too. It was a good meal. Best I've had in a long time."

"I would invite you in, really—but I must rise early. I truly hope that you will call me again." He kissed her on the lips as she went inside. Did she really want to see him again? He thought so, but wasn't sure. He drove back to his apartment about five miles away and continued to think about her.

He sent her a different floral arrangement every day for the next six days. She called to thank him and asked him if he wanted to go out again. They agreed on some take-out food at his apartment and a play—Arsenic and Old Lace.

Chapter Sixteen

On the surface, it seemed to Alex that he and Bonnie had little in common. He was used to living the fast life in Nashville, going to clubs, concerts, and other activities. Bonnie was more interested in quiet pursuits such as reading and outdoor activities. On a deeper level, though, they shared a love of science and passion for learning new things.

She was unbeatable at any games which involved discrete numbers or words. She was also quite adept at strategy games such as chess, where Alex couldn't defeat her, despite years of playing. For some reason, she had no interest in card games, despite being an expert at card tricks. Both, however, were severely cooking-impaired, and between them had difficulty creating an adequate meal.

Later, they were over at her condo after coming home from a show and were relaxing in her bedroom, where the lone TV set was located. Alex picked up one of her blue Prada pumps lying on the bed and noticed the number "4" marked on the inside.

"Why do your shoes have numbers on them?" he said as he twirled the shoe in his hand. "Four can't be the size."

"*All* my clothes have numbers. The blue shoes are category four and may only be worn with category four clothing."

"Why? Are you color blind, too?"

She laughed. "No—I can read an Ishihara chart as well as you. But certain colors, when combined, produce odd sensations. I'm told my own clothing combinations are . . . shall we say, unappealing. I disagree, of course."

"Is that a synesthesia thing?"

"Yes—the combination of burgundy and lime green, for example, evokes a delightful strawberry aroma. Orange and violet together taste like chocolate ice cream."

He stuck his tongue out. "Yuck. So, someone picks the clothes out and numbers them so they match."

"My mother does that. She wants me to look nice."

That she did. He marveled at what was the most remarkable human being he had ever met. She had overcome numerous obstacles and came out on top every time. How could he do the same to live up to his potential?

• • •

Bonnie told him she was a little nervous later that evening, as they had been out five times with a certain subject never having been brought up.

"I know you're probably anxious . . . I would like you to stay tonight, if you wish."

"Tonight? Are you sure? I don't want to push you."

"No, I'm sure about it."

"It's important to me you feel comfortable with it."

About fifteen minutes later, she showered and put on an attractive nightgown, but was obviously nervous.

"You look really beautiful."

"Thank you. But you need to know something—I haven't done this very much and don't have much experience."

"That's okay, there's nothing wrong with that. I'm here for you."

"I'm just a little nervous."

He didn't want it to be obvious he was very anxious as well. As they went to bed together, he anticipated a wonderful night of love. He wanted nothing more than to reassure her and be gentle.

However, something went wrong again. Some of the other times he'd been drinking too much, but not tonight.

"What's wrong, Alex?"

"I'm sorry. I'm just having a little problem tonight."

"Do you need more time? There's no hurry—we have all

night."

"It just . . . isn't working." He was used to his companions being fairly insensitive to his problem that was becoming more frequent.

"Is it me? Have I done something wrong?" She got up and walked across the room. "I know it's probably me."

"What do you mean? You're a beautiful woman. It has nothing to do with you."

"I hope that's the truth."

"I'm sorry. I'll go if you want."

"What? Why do you think I would want you to leave?" She got back into bed and hugged him.

"Well, nothing's going to happen tonight, I'm afraid."

"I hope you don't think me such a shallow person that I wouldn't want you here because of that. We can still share a special experience. The other isn't that important. It'll be all right next time."

"What if it isn't?"

"Then we'll deal with it. Sometimes our physical body doesn't do things the right way, and I know all about that. It's what's up here that's important," she said, tapping on her forehead. "Whatever is going on, I will help you with it. We don't need to fret about tonight."

She said the act of love itself wasn't as important to her as reassurance she was still wanted by him. He thought about it as they went to sleep. Why had it happened again? He wasn't especially tired, and was in the best physical condition he had been in years.

He'd never really been with someone he felt was both a physical and intellectual equal—the possibility of failure was therefore very disturbing to him. But Bonnie was a much deeper person than he'd realized. She was someone who had lost physical abilities, and she didn't dwell on it.

It was nice having someone close to him for the night, someone whose name he would remember in the morning. Despite his sexual difficulties, it was probably the happiest night he had experienced in a long time.

Chapter Seventeen

Detective Lt. Marcus Owens and his partner arrived at Anne Markham's home, a large Tudor-style home in an older neighborhood. She answered the door.

"Mrs. Markham," Owens said. "We have a search warrant for your home."

"My attorney told me to expect you. I don't have anything to hide," she said. Her attorney, Tom McDonald, was there as well. She definitely was not pleased as she watched them search the premises. They went through all the closets, emptied out drawers, ruffled through clothing, and generally made a mess of things.

After about an hour, one of the officers called out to Owens. "Marc—this is interesting." He showed Owens a box containing rat poison containing arsenious oxide as the active ingredient. Another officer found some books on poisoning in the study.

Owens then confronted Anne. "You should know. We found rat poison containing arsenic in your house. And we discovered that you had several books on poisoning purchased over an Internet retailer."

"I have rat problems. I also have an interest in crime stories and entertained being a writer at some point. It's no crime to own those books. I have lots of books on true crime, as well as fiction books."

"This house can't be more than five or six years old, and I doubt there's a big rodent problem here. Not in Southern California," Owens said as he continued looking around the living room.

Tom McDonald rose from his chair and spoke up. "Anne, I'd

advise you not to say anything further."

"What's going to happen, Tom? Are they going to arrest me?"

"Probably," McDonald said. "I'm sorry, but it's a high-profile case, even though the evidence is circumstantial. If I were you, I'd clear up any loose ends before they get back."

Owens and his group gathered and prepared to leave. "Mrs. Markham, I'd advise you not to go anywhere. We'll be back, as the good counselor said."

● ● ●

Alex and Bonnie were consuming take-out Chinese food at his apartment, which was relatively Spartan in furnishings, except for the latest in high-tech electronics. A sixty-inch plasma screen television was the focal point of the living room. They were watching a sports show, where a well-known, incendiary baseball manager was conducting a post-game interview.

"I've always wondered about something," he said.

"What?"

"When they bleep out the profanity, can you read their lips and tell what they said?"

"Yes, and it can be quite entertaining. Now some of the shows pixelate the mouth so as not to offend the deaf. Just another thing taken away from us."

"Anyway, the Markham case is going somewhere, right? I told you those CT images were digitally altered. They find out if it's really Anne Markham who did it?"

"A woman came forward with a voice recording, which matches Anne Markham's exactly. The detectives searched her house and found arsenic-containing rat poison."

"Have you ever done any work where it was the poison?"

"One. It's an excellent poison, but rarely used today because it can be easily detected. There are many organic compounds that can kill easily, but degrade rapidly."

"He didn't have the typical symptoms, though—delirium, diarrhea, abdominal pain."

"If the arsenicosis was chronic, the specific symptoms would be less pronounced, Alex."

"So, will they arrest her and charge her with Markham's murder?"

"There may be probable cause at her home to arrest her, but a grand jury will have to indict her if that's not the case. The latter will be challenging."

"But arsenic is so corny. It's been done to death."

"Of course, it's one of the oldest known poisons, dating back to 700 A.D."

"I was happy you found something in the cremains, but if you were going to alter radiographic images at the machine level, wouldn't you use something a little more sophisticated than arsenic? How tacky."

"One may also debate that it is so obvious no one would think of using it. And, if your nicotine-enhanced brain had not been up all night analyzing images, it would never have been discovered."

"If not for that, we wouldn't be together in the first place. Markham actually did us a favor. No more nicotine for me, either. I've quit."

"Good, but I think you're paranoid. And why do you care so much about Markham, anyway? You didn't even know him."

He didn't know the answer to that question. He just believed he'd discovered something that he shouldn't have, done by someone who thought he or she was smarter than everyone else. And he didn't like to be outsmarted. He contemplated the ways he would've poisoned Markham if it had been his plan—something much more elaborate than that. Something worthy of a talented adversary.

• • •

Owens and his partner returned to Anne Markham's home the next day, as the attorney had predicted, with an arrest warrant signed by a judge, citing probable cause based on items found in her home earlier.

"Anne Markham, you are under arrest for the death of your husband." He read Anne her Miranda rights, and she was taken into custody. Officers actually were not required to read suspects their rights at the time of arrest, only before an interrogation. This was likely to be a high-profile case, however, and they didn't want anything to be thrown out of court if she started talking spontaneously.

"Tom . . ." she said as she turned pale and started trembling.

"I'll get down there right away and set up a bail hearing for you," McDonald said as Anne was led to the unmarked car and taken to jail.

• • •

The bail hearing was the next day. McDonald was able to get bond set at $100,000, given that she had no prior record and was neither felt to be violent nor a flight risk.

McDonald arrived to pick her up and they drove from the jail in his car. "Look, Anne, I'm trying to help you, but you have to be honest. I went through your records as you instructed me to do. I'm worried about the poisoning books you bought. It's pretty creepy."

"So what, Tom? Like I said, I wanted to get into writing crime stories. But I didn't poison John. Yes, there were times I wished he was dead, but I can't remember saying that to Pam. And I never would follow through on something that horrendous. Do you think that, if I really wanted to poison John, I would've been so blatant about it?"

"Who has access to your house? Does your daughter have a key?"

"Kristin? Why would you suspect her? And, no, she doesn't have a key. Neither does Stephanie. We don't really speak a lot any longer since John passed."

"Is there anyone else that would want to set you up?"

"I don't think so. The phone conversation with Pam—it was almost like she was goading me into saying that stuff about wanting to kill John. I just blurted it out, I think. I really don't remember much about it, I was so angry."

"Let me just tell you, the DA is going to argue you would be divorced soon, probably before he would've died of natural progression of his cancer."

"But there's no motive. We were married for thirty–five years, and there was no prenuptial agreement. I would've gotten half of the estate, anyway."

"Anne, I'll get the best criminal defense team we have to help. We'll get rid of this."

"I hope so, Tom," she said, trembling. "I've never been so scared in my life."

Chapter Eighteen

Alex and Bonnie spent an extended weekend together in the mountains in early August. Saturday would be her thirtieth birthday, and he had brought several special gifts. Her parents were out of town, and would have a party for her in a few days. He had rented a cabin about twenty miles outside of town; it was well-equipped with modern amenities, save computer connections, as he didn't plan on needing the Internet much this weekend. He certainly hoped this little sojourn would be something to remember.

It had been almost two weeks since their first attempt at lovemaking; he had earlier avoided the subject, but wanted to try again that night. He had, reluctantly, decided to see an internist about his problem last week. His laboratory tests were all normal, confirming his feeling that the problem was psychological. The fact it wasn't physical didn't make it any less difficult to treat. But he was now with a person who understood about being patient.

They did successfully consummate their relationship that night, and it was a much more meaningful experience than he'd expected. After all, most of his prior sexual adventures had been very superficial, and his previous lifestyle of one-night stands seemed strangely distant. Part of the warm feeling was a physical attraction, to be certain. He learned she was a very physical and sensual individual, although less experienced in intimate matters. But Bonnie Mendoza was, in totality, more woman than he'd ever been with before. Afterwards they relaxed and drifted off to sleep. The best sleep he'd had in many months.

• • •

The next morning, Alex woke up and tried to fix breakfast. He managed, with some success, to create a digestible meal of eggs, bacon, toast, and pancakes, and brought Bonnie breakfast on a bed tray.

"Breakfast in bed—how exceptional. Thank you. I have not had that for a long time."

"It's August sixth, your birthday, so I hope that it meets your standards."

"My standards are not very high. I am a poor cook, a genetic trait passed from mother to daughter. Oxygen and a defibrillator are mandatory accessories for our meals."

"So, do we do anything special for your thirtieth birthday, since it's two times fifteen? Another passage of womanhood?"

"Just passage into middle age, unfortunately."

"That's not true. Middle age is around fifty, fifty–five."

"How many people do you know who are a hundred? Not many."

They ate breakfast and lounged around for awhile. He eventually went to his suitcase and pulled out a small gift box.

"This is for you—happy birthday."

"What is it?"

"Open it and see." She opened the box, which contained a beautiful bracelet of eighteen-karat gold with diamonds and rubies. It had set him back a pretty penny.

"I can't believe that you purchased this. It's one of the most spectacular gifts I've ever received."

Alex removed the red metal bracelet from her right wrist and applied the other bracelet.

"It fits perfectly. You can wear it instead of that red one."

"Oh, no—I'm now like Samson without his hair, or Popeye without his spinach."

"You really can't tell right from left without it, can you?"

"Very poorly. After a minute or two, I can usually figure it out. Did you pick the bracelet out yourself?"

"I had some help." Wendy had helped him select it, since his knowledge of jewelry was equivalent to his culinary skills.

"Thank you so much. It's a very special gift."

They showered, changed clothes, read and watched television for awhile, and he thought more about her odd "hobby."

"Anyway, tell me about the magic stuff. Why did you get into that? It doesn't seem very scientific."

"When I was in rehab they wanted me to do things to help me regain hand-eye coordination, so I tried that. Eventually, I became quite skillful and am now a master class escapologist."

"About that—I used to think an escapologist was one who diverted his or her mind to purely imaginative activities."

"No, that's an escapist, or a person who gets away from it all by going off in his or her mind. Daydreaming. Escapologists escape from things."

"As I have learned. Why do you do that?"

"I guess I like the seeing the shock on people's faces when I escape from things. They don't expect it."

"There must be more to it than meets the eye. At first glance, it doesn't seem to be much more than trickery and sleight of hand."

"It can be highly elaborate. Much of it demands very high strength to size ratio and flexibility. The rest depends on an intricate knowledge of the devices, which can be complicated."

"How do you do that, though? Flexibility's one thing, but you can't bend through steel."

"Perhaps some day I will tell you my secrets, if you become an apprentice." He started laughing heavily. "What is so funny?"

"Well, on our first date, I saw Big Box O' Cuffs in your apartment and you playing with them. I thought they were for something else, though."

"What other purpose would there be for owning those?"

"I thought they were some kind of, uh, adult toy."

"Huh? They're real, not toys." She pointed a stern finger at him. "Listen up—toy ones will break and you'll be in a pickle."

He was now wise to the fact that her playing dumb was just an act. *No one*, least of all a forensic scientist who had done CSI work, could be so ingenuous. "Stop joking around. I mean a sex toy."

She displayed that inscrutable expression again. "Oh, I see, to play 'cops and robbers.' I've been called to rescue a couple of friends and neighbors who have gotten stuck playing that. Would you like to do that, robber?"

"Cops and robbers, right," he snickered. "Not the kind of game you probably played as a kid. But I can show you how to play the grownup version."

"If *you* are suggesting it, this activity must be very depraved."

"You're getting more perceptive. And you don't fool me with all this escape artist stuff—I think it's all repressed sexual energy. You secretly fantasize about it, don't you?"

"I do? Are you Dr. Sigmund Freud now, extracting my dark, subconscious desires?"

"Something like that." Why did she often answer a question with another question? "But you didn't answer me."

"The unknown is always more exciting. If you violate me, though, Doctor, I'll make certain you're reported to the medical board. I will also arrest you for assault when you are finished with your activity."

"You aren't a sworn officer and can't arrest anybody, so there. I know the law."

"Wrong—I can make a citizen's arrest for a felony committed in my presence. It seems there will be many infractions tonight."

"This is true."

"And you've already halfway unbuttoned my blouse, you pervert," she said as she thrust out her chest. "I even wore something special for you."

"What is it? A bustier? A teddy?"

"Better than that—it is custom-made and very expensive." He excitedly opened her satin blouse the rest of the way, like a boy opening a Christmas present. Underneath he found a tight-fitting royal blue spandex garment emblazoned with a stylized "M²" emblem on the front.

He felt the slick, shiny material. "How did you know I wanted to molest a superhero?" He then took out two red silk scarves.

"Silks? *You're* going to show *me* a magic trick? How comical."

He laughed. "Oh, yes, a trick we'll both enjoy."

"So, what dastardly thing have you planned for me? Do we engage in amorous dalliance after you affix me to the bed?"

"I don't know what 'dalliance' means, but it sounds fun."

"I hope you remembered to bring insulators."

• • •

Alex and Bonnie stopped for lunch at a seafood restaurant on the drive home. He ordered his usual beverage of iced tea as they waited on their meals.

She stared at his drink "You seem to avoid the subject of your obvious abstinence from ethanol. Why is that?"

"It's daytime and I'm driving. What's it to you?" The dysfunctional genie was poking his head out of the bottle.

"I was merely asking. You don't need to bite my head off."

He looked down at the table. "Sorry—I'm a bit sensitive. It took me a while to admit it, but I have a drinking problem," he said after some hesitation. He figured she probably suspected that, anyway.

She touched his hand. "I'm sorry. You doing okay with it?"

"Sometimes not. It's difficult—I haven't taken a drink in three months."

"It takes a lot of courage to do that, Alex," she said as she smiled and squeezed his hand. "The hardest part is admitting you have an addiction."

He opened his mouth wide. "Thanks for the pat on the back, but . . . that's pretty easy for you to say."

She pushed herself away from the table and put her hand over her chest. "Is it? How do you know? You think you know everything about me, do you?"

"*You* have an alcohol problem? The perfect wholesome girl?"

"No, not that—I enjoy an occasional drink. But I'm far from perfect, and not nearly as wholesome as you might believe. I have my own addiction for which I am still in counseling."

"Right," he laughed. "What did you do? Go on too many shopping binges at Police Supply Superstore?"

"You made a joke on our first date that I should gamble—how ironic. I can look at a deck of cards and, knowing what cards were dealt, automatically calculate the odds of any hand. The ability to instantaneously calculate probabilities is sufficient to win often enough to be in the money. Blackjack, poker, craps—anything that depends on mathematical odds. It always works, and I never make mistakes."

He stared at her for several seconds. "You're a compulsive gambler? What happened? I assume you lost a lot of money."

She frowned. "On the contrary—over several years, I won more money than you can imagine. You think my condo is nice? Well, I cannot afford that in San Diego on my salary, trust me, even with my brother's help. Las Vegas paid for the down payment, plus my student loans. Money is one worry I don't have."

He was perplexed. "What's the big deal, then? Thirty years old, with absolutely no debt. I'd be ecstatic if I could do that."

"What's the big deal? It became an obsession, that's what—all my time off, going to Las Vegas or wherever. And the Internet, which was even worse. Did I need the money? Was it for fun or recreation? I'm sure losing money would've been worse, but at least then I might've stopped. I didn't keep myself as healthy as I should have. I neglected relationships, my family, and finally gave it up. I play games of chance only for charity performances or for fun."

"You shouldn't feel guilty about winning money. It's not illegal or anything."

"Do you still not comprehend this? It's not about the money! It's the time taken away from things that are really important. God took away some abilities, but gave me other unique ones, which I should use to help people."

He shook his head and threw down his hands. "There you go with the God thing again. God looks after you, you think?"

"Of course God looks after me. He does after all people. If you wish to be a part of my life, you must try to accept God in some fashion—it's part of who I am. And if you want to continue an intimate relationship with me, we must have a commitment."

"Look, I'm not ready to get married, if that's where you're going with this."

"I didn't suggest that—I'm not, either. But understand I know much about you from your sister and how you don't like commitments."

"It's unfair that you know things about me from Wendy. I don't have the same advantage."

"Maybe that's true. But I think that we should promise to see only each other."

"I . . . don't know if I'm ready for that." He hadn't been with anyone else since they started dating, but he didn't like ultimatums.

"Well, that's the only way I can do things, Alex. I'm sorry, but you'll need to eventually make that choice."

"I'm also not ready to 'see the light' and forsake material things," he said as he finished his tea.

"Again, you blow everything out of proportion. I like many material things, such as clothes, books, computers, and fine jewelry. I just don't want my whole life to be about money. It's what you are inside that's important, rather than your accomplishments. You go see poor children in Mexico or South America, you see people who have nothing. Open your eyes."

"I can't help I wasn't poor—you weren't either, from what I know. Your idyllic family's right out of a 60's sitcom."

"Yes, but you can help being arrogant. You have more potential for doing good than you realize. Don't waste your gifts."

"I don't know—Wendy's like her mom. I'm my father's son."

"You're not at all like Conrad, and you and Wendy are much more alike than different. I'm not that dense. Deep down, she wants to help people, but she has her own self-serving motives. We all do."

"How do you know anything about my dad? You met him only once, you said."

"I can tell a lot about a person, and Conrad almost has an aura of maleficence. I felt very uncomfortable around him. I don't think I want to know him very well."

"He's just a crazy old man. You're exaggerating."

"You aren't like that, Alex. Maybe about some superficial things, but not deep down, and you can help many if you choose to do so."

He reflected on what she'd said, and much it was true. He'd never seen things in that light before, and she certainly had given him a lot to think about. Monogamous relationships might be worth a try; the other ones certainly hadn't worked out very well.

Chapter Nineteen

Alex and Bonnie returned to town and arrived at her home. Shortly after they began to unpack, her pager began vibrating loudly and emitting bright strobe flashes, a feature which existed in the event she didn't "hear" the beeping. She recognized the number as one belonging to police headquarters, and pulled out her cell phone which had a special cord that plugged into the speech processor of her left ear. She did much better with a direct connection to telephones than to try and deal with the added distortion of handsets.

"This is Bonnie Mendoza."

"Mendoza," Lt. Marcus Owens said, "we just got a call from the neighbor of a Dr. William Underwood. A gunshot was fired. Doc's dead, with a gun in his hand, they said."

"Who is this Dr. Underwood?" she asked.

"Markham's oncologist. It looks like a suicide. I know you're not on duty and it's not your job any more, but I know you have an interest in the case. Why don't you go out there and supervise the evidence handling? Unless you're busy."

"Thanks, I will be there as soon as I can. What's the address?"

"2626 Mockingbird Lane," Owens replied. Bonnie opened her GPS-enabled personal digital assistant, which provided a map.

"What happened?" Alex asked as she closed her cell phone.

"This Dr. Underwood was found dead at home. The neighbor heard a gunshot. Looks like a suicide."

"*Underwood*? He was Markham's medical oncologist. I have to come with you."

She pushed him back. "No, you aren't. It's a homicide scene, and you're not allowed."

"I won't bother anything."

"You're absolutely correct—because you're not going."

• • •

Bonnie and her CSI kit traveled with her driver to Dr. William Underwood's home. The collection of uniformed and plainclothes officers nervously parted like the Red Sea after spying her coming up the curved sidewalk.

The tan-suited woman entered the house and was greeted by Ray Lattimer, the homicide detective on duty.

"Wow, when we called for an investigator, I didn't think we'd get Bonnie Mendoza herself. To what do we owe this honor?"

"I have a special interest in this one. Owens tipped me off and asked if I wanted to come."

"It looks like this Underwood guy killed himself with a single shot from a thirty–eight caliber revolver. The body's in the den."

She picked up the weapon after donning gloves. Five rounds still left in the chamber, standard ammunition. A handwritten note had been found by his side.

"What's this? Suicide note?" she asked.

"Yeah," Lattimer said. "Real original."

She looked at the note, written on yellow legal pad paper, and read it:

"Please forgive me, but I can't live any longer with my disgrace. I must end it all today. Bill Underwood. "

A rather generic "suicide note," indeed, but creative writing may not have been Underwood's strong suit. "Is this firearm registered to him, Ray?"

"No, it's unregistered, but it would seem to be his."

"We can't assume anything," she said as she looked around for other clues. He'd been holding the gun in his right hand, and the entry and exit wound were consistent with the shot fired. Lattimer had found the bullet imbedded in a piece of paneling across the room after it exited the left side of Underwood's head. She picked the lock to the credenza and discovered a second handwritten note, which contained the following series of numbers plus a cryptic message:

10-5   34-6   43-12   2-8   82-4   91-3   102-10   23-5
67-7   43-2   45-8   118-11   54-9   47-5   6-12

PICKETT ATE NINE AND A HALF PIES IN HIS FIRST
LOG CABIN AND LISTENED TO A CD

"I have no idea what it means," Lattimer said. "It's right up your alley, though."

"It's meaningless to me. The first note is too stereotypical, the second is gibberish. Who is this Pickett?"

"Your guess is as good as mine. Maybe he was nuts, or high on crack or meth or something. Seen doctors be users before."

She noticed something else next to the note in the credenza. A word puzzle book—"Giant Mensa Super Puzzle Challenge"— obviously meant for people belonging to that exclusive high-IQ society. This version was published once monthly, and was only two weeks old.

They dusted for prints as she took the note, sealing it inside an evidence bag. She would likely be able to verify later if Underwood in fact had written the note.

"Looks to me like just a suicide. No sign of forced entry. You can look at the prints, but I don't see much here," Lattimer said.

"Very odd, the numbers and the book. I've never seen anything like it." Was this doctor high or crazy, or did the message have a hidden meaning? She had no idea.

• • •

Bonnie took her evidence back to the SDPD lab for analysis, where ballistics on the bullet matched that of the unregistered pistol he'd held in his right hand. The powder residue found on his right hand was also consistent with that mechanism of death.

She also analyzed the handwriting and deduced from samples

provided by the hospital that the handwriting resembled that in his "suicide note," but was almost *too* perfect. The ink used in his fountain pen was interesting, as the spectral pattern didn't match any known ink composition. She wrote up her preliminary findings and submitted them to Owens, but she didn't know what to make of the word puzzle book. Both notes contained only Underwood's fingerprints, while the book had others, likely from persons who had handled it before it was mailed and/or sold.

She later discovered the ink in the suicide note didn't match that in the fountain pen. The writing looked like Underwood's (after comparison from other written documents found in his home), but was remarkably regular. This might have not been unusual if he had used a ballpoint or gel pen, but fountain pens didn't produce such regular strokes. The spectral pattern of the ink in that note matched that from a well-known computer ink manufacturer; it apparently had been printed to look like he'd written it. But the ink in the second note from the credenza—with the numbers and riddle—*did* match that of the pen. Very strange.

• • •

Bonnie later invited Alex to her office to review the findings, since he had an obvious interest in the case and might be able to provide further insight. He looked at the heavy Rettermann fountain pen nib under a magnifying glass.

"If this is his pen, he's not right-handed. He's a lefty," he said.

"You can determine that solely from looking at the pen?"

"Sure. My dad's a lefty. If he'd been using this pen very long, one tine would be worn slightly more than the right. That's one reason southpaws don't do well with pens previously owned by right-handers."

"It appears to be very old—spectral analysis suggests that it is made of an old type of plastic called celluloid dinitrate or pyroxylin. What if someone else had used it before, but had given it to Underwood as a gift?"

"Yeah, it's from the 1920's, I think—it looks like some of my dad's old ones. I suppose that's possible."

"We know the suicide note was printed on a computer to

approximate his normal handwriting. The gun was in his right hand. If he shot himself, and he was indeed left-handed, it should've been in his left."

"Then this wasn't a suicide. Someone wanted him dead."

"That's a bold statement, Alex. Who would want an oncologist dead? And what of these clues in the credenza?"

"I don't know. But I'm going to find out, you can be damn sure. Does the name Pickett mean anything to you?"

"No. Pickett, pies, log cabin, CD . . . peculiar."

"Log Cabin syrup, Pickett . . . what if Pickett's not a person, but a company or something?" He sat on a computer terminal and logged onto an Internet auction page and searched for items matching "Pickett."

"Wilson Pickett the singer, Pickett china, Pickett records—those things aren't significant to me," Bonnie said.

"Lots of Pickett slide rules. Don't see those any more."

"Slide rules. I'm sure I have one of my Mom's, if you want to reminisce."

"You're kidding. That would really turn me on."

"If *that* stimulates you, then I have many other items to show you later at my place, such as my element collection. The building blocks of matter are relaxing to look at after a long day."

"I can't wait for that."

Chapter Twenty

Bonnie met Alex and Wendy for coffee at five–thirty two days later on the hot mid-August day. Wendy kept bugging her for details while drinking her fourth espresso on the outdoor terrace.

"It appears he just blew his head off. I don't know why," Bonnie said. "Odd message he left. Bizarre references to numbers and pies and log cabins."

"Any idea what it means? Wendy? You knew him a little bit," he asked.

"I have no clue at all," Wendy said. "I always liked Bill, although he seemed depressed sometimes. I know he didn't have much of a social life."

"What about the word puzzle book in the credenza? Do we really think he was doing word games right before he killed himself? And that crazy log cabin riddle?"

"I don't know—I turned it in to the evidence room," Bonnie said.

"I'm sure the numbers could represent some sort of clue."

"You think, Sherlock?" Wendy said sarcastically. "What are you, a cryptographer?"

"Sherlock?" Bonnie asked.

"Sherlock Holmes. It's a metaphor," he said.

"Of course—the fictional British sleuth. But what Wendy described was a simile, not a metaphor. A metaphor says you *are* Sherlock. A simile relates two things that are essentially unlike, but alike in one way." She laughed. "In most ways, such as being clever, brilliant, and astute, you *hardly* resemble Holmes, and therefore it is—"

"Here's fifty cents. Go call someone who cares." For someone with a speech problem, she sure liked to talk, he thought as he tossed two quarters into her right hand.

He watched as she opened her hand and two gold dollar coins appeared in their place. "Thank you, cheapskate, but your ancestors would be ashamed you can't use your own language properly." He'd told her before that his and Wendy's descendants were English; the name Darkkin was brought to England in the migration that followed the Norman Conquest of 1066.

"My most recent ancestors were far more concerned about making moonshine than using proper grammar. Anyway, can we get that word puzzle book back?"

"Not that one, as it's evidence. But I happen to get the same book as a member of Mensa." She pulled a copy out of her purse.

"Great, let's look at it."

"Right after I powder my nose. I have had too many cups of coffee today." Bonnie got up and went inside. "Be back soon."

"So, did this Underwood have any friends?" he asked Wendy after Bonnie had left for the restroom.

"He did have one good friend, I remember. You might go talk to Dr. Monte Buechler—I think he was Markham's internist, come to think of it. He and Underwood were pals. A doctor's doctor. President of the medical staff, as you know."

"Sounds like I should talk to him. Speaking of the medical staff, how are the meetings and task forces going?"

"I thought you didn't care anything about that stuff."

"Well, maybe you were right before. I have a stake in this place, too."

"But, about the findings—not much improvement. They've done 'root cause analyses' to try to find a systematic component to the problem, without much luck. Most of them appear to be random errors, many them blamed on the residents in training."

"Do you believe that?"

"No, our residents are as good as anyone's. It's just easy to blame things on them because they're trainees."

They continued to discuss the politics of the hospital for a few more minutes until Bonnie returned. He started looking at the word puzzle book.

"I warn you, Alex, this series of puzzles is very challenging," Bonnie cautioned. "They are not for the average person."

"Yeah, sure. What do you think I am, a dummy?" He looked over the book hurriedly and frowned. "These usually list the words you have to find, but this one doesn't—and there are no answers. How the heck am I supposed to do this?" Each page had 20 words to find, with 120 total pages—a total of 2,400 words.

"I told you, it's very advanced," Bonnie said. "The answers will be published in the next issue, which is not yet available."

"I suppose this means Underwood left his secret message just in time, before something happened to him. Was he a member of Mensa?"

"No, he's not in the member directory. I looked him up."

"Maybe he left it for you or someone like you to find," he laughed.

"Do you need your secret spy decoder ring to decipher your little message?" Wendy asked as she drank another espresso.

"I don't need help from someone who can't find words in a dictionary." Medical spell-checkers had saved his sibling from a life of medical illiteracy.

"I don't mean me," Wendy said, plucking the book from his hands and giving it to Bonnie.

"What do you want me to do with my puzzle book?"

"Alex needs help finding the words," Wendy said, handing her the book and a pen. "He's too arrogant to ask you himself."

She pressed the power buttons on her aural processors to go "offline," and he watched in astonishment as she stared intently at the pages and closed her eyes slightly, as if in another world. She picked out and circled a word at the rate of roughly one every two seconds, or about one minute per page. Words in vertical, horizontal, diagonal, forward and even backward orientations. Three minutes later, she had completed 10 of the 120 pages, and then switched her processors back on.

"How . . . did you do that?"

"The words have colors and sounds. The letters jump out and form words as a projection in my field of vision. When the letters form a word I know, I see a characteristic pattern or hear a sound, like a melody."

"Sounds? You can't 'hear' anything with your processors off."

"It's synesthetic sound, derived from visual stimuli. Frequencies which are far outside my implants' range."

"And the text isn't colored, it's black and white," he said.

"It's difficult for me to explain, but to me it's colored. Zero is red, one is orange, two is yellow, three is green, and so forth."

"Sort of like the spectrum of visible light — red, orange, yellow, green, blue, indigo, violet. Roy G. Biv."

"I suppose so. But when they form a word, I hear a chord or melody, or sense a smell. This word is a sweet, gentle one. Others are harsher. But these words form no meaningful sentences."

"What if the numbers represent some type of code, to look for a meaning in the circled words? The first number could correspond to a page, and the second to a word on the page. There are fifteen words on each page, and the second number never exceeds fifteen."

"But how do you know which word corresponds to the respective number?" Bonnie asked.

"Right to left, top to bottom, I assume. Ten pages. That gives us three letters, if I'm right." He looked up the corresponding words on the pages. "Sartorial, penultimate, ephemeral — SPE. Speck, special, spectrograph, species."

"I'll need about a half hour to do the rest of the words, Alex. I'll try to get it done by tomorrow."

"By the way, did you bring my slide rule?"

"I did, since you are so obsessed. Don't you have better things to do?" She removed the thirteen–inch long yellow metal slide rule from her small purse and handed it to him.

"What the — how did that fit in your little handbag? No way."

"My purse, like me, always contains more than meets the eye. There are many surprises."

"Yeah, I see a couple of magic items we can utilize later." He studied the smooth gleaming yellow object. "A vintage Pickett slide rule. What if Underwood was referring to that? 'CD' could mean the C and D scales, and 'first log cabin' might refer to the first logarithmic scale, or LL1."

"You're nuts," Wendy said. "That's really stupid."

"No, I'm serious. I stayed up all night thinking about it. 'Nine and a half pies' could mean 9.5 π."

"There's a π value on both the C and D scales. Which one do you use, Euclid?" Bonnie asked.

"Don't know—I guess I'll do both." He lined up π on the D scale to 9.5 on the C scale and read the corresponding value from the LL1 scale after moving the cursor line. "About 1.032."

"What does that mean?" Wendy asked.

"No clue." He did the same manipulation, this time lining up π on the C scale to 9.5 on the D scale. "1.107."

"Two more meaningless numbers. Your discovery has unlocked the mysteries of the universe," Bonnie said dryly.

"At least it was fun. Meanwhile, I'll go see this Buechler guy."

"Who? I see you both have plotted something during my brief absence. Alex, leave this to the police. You have no experience."

"Where do I find him?" he asked Wendy, ignoring Bonnie's harsh admonition.

"I'll give him a call and tell him you're coming," Wendy said.

"*You* have no business getting involved in this any further. I mean it," Bonnie said, turning to Wendy. "And *you*, encouraging him. I'm disappointed in you both."

"I'm not doing anything wrong—I just want to know more about this Underwood guy, that's all. Heck, he was a partner in the oncology practice. Besides, without my help, you wouldn't have anything right now, anyway."

She stuck her finger in his face. "We have nothing at all except traces of arsenic in exhumed cremains and much aggravation, thanks to your meddling. But, I should know better than to try and stop you. You are obsessed with John Markham, even though there's no evidence Underwood's death is connected to him in any way."

"You're not my boss."

"You think not? We will see about that!"

• • •

Despite Bonnie's edict, Alex made an appointment to talk to Dr. Montgomery Buechler the next day. Buechler, a nice-looking man in his late forties, was Markham's internist for about fifteen years. Markham had seen oncologist Bill Underwood most recently, but Buechler had been his primary physician for the last eleven years. His office was located on the outskirts of town, a few blocks from Underwood's oncology office. Wendy said he was divorced and had no children.

"Alex, welcome to San Diego," he said, extending his hand. "Wendy's said so many good things about you. Your credentials are impeccable, and we're glad to have you with us. Sorry I haven't met you till now."

"Same here," he said, shaking his hand. "Thanks for seeing me. I know you're busy." He sipped the coffee the receptionist had given him. It was a large step above what was available in the police station.

"It's good of you to fill in for Bhavin, too. I'm sure they can make a spot for you permanently when he comes back."

"That's interesting—I'll have to think about that. But what can you tell me about John Markham?"

"John was a fascinating man," the six-foot, 170-pound Buechler said in his high-pitched voice. "I knew him for years. Passion for finer things. He really liked to collect fountain pens."

Alex pulled out a large fountain pen from its holder on the desk. It was bright blue and made of hard celluloid resin, and he examined it for a minute or so.

"John was especially fond of big Rettermanns, like this one, from the fifties. He had lots of older ones in his collection—they probably were sold at an estate auction; like most German fountain pens, they load ink with a piston mechanism. This one's newer and uses a plastic resin. The older ones had cork in the piston and seals; when not in use, you can't leave them dry. Generally you had to keep some water in them so they wouldn't dry out."

Alex remembered about Underwood's left-handed fountain pen, and thought it likely Markham had given that to Buechler. He carefully examined the one Markham had given Buechler—the tines appeared to be worn equally. "I see you're right-handed."

"Most people are, but how would you know that?" Buechler asked curiously.

"The right tine on the nib's worn down a bit. Markham was a lefty, I found out. It looks symmetrical now, with both sides of the nib appearing equal. Ink stains on your right hand, too."

"Interesting observation. But, anyway, Bill really wanted to help John. You know that he was on that new experimental drug."

"No, I didn't know that. Which one?"

"I can't keep up on all the new cancer drugs. Some platinum derivative, I think."

Alex had a good memory, and Markham's records hadn't mentioned anything about an experimental drug trial. "Was there anything unusual about Underwood?"

Buechler grinned and leaned forward in his chair. "Where do I start? He was a real odd duck, into the metaphysical and expanding his mind. Artificial intelligence, ESP, and all that garbage."

"I guess he didn't achieve his goals. Another weird question— do the numbers 1.032 and 1.107 mean anything to you?"

Buechler pondered a minute, fondling the blue pen with his right hand. "No. Is there some reason they should?"

"Just a hunch."

"Well, since we're talking about Bill, I'd look at their association with gambling. Odds on some race or something."

"Gambling?"

"Look, Alex, I probably shouldn't say anything, but Bill's dead and it won't matter. I found out by accident and confronted him about it."

"What?"

"Bill was a good doctor, gave the best to his patients, but had some bad addictions. He was a compulsive gambler and was in debt up to his eyeballs. His credit score was about 450."

Most compulsive gamblers ended up that way, it seemed, with the exception of a certain magician intimately known to him. "Okay, but I don't see what that has to do with this."

"Figure it out—he wanted to try and get more trials to get more money. Wouldn't have surprised me if he tried to forge data to get the results he wanted, or if he even engaged in illegal trials."

Illicit clinical trials—he knew they sometimes took place in other countries but had heard only rumors about them occurring in the United States. Patients received access to experimental drugs in response to a fee. Doctors were paid by the drug companies to participate, and the whole sordid process took place under a cloud of secrecy.

He shook his head. "I can't believe that. Underwood wouldn't risk ruining his reputation, would he? There's nothing worse a researcher can do than fabricating data and doing studies outside of the IRB." The IRB (Institutional Review Board) at each institution was empowered to oversee all research on human subjects. There was no such documentation in Markham's files.

"Well, for a man who's desperate—getting another article published, another grant—means more money to gamble away. Hey, he's dead. Probably was about to get busted up by the loan sharks. You seem to be interested in Markham, though, from what I understand. Why don't you ask some other people?"

"I might do that. Next question—do you think Markham died of cancer?"

Buechler looked puzzled. "Of course. Why would you think otherwise? I don't believe any of that bunk in the news about Anne poisoning him with arsenic. Anne was a witch, but John was no saint, either. She wasn't capable of anything like that."

"What about the daughters? Would they have done something like that?"

"Stephanie, no way. She didn't come a lot, but she was very loving towards John when she did come. Kristin came to most every visit, but was always on her cell phone or laptop or something. She's a pretty emotionless character, but, murder . . . that's a stretch."

"What do you make of this note he wrote?" he asked, showing Buechler the note with the numerical codes and word riddle.

Buechler looked at it for a few minutes. "I have no idea. Codes like these could relate somehow to study patients. About the urine studies on Markham, perhaps he tried to cover something up. Don't know about the words."

He paused. "I don't know anything about Underwood having urine studies on Markham. Why would you mention that?"

"I said that because I suspect he was making up data, and assumed there might be some studies that didn't match up.

Platinum chemo drugs can cause kidney failure, Alex, you know that. Urinalyses would be the most likely data to have been fabricated."

He thought for a moment as he fondled his coffee cup. "Okay, I suppose that makes sense. Anyway, I've taken up too much of your time, Dr. Buechler. I'm sure we'll speak again over a patient or something."

"Anytime—and please call me Monte. Let me know if I can help further. Bill was a good friend, and I want to do right by him."

He shook hands with Buechler and left. The suggestion about the illegal clinical trials made sense now. Maybe Underwood was involved in some way, but he was dead, so that would be hard to determine. Buechler was a leader in the hospital, Wendy maintained. If anyone wanted to save Parkwood, it was him.

Chapter Twenty-one

Bonnie was in Alex's modest office after they ate lunch, on semi-official business. She looked like a large robin in her black suit and orange silk blouse.

"I can't believe you actually went to see that Dr. Buechler. You had no business doing that."

"Okay, but I just needed to get some information," he said as he rose from his desk chair. "You're also here to search Underwood's office, right?"

"Yes, I'm authorized to gather any evidence necessary. You may observe but may not touch anything without permission. I am in charge here."

"Did you finish the puzzle book?" he said as he saluted her.

"I did." She handed him the book with twenty words circled on each page. Alex sat down and tried to match the words up. He wrote the word corresponding to its left-to-right number order from each page on a slip of paper, and stopped after eight pages:

SARTORIAL
PENULTIMATE
EPHEMERAL
CARTOGRAPH
INCANTATION
FASTIDIOUS
INTEGUMENT
CRETACEOUS

"If the first number in his note is the page, and the second is the number of the word in the puzzle on that page, the first eight letters spell *specific*. Weird."

"What about the rest?" she said as he wrote down the next set of words:

GARGANTUAN
REPULSIVE
ACTUARIAL
VEHEMENCE
ITERATION
TUMULTUOUS
YTTRIUM

"*Gravity. Specific gravity.* What the hell does that mean?"

"Specific gravity is a physics term—the relative density of a liquid to water. Pure water has a value of unity, for example, and—"

"I'm not stupid—I know what it is." He shook his head. "But in what context do we take this, and is that the correct combination of letters?"

"The probability of a random assortment of letters forming two meaningful words is extremely remote."

"Like monkeys writing the classics, I know."

"No, actually, the probability of those letters forming those words is exactly one in 17,283."

He rolled his eyes. "Whatever. But what is it? A declaration? A clue?"

"I don't know. Perhaps additional clues exist in his office."

They went into Underwood's office on the floor above, the door marked with crime scene tape. After donning a set of gloves, she discovered a safe behind a photo on the wall.

"Great. How do you get that open?"

"Luckily, I can open virtually anything that locks mechanically." She explained how she would apply a small transducer to the safe door that would show the contact points of the wheels. The left and right contact points would converge at several points, leading Bonnie to a narrow range of numbers that held the correct combination. She would then mentally sort all the possible combinations and try each one on the safe's lock. After five minutes it was opened, revealing a disorganized pile of lab reports.

"I don't believe it—a safecracker. Are you really allowed to do that?"

"A man just shot himself, and I am empowered by the court to gather any evidence necessary. Do you truly believe I would do anything illegal?" She took out some papers, wearing latex gloves. "Urinalyses on John Markham—they appear as if they were done in a portable analyzer." She looked through the papers. "The specific gravity of the in-house result is 1.070, so the decimal point must be in the wrong place. It should be 1.007, rather than 1.070. That's correct, yes?"

"I reviewed the hospital labs, and agree that the calibration or something must've been off. The hospital labs showed dilute urine, and none of the specific gravity levels were remotely that high. I remember his sodium and serum osmolality levels were a bit low, actually." Osmolality was a measure of the number of ions and other particles dissolved in a solvent; the greater the quantity of particles, the higher the value.

Underwood had circled the abnormal values; Bonnie quickly scanned the handwriting and verified it belonged to Underwood by comparing the images to her previous analyses. They also found two other lab slips from previous weeks showing similar elevated urine specific gravity levels.

"Machine's probably broken. But, the reference to 'specific gravity' in the puzzle book—what do you think he meant by that? Was he simply being metaphorical, or was he trying to point us in the direction of the lab slips?" He hoped he had the metaphor thing right this time.

"Is it even physiologically possible to have a urine specific gravity that high?"

"No, I don't think so. The kidney can concentrate urine up to about 1.030, but anything over that would have to be caused by an unmeasured solute. Glucose can do it, but he didn't have diabetes, and there's none in his urine. Radiographic contrast dye could've raised it, but it wouldn't have been repeated on several occasions."

"Is there anything else odd about the urine studies?"

"Yes. The urine osmolality measures the number of osmotically active particles. The higher the osmolality, the more concentrated the urine. Almost always, osmolality and specific gravity go together. But his urine osmolalities are in the range of 200-250 milliosmoles per kilogram of water—extremely dilute. It doesn't make any sense."

Bonnie turned on Underwood's computer. The data files on his hard drive revealed a statistics spreadsheet containing dozens of urinalysis data values. Alex was easily able to easily crack the encryption with a utility he carried on a portable flash drive. The file contained the header, "Study # 436557B9. Analysis of Moxplatin in Patients with Metastatic Lymphoma."

"What is this moxplatin substance?" she said, twisting a strand of black hair in her hand. "I am unfamiliar with it."

"A platinum-based chemo drug, similar to cisplatin. Buechler said he might've been on it. But, look at the urine—the specific gravity values in these studies range from 1.003 to 1.009. Very dilute, and nowhere near 1.070."

"I suppose this explains the platinum in his cremains. Perhaps Underwood forged some of the data, though," she said.

"That's what Buechler suggested—but why would Underwood do that?"

"Just out of curiosity . . . who manufactures moxplatin?"

He looked it up on the computer. Moxplatin was not an FDA-approved drug, but was available in India. Only preliminary research data were available, and there was no IRB-sanctioned clinical trial at Parkwood. "Get a load of this—moxplatin is made by Pyrco Pharmaceuticals, and they have operations in India."

"The same company that Clystarr merged with, correct?"

"That's right," he said excitedly, jumping to his feet. "So, how about this? Underwood does a study for Pyrco for money, maybe with Kristin's knowledge. Markham's urine studies are outliers, so he makes up data and puts someone else's pee in there for the study. In addition to an unethical study, he's fabricated data. He figured he was going to be found out and decided to end it all."

"A bit extreme, don't you think? And you have no evidence to suspect Kristin."

"Maybe, but for an oncologist with a distinguished career . . . I guess the potential negative publicity from this was enough to decide life wasn't worth living."

"Did Underwood have a family?"

"No—divorced from his second wife, no children. Lots of debt from gambling. Buechler said his credit score was in the crapper."

"*Crappie*? A freshwater sunfish indigenous to the Midwest?"

"Crapper. Toilet." He gave her a thumbs-down sign as he drank the orange soda he'd brought in.

"Oh. Well, why is this enough to commit suicide over?"

"Maybe he believed something stunk about Markham and his 'metastatic cancer.' Or he couldn't live with the disgrace over what he's done, but was trying to leave clues, anyway. Why else would he do it?"

He thought about the urine studies for a few minutes before they moved to the rest of the office.

• • •

Alex and Bonnie dismissed the odd laboratory results for the time being and looked through the remainder of Underwood's cluttered office. They then spied the four-cubic foot refrigerator in the back. His stature had afforded him the luxury of a private bathroom and kitchen area—a nice area for a man whose net worth after nearly thirty years of practice was a negative number.

"For a physician, this refrigerator is a disgrace," Bonnie said. "How unhealthful."

"You should know—it looks like yours."

"There are many similarities, I'm ashamed to admit," she pouted as she examined the contents. "Fairly unremarkable. Soda, moldy cheese and sandwiches, and a few bottles of water." Three sixteen-ounce bottles of water stood in the rear. One was a bottle of "Quattra" water, the other two a different, cheaper brand. She began to close the door, but noticed that the water in the Quattra bottle was frozen, while the other two were liquid. The thermometer in the refrigerator (required by regulatory standards to ensure food didn't spoil) read thirty–seven degrees Fahrenheit.

"What is it?" he asked.

"Horrendous news—I cannot locate his temperature log, and it's too cold. Perhaps he killed himself because he knew he'd be in trouble with OSHA (Occupational Safety and Health Administration)," the officious scientist said. "But, come here—one bottle is frozen, while the other two are liquid. 'Quattra Super Premium Arsenic Free Water.' I suppose Markham should have consumed this instead of the arsenic his wife gave him," she chuckled.

"Actually, he did drink this brand of water," he said confidently.

She squinted at him. "What? How would you know that?"

"I know a *lot* about John Markham. He was obsessed with health and only drank certain types of expensive drinking water. Quattra, by the way, is made by a Clystarr subsidiary."

She took a mercury lab thermometer and thrust it into one of the liquid water bottles. "Three degrees Celsius." She converted the temperature to Fahrenheit in less than a second without a calculator. "37.4 degrees, just like the refrigerator." She finally put the thermometer into the frozen bottle. "Same temperature, so this ice should be liquid."

"Maybe there's vodka in there, too, to drown the sorrows of losing all those paychecks."

"*Vodka*?" She stared at him in amazement, hands on hips. "Where did you learn chemistry, Doctor? Ethanol-water azeotrope freezes at a lower temperature than water, not higher, and would be liquid at that temperature."

He pondered for a minute. "Fill up that sink with water."

"Whatever for?"

"Just do it."

She filled the small sink halfway with water from the tap. He put the frozen bottle of Quattra water into a plastic bag, sealed it after expelling the extra air, and dropped it into the half-filled sink. The frozen bottle sank while the other two floated.

"That's impossible. Ice is less dense than water," he said. He then took an ordinary ice cube from the freezer and put it in the sink. It floated. He took the plastic-bagged bottle from the sink, opened the cap while holding the bottle inside the bag, took out his pocketknife, broke off a piece of the ice from the frozen bottle, and finally put it in his mouth.

"Alex! That was a tad reckless, wasn't it? You are contaminating the evidence."

He pondered the ice he'd just consumed. "Frozen at thirty–seven degrees, sinks, yet tastes like water. I don't get it."

She paced around the office for a few minutes, chewing on a pencil. "Well, you *should*. Haven't you ever seen ice cubes that sank instead of floated?"

He pondered a moment as he walked over to the window. "Yeah—with those kids at the children's hospital, as part of your magic act. I still haven't figured out how you did that."

"Think—what's pure water, but heavier than water?"

He studied the riddle for a couple of minutes, walking around. There was only one explanation, but it seemed absurd. "Only one conclusion's logical, of course—it's frozen deuterium oxide, or heavy water."

"Correct. It's chemically water and tastes the same."

"But I saw you drink it on stage."

"Yes, and you probably just consumed a chunk of heavy ice, which is non-toxic in small quantities. About one in 6,000 water molecules occurring in nature is actually heavy water, or D_2O, just like other isotopes of elements occur naturally. I imagine, however, that you would have to drink a lot over a long period of time to cause ill effects."

"So what? Why would Underwood have had that in there? I doubt he was into magic tricks." After a minute he remembered something and opened his mouth wide. "Do you know the specific gravity of deuterium oxide?"

"I believe it is approximately 1.10. Look it up," she said, directing him to the bookshelf.

He busily opened a musty Handbook of Chemistry and Physics he removed from the shelf. "1.107—one of the numbers I got from your slide rule when I lined up the numbers from Underwood's riddle."

"Come on, Alex—that must simply be coincidence."

"It can't be. 1.107 is higher than, but similar to, the values in Markham's urine labs in the safe. What if the two are connected?" he asked excitedly, remembering information from his nuclear physics courses. "What if Underwood gave him large amounts to kill him?"

"Why would Underwood do that, then leave the clues to incriminate himself?" Bonnie asked.

"I don't know—it doesn't make sense. Maybe someone was trying to set him up, too."

"But we must analyze it first before we jump to conclusions. I'm taking it to the lab, if you don't mind."

"I'm going with you," he said as Bonnie sealed her evidence in a plastic bag. They went to the lab, bringing the computer files that had been placed on a flash drive.

Chapter Twenty-two

At the SDPD laboratory, Bonnie analyzed the contents of the three bottles of water found in Dr. Underwood's refrigerator.

"What do you have?" Alex asked, peering over her shoulder.

"Unbelievable. As we predicted, mass spectroscopy reveals the liquid in the 'Quattra' bottle to be 99.4% deuterium oxide. Also, it contains trace minerals such as boron, phosphorus, iron, and zinc—similar to what would be found in any commercially available bottled water."

"What about arsenic?" he asked.

"0.12 ppb (parts per billion)."

"How does that compare to the analysis of the other waters, and do we know the mineral composition of Quattra water?"

"Most bottled waters contain 0.30 ppb of arsenic or less. The other two have mineral contents consistent with their brand, 0.28 ppb arsenic—not enough to be even remotely toxic. And, those other two are, otherwise, pure light or regular water. Even stranger, the mineral content of the 'Quattra' water is identical to what the Institute of Plant Nutrition and Soil Science has published for it. But it's heavy water. Quite bizarre."

"So it appears as if someone isolated the exact anhydrous components of Quattra water and added it to pure D_2O, is that what you're saying?"

"That appears to be the case. It certainly was not manufactured that way," Bonnie said.

"So, if simple chemical tests were done, it would appear to be plain water."

"Of course—it's chemically water, and the two would be indistinguishable. Only by using mass spec, measuring specific gravity, or some odd test like that would you be able to tell them apart. And the difference in melting point, of course, which led us here."

"And if his fridge had been at the OSHA required forty degrees Fahrenheit, we wouldn't even be here, because the heavy water would've been liquid like the others. Amazing."

They walked downstairs to get some coffee after cleaning up and then went back to her office and sat down at the conference table.

"So suppose the urine specific gravity levels in Underwood's reports in the safe are right," he said. "Markham would be two–thirds deuterium oxide. It wouldn't show up in any lab tests other than the urinalyses, which could've been altered in the 'official' medical record."

"But you said the osmolality was low."

"That's right—the urine itself was dilute as it had very few dissolved substances, hence the low urine osmolality. The specific gravity was high not because of things dissolved in the water, as is usually the case, but because the water itself had different physical properties. That could be how he died, not the cancer."

"Alex, that is ludicrous. It would take a very long time to kill someone with heavy water, if it's even possible. My guess is, you need a large body burden of deuterium before it becomes toxic."

"There's a first time for everything. But we don't know the effects on a human being for sure, you concede that."

"I haven't written a dissertation on that, no."

"What types of poisons are typically used in murder?"

"Well, arsenic, of course, but we've discussed that. The other common ones are strychnine, cyanide, thallium, you know most of them, being a doctor. The best would be sophisticated organic compounds that would vaporize."

"But I learned from his medical files he had obsessive-compulsive disorder and would only drink certain kinds of bottled waters and eat certain foods. I suppose, at the end, when he couldn't drink, it could've been substituted for light water in his intravenous fluids."

"What you are suggesting is inconceivable—that, instead of a poison being placed in his water, the 'murder weapon' was the water itself? And later add the minerals to make it look like real bottled water? That's an outlandish hypothesis."

"No, it's not. Picture this—Kristin plans to kill off dear old Dad to take control of Clystarr and sell it off, reaping the profits. He has cancer but isn't going to die soon enough. She had already cooked the books to make it look profitable, when in fact Clystarr is drowning in debt. She has heavy water placed in his supply of Quattra, which he obsessively drinks. Over time, he deteriorates by what everyone thinks is the natural progression of his cancer. The false images are then placed into the imaging system."

"What about Underwood? Why would he leave the frozen heavy water in his own office refrigerator for someone to find?"

"Look at that office—he's a slob who likely didn't even know it was in there, like the hundreds of other bacterial and fungal cohabitants. My guess is that Markham left it behind on an office visit, and someone else put it in there with the other leftovers."

"A doctor killing his own patient? Why?" She stood up and opened her arms wide.

"Buechler said his finances were really bad. Maybe that's why Underwood would've been in cahoots with someone to kill Markham."

"Does that make sense? He would've been giving something to foul up his own clinical trial."

"Maybe he was double-dipping. And this caper would have required the expertise of someone with high-level medical knowledge. Someone who would've known the only commonly used test to detect it would've been impossible to perform."

She walked over to the window and looked out. "Magnetic resonance imaging?"

"Yeah—heavy water doesn't show up on MRI."

"Why did he never have an MRI scan?"

"That's one of the first things I asked myself when I first looked at his file. He had a metallic hip replacement and couldn't have one." MRI exploited the behavior of hydrogen nuclei when exposed to a strong magnetic field. At rest, the nuclei were oriented at random. But when exposed to a magnetic field, the nuclei would polarize and oscillate at a certain frequency unique to each atom. Deuterium, however, although chemically hydrogen, had a different magnetic moment, and would appear essentially "invisible" to MRI.

"Why, then, is there such a discrepancy between the urine specific gravity readings in the actual medical record and the lab slips we found in Markham's safe?"

"The only explanation is that someone altered the records in the hospital medical record. He's cremated, and there's no way to detect heavy water since it would've been vaporized. Someone knew about Anne Markham mentioning about poisoning him, and set her up. They knew she wanted him cremated, which made it look like she was covering up evidence."

"I'm not buying this, mind you, but if he was indeed killed by deuterium oxide, then where did the arsenic come from? In California, ashes can be scattered. If Anne Markham gave him arsenic, it would've made more sense for her to scatter them."

"I don't think she did it. If I were planning a murder, I'd do things to throw people off. Suppose the arsenic plan was fabricated just for people like us who discover the altered CT images. He either was given enough arsenic to be found in the cremains, or Kristin paid off someone to add metallic arsenic later."

"I will be the devil's advocate here. Why not just really kill him with arsenic? And, it could have been any of a number of people other than Kristin Markham."

"Arsenic could've been detected. We wouldn't have suspected the Quattra water at all had it not been for Underwood's faked labs and the frozen bottle of water in his fridge. Kristin, Underwood, or whoever, and some other unsuspecting people probably drank small quantities not to arouse suspicion."

"But where would someone get that much? I have a liter here, but that's not nearly enough."

"I don't know—but Clystarr makes radiopharmaceuticals for diagnostic and therapeutic use, and could have a reactor."

"Alex, before you get carried away any further, you must determine what published information is available on deuterium oxide's effects on humans. As a scientist, I demand proof."

"That's just like you. I'll get it for you, then, if it kills me."

Chapter Twenty-three

Alex performed a quick Internet search of medical databases at a workstation in Bonnie's office. His queries revealed no cases where deuterium oxide had been used as a poison; surprisingly relatively little information even existed on its toxicity in animals. He turned his interest back to the bottle they had discovered.

"Can you take prints off the bottle?"

"What kind of a police scientist do you think I am?"

"How will you know if Markham's are on there? I doubt he has any on file at the police department."

"I'm sure he traveled much as a corporate CEO, and was likely in the transit authority's Expedited Traveler program." He'd heard of that—in exchange for some personal information and having biometric information on file, travelers could pass through security checkpoints much faster.

She had the technician analyze the prints. The procedure was much simpler today with scanner and computer technology than in past years. Fifteen minutes later, she obtained the results.

"There are three sets of prints on the bottle. Markham's left hand and two other unidentified persons not in my database. Probably the housekeeper or whoever found the bottle and put it in the refrigerator, and perhaps someone at the store where it was bought. Do you know if Markham was left- or right-handed?"

"Actually, he was left-handed, like Underwood. He saw a neurologist several times, and that info was in his records."

"That would be consistent with holding it with his left hand."

"It also means, if Markham gave him that pen, two lefties had used it. Further evidence that Underwood was murdered, since the firearm had been in his right hand."

"Unless Underwood was ambidextrous."

"About the pen, though—you said the ink didn't match any known spectral pattern. What kind of pattern?"

"Colorimetric. Inks are made of different pigments, and most fountain pen ink compositions are on file. This one didn't match any of those. He could've mixed his own ink from pigments and solvent."

"Yeah, Buechler said that Markham did that, and must've given Underwood some ink. Did you ever write with it?"

"No, it was evidence, so I didn't."

"If it was Markham's pen and he mixed the ink, perhaps the solvent's deuterium oxide as well."

"That's ridiculous, Alex. If heavy water is in Underwood's pen, then I'll do whatever you want this weekend."

"*Anything?* Better be real sure about that."

• • •

Bonnie had retrieved the Rettermann fountain pen Underwood had supposedly used to write his "suicide note." She had earlier discovered, however, that the note contained ink matching the composition of a common computer printer manufacturer. The note looked virtually perfect, which was the problem—it was supposedly written with a fountain pen. She knew that fountain pens generate different weights of strokes, depending on the user. Although the inks looked the same, the color spectral analyses were slightly different. Bonnie was now preparing to review the mass spectroscopic analysis of the inks.

"As you can see, Alex, the colorimetric spectrograph of the note he supposedly wrote compares favorably with that of the ink in the pen, although it is chemically different. The ink in the suicide note matches that produced by the Capstan printer company. Interestingly, an empty Capstan ink cartridge was found in his garbage."

"What about the solvent of the ink in the pen?"

She sighed and put her head down. "As you remarkably

predicted, mass spectroscopy demonstrates a ninety–five percent peak at twenty Daltons, the mass of deuterium oxide. The other five percent is at eighteen."

"Light water. What about the second handwritten note? The one with the numbers and word riddles?"

"That ink's identical to the one in his pen, and the irregular strokes are consistent with a left-handed fountain pen user, as you suggested."

"So it's further proof Markham was killed with heavy water. He gave his own physician a pen with heavy water-based ink."

"Your conclusion is flawed, as there could be many other explanations. Underwood or someone else could've put heavy water in the pen. It also doesn't prove heavy water killed him."

"But it's very suggestive of that, you must admit."

"Possibly. But I'm very skeptical, I must tell you."

"Back to the first note—you said that this was printed electronically to simulate his handwriting? How?"

"You can program a computer to perform handwriting in this fashion after analyzing enough samples. It is sort of like speech recognition."

"Is it better than plain forgery?"

"Almost always. A good forensic scientist can detect subtle differences in handwriting. But this imitation is state of the art. The authenticity of the note wouldn't be in question were it not for the regularity of the writing, which could not have been produced with a fountain pen."

"But the fountain pen with deuterium oxide-based ink wrote the number and Pickett pie note. Why was the first written by computer, the second by hand? Do we go back to Owens with this?"

"I suppose that we must. He'll be skeptical, but we have no choice."

"You're forgetting something. We had that little bet . . ."

Chapter Twenty-four

Bonnie took Alex to see Lt. Marcus Owens at the police station, where they also met with Richard Sheldon, assistant district attorney. At least things had progressed enough to warrant an audience with the DA, Alex thought as they went into the conference room. An assistant served coffee and soft drinks as he began telling his theory of John Markham's demise.

"Run that past me again, Doctor," Sheldon asked in a loud voice. He was a short, stocky man with dark-rimmed glasses, a sharp contrast to the gangly Owens.

"Heavy water—they killed him with it."

"What's heavy water? You mean hard water?" Owens said, pointing at Alex. "We drink hard water every day. So what?"

"No—hard water is just 'regular' water with minerals in it. Heavy water's the same chemical composition as normal water, but is made from deuterium or heavy hydrogen. It's generally only used in nuclear reactors and the manufacture of atomic weapons, with a few limited medical uses."

Owens' mouth opened wide. "*Atomic weapons*? Radioactive stuff like what they poisoned that Russian spy with?"

"No, that was polonium. And heavy water's stable, or non-radioactive. Superheavy water, or tritium oxide, is radioactive, but that's even rarer. If you ingested enough heavy water a long period of time, it could kill you, I think."

"You *think*? I suppose there are lots of cases of people being killed with it?" Owens asked dryly.

"Well, it's never been documented. You'd have to administer

it over several weeks, and essentially control the victim's water supply. And you're the one who brought up Litvinenko—people would've thought it absurd a year ago that a spy could be killed that way. But it happened."

"I *still* don't understand," Owens said. "You say it's water, but a different kind?"

"Yes." He removed two small plastic vials from his pocket—one containing light water, the other pure deuterium oxide. "Both look and taste exactly the same, since they're chemically both water, but have slightly different physical properties. Small amounts occur in nature and aren't harmful. There's probably about ten grams in your own body."

"I'll take your word for it. But so what? Even if it's true about this fantastic stuff that you can't even document is lethal," Owens said, tapping his pen on the desk, "what the hell did they do, pipe it into his house?"

"No, I think they did it an easier way. Markham was obsessed with drinking a certain type of water." He pulled a bottle of Quattra water from his pocket. "He apparently only drank this stuff, the heavy water version of which we discovered in Underwood's refrigerator. He had cases and cases of it around the house, from what I understand—because his own company made it. When he became too incapacitated to drink, it was probably placed in his intravenous fluids."

"That's stupid—no one would do that," Owens said, throwing down his hands. "Kill a man with his own bottled water?"

The shorter Sheldon held up his hand. "Wait a minute, now—this is interesting. How easy is this material to get?"

"Most labs can obtain a small amount for experimental use," Bonnie said. "In small amounts it is not harmful at all—it actually can be used as a tracer in clinical drug trials to test compliance."

"Tracer?" Sheldon asked.

"Yes," she said. "Minute amounts of heavy water can be added to liquid medications and assayed later in the patient's urine to assess compliance. But getting the amount to cause toxicity would be very difficult for the average individual. Probably at least twenty liters, by my estimation."

"Suppose what you say is even true," Owens said, "again, the chain of evidence is broken. Just because you found this heavy water stuff in his doctor's office and fountain pen doesn't mean he ever drank it, Darkkin. Markham's wife poisoned him with arsenic, we think. That was your great discovery, as I recall, Mendoza. Why can't you just leave it at that?"

"But what if that's wrong, Owens? Don't we all want the truth here?" he said, pointing up at the taller man.

"And we're just brainstorming here, colleagues," Bonnie said loudly. "I'm not sure what to do with this either, but brought Dr. Darkkin here to share this information with you. Don't give us such a damn hard time."

"Holy smokes—Bonnie Mendoza said 'damn.' Can you believe that, Richard?"

Sheldon shook his head at the tall detective. "Marc, don't start something."

Owens ignored the short man and pointed at her. "Maybe I'm giving you a hard time because I'm a detective and you're not," he blurted out. "You're wasting our time. Why don't you just go back to your lab and mind your own business?"

She snarled angrily at the six–four detective and clenched her fists. "For your information, *Detective*," she sputtered, "I have been on the front of a Wheaties box and you have not!"

"Atta girl!" Alex exclaimed. "That'll fix him."

"What does that have to do with anything, Mendoza?" Owens said, perplexed. "You're really weird, you know that?"

"And whatever issues you had with my father have nothing to do with me. I would appreciate you giving me the respect I have earned," she said as she stared up into his bifocals. "Is that satisfactory to you?"

Owens paused for a moment, then sat down. "Yeah. Sorry."

"But, Bonnie," Sheldon said, "Marc does have a point. Your theory's intriguing, but there's no physical evidence linking anyone to this. The only identifiable prints on the bottle belong to the deceased, and there's no way I can charge anyone right now."

"I don't know who did it, that's your department," Alex said. "But this would take someone with a lot of access to Markham. I'd say Kristin Markham would be a good bet—she had a lot to gain from his early demise. I also wouldn't dismiss Underwood."

"What about the Anne Markham case, then?" Owens asked.

"I don't want to prosecute an innocent person, if any of this is true," Sheldon said as he paced around the table. "We have to disclose these new findings to the defense, as it could be exculpatory evidence. I think this new info provides enough reasonable doubt to exonerate Anne Markham."

"Can you at least *talk* to Kristin Markham?" he asked. "Expediting her father's death would've been in her best interest, for the merger with Pyrco. Most people, I understand, believe that she and Dad didn't get along too well."

"Okay, Darkkin—we'll look into these suggestions," Owens said. "Lots of little pieces here, but not anything concrete enough to build a case."

"Then I need to get more information, it that's what it takes."

• • •

Alex drove home in his SUV the next day and continued to think about the theory he had concocted. He looked at the sun to his left and thought of the significance deuterium had in his daily existence.

Deuterium was, of course, the fuel that powered the stars; although the nuclear equations were somewhat complex, the sun's energy was derived from a series of reactions that converted the hydrogen isotopes deuterium and tritium into helium, releasing tremendous amounts of energy. But was it really possible John Markham was killed by deuterium oxide? It seemed outlandish, but the only plausible explanation. Alex, a childhood fan of Sherlock Holmes, remembered a quote from Holmes' author, Sir Arthur Conan Doyle:

"Once you eliminate the impossible, whatever remains, no matter how improbable, must be the truth."

It was clear a collection of lab reports hidden in the safe of a dead man and a bottle of heavy water in his refrigerator would be insufficient proof for the San Diego Police Department. Even the heavy water-inked pen was circumstantial evidence. The police had already searched Markham's empty estate, and no deuterium oxide had been found.

He then thought about Markham's ashes as he drove down the highway to collect his thoughts. Bonnie maintained there were no methods of detecting deuterium in the cremains, since the heavy water would've been vaporized. But no one—not even Mensan Bonita Mendoza—knew everything. The ever-skeptical radiation oncologist, as usual, set out to determine for himself whether or not that was actually true.

It then dawned on him—he was in California, for heaven's sake. He hurriedly pulled over to a gas station, opened his laptop, and visited several environmentalist forums using his satellite network card. The Greenpeace people were always interested in emissions that could increase air impurities. To his surprise, he found several Web sites actually devoted to cremation and air pollution. It seemed there were growing concerns about plastics from coffins and mercury from amalgam dental fillings entering the atmosphere and killing people.

He found the Web sites of various cremation equipment manufacturers. He didn't realize that cremation was such a high-tech industry until he discovered Henderson Technology's Cremation Division product line of human and animal cremation equipment. The new standard for cremation equipment seemed to be the "Super-5000" model, which "represents the very latest in cremation technology, designed for fully automated operation." The Super-5000, according to the manufacturer, cut down on "toxic emissions" and was "environment friendly." Emissions were diminished by interchangeable filters that removed toxic chemicals before releasing harmless smoke into the environment. It seemed too ridiculous to be true, but there it was.

He then pulled up John Markham's death certificate on the Parkwood electronic medical record, which contained the name of the funeral home—Raintree Funeral Home and Crematory. He located the address and telephone number and made an appointment to talk to the funeral director, Ben Tucker. Bonnie didn't need to know about this new discovery yet. It would be a surprise he would share later.

• • •

The next morning, Alex drove to Raintree Funeral Home and Crematory, located on the outskirts of town. He was greeted by a receptionist as he went in, and was seated in the director's office.

"Doctor, I'm Ben Tucker," the smallish, dark-suited man said. "It's a pleasure to meet you." The receptionist handed them coffee in elegant crystal cups.

"Thank you, sir. I just have some general questions."

"What can I do for you?"

"Like I said on the phone, I'm a physician who took care of a deceased patient, and I have an interest in the cremation process and how it works. He may have received a drug that we didn't know about, and we were concerned if the substance could be detectable afterwards."

"I'm happy to take you to see our process," he said as they sat down their coffee and went downstairs to the crematory area. Their primary model was a Henderson Super-5000, as he had seen on their Web site—the top of the line model.

"How does this device cut down on toxic gases?" he asked. "As an environmental advocate, global warming concerns me greatly, and we must take better care of our great planet's resources." The gas-guzzling SUV-driving Alex actually cared little about polluting the environment, unfortunately.

"I agree. A series of filters remove toxic gases—benzopyrene, for example."

"Yes, I was especially worried about that particular carcinogen. How long has this wonderful technology been available?"

"About two years."

"How long do the filters last?" he asked, looking at the massive chrome device.

"About a week or so, then we change them."

"So, for someone cremated about four months ago, you would've changed them about twelve to fourteen times, correct?"

"That's about right, yes. Maybe a little bit more."

"And, the substances collected would still be on there after all this time?"

"I'm no chemist and can't testify to the compounds' stability over time, but I would assume that to be the case."

"What happens to the filters after use?"

"They're stored in a drum for later disposal. If it's a few months ago, we probably still have that one."

"We might be interested in that information. I'll let you know."

"Please contact me if you need anything else. Raintree Funeral Home and Crematory is here to serve."

"I will. Thanks." He shook hands with Tucker and left in his SUV to share the good news. He just knew how excited Bonnie would be about it.

Chapter Twenty-five

"Please repeat that, Doctor—slowly. It sounded something like: 'I journeyed to Markham's crematory to examine hydrocarbon residues in the air filters. Hooray! Please analyze them for deuterium.' But I know that could not possibly be correct, since you are seemingly an intelligent man and not an imbecile."

"That's what I said," Alex said proudly as he took a seat behind Bonnie's desk. "It's *not* your processors malfunctioning."

"Why? You are really exasperating, do you realize that?" Bonnie said as she poked him between the fourth and fifth ribs.

"Ow, that hurt. But I know some things you don't. For example, modern cremation equipment has filters to remove the toxic chemicals given off by cremation." He put his feet up on her desk.

"That's absurd. I can't believe cremation is a legitimate environmental hazard. And get your big ugly feet off there."

He didn't move. "Nevertheless, it's true. The man at the crematory claims they still may have the filters from when Markham was cremated. They change the filters about once per week. They don't have a storage problem, so they tend to let them accumulate."

"Well, how many do they cremate per month?"

"About eighty or so."

She put her right hand on her hip and stared out the window. "So, in Markham's batch, there would be residue from at least twenty other bodies, is that correct?"

"I suppose so."

"Look—we've already been to Owens, and it's now an official

police matter. Do you have any idea what could happen if you incorrectly obtained evidence? It could be thrown out, even if it were valid."

"I was just asking questions. I'm a private citizen with the right to do that."

"Just the same, you do *not* represent the police, and you can get in trouble. And who will be blamed for it? Me. You could also be accused by the Markham family for invasion of the deceased's privacy."

"Are you a lawyer now, too? I assure you—I didn't touch any evidence or divulge his name. I'm not that dumb."

"I must disagree with that last statement."

"Well, are you going to act on this information or not?"

"I suppose I must," she sighed. "I'll call Owens and have him procure the crematory filters. But I still don't believe it—millions of Californians are polluting the air with smog, and a corporation markets and manufactures a high-tech, environmentally-friendly cremator."

"Only in America—anything to make a buck."

• • •

Three days later, after obtaining the Raintree crematory filters, Bonnie had completed a preliminary analysis and met with Alex in her office at noon.

"The primary residue is benzopyrene, a product of incomplete combustion of organic compounds, such as charbroiled foods. It's also the chief particulate component of cremation smoke," she said as she took a bite of her grilled bratwurst.

"What else do you find?" he asked as he drank his coffee.

"Mass spectroscopy demonstrates a large peak at molecular mass 252.3 Daltons—the mass of benzopyrene. There are a few slightly higher peaks at 1/100,000 the concentration of the dominant species, consistent with other natural isotopes of carbon, like ^{14}C, as well as naturally occurring deuterium."

"What about higher masses?"

"There are several molecular mass spikes at 256.7, 260.2, and 264.4 Daltons, each 1/100 the peak of normal benzopyrene. Far greater than can be accounted for by the occurrence of natural deuterium."

"How many hydrogens are there in benzopyrene?" Organic chemistry was a dim memory of his undergraduate past.

"Twelve. 264 is therefore the mass of benzopyrene with deuterium atoms in all positions instead of light hydrogen. The other spikes correspond to several distinct species of benzopyrene containing varying amounts of deuterium."

"So, you're saying he was mostly deuterium oxide when he was cremated."

"Yes. He or someone in that batch contained a significant body burden of deuterium, which didn't exist as free heavy water—the deuterium must have been incorporated into proteins to have produced deuterated benzopyrene upon combustion. Those higher peaks aren't seen on the other filters."

"You can't detect any other poisons?"

"No, but any organic compound would've been vaporized. The deuterium was detected in the new compound, benzopyrene, which was created by combustion of the body and casket."

"So Markham was killed with deuterium oxide, as I predicted. It seems you owe me an apology."

"I admit I was unfairly skeptical of your theory. But this does not prove the deuterium oxide killed him."

"So what do we do now?"

"I shall show Owens this new evidence, but you must conjure up data to support your argument of toxicity. The DA won't proceed with anything that can't be backed up in court. Put up or shut up, Alex."

"Wait a minute—you're actually *encouraging* me now?" He put his hand over his heart in astonishment.

"I suppose we have no choice. For lack of any other options, I guess it is you."

"Great. But right now I'm hungry. A nice charbroiled ribeye steak sounds good."

She grimaced, stuck her tongue out, and threw the rest of her sausage into the trash can. "That's disgusting. I have lost my appetite, thanks."

Chapter Twenty-six

The amazing Bonita Mendoza insisted on the "scientific method" in any investigation, which meant she wanted proof about deuterium oxide toxicity before expending further cognitive energy on its having killed John Markham. Alex's quick initial search at the police lab had yielded no useful information, so he now perused more elaborate medical texts and online resources at the university library. He quickly discovered there was absolutely no such information in the standard treatises on toxicology, as his companion had claimed. His investigation of traditional scientific journals also revealed little about heavy water toxicity in humans or animals.

The existence of deuterium was predicted in 1926 by scientist Walter Russell, who developed controversial theories of the origin of the universe. Another scientist, Harold Urey, won the Nobel Prize in chemistry for discovering deuterium; in 1931, he distilled five liters of liquid hydrogen to one milliliter of a liquid that contained small amounts of a substance with chemical properties equal to hydrogen but with an atomic mass of two (compared to one for "light" hydrogen). Gilbert Newton Lewis isolated pure deuterium oxide in 1933, where it was used for radiation experiments. Although deuterium was relatively uncommon on Earth, it was a major constituent of the sun; according to physical cosmology, it had been produced by primordial nucleosynthesis, more commonly known as the "Big Bang."

The discovery of heavy water also heralded the glorious "atomic age." A major coup in American history was the destruction of the first heavy water plant, built by the Germans, in 1934. Heavy water was necessary for nuclear reactors and the enrichment of nuclear fuel at that time. It acted as a neutron moderator to slow neutrons so that they could react with the uranium in the reactor.

A more sinister use of the substance was in heavy water production reactors, which could be designed to turn uranium into weapons-grade plutonium without requiring enrichment facilities. Pu-239 was one of the two known fissionable elements that could sustain a critical chain reaction for a nuclear explosion, the other being uranium-235.

After many hours he finally ended up at the veterinary college library, where he pored over many esoteric treatises not contained in the standard online databases. He eventually found the writings of a physiologist, Dr. Carl Rensselaer, who had published three scientific articles on animal toxicity of deuterium oxide. He pulled up his faculty profile on the Internet. He couldn't wait to share this new information with Bonnie that evening.

• • •

"I have to know more about this," Alex told Bonnie while they were out for coffee later in the evening. "I'm going to see this Rensselaer guy at his university."

"I hate to ask, but where is this famed deuterium scholar located?" she said, nibbling on a chocolate biscotti.

"University of Iowa."

"Maize country. I regret I will not be able to go, since I who must toil at a real job have no time."

"I really bet you regret it. I assume I have your permission to go, then?"

"I suppose so. It will give me a holiday from hearing about Markham and his heavy water."

"I'll get Crazy Jim to go. It sounds like a road trip he'd like to make."

"Crazy Jim? Who's that? He's not really crazy, is he?"

"My old college friend. And, yes, he's a little unhinged. But just the person I need to help me right now."

• • •

Alex dialed a phone number in Houston at nine o'clock in the evening in late September. A deep voice answered the phone after six rings. "I don't believe it. That you, Darkkin?"

"Yep, it's me, Jim," he said. "What's going on?"

"Not much. Doing some consulting work. Other stuff on the side, you know how it is. Same old routine. How's California? Haven't talked to you in a while."

"Job's great, lots of sun. I forgot how much I liked the ocean."

"What's up, anyway?"

"I need some help. I'm involved in something a little bizarre and need to make a trip."

"Bizarre is always good for us. Where to? Any place good?"

"The University of Iowa. Iowa City. Ever been there?"

"Uh, nope. I'd hoped for some exotic location—Hawaii, the Bahamas, or the Grand Caymans."

"Sorry. I can fly in to Houston and we can fly there together."

"Well, that depends. Are you paying for it? Four-star hotel and everything? Meals? I have expensive tastes."

"Don't know if they have a four-star in Iowa City, but I'll do my best. The world's biggest truck stop is nearby, I found out."

"Oboy—I'll get packed. Let me know the details."

• • •

Alex and his college friend Jim Krakowski had stayed in contact over the years and got together at least twice a year. He explained after his arrival in Houston that he wanted to go there to investigate the possibility of deuterium oxide poisoning.

He had met Jim while they were undergraduates at Vanderbilt University. Jim was a similarly gifted individual with an exceptional talent for computer hacking and mischief. On one occasion, Jim decided all test answers should be in the public domain. Thus was born the non-FCC-sanctioned "Radio Free Test Answers" radio station in which he, as an anonymous benefactor, broadcasted exam answers over various AM and FM radio bands, creating a cheating nightmare. He stole answers to test questions the night before, which, when transmitted, could be heard by any student with a simple radio. Officials resorted to confiscating all radio devices for students entering a test area. Jim had no self-serving motives for this activity, since he was an excellent student—he just enjoyed being a pain in the butt.

Fortunately, Jim was clever enough to cover his tracks so he was never caught; the penalty would've been immediate expulsion and a dismal career flipping burgers in some fast-food restaurant. School officials searched fruitlessly for the broadcasting site, but never found it. What they didn't know was that the transmitter had been hidden in the trunk of an old sedan Jim drove around campus and hid in a storage shed when not in use.

Jim's crowning demented achievement was the construction of a voice synthesizer and real-time audio capture device designed to intercept the dean's commencement address. His friend Alex Darkkin was happy to fund that worthy project; like Jim, he had disdain for authority, and the dean represented the pinnacle of academic pomposity. That particular endeavor depended on the dean using an FM wireless microphone at the podium. The audio stream was captured by an FM receiver, computer analyzed, and re-encoded using a sophisticated computer algorithm developed by he and Alex, who were, of course, in the honor roll group about to receive their baccalaureate degrees.

They then decided to alter the content of the dean's speech, adding certain off-color words and inflammatory comments as he spoke. The hidden computer captured his speech, performed speech recognition, and re-coded it with new, added words that were then transmitted for all to hear. He was several minutes into his speech before he could be stopped; he was so self-absorbed that he didn't notice. This created severe chaos during commencement, and guests were mortified.

Alex looked forward to some "male bonding" time with his old friend. He packed a change of clothes and left to meet him in Houston.

Chapter Twenty-seven

After leaving Houston's Hobby Airport, Alex and Jim began their journey to visit Dr. Carl Rensselaer, professor of physiology at the University of Iowa. U of I was a Big Ten university located in Iowa City, with a population of approximately 65,000. Iowa City had no commercial airport, so they had to fly to St. Louis and then catch another flight to Cedar Rapids, IA, where they drove a rental car to the university. The five–ten, 210-pound Jim was perpetually half-shaven and balding. He wore a wrinkled golf shirt and khakis with sneakers.

"So, what's been going on, Alex? Haven't kept up with your personal life. Anything exciting happening?"

"I'm involved with someone," he said as he drove the rented Lincoln Town Car down Interstate 80. "I think it's serious."

"No way—not *you*. Tell me a little bit about her," Jim said as he slurped a sixty-ounce cherry milkshake.

"She's an old friend of Wendy's who was born and raised in San Diego. Deputy director of the police lab."

"Police? You, with a cop? That's distinctly unlike you."

"Bonnie's not a cop. And I did date a cop for a while in Frisco, by the way."

"Bonnie? Ah, I can picture her beauty now—a petite, red-headed Scottish lassie."

He laughed. "Boy, are you way off base."

"But still . . . you, Mr. Anti-Establishment, I can't believe it."

"She provides my life with structure."

"If you say so. Not to change the subject, but what is it we're doing again?"

"I have to talk to the world's expert on deuterium oxide's effects on mammalian physiology."

Jim nodded. "Deuterium oxide? That's too heavy for me, man. Heavy—get it?"

"Yeah, real funny. No one knows much about its effects, though."

"There's probably a good reason for that, son. Who gives a rat's ass?"

"I do. I think a patient was killed with it."

"Cool. Is that even possible, though?"

"I'm certain it is if you drank enough. We'll see in the morning."

"Boy, I can't wait for this one. I know how you are when your mind gets fixated on something." Jim finished his 3,000-kilocalorie beverage, reclined his seat back, and dozed off.

• • •

Alex and Jim spent the night in the university hotel and walked the next morning to Bowen Science Building, where Dr. Rensselaer's office was located. The professor greeted the two men after a short wait and took them back to his inner office.

"Welcome—it's not every day I get people wanting to talk about my research on deuterium oxide toxicity," the small, fiftyish scientist said. "In fact, you're only the second people to come around."

"As I mentioned, Professor, I'm a radiation oncologist, and am interested if there have been any reported cases of human poisoning with deuterium oxide," Alex said.

They took a seat as his secretary offered them coffee. "No. It would take weeks, even consuming pure D_2O, for sufficient deuterization to cause death. It wouldn't be a very practical agent to use, as you should know."

"This is a dumb question, Professor," he asked. "But why study it, then?"

"You're a scientist, so you should know the answer—because it had never been done before, and it might have other uses, such as treating cancer or infections. But that doesn't appear to be the case."

They went into his lab, where he showed them multiple graphs and video clips. "These are examples of my mammal research. Rats and dogs, mostly. The dogs showed no ill effects at twenty percent deuterization, although they did exhibit some sterility. Thirty percent appears to be the limit of reversibility, which takes several weeks. At forty percent deuterization, they begin to show ill effects like neurological impairment, which appear to be permanent." The dogs looked extremely emaciated and could hardly stand. "They die at fifty to fifty-five percent."

"They look extremely cachectic. Is it painful?" he asked.

"Yes, it seemed to be painful to them. Don't mean to be cruel, but it's better to experiment on animals than on humans," he said. "I hope you aren't some animal activist people, we don't need any more of that. Mine are legitimate experiments."

"No, sir—we just want some information on heavy water toxicity in animals," Jim said.

"Interestingly enough, some bacteria and algae can grow in pure deuterium oxide after a period of adaptation. But not multicellular organisms. It's lethal to them."

"They look like they're dying of cancer," he said.

"It's *exactly* like cancer—you're very perceptive, Dr. Darkkin," Rensselaer said. "The mechanism of death appears to be cytotoxic, like with chemotherapy or radiation, which you would know about. Deuterization in excess of thirty percent inhibits cell mitoses. They die of bone marrow failure, diarrhea, etc., just like cancer patients."

That answered one question. Bonnie said there were dozens of undetectable organic poisons that could've been used. But none of those would have exactly mimicked the painful death of metastatic cancer on a cellular level. Whoever did this wanted Markham to suffer.

"I have an interest in their laboratory studies, Professor. What abnormalities occurred in the dogs?" he asked.

"Serum hematology and chemistry values were perfectly normal. Although the urine was very dilute, the specific gravity was high, because the urine was mostly deuterium oxide."

"So, if someone deuterized a human being, it might appear he died of cancer. Hypothetically speaking, of course."

"I suppose so—I never thought of that. That concept sounds pretty radical, though, don't you think?"

"Yeah, it's crazy, but, offhand, how much heavy water would you say it would take to kill a seventy-kilogram human?"

"Acutely, I suppose you'd have to drink at least fifteen to twenty liters, or four to five gallons, to have toxic effects. More to be lethal. Chronically, it would require more, as the body would have time to eliminate it."

Dying of heavy water poisoning wouldn't have been a pleasant experience for Markham. Despite being chemically water, the extra-large water molecules wouldn't allow body proteins and chemicals to function normally. It was, paradoxically, like dying of extreme dehydration. For all practical purposes, however, it would appear, as Rensselaer said, no different than natural death from metastatic cancer.

He remembered something the professor said earlier. "You said we were the *second* folks to inquire about your research."

"That's right. As you may imagine, my little research interest hasn't been very popular. But a young woman came and saw me about a year and a half ago. She also had questions about what would happen if you gave it to humans. She spent a week with me in the lab helping with work on the dogs and rats."

"Who was she?"

"Let me see . . . Miller, I think." He went to a notebook on his desk. "Cathy, no, Cindy Miller, it was. Said she was a graduate student doing a similar study. Not at this school."

"Do you remember what school she was from?"

"I don't. We're very informal here. She didn't ask for any credit or references, so we took her on her word. It certainly wasn't classified research."

"Do you have any information on her at all?"

He went to his office and pulled out some files. "We frequently have student visitors and sometimes take photographs of them. I have a picture of her, not very good, but here it is. Cindy Miller." The young woman in the fuzzy Polaroid photograph appeared perhaps twenty–five years old, and Alex photographed it with his small digital camera.

"Do you remember what she did when she was here?"

"I remember she was particularly concerned with the effects of deuterium oxide on some of the laboratory values, just like you'd asked. Urine specific gravity, for example, plasma electrolytes, blood count, urea nitrogen."

"Dr. Rensselaer, we thank you for your time. You have given us a lot of valuable information."

"You are certainly welcome, gentlemen. Thanks for coming by—I welcome inquiring minds." Alex and Jim left the science building and walked to the parking lot.

"Well, that was fun. I've learned a whole heap about heavy water today. What do we do now?" Jim asked. "After we eat, of course."

"Let's go back to the hotel and see what we can find out about that girl from the name and picture." He looked at the photo on his PDA.

"Alex, she was probably a legitimate student. Do you know how many students a good professor gets? That's a common name, too, if it's even real. I don't think we'll turn up anything, but as long as it's on your dime, I'll play along."

Who was this "Cindy Miller," and what was she doing in Iowa City eighteen months ago? And how was she connected to John Markham's death? These were the questions facing him. Was she really a graduate student, or someone gathering information on how to kill John Markham with heavy water? There was no way to know for sure from the information at hand. He turned on his laptop and e-mailed his query and the attached digital photo to Bonnie.

Chapter Twenty-eight

Bonnie, Alex, Wendy, and Jim were discussing the situation in the family room of Wendy and Stan's Colonial-style house two days later. Alex had asked his ex-hacker friend Jim to stay after their journey to Iowa City. The conservative Bonnie already had expressed her opinion of his Bohemian buddy. She said he had a muddy-brown color and smelled like old *cerveza*. Looked like crap, with the odor of stale beer—you sure didn't need synesthesia to know that about Jim Krakowski.

"I still think it's Kristin Markham, or maybe Underwood," Alex said.

"Again, we always return to Kristin. Why do you persist? And Underwood is dead," Bonnie said sarcastically.

"Who else had the motive to do it, then?" he said as he took a handful of pretzels from the bowl on the table.

"Look, comrade," Jim said, "I know you're the big doctor here, but let me be an impartial third party. Are we sure the Markham dude didn't just die of, now, this is out there, but—cancer, maybe? Look, even the police are moving on."

"Oh, Jimmy, that would just be too simple for him," Wendy said as she stared at the plasma TV and flipped through channels.

"No!" He pointed his finger at Jim. "I've reviewed the case, and there's no other way to explain finding the heavy water. Maybe the picture of this 'Cindy' will help us somehow."

"Or maybe she was just a legitimate student. What about Markham's older daughter? Why aren't you the least bit concerned about her?" Wendy asked.

"Stephanie Farren? She doesn't even live around here, and she's not involved in Clystarr. Lives in San Francisco, she's an artist or something. I can't imagine what interest she would have in that. According to Buechler, Farren was the caring, loving daughter, and Kristin the cool witch."

"Sometimes looks can be deceiving, Alex," Jim said.

"But, how could they have cracked through the encryption? It's 512-bit."

"Back door—that's one possibility," Jim replied. "It would take forever with conventional hacking, and I should know that better than anyone. It would be possible, though, to hack into it using brute-force attacks with a quantum computer."

He pondered for a minute. "Quantum computer? That's years away, isn't it? I thought there were working prototypes, but no one had actually built a working model."

"That's right—only crude prototypes exist. I suppose it's possible someone built a working model, or is working on one."

"How much do you think it would cost to build this hypothetical quantum computer?" he asked.

"At least ten to twenty million to start. Maybe even a hundred. The good news is, the world of elite computer hackers is pretty small. It might be possible to narrow the list down to a handful of known criminals who could've engineered this."

"It would still take a lot of computing power to crack the Complete Data Systems codes, quantum computer or not."

"Maybe they have an army of autistic savants working for them," Jim said laughingly.

Bonnie pondered their ramblings. "Okay, boys, suppose your preposterous hypothesis is true. Why would someone hack into a medical database, alter a man's medical records, just so someone could kill him with heavy water? It would cost more to construct your purported quantum computer than the money that would possibly be obtained. And what of value would be accomplished? Death a bit sooner than expected?"

"People do lots of stuff that seemingly has no value," Jim said. "Alex and I did all kinds of weird crap. Did you tell her about—"

"Not now, Jim," he said as he stroked his index finger across his neck. He was certain Bonnie wouldn't have approved of their previous collegiate activities. "But, like I said earlier—suppose I'm Kristin. Clystarr's stock is on the decline, but we still have a couple of good products in the pipeline. I want to sell the company off and merge with someone else. But Daddy doesn't want anything to do with that, company loyalty and all. Unfortunately, Dad's cancer isn't going to kill him fast enough, so I'll just do him in myself and make it all look like the natural progression of his illness. Arsenic thing was to implicate the wife in case she made a ruckus with the merger."

"Alex, what do you know about money? Did you secretly go to business school?" Wendy said, tossing cheese puffs into her mouth.

Stan was passing through the room to get a snack and heard Alex's analysis. "Hate to agree with Alex, but he's not that far off. Clystarr was in fact going down the tubes. If Markham had died two or three years from now and they didn't sell off, the shares would have been worth a fraction of what they sold for in the merger."

"See?" He patted his brother-in-law on the back. "Thanks, Stan. Anyway, if it were me, I would use the information to hack into all sorts of databases. You could use the information to blackmail people. Or, do a lot of rotten stuff. The list of possible uses is limitless."

"How sinister! How could you even think that?" Bonnie said.

"It helps to think like a criminal. Don't tell me you don't sometimes put yourself in the criminal's mind when you're analyzing the case."

"Well, stop it—you are playing a *very* dangerous game here. Trust me, if even a fraction of what you say is true, these people are very, very dangerous. You are not a trained professional and have no idea what you are getting into," she said as she poked him in the abdomen.

"I told you to stop poking me. I just want to find out more about the criminal mind, that's all. What's wrong with that?"

"If that's all you desire, you may wish to sit in on one of this man's classes. He is rumored to be an excellent professor. I don't know, as I have never had one of his classes."

"I did," Wendy said, holding up her hand. "For an elective.

Pretty tough."

Bonnie handed him the professor's business card. It took much to satisfy his curiosity, and it was time for more information gathering.

• • •

Alex went the next morning to the campus of San Diego State University to sit in on a session of Criminology 343—Criminal Behavior and Psychology. He was vaguely familiar with the campus his sister had attended as an undergraduate.

He took a seat in the rear of the old lecture hall, where he learned this session would be about the "narcissistic personality." There were many psychological profiles of the criminal mind: those who were maladjusted, paranoid, or even psychotic. But, as the professor illustrated, the narcissistic personality was one of the most dangerous. Those individuals actually believed their importance outweighed anything else. They weren't usually as grandiose as, for example, a bipolar individual in a manic phase, but that made them even scarier; their self-importance was so great they would do nearly anything to achieve their goal.

The session ended with a pop quiz for the fifty or sixty students in the auditorium, who groaned. The sixty–year old professor gave him a copy of the fifteen-question test.

"That's okay, sir. I don't need one."

"Oh, nonsense. I'm certain you want to get the whole experience, don't you, son? Surely a man of your stature can compete against a bunch of college kids."

"I guess so." He answered the fifteen questions as best he could and passed it back to the front.

"Everyone remember, your midterm papers are due next week. A letter grade off for each day late." Moans and groans reminiscent of an old Halloween record filled the room as he went to the front of the room to turn in his paper.

The professor pulled out his paper. "Let's see how you did." He took out his red pencil and made many broad marks. "Oh, Lord—five out of fifteen. That's an 'F', I believe. I told my daughter to only date smart guys. Guess she didn't listen." Dr. Carlos

Mendoza Saldana stared at him intensely for several seconds, then broke out in laughter.

"I assume Bonnie told you I might be coming."

"No, but you kind of stick out in a room full of college kids."

"Anyway, thanks for allowing me to sit in. It was an interesting lecture."

"So, you've acquired an interest in criminal behavior?" Carlos said as they sat down in two chairs on the stage.

"A little bit. We've been having some weird stuff go on at the hospital. Someone hacking into medical records, I think."

"That's sick. What do you think they're after? Money, I assume?"

"That's just it—I'm not sure monetary gain is the goal here."

"Well, then, it's fortunate you came today. Most crimes are committed because of money, power, lust, or something tangible. Unless the criminal's a psychopath or wants one of those things, he or she probably has a narcissistic personality."

"Someone doing something just because he can, to satisfy his own ego?"

"Exactly. It's a personality disorder. The true narcissist has a grandiose sense of self-importance, dreams of unlimited success, power, and brilliance. He believes he's special and unique and can only be understood by other special or high-status people. Their arrogance demands extensive admiration, and they have a strong sense of entitlement."

"How do you recognize them, then?"

"It's very difficult. Many of them can play the game very well, and are intelligent enough to manipulate the system."

"Difficult to deal with?"

"They're some of the hardest. Sure, it's easy to figure out if someone wants to rob a bank or murder his rich wife. But the narcissist—his motives aren't so clear, unless you can think like him. Can you?"

"I don't know. Maybe a little bit." He knew he probably had many narcissistic personality traits. A lot of physicians probably did, from what he just learned.

"Just remember—these people were born this way and have been practicing since childhood. They can sense when someone is getting close."

"But everyone has an Achilles' heel."

"You're right. The narcissist's is that he thinks he's smarter than everyone else. No one can figure out his scheme. But if he gets up against an adversary who understands his thought processes, he's met his match. He loses his edge and gets angry."

"Angry?"

"We're at our weakest when we're angry. Contrary to popular belief, most narcissists don't get upset over little things. It draws too much attention to them, which is what they want to avoid. But if you get them upset, they let down their guard."

"I guess it would be helpful to know who the adversary is."

"Ah, but that's the very problem, isn't it? And if you aren't prepared, you have no business playing this game with a criminal. I'm happy to talk in generalities to you, to satisfy your own curiosity. Maybe you want to write fiction or something. But you have no business, Alex, getting involved in this kind of thing."

"I'm already involved in it."

"And I understand you've been very helpful to the authorities. But try to stay a distance from it. I wouldn't pretend to sit in on a few classes and start practicing medicine."

He laughed. "Your point is well taken. Thanks, Professor. I appreciate your time."

"Sure, glad to help. You need to come over sometime. We'll play golf or tennis."

Everyone was trying to discourage him from becoming further involved: Wendy, Bonnie, and now Carlos Mendoza. Maybe they were correct, but he still had to push on in his quest.

It took someone with an inflated self-esteem to fully comprehend his opponent's mind. Carlos said the best adversary for a narcissist was another narcissist. Someone with heightened ego development, who thinks the world revolves around him or her. And he understood that better than just about anyone. That's what scared him.

Chapter Twenty-nine

Alex was again a guest at the San Diego police laboratory in Bonnie's office, and they were sitting at her conference table the next day.

"We never did find out who the girl was up at the heavy water expert's lab in Iowa City," he said. "Cindy Miller." He had sent her the scan of the blurry photo Dr. Carl Rensselaer had shown him.

"Actually, that's interesting," Bonnie said. "We ran the photo and compared it to some people in the database."

"You can do that?"

"Certainly. Facial analysis has become quite sophisticated nowadays. The photo matches that of a nineteen-year old who was arrested six years ago for misdemeanor cannabis possession."

"Marijuana? Big deal. What's her real name?"

"Cynthia Gottesmann. Not much other information."

"Did you compare it to our rogues' gallery?"

"Yes, but it's odd. There's a partial similarity between Cindy Miller, Kristin Markham, and Stephanie Farren. The similarities between the sisters is about seventy percent, what you would expect, but there is a thirty percent concordance between Cindy and the Markham sisters."

"What about a half-sibling? Is that possible?" he asked.

"There aren't any half-siblings," Lt. Marcus Owens said as he walked into her office.

"Not any we know of, but one could still exist," he replied. "What about Cindy's photo and Underwood's?"

"I didn't analyze him, since we just now began talking about this," she said.

"Do we have a photo?"

"I do not. Sorry."

He went to a workstation and sat down. "I'm going to use this. Okay with you?" he asked dryly.

"Oh, I suppose—but please don't download viruses or spyware and crash our servers."

He pulled up a Web page for the Parkwood hospital staff. The physician directory was available online, with photos available of the staff members. The hospital appeared to be a little slow in removing photos of dead doctors; he found a JPEG image of Dr. William J. Underwood and downloaded it.

Alex and Owens then watched her analyze the photo. Her software utilized the concept of "eigenfaces"—a set of standardized facial features. Any human face was considered to be a combination of these standards. The program then created a set of "eigenvectors" derived from extensive statistical analyses of pictures of faces. These eigenvectors would then be used to create a covariance matrix and probability distribution of all potential faces of human beings. It was not, for example, as accurate as fingerprinting or retinal scanning, but was a useful tool when properly utilized.

She received a result after ten minutes. "Underwood's and Cindy's faces reveal no significantly higher association than would be expected by chance."

"How about John Markham himself and Cindy?"

"What potential connection are you looking for there?"

"It's one possible link between the sisters and Cindy."

She found a portrait of John Markham on a Web site, downloaded it to her desktop and performed a facial recognition analysis, which took ten more minutes to complete.

Her mouth opened wide. "The result demonstrates a much higher than average eigenvector probability relationship between Markham's photo and Cindy."

"There's only one explanation, then. If the sisters match Cindy, and Markham does, then Markham is Cindy's father," he said.

"That's illogical, Alex. You know all there is to know about Markham. There *are* no other children."

"None that we know about—we know Markham messed around. Just suppose this particular one produced a child. One he didn't know about."

"Okay, but, assuming you're right, who would the mother be?" Owens asked.

"I don't have a clue," he said. "I guess we'll need to keep on working."

"I'm sorry now I wandered in here, Darkkin. I feel like I'm in some damn crazy house. Arsenic, heavy water in fountain pens and bottled water, and Markham has another daughter."

"Owens, just do me a favor. Try to see if any of the Clystarr or Pyrco subsidiaries, either domestic or abroad, have a heavy water facility."

"I think I'm wasting my time, but . . . in for a penny, in for a pound, I guess. You guys are persistent, I'll give you that."

Bonnie had to attend a meeting while he went back to the medical center to see some patients that afternoon. The disjointed clues would have to wait a while longer.

• • •

The thin, dark-haired, late-fortyish man walked down the street towards run-down Ranty's Coffee Shop at 5:03 AM. He went in, ordered a cup of black coffee and a chocolate doughnut from the elderly waitress, and began reading his morning newspaper.

Five minutes later a thin blond man sat down across from him in the booth in the corner. He was obviously not in a good mood.

"What the hell is going on?" Terrell Lewis asked in an irritating British accent. "Why bother me by calling me up here?"

"I need to give you some information, Lewis. What you decide to do with it is up to you," the thin, well-dressed American said.

"My time is valuable, boy," the Brit said. "Well, lay it on me, since you dragged my ass out here."

The dark-haired man grabbed him by the shirt. "First of all, don't call me 'boy.' You wouldn't have jack shit if it wasn't for me. You take the orders, I give them."

The British man laughed for thirty seconds. "Right, Harter— I'm really terrified of you. What is it you want to tell me?"

"This guy keeps coming around asking about Markham— some doctor from Tennessee working here for a few months. I overheard him going around questions about heavy water, and then Underwood goes and shoots his head off. It's pretty shitty timing."

"So what? You've covered your bases, and no one needs that fool Underwood any more—good riddance. And you can't honestly be worried about some hillbilly."

"I don't know, but he makes me nervous, Lewis. Just thought you should know about it."

"You said we wouldn't have any trouble. It sounds like you've taken care of things, so who cares?"

"Well, I may be in charge of the big picture, but you're the one who engineered the software aspects. You said nothing could be detected. You're wrong,"

"Don't get a big head, Harter. Anyway, Markham's death can't be linked to us."

"Look, I don't want anything bad to go down either. The guy's name is Dr. Alexander Darkkin." Harter handed Lewis a folder containing information. "There doesn't appear to be anything unusual about him. Just some wise ass sticking his nose out where it doesn't belong."

Lewis looked through the papers. "Big goddamn deal. Just cool it, Frank."

"He also hangs out with this Flores *chica*. She's some friend of Darkkin's sister. I found out all I could on her." He handed Lewis another folder.

"Yes, they appear to be a huge threat," Lewis said as he looked at the information in the folders for a few minutes. "But some of this information is interesting. It may be something we can use."

"I'm not telling you so you can do something to them, just so you can be on the alert. If something happens to this Darkkin, it could make me look bad—his sister has a lot of connections. You just keep your eyes open."

Lewis stood up and pointed at him. "If anyone finds out certain information, you'll go to jail for a long time, so don't *ever* tell me what to do, you asshole." The British man ordered another lousy cup of coffee and drank it quickly. "By the way, you need to get that perverted stuff off our servers. For someone with my high standards, it offends me."

Frank Harter knew he had to continue to help as he left the deserted coffee shop and walked back to his car. His obsession with pornography would ruin him if anyone found out. Chills went down his spine as he remembered the "colleague" at Parkwood who would enjoy nothing more than to disseminate that information to everyone.

Chapter Thirty

Kristin Markham came to SDPD headquarters voluntarily to answer questions from Lt. Marcus Owens and the assistant DA, Richard Sheldon. The diminutive, navy-suited executive was accompanied by her attorney, Janelle Funderburke, in a conference room.

"I want to be clear that my client is here voluntarily," the deep-voiced Janelle demanded. "You guys really are on a witch hunt for the Markham family, you know that? We should sue you for harassment, Owens."

"Relax, Janelle," Sheldon said. "We just asked Ms. Markham up here to talk. I think we want the same thing here—resolution of Mr. Markham's death. This isn't an interrogation."

"I don't know anything about my father being murdered," the mid-thirtyish Kristin said. "Why don't you ask my mother? She's the one who was arrested for poisoning him with arsenic."

"As you know, there was insufficient evidence to continue that case," Sheldon said. "You don't know anything about his water being poisoned, you say?"

"I have no idea what you're talking about," Kristin said.

"What did he usually drink? Bottled water?" Owens asked.

"Yes. During his last year, he went on a health kick. Only drank a certain brand of expensive health water. A lot of good it did him, don't you think?" she said sarcastically as she took a sip of her own water.

"Ever hear of heavy water?" Sheldon said.

"Yes," Kristin said. "I have a pharmacy degree, as you may

know. It's water of a higher molecular weight than normal. Used in some nuclear applications, I think. What does that have to do with anything?"

"We think someone poisoned your father with it."

"How? By giving it to him in a drink or something?"

"It would take weeks of continuous dosing to kill someone. We think someone substituted heavy water for his bottled water," Sheldon said as he placed a sixteen-ounce bottle of Quattra on the table.

"Quattra? My dad drank that, sure—but what you're suggesting is preposterous."

"I don't suppose *you* ever drank this brand of water?" Owens asked.

"Yes, I did, actually. I frequently drank it when I was at his house, which was quite often. He had all these other expensive nutritional supplements flown in from Europe."

"Can you tell me where he bought it, Ms. Markham? The grocery?" Sheldon asked.

"No, he had it shipped here by the case from Wisconsin. We were the parent company of the manufacturer, so that was easy. You could buy a case or two at the specialty grocer, but for him, it was easier just to have it delivered."

"Who brought it in?" Owens asked.

"I don't know. Servants or delivery men, I suppose. Surely you don't think they put this stuff in the water, or that I had anything to do with it."

"It's not something 'put in' the water, Ms. Markham. The water itself 'is' the poison, if that makes any sense," Owens said. "But we have something else to talk to you about."

"What's that?" Kristin asked.

"You know what Bertaxy is?" Owens asked.

"Of course—it's an Indian chemical and pharmaceutical company. We owned a majority share in it, and we're going to sell it off in the merger."

"Do you know what one of their major products is?" Owens asked.

"They have many products—chemicals, industrial supplies, some biotech. Please be more specific, Lieutenant."

"They also manufacture heavy water," Sheldon said.

"What does that have to do with me?" Kristin asked.

"We have the records—large shipments have been sent out. We don't know where," Sheldon said.

"Surely you aren't suggesting it was sent here from India?"

"I don't know—that's a lot of heavy water missing. And someone at Clystarr could've controlled that company's exports and placed it into his Quattra supply," Sheldon replied.

"God, that's ridiculous. First of all, if I were poisoning him with Quattra, why the hell would I be drinking it myself?" Kristin asked angrily.

"We're not necessarily accusing you," Sheldon said as he leaned back in his chair. "We're only looking for information. And there's no proof you drank it."

"It sure sounds like you're blaming me." Kristin stared out the window for a few seconds. "If I drank it, would any of my lab tests be abnormal?"

"Very few," Sheldon said. "A part of the urine test called the 'specific gravity' would be off. Why?"

"I had a really bad urinary tract infection a while back, and my doctor did several urinalyses. He said some of the values were really off, and dismissed it as lab error."

"It would be helpful to look at the records of someone else who drank that water. Can we look at your file?" Owens asked.

"I'll sign a consent form and have you review them, if you think they'll help. You may not believe this, but I want the truth as much as you do. So, you don't think my mother killed him?"

"As I said, given this new heavy water evidence, there's reasonable doubt to continue the case against her, so it was dropped," Sheldon said. "There was other evidence a judge would've thrown out, so we decided there's not enough there to prosecute your mother."

"You say the urine would be abnormal with this type of poisoning?" Kristin asked as she stood up and walked around the table.

"There haven't been any reported human deaths from this substance, but my expert says the urine would be abnormal, yes," Sheldon replied.

Kristin looked out the window for a few seconds. "I remember Dr. Underwood's weird behavior when my father passed. He made sure to get Dad's urine catheter bag before he stepped out. He said something about it being a 'biohazard' because of his previous chemo and radiation therapy. I was upset at the time and dismissed it, but it sounds odd. I don't believe that's possible."

"I'll have to ask my expert about that," Owens said. "We did find the stuff in a fountain pen your father reportedly gave him." He held up a big German piston-filled fountain pen.

"I can't think of why it would be in there," Kristin said. "That makes no sense."

"Someone said your father mixed his own ink. Would he have used bottled water for that?"

She leaned forward. "You know, that's possible. He wouldn't use tap water in those dumb old things, he was so worried about 'contaminants.' He even had his own 'pen room' for filling them. I don't know much about it."

The heavy-set female attorney spoke up. "So let me make sure I understand, Richard. You don't know for sure this material is even toxic, yet you continue to harass the family about his death. When are you going to let it alone?"

"Animal research demonstrates the substance is lethal, given enough of it, and its victims die a death similar to Mr. Markham's," Sheldon said. "We have to follow all avenues."

"Do you need anything else?" the attorney asked.

"No, that's all for now," Sheldon said. "Again, we're not accusing you of anything, yet. But something pretty weird happened to your father. If you find out any more information, let us know." Kristin and her attorney left the building, and Sheldon and Owens went to work on getting Kristin's laboratory reports to Dr. Alexander Darkkin.

• • •

Alex reviewed Kristin Markham's medical records the next day, and determined she had several physician visits during the time interval when Markham could've been poisoned with heavy water. Most were to her internist, Dr. Singer. One was to a derma-

tologist, where she had a visit for some type of dermatitis. There were two urinalyses dated three months apart. The urine specific gravity readings on the two specimens were 1.027 and 1.022, respectively. They were otherwise unremarkable, and the words "laboratory error" were written on both reports in red ink.

"What does it mean?" Owens said to Alex and Bonnie as they perused the reports in her office. "I figure you know more about this stuff than anyone else, Darkkin."

"It looks like Kristin had drunk enough heavy water to elevate her urine specific gravity, but not enough to cause permanent harm," he said. "Doesn't this prove her innocence? Why would she consume something she knew could be harmful?"

"Unless she knew what she was doing and knew not to consume too much," Owens said. "Damn, this is driving me fricking nuts. It all looks encouraging on the surface, but it really leads nowhere. No jury is going to convict someone who consumed the same 'poison' as the victim, Darkkin."

"Then you have to look for the person who did. You mentioned Kristin described Underwood being in a hurry to dispose of Markham's catheter bag. If it contained deuterium oxide, that could be a reason for him hastening its disposal, and that's further proof that Underwood did it."

"Or they were both involved in it, with or without Anne Markham," Owens said. "One or all of those three seem to be likely culprits. Also, Kristin said Underwood had to dispose of the urine because it was a radiation biohazard. Is that true, Darkkin?"

"No, I don't know why he would've said that. The last radiation he received was months before his death, and external. There wouldn't have been any internal buildup. He obviously fabricated that story."

"What of this 'Cindy Miller'? From my photo analysis, she may be a first-degree relative of the Markhams," Bonnie said as she stood up.

"I looked at that, Mendoza. First of all, that's probably not even her real name. Secondly, do you know how many 'Cindy Millers' there are in the country? Over 12,000. How are we supposed to work with that?"

"Her real name is Gottesmann, we think," he said.

"Miller, Gottesmann, whatever. Doesn't help much, anyway."

"So, we have a death, a mechanism of death, and probable motive, we think. But not a clue about who did it," he said.

"That about sums it up, Darkkin," Owens said as he picked up his briefcase. "It's another dead end unless something turns up. I'm putting it on the back burner for now."

"Don't worry, Owens. I'm sure something else exciting will happen soon."

Chapter Thirty-one

Alex and Bonnie had spent another weekend together in the cabin in early October. They were walking down the street after they had dinner in a small town at a roadside diner. It was about eight-thirty PM, and they were getting ready to return to town. They got into his Navigator SUV and were rudely greeted by two men with guns in the back seat.

"Don't look back. I swear I'll blow your head off right here and now if you do anything—either of you." He felt the cold steel of a pistol at the back of his head, and had never been this scared in his life. Part of it was fear for his own life, the rest was legitimate concern about what his better half might do. She might try to disarm one guy, but hopefully not two. Fortunately, she sat calmly.

"What do you want?" Alex asked shakily.

"Just drive where I tell you to."

He desperately wanted to know what was going on, but the two men didn't look like they wanted to make conversation. He considered his options and decided he had none at the time other than to cooperate. Just then, his satellite cellular phone rang.

"Cell phone? It shouldn't work out here," the first man said.

"It's a satellite phone. It'll work most anywhere on Earth."

The man looked at the phone and its caller ID. "It says 'Jim.' Who the hell is Jim?"

"My best friend."

"We'll just let him think you forgot your phone and left it on."

"He knows better than that. You'd better let me answer him or he'll get suspicious."

The phone continued to ring. "Okay, Darkkin, but you'd better put him off. I mean it, or Ill blow the girl's head off."

"I promise. I won't try anything." He answered the phone. "Jim? That you?"

"Hell, yeah. What's the deal, man? Fifteen rings?"

"Been busy. What's up?"

"Where are you at? You haven't been answering your e-mails or anything."

"Bonnie and I took a few days off. We're going to do some hiking up in the mountains."

"Yeah, I understand you're quite the outdoor guy now. When are we going to get together? I have to get back home in a couple of days."

"Maybe you'd better take off, Jim. We'll be a few more days, you know how it is."

"Okay. You guys do anything fun?"

"We found a couple of good Mexican places to eat, you know how Bonnie is always wanting good Mexican food."

"I guess that makes sense. Well, I'll see you, I guess, buddy."

"Right. If you talk to Mary, tell her we'll call her and Stan when we get back. We'll fly up soon." He hung up the phone.

"I guess you did okay with that, Darkkin. But no more phone calls."

They drove about twenty miles out of town to a deserted lake. "Pull over there." A plain white panel truck was parked right next to the lake. "Get out."

They got out and the larger of the two men searched both of them for weapons while the other held a gun. Each of the men wore ski masks. The larger man took out two pair of plastic handcuffs and restrained them with their hands behind his back. He then put a piece of duct tape over their mouths and blindfolded them. He then escorted them over to a panel van and told them to get in. The larger man put a wooden block on the accelerator of his SUV, put it in gear, and watched it drive into the deep lake. It was totally covered before the engine died.

They traveled for what seemed like a half hour to their destination. Neither he nor Bonnie had any clue where they were, since they were blindfolded. The ride was bumpy, so he assumed they were still in mountainous country of some type.

• • •

Alex and Bonnie were finally taken into the old building and their blindfolds removed. The large man took the tape off his mouth and took him to one room, while the other took Bonnie to another room. They removed her watch, but left her transceivers and aural processors attached. "Get in there, Darkkin, you piece of shit." The large man motioned for him to sit in a chair.

A tall, thin blond man, perhaps forty years old, came into the room. "Good evening. My name's Lewis. Do you know why you're here?" the British man said.

"I'm not sure. I think I paid my taxes on time, so I don't think that's it. Could it be—something to do with John Markham? Just a wild guess."

The man slapped him in the face. "Smart ass—you think this is funny? Well, it's not. And I don't know anything about any Markham."

"Yeah, right. Quattra water—the drink of champions."

"I wouldn't know about that."

"The police know about this. You certainly must know that."

"You sound like an old movie serial. But I'm not sure whether to be angry at you or to thank you, since you have the pitiful authorities running around in circles. Despite your efforts, what real proof do you actually have? There are at least three different suspects. If you had real evidence, we would've known by now."

"You have it all figured out, so what do you want from me?"

"You're a big pain in my ass, but we wish to go on with the original plan. You know, I'm now $2 million richer—my fee for helping hasten the inevitable Clystarr-Pyrco merger."

"Congratulations—you sure deserve it. But isn't that enough?"

"To some, perhaps, but not to me. This caper is just the tip of the iceberg—the ability to hack into medical information systems opens up a plethora of fantastic opportunities that can be exploited. Can you think of any, Darkkin?"

"Sure. If it were me, I'd think about organ trafficking and

blackmail. Lots of other stuff. But first tell me if Kristin Markham was involved."

"Of course Kristin's involved. But I thought you had figured that out already, Darkkin," Lewis said. "Don't you think it's ironic—Daddy's little girl finishing him off to have the company for herself?"

"So you *do* admit you had something to do with Markham."

"Okay, whatever. But there's no way you or any one else will ever prove it. I'm curious about one thing—why do you care, anyway? No one gives a shit he's dead—least of all his family."

"Kristin Markham might be a bitch, but I don't believe she's capable of orchestrating something of this magnitude."

"Well, it really doesn't matter what you think, because you're going to be dead soon, Darkkin."

"That answers my next question—why you're telling me all this so I can tell others later. I imagine you don't plan on letting me leave here, do you?"

"Goddamn, what an Einstein. Bruce, isn't this guy brilliant?" He gestured towards the large man who was holding a Smith & Wesson semiautomatic weapon. Bruce's cerebral cortex didn't appear to have a high density of functioning neurons.

"I don't care what you do to me, but leave my sister's friend out of it. She doesn't have anything to do with this—all this was my doing."

"Ah, but she has caused great trouble, too, your intrepid Ms. Flores," he said. "I'm not stupid—you care about her *so* much."

"I don't really give a shit about her. I'm a doctor, though, and don't want anybody to come to harm if I can help it." He paused for a few seconds. "But I've already guessed Markham's death wasn't your primary goal. You plan to hack into other databases, but you'll hit a wall soon. They'll strengthen the encryption once they figure out what is going on."

"We're working on that, Darkkin. Pretty soon, that won't be a problem anymore."

"I'd be building a quantum computer, but that's just me."

"That's right—I hoped you'd be smart enough to think of that. I do, in fact, have designs for a practical quantum computer. A quantum computer has the ability to conduct extremely fast searches, and means that key lengths now considered effectively beyond any brute force attacker's resources would then become practical for me to exploit."

"But *why*? You have enough technology to do what you want, don't you?"

"For now, maybe—but not for the future. You have to plan ahead, Darkkin. Quantum computing leaves no trace something in the conventional computer system has been hacked; the technology is so infantile, no one would suspect. We'll start building it in the next few months. Not around here, of course—too dangerous."

Jim had discussed the possibility of such technology. He didn't know much about the specifics, but could bluff for a little while with information Jim had given him earlier. A quantum computer would obviate the need for cracking algorithms; it would be so powerful it could do brute-force attacks—guessing at passwords until one is found that works—in days that would take conventional computers hundreds of years. Lewis certainly appeared to be quite the grandiose dreamer.

"This 'quantum computer' would cost you at least a hundred million just to build, assuming it even does what you want. How rich do you need to be, anyway?"

"You're right. At some point I want to leave here and get out of the country. But I need way more than two million for that."

"Wow, you don't miss a trick, do you? But, again, I'm not trying to be dense here, but what is it you want me to do?"

"Despite the genius of my associates and I, we lack a certain, well, medical software sophistication. I was hoping you would help me with your vast knowledge of medical information systems. Obviously, you discovered the inconsistencies between Markham's digital image files and the real thing. Great minds think alike, Darkkin, and you've already come up with some good suggestions. Most of them we're already doing."

"What makes me think I would help you?"

"Well, I could just blow your head off."

"You'll kill me anyway, you said."

"Excellent point—however, there are many ways of dying. For your friend, too. My colleagues are quite skilled in using knives and such. Knocking all her teeth out would be nice. There must be something else we could do to get you to help us."

"You overestimate me. I'm just an informatics expert. I don't know about hacking or espionage."

"You're too modest. I think you're capable of so much more if you just think outside the box."

"They'll know I'm gone and look for me."

"I doubt it. Bruce says you convincingly reassured your friend that you and Ms. Flores were on holiday. They won't be looking. And, if they do, how do you think they will locate you? We're out in the middle of nowhere. And I don't think your friend will cause us much trouble. You both should have minded your own business and stayed out of ours."

He tried to stall for time. He certainly had no interest in helping with computer terrorism, whatever their game was. But he was sophisticated enough to think of some ideas. It seemed unlikely they would be released alive, but as long as they had some use for him, he could buy some time. And that was the *second* time he had mentioned Bonnie by her rarely used second surname, and he wasn't sure what that meant.

"There are lots of things you could do just to be a bastard, Lewis. You obviously wouldn't just be in this for the money, or you would've just stolen that. Anyone you really hate?"

Lewis thought for a few minutes. "I hate lots of people, like you doctors. But, since you are waxing philosophical here, do you mean a particular person, or class of people?"

"Group of people."

"Athletes," the British man said. "Don't do a damn thing for their money. Make millions for throwing a ball in a basket or kicking a football. Get all the women, too, the sons of bitches."

"I hate those assholes, too. We could do something about it," he said with a gleam in his eye. The horrible ideas that popped into his head scared him to death, but he might be able to make good use of them.

"What the hell do you know about it?"

"Take Jerome Worthington—wide receiver for the Titans. He just injured his knee. He's to get an MRI, according to the news."

"So what, Darkkin? Who gives a shit about your American

football players? Soccer is *real* football."

"Suppose I alter his MRI so it shows a tumor instead of the anterior cruciate ligament injury he probably has. He gets a biopsy. I hack in and put in pathology slides of malignant tumors instead of benign ones. They tell him he needs to get his leg cut off. His career's ruined, and none of it's even true. And no one can find out. That sounds like something you'd like to do, Lewis, just to be an evil miscreant."

Lewis paused for a moment. "That's . . . really quite brilliant. Damn. I knew talking to you might be a good idea."

"Lots of other things you could do. Someone you hate? Politician? Banker? Magically make him HIV positive and send the results to the wife." The scary part was that these things could actually be accomplished, with his creative knowledge and Lewis' resources. "Or, a patient with a metallic plate in his head would get an MRI, and the magnet would be powerful enough to kill him."

"Now *that's* a great idea. I have a clip in my own head from an aneurysm they found ten years ago. How ironic for someone else to die that way."

"I think it would be really cool to watch."

"Darkkin, I'm not an idiot like some of the people I work with. If you try anything stupid, my guys have orders to kill your girlfriend instantly."

"I told you, she's not my girlfriend."

"We've seen you out together."

He was scared, but quite intelligent, and was willing to match wits with his adversary, since it seemed he hadn't much to lose. "You really think I'm interested in her? Hell, I only needed her to get some information."

"You're lying."

"No, I'm not. I never planned on doing anything criminal, but I'm sick of what I'm doing now. That girl's just a friend of my sister. For all I care you can harvest her organs."

"Another good suggestion. But, was she good, Darkkin?"

"Not really, I've had better. I just happen to like diversity, and she was my flavor of the week." He wished he could tear Lewis' head off, but he figured his and Bonnie's best chance at survival was to play psychologist. He was a pretty convincing liar, an unnerving trait he had discovered during his college years during the many stunts that he and Jim had engineered.

He was taken back to the holding area at night where he was handcuffed to a cot with Bonnie across the room. She appeared to be unhurt and was doing fairly well. He didn't say much since he didn't know if the room had sound monitoring or not. He had a lot of time to think about what he was going to do next.

• • •

The next day, Alex was allowed at the computer keyboard in the cluttered control room of Lewis' headquarters. He would help them hack into databases to try and carry out what he'd proposed the day before. He knew they were watching him closely to prevent him from sending any messages; he doubted that their network servers could be traced, as they were likely routed through some dummy servers.

But he had an emergency tool, one he hadn't used for over ten years—the "panic worm," as Jim Krakowski had called it. The covert applet would allow a message to be transmitted to Jim's server after opening up a seemingly innocuous browser window. But the message had to be something no one like Lewis would detect.

Bonnie had made him memorize a multi-digit number which he entered into the search browser. They had taken her watch (a small GPS device used for direction mapping) which showed longitude and latitude. It wouldn't work very well in the van, since the GPS device required direct view of the equatorial satellites to the south. But it had fixed on the location when they were removed from the van, and was stored in its flash memory. After they exited the van, she had just been able to see the reading under her blindfold and commit it to memory before she pushed a button to clear the settings.

"What the hell are you looking for, Darkkin?" Lewis asked.

"I need the DNS (domain name server) of the Web site I'm looking up," he said. "I'm entering the hexadecimal code." The DNS translated a Web address (URL or uniform resource location)

184 J. Matthew Neal

into an IP (Internet protocol) address. It was a long shot, but Crazy Jim was a pretty resourceful guy.

"Let me see that," Lewis asked. "It's not hexadecimal code, Darkkin. It's decimal."

"It's hex, there just aren't letters in that. Back door to Complete Data Systems' electronic medical record. I'm just trying to do what you want."

He was able to show Lewis the thousands of medical records in the database. Terabytes of confidential information that could be accessed, manipulated, and exploited. Killing people using "medical errors." For example, a patient with pneumonia has an allergy to a certain antibiotic. He could purge the system of that information, which would then allow the person to receive the medication, resulting in death.

It then occurred to him that Lewis had probably already been doing that. Were the medical errors at Parkwood actual mistakes, or cleverly crafted alterations done to mimic errors? Why would they do that? The Markham death might have yielded financial rewards to someone like Kristin Markham, but what about the others? And what did they want him to help him with? Organ trafficking? The possibilities seemed endless.

He turned his thoughts to something else that sent a shiver down his spine. He was a skilled software engineer and pretty decent hacker, but they could probably find someone else like him to employ. He was arrogant enough to assume it was all about him, with Bonnie just unlucky enough to be along, but could it be the other way around? She had amazing mathematical skills which could be exploited for cracking passwords, just as Jim had said. But he had no idea how they would apply that knowledge. He hadn't been allowed around her a lot, and was concerned she was naïve enough to unwittingly help them.

He wasn't serious about going through with his plan to help Lewis, but merely displaying his potential to Lewis to buy some time. If only he could obtain confirmation that Jim had received his cryptic message. He hoped that his old friend was looking for him.

Chapter Thirty-two

Jim Krakowski had been looking for Alex for several days until he finally reached him on the satellite phone. He still thought it unusual for the compulsive "master of technology" not to return a message, even if he was on vacation. Something about that earlier conversation just didn't seem right. And he had Alex beat when it came to paranoia.

He knew Alex's rented Navigator SUV had a GPS device in case of theft. He didn't know the password, but that was likely retrievable given the personal information he already knew about his friend.

He went online to the Web tracking site and logged on; he found that, four days ago, his SUV had been heading east, out of town towards the mountains—but then it stopped, in the middle of no particular place. Why would he go to the middle of nowhere and stop? He wasn't the outdoors type, anyway. Maybe Bonnie was, but the location was disturbing. He went to an Internet satellite map utility and looked up the landscape corresponding to the exact point on the GPS. It looked like an old road near the base of a mountain, ending in a lake, but the resolution was poor. The photos on the Internet search engine were likely a year or two old.

Alex was peculiar, but usually dependable. Jim came to the stark realization something may have happened to Alex, who was, after all, messing around with dangerous stuff. Could he have been killed or kidnapped? He thought briefly about going to the police, but changed his mind. He had a native distrust of the authorities, and it occurred to him there might be someone on the inside working with whoever killed John Markham. If someone had actually done Markham in, that is; he still had doubts about Alex's bizarre theories. But a strange e-mail message reminiscent of the past convinced him that he had to do something.

He pondered his choices and decided to call one person out of two or three in the world he knew he could really trust. He pulled out his cell, but then decided to go to a pay telephone, after realizing that someone could be monitoring his phone conversations. He dialed the number nervously and waited for an answer.

"Hello. Who is it?"

"Stan? This is Jim Krakowski."

A long pause. "What can I do for you?"

"I need to talk to Wendy, Stan—right away."

"She's putting our son to bed, Jim, and it's very late. Can't she just call you tomorrow?"

"No. It's an emergency. Please put her on."

"What's this about? And why are you calling from a pay phone?"

"I can't tell you."

"Dammit." He put the phone down, and after a couple of minutes, his wife picked up the receiver.

"Jimmy? What's wrong?"

"Alex has been missing for days. Did he go anywhere that you know of?"

"Missing? I think he and Bonnie went up to a cabin in the mountains for several days. They've been doing that a lot lately, so that probably explains it. Did you try her cell phone or home?"

"I don't know her number. But I finally got Alex on his cell, and had a strange conversation with him."

"So what? I have lots of funky conversations with him."

"Wendy, he has OCD and can't go over two hours without checking his e-mail. He's always bugging you about something since he moved here, isn't he? Have you heard from him?"

"You have a point, come to think of it. But Bonnie evades technology when she's off, so they may be disconnected from the world. What is it exactly that you want me to do about it?"

"Meet me at the bus stop outside Balboa Park in 30 minutes."

"What? Are you out of your mind?"

"Maybe, but you have to come. I don't want to talk about anything else on the phone."

She paused for a few seconds. "Okay, but I have one final question," she said sweetly. "Do you have good health insurance in your current job?"

"Huh? Yeah, but what does that have to do with anything?"

"Because, if this is a joke, you're sure going to need it during your long stay on the orthopedics ward. I'll be sure to send you flowers."

• • •

Jim grimaced as he watched the intimidating figure in the dark blue Chargers sweatshirt get out of the silver minivan and ramble up to the bus stop. She didn't appear particularly happy.

"Okay, Jimmy, what's with the cloak-and-dagger? You're creeping me out."

"Sorry. I don't know what else to do. I don't trust the police."

"You crazy? Why don't you trust them, of all people?"

"Because Alex has been working on this case with them. If something's happened to him, I bet they're involved. This is bigger than you or me."

"My brother's rubbing off on you. You sound like a tacky mystery novel—you're paranoid."

"Damn straight I am. He could be dead or something. And your friend too."

"He said they were going away for the weekend, and you even talked to him. What more do you want?"

"That's what's strange. He ended by saying something like, 'tell Mary I'll call her when I get back.' He never calls you by your first name."

She paused for a few seconds. "That's odd, I must admit. What else did he say?"

"Not anything unusual. Something about going to a couple of Mexican places that Bonnie liked."

"Now *that* can't be true. She doesn't like Mexican food."

"What? How could she not, with that name?"

"She just doesn't. Do you like Polish food?"

"I like food in all forms. You look like you could miss a couple of meals, too."

"Oh, real funny, Jimmy. A couple of odd things, I must admit, but they're both a bit eccentric."

"Then you can chew me out if I'm wrong."

"I just think you're overreacting."

"Do you think I'm making this up?" He showed her the satellite photo of the last known GPS location of his SUV. "His leased vehicle had Sat-Track, and the signal stopped in that lake. I doubt he drove it in there himself."

She looked at the photo for a couple of minutes. "Who else have you told about this?"

"No one, as I said. I need someone who has some contacts and can get stuff done."

"But why call me? I'm a pediatrician. My husband is a finance professor."

"*You* know who. I want you to call Rad. I can't find his number, it's unlisted."

Her eyes and mouth opened wildly as her big mezzo voice increased an entire octave in pitch and tripled in intensity. "What the *hell* are you thinking? I don't trust him, and he's brain-damaged. I don't know the number, anyway—he changes it all the time."

"How much harm can your dad do? He knows people."

"There's just something rotten about him. Lots of people are scared to death of him."

"Rad's a huge dude, is drunk most of the time—who wouldn't be scared of him at first sight? You got a better idea?"

"*Any* idea's better than that. I know one person, and I'm pretty sure we can trust him. God, I can't believe you."

• • •

Wendy and Jim left in her minivan at ten PM and drove the five miles to the nice suburban ranch house that she had been in many times. They went up to the door after she parked the car.

"I didn't know we were going to a dinner party. I left my tux at home."

"Shut up." She rang the doorbell, and a late-fiftyish Hispanic woman answered the door half a minute later.

"Hello, Wendy," Elisabeth Flores said, wearing pajamas and a robe. "It's awfully late. Bonnie isn't here—can I help you with something?"

"I know, Elisa, I'm sorry to bother you at this time of the evening, but I need to talk to Carlos. It's urgent."

"Of course, come in. Would you like something to eat?"

"Uh, no, thanks. We're not hungry." She didn't need a flare-up of her acid reflux right now. A few minutes later, Carlos Mendoza came into the living room.

"Carlos, this is my friend, Jim Krakowski." Jim shook hands with the six-foot, athletic-appearing man.

"What's wrong, Wendy?"

"I apologize for the intrusion, but I'm a bit worried. We're looking for Alex and Bonnie. Have you heard from her in the last few days?"

"No, I haven't heard from her in over a week. I know she took some personal time off."

"She went with him to a cabin that he rented outside of town."

"They've gone up there before, I think, so why would this particular trip bother you?"

"He's pretty compulsive about checking messages. And we haven't heard from him, except for an odd phone call Jim had with him earlier today."

"You know who John Markham is?" Jim asked.

"The pharmaceutical chairman, everyone knows about that. They thought he died of cancer, but I heard his wife had poisoned him with arsenic or something."

"Do you know much about the investigation?"

"I'm vaguely familiar with it through the grapevine. I know Marc Owens is on the case."

"Alex discovered that he was poisoned with deuterium oxide," she said.

"Deuterium oxide?"

"Heavy water. Used in nuclear reactors."

"I don't know much about that. Is that even possible?"

"Alex is pretty sure, but he thinks it would be a mighty hard thing to pull off. I guess it would kill you if you drank enough," Jim said.

"Why haven't you gone to the police?"

"Because we're suspicious the police might be in on it. We think they've been kidnapped," she replied.

He stuck his palm out. "Whoa, hold on, Wendy—you don't know anyone's been kidnapped."

"But suppose they were. Wouldn't we also suspect the police?" she asked.

"What possible motive would the police have for being involved in your theoretical abduction, and why would they care about John Markham?"

"I don't know, it's just that they knew about it."

"Who else knew about what they were investigating?" Carlos asked.

"A couple of people at the hospital. People I trust in administration."

"Well, I doubt the police are suspect. But I was in Internal Affairs before going into academics—I suppose anything's possible. I do know Marc Owens would never do anything like that. We never liked each other, but I have complete respect for his integrity."

"Besides, to lend credibility to our kidnapping theory," Jim said, "I received an e-mail message from 'Stu Mulligan.' That's a fake name Alex and I used to send secret messages back in college. It's untraceable, and no one else would know that."

"What was in the message?"

"A numerical string. I don't know what to make of it. I also tracked Alex's SUV into the mountains where it stopped in the middle of a lake. The GPS system was either disabled, or the vehicle was destroyed."

"I'll try and help, but what exactly is it you want me to do? I'm not an officer any longer."

"I need some resources and equipment. More technology than I have," Jim said. "Wendy says you might still know someone in the business."

"*What* business?"

"The federal law enforcement business."

Carlos paused for a few minutes. "You say they're out of town at least twenty miles? Are you certain?"

"I believe so, from my calculations. They could've been taken somewhere else, much farther away than where the SUV stopped. I don't know for sure."

Carlos turned to his daughter's friend and looked up, pointing his index finger. "Wendy, this fellow had better be on the level. I'm not doing something idiotic."

"Look, Jimmy's a little odd, but Alex and I have known him a long time. I trust what he says impeccably when it comes to computers. If he says it's true, I would believe him."

Carlos looked at Jim and sighed. "All right, I know a guy in the FBI who might be able to help. Give me a few minutes." Carlos went into the other room to call his contact.

"Wendy, I hope this is the right thing to do. Calling your dad might've been a better idea."

"Yeah—if you want to end up dead. I'm sure he would have concocted some insane scheme. Trust me—you don't want anything to do with him."

Carlos came back into the room. "Ken Thornton—old buddy from the FBI. He'll be here in the morning. Took some fishing trips with him in the old days."

"I'm just worried to death about them," she said. "Alex is an arrogant blowhard, but he hasn't ever been in any real danger before. And who knows what fool things Bonnie might do. She's not loaded with common sense."

"The blind leading the blind," Jim said.

"Correction—the deaf leading the blind."

Chapter Thirty-three

The blue cable television van pulled up to the seedy Hilltop Motel at five AM the next morning. The two dark-clothed men got out, walked up the rusty, rickety metal stairs, and knocked on the door of room 211, where Carlos Mendoza and Jim Krakowski were waiting. Carlos had remote concerns that someone might be monitoring his house and decided to stay at the decrepit old motel, one that he was familiar with from his two years on the vice squad before he transferred to Internal Affairs. He trusted Marc Owens, but he couldn't be entirely certain a leak hadn't originated from someone else within the department. He also didn't want to involve his son Mike, a police sergeant, who was likely to be emotionally involved where Bonnie was concerned. Moreover, neither Mike nor Owens was skilled in this type of maneuver. One family member being involved in Alexander Darkkin's grandiose escapade was enough.

"Hey, Carlos, it's been a while," FBI Special Agent Kenneth Thornton said. Thornton, about five–eight with a stocky build and graying brown hair, had known Carlos from his days in the San Diego Police Department, before he left for academia. Thornton was Special Agent in Charge of the San Diego Division and was four years from the mandatory retirement age of fifty-seven. He planned on doing private consulting work for the government after his career with the FBI.

"Yeah. I'm not here to reminisce about old times, though."

"This whole deal sounds crazy. Are you sure this is right?"

"Come on, Ken—have you ever known me to embellish or

have inaccurate information?"

"I guess not—you've always been pretty straight. But who the hell is this character?" he said, pointing to the unkempt Jim. "Doesn't look like the kind of fellow you'd be hanging out with."

"I can vouch for him, despite his appearance. He's one of the best at computer technology, from what I know."

"I have something to show you, sir." Jim showed him a printed copy of the e-mail message he had received earlier:

> From: Mulligan, Stuart G.
> To: Krakowski, James A.
> Re: 222227325531329223311323333

"Who the hell is Stuart Mulligan?" Thornton asked.

"He doesn't exist. Alex and I used that name to send secret e-mails to each other in the past. No one knows about it."

"And what's this number? An encryption key of some sort?"

"I don't know. It isn't anything significant to me, except that they appear to be several sets of prime numbers."

"Primes? I'll send it to crypto." Thornton sent the number back to the cryptography lab. "Get as many computers as you can on this," he said to the analyst on the other end. "Might as well hang out, boys. It'll be a little while before they can get that information."

They consumed stale coffee and doughnuts from a nearby café for two hours. Finally, Thornton received the long-awaited call from cryptography.

"What do you have?" Thornton asked.

"I'm not sure, Ken," the agent on the other end said. "The string of numbers, twenty–seven digits, isn't the proper length for an encryption key. And, if it were, it should contain some hexadecimal digits as well as decimals. The only thing that makes sense is—they're sets of prime numbers."

"Hell, we already know that. But what do they mean?"

"We had the computer try every manipulation of them. The only logical one is this—if you multiply all the primes into each other, you get one eight and one nine digit number."

"What are they? Phone numbers? Social Security?"

"They aren't phone numbers as far as we can tell. The numbers are '32422539' and '116313981', which could represent a longitude and latitude."

"Where?"

"Believe it or not, those numbers correspond to an area about forty miles east of you. Check it out on your end." He opened up a window in an FBI satellite tracking program.

"Damn," Jim yelled. "Is it possible this message is a location of Alex's whereabouts?"

"Look, Carlos, I don't know about this. For all I know, this guy is an idiot. And why would anyone want your friend, Krakowski? What's so special about him?"

"He was getting close to solving the crime," Jim said. "I assume they want him out of the way. He's also pretty good with computers. Maybe they want to use him to help."

"From what you've told me, there isn't that much concrete evidence, and he was far from solving anything. Why do this when just leaving him alone would've been less risky?

"Well, he's gone, and wouldn't have sent this message otherwise," Jim replied.

"I can't imagine why someone would kidnap a radiation oncologist—does Darkkin have the skills to put together a nuke or something?"

"I don't think so. His dad, maybe."

"Who the hell is his dad?"

"Dr. Conrad Darkkin. He's retired now, but he was a nuclear physicist, a big shot who did classified stuff at Oak Ridge National Laboratory. He might know something about nukes."

"Conrad Darkkin, huh? I'll have to find out more about him."

"Maybe that's not what they want at all," Carlos said.

"What does that cryptic statement mean, Carlos? What other possible reason is there?" Thornton asked.

"Maybe they have an interest in my daughter."

"Your daughter? What use is she to them? She's a forensic scientist and is on that dumb kids' TV show, right? So what?"

"Bonnie might be of tremendous value to computer hackers."

"Why?"

"She is extraordinarily gifted with numbers and words—to a

level that would astound you."

"Dr. Mendoza's right," Jim said. "Alex said she is able to pick scrambled words out of puzzles and do mathematical computations almost instantaneously."

"Why would anyone give a crap about that?" he asked.

"Someone wanting to find out new ways to crack computer algorithms. It's at least a thought. A hacker with that ability could expand his abilities enormously."

"So she can compute numbers rapidly. They can duplicate that with a computer."

"You don't get it, Ken. A simple savant can do calculations, play music, or recall π to ten thousand digits. But they don't understand the mathematics behind it. My daughter understands the underlying mathematical theories to an extent neither you nor I can comprehend."

• • •

The next day, Alex sat at one of Lewis' computer terminals to work on several sinister projects. He'd been convincing enough presenting his new ideas that they at least weren't guarding him continuously. They still had Bonnie in the other part of the warehouse, of course, to ensure his compliance.

Alex was able to log on to the video feeds of the security cameras for a few seconds. He turned off the tracking applet so that his whereabouts on the terminal couldn't be seen. He saw a number of different rooms, one of which appeared to be an operating suite. He wasn't certain what that was for, but he had a pretty good idea.

Another type of room really caught his eye—a large room that appeared to be some type of recreational area, complete with king-sized bed. Probably an adult play area for Kristin Markham, he thought.

He made sure he wasn't being watched as he continued his virtual tour of the complex. He found the room where Bonnie was located. She appeared to be lying on a cot, and was writing something in a paperback book. One ankle appeared to be shackled to the end of the small bed frame. He watched the routine. There were always two guards that came in, a smallish woman with dark hair and a medium-sized man. She was allowed up several times per day to eat and to go to the bathroom. During that time the woman removed her cuffs while the man held a gun. It didn't appear she was being mistreated, at least for the time being. But he couldn't see any way to get her out of there without someone seeing the security cameras.

They took him back to the cell to join Bonnie in the late evening. He would be secured to another small bed.

"Are you all right?" he mouthed to her. He didn't know if there was audio in the room, although it didn't appear to be the case from new observations. The cameras appeared to be simple wireless surveillance cameras easily purchased from security stores.

"I guess so, Alex," she replied softly. "They have neither hurt me nor treated me badly. I know I could escape from here, but don't know where to go. What is it they want?"

"I don't know. It appears they want me to help them with some computer espionage."

"Have you?"

"I've had to give them some things. Not a lot they didn't have. Just discussed some ideas. But this is all pretty weird. What is it you were reading and writing in?"

"They gave me some crosswords and number puzzle books for something to do. There is a small television in the corner but I cannot hear it very well."

He wondered why they would give her those things to do. Perhaps they were testing her abilities to see if they were real. "Did you do them?"

"What else am I to do? It is pretty boring in here, and I'm really scared, Alex. What are they going to do to us? I have done as you asked, and have not tried to get out."

"I don't know what they have planned. I sent the message out and just hope that someone got it."

Chapter Thirty-four

The eclectic ensemble of Jim Krakowski, FBI Special Agent in Charge Kenneth Thornton, Professor Carlos Mendoza, and a second agent drove the blue van up to the location of the longitude and latitude numbers, 32°42'25.39" N and 116°31'39.81" W, which corresponded to an old abandoned warehouse about 40 miles outside town. Thornton had few reservations about taking Carlos, a former police lieutenant, along. He did think twice about taking a civilian on an investigation. But, even the FBI might have a need for Jim's specialized knowledge, and he would be nowhere near any real action.

He pulled the van onto a hilltop about two miles away from the warehouse. A highly directional antenna was connected to Jim's laptop, giving them line-of-sight to a radio tower on top of the old warehouse. A skilled hacker, Jim said he could probably get into the wireless network from the outside, but would likely need some other types of surveillance equipment. Jim started his Wifi-Stumbler program, which he said he often used for "war driving"—gaining unauthorized access to computer networks.

The SSID (network service set identifier) TORNADO, the default for a Rantel access point, came up on the screen. The people inside hadn't even bothered to change the default SSID or turn its broadcast off. 128-bit encryption—Jim said he would need 20 minutes to crack it, and he could scarcely believe how insecure the network was.

They discovered the old warehouse had belonged to Clystarr and had been abandoned two years earlier. Clystarr had installed wireless video surveillance transmitters in the rooms; not the most secure devices, but useful for setting up quick cameras.

Jim hacked into each of the video cameras and found thirty enabled in the warehouse. The normal range of the network was about two hundred feet, but the FBI high-gain antenna allowed a several mile range. The network was designed to automatically assign him a network IP (Internet address) to Clystarr's subnetwork—even better for him. The more secure networks only assigned IP addresses to a specific computer's address, effectively preventing someone from doing what Jim was attempting.

"Very poor security," Jim said. "The dumb ass in charge of this should be fired." He came to the room where Alex and Bonnie were being held.

"I doubt they're on the payroll. I assume that's them, correct?" he asked Jim.

"Yes." They came to a second camera outside which showed the woman guard sitting in a chair. The male came up occasionally to talk to her.

"Damn stupid wireless cameras. Video only, no sound. I guess it wasn't built to withstand high security," he said. "Okay, I guess we have something. Kidnapping, at a minimum—enough probable cause to send a team in there."

"Can't you go in there and get them now?" Jim asked.

"That would be damned dangerous. Getting them out without them being hurt or killed will be a huge challenge. And they don't appear to be in any imminent danger. We should bide our time and gather more information."

"What about this, Agent Thornton? I can capture some footage from the room where they are. It can be replayed as an endless loop back to the server so that it would appear that they were still in the room."

"What good does that do, Krakowski? How would they get out of there?"

"We buy them some time. Bonnie can take care of the guards and get them out of there," Carlos replied.

"Are you nuts? How?"

"She's a master class escape artist. One of the best."

Thornton rolled his eyes. "You've *got* to be kidding. But this isn't some damn TV or stage show where everything is planned. You don't want them to get killed, and I don't want to endanger anybody. If we rush in there, I'm sure they will be."

"It's just a plan. You're in charge, obviously," Carlos said. "I just want to get them out as quickly as possible. I don't see what we lose by doing this."

Over the next few minutes, Thornton pondered what they had suggested, and reluctantly reconsidered it. "Even if what you say is possible—we feed in some footage so it appears to the main room that they're still lying there. They don't know that. How would we signal them?"

"Sorry, I didn't think of that." Jim paused for a minute. "But there's a status light on the camera that can be turned on or off through the wireless applet. It's simple."

"So? What good does that do?" Thornton asked.

"Morse code. It can be toggled on and off rapidly enough to do that," Jim said.

"Who the hell knows Morse code?"

"Alex is an Extra Class amateur radio operator and knows Morse code. In any case, I don't see what harm it would do."

"But it still won't work," Thornton said. "Assuming he can decipher our message, how would they signal us back, assuming this even works? We can't still see the live camera, can we?"

"We can see it briefly until we get a signal," Jim said. "I can clone the MAC (Media Access Control) address so our redirected transmission will appear to be coming from the original camera. There'll be some mild signal attenuation, but it would take some-one pretty perceptive to pick up on that. But, if I keep the original camera on, there'll be two signals. I can change the channel and encryption on the original to send back to us, but they'll eventual-ly see two, and they could figure it out. It would be safer to black it out altogether after a few minutes."

"I agree with you. But if you black it out immediately, then we don't know what's happening in there," Carlos said.

"I can get some men in here in about a half hour or so. We need to know if they're out of that room, so we keep the other camera on till they're safe. I don't want to send anyone in until I'm sure it's clear."

Jim set up the computer to automatically record several minutes of footage. They saw a small woman standing outside the room. The man came up to relieve her while she went to the bathroom or something. Jim would set it to record both and then play it back in an endless loop, instantaneously deactivating the original cameras' signal to the criminals.

"What message do you recommend we send?" Jim said.

"A short one, like, 'FBI outside, cameras off.' What's Morse code for that?"

"Heck if I know — I don't know Morse code. I'm sure your men can get it."

"Do those cameras have sound?"

"That model doesn't. Some jurisdictions don't allow sound."

"I don't think they're particularly worried about the legal ramifications here, Jim," Carlos said, patting him on the back. "I think they have enough problems to be concerned about."

They prepared for Jim to switch the feed. There would be a split-second transition between the two video streams. Hopefully, the degradation would be imperceptible.

• • •

The signal on the camera began blinking in Morse code according to the algorithm Jim Krakowski had programmed to repeat. They were still on a live feed until they got some acknowledgment back that they understood. Jim could blink the status light while the camera was still live. Alex and Bonnie were each cuffed to a metal-framed cot by all four extremities, and didn't have much freedom of motion.

It took a few minutes for Bonnie to see the blinking light, which was out of his field of vision at the angle the camera was placed. He knew that hearing-impaired people often noticed small visual clues that others wouldn't.

"Alex, a light is blinking on that camera at regular intervals. Short-short-long . . . I don't know what it means."

"Was it blinking before?"

"I don't remember, but I'm awfully tired. I don't believe so."

"It sounds like Morse code. Are you sure?" She described the pattern of the blinking to him. "F . . . B . . . I. FBI outside, I think. No . . . sound. Camera . . . off. What does that mean? I don't even know where we are. Are you certain that's correct?"

"I think so. How is that possible?" Bonnie asked.

"It's a wireless camera—Wi-Fi. It would be possible for someone outside to control it. I sent the worm with your prime-factored GPS address. If the Morse coded message is correct, the FBI could be out there."

Another series of signals came through. She described the pattern to Alex. "S-I-G-N-B-A-C-K," he said. "Sign back. They want you to sign back, acknowledging receipt of their transmission."

"I can't sign like this, that's ridiculous."

"You can move your hands a little bit. Can't you send some purposeful message?"

"I'll try." She moved her hands to form the letters meaning "O-K," "O" being a fist with thumb in, and "K" being index and third finger up with thumb straight up ("peace" or "victory" sign).

A few minutes later, Tomas, the male guard, heard a low-pitched cry from the holding room. He came into the locked room and saw the sandy-haired physician having a seizure, his hands and feet still cuffed to the bed frame. He was flailing, almost lifting the cot off the ground, his pants soiled with urine.

"Please help him, he's dying!" Bonnie said.

"What's wrong with him?"

"He has seizures—you must get him some medication."

"I don't know what the hell to do," Tomas said as he reached down to look at the flailing man. "If you're trying something, I swear you'll be sorry."

"I'm not trying anything. Please—I am certain your boss wants us both alive."

"Shit. I have to make a call." After Tomas seemed satisfied she was still secured to her metal cot, he pulled out his radio and looked away from her for a few seconds. General Sun Tzu was right—a bad decision could have terrible consequences.

Alex awoke from his "seizure" to hear the sickening sound of steel splintering bone and teeth and observe 6,000 Newtons of highly focused force transform the man's face into an unrecognizable crimson glob. Tomas apparently had missed the episode of *Science Squad* where kids learned force equaled mass times acceleration. Because of the latter property, *Mendoza Milagroso* had far greater punching power than her co-stars *Chemical Cowboy* and *Admiral Ampere*. Two strong fists, each using loose handcuffs as "brass knuckles," pummeled him with sharp ratchet teeth in an incredibly efficient transfer of momentum. He was probably beginning to understand the physics concept now.

"Stay down, or I swear to God I will kill you! I will give you one more chance."

"What the hell did you do to my face, you goddamn bitch?" Tomas said almost unintelligibly, as most of his teeth and maxilla had been destroyed. Bonnie easily dodged his clumsy swings and finally struck him with a right uppercut that lifted him off the floor, spewing blood across the room and knocking him into the wall.

"So be it. You will have to live with your choice, then." She took his head, smashed it against the cinder-block wall, and twisted it sharply to the left. He dropped to the ground and started seizing—for real. She had severed his spinal cord at the second cervical vertebra—a "hangman's fracture." He would never breathe again. "Sorry—'live with your choice'—my bad."

"*Holy shit*," Alex gasped as he looked at the bloody heap on the floor that had once been a man. He was *really* glad now he had made wise choices on their first date. "Is he dead?"

"Duh! Does a doctor not know a dead man when he sees one? I assure you, he would have killed us, and I told him to stay down."

"I know, but that was pretty vicious. He was just a flunky."

"Excuse me, but who is rescuing whom here? And was it truly necessary for you to pee on yourself?"

"I wanted it to look realistic."

She replaced the plain gold ring on her right finger. A few minutes earlier, she had removed it, which contained, in a hidden compartment, a highly coiled strip of stainless spring steel. A magician would call it a "shim." She had demonstrated once at her apartment how, when uncoiled, it could be inserted between the pawl (internal locking mechanism) and ratchet teeth of a handcuff, allowing it to be opened. It was child's play to someone who had actually disassembled the locking mechanisms of hundreds of different restraints. The shim wouldn't work if the cuffs were double-locked, but she had a solution to that, too—the ring also contained the working end of a key which folded out of another compartment.

She had earlier opened one handcuff, then the other, then the leg irons. They were then seemingly "re-closed" by bending the single strands with the ratchet teeth enough so that they moved just outside the pawl rather than engaging it—to the casual observer they would still appear locked, but could be easily pulled open. An old policeman's trick for escape in case the officer was cuffed with his or her own cuffs—she was able to instantly pull free when the time arose.

"Do your stuff and get me out of these." She found the keys and removed his right handcuff, allowing him to remove the other three. It would be quicker for him than the shim, which took some skill. He was removing the cuff on his left wrist when he started cursing. "Dammit."

"*Now* what have you done?"

"I sort of broke the key off in the lock. Give me another one."

"That won't help, because you've clumsily sheared the flag off inside the lock casing, and a new key won't work. I'll remove it later." She took another key and removed its mate from the cot, and he would have to wear the broken set for a while.

"I'll shoot it off, then." She then removed the ankle cuffs.

"That's smart, if you enjoy practicing medicine with one hand. You can't shoot it off with a nine millimeter, anyway. That's just in the movies. I've done tests, but don't believe *me*."

"Okay, I believe you." He got up and went through a box that had some items he could use. He found an old 35mm camera, an electronic flash, and AA batteries. "I can use this."

She laughed. "What for?"

"The capacitor in this flash generates over 100,000 volts. Like a stun gun, except it all dissipates in one dispersion. It takes a few seconds to regenerate, but it's still a big jolt." He broke open the casing and disconnected the wires from the flash tube.

"We have his firearm and don't need your crude toy."

"What's the combination to the door?" The combination lock had closed behind them.

"9-8-3-5-6-2-3-7." She had seen it entered several times while she was held there and had instant number recall. As they exited, they were met by "Cindy," the smallish woman, who rushed into the hallway. He was in front of Bonnie, who was holding the semiautomatic weapon. Cindy pointed an identical gun at them, holding it in her right hand.

"Get back in there, I mean it," Cindy said to them.

"Uh, I don't think that's a good idea," he said.

"Get back in there or I'll blow your head off." Cindy obviously appeared nervous, and he deduced she was not very experienced at this type of activity.

"Your accomplice is a bloody pulp. Do you also believe you are the one in five thousand who is faster than me? Are you willing to find out?" He heard Bonnie disengage the safety.

"Last time . . . I'll ask you, retard."

"Then I guess we have a Mexican standoff. Hahaha, Mexican—get it?" Bonnie rolled her eyes and laughed in a baleful tone as she slowly approached Cindy, who was now trembling.

"You know, we could really do without any more of your awful quips right now. Comedy's just not your thing."

Bonnie moved forward again and grabbed the pistol from the small woman's hand before she could blink an eye. "That is dangerous for such a small waif to have. Give it to me!"

Cindy tried to run, but he grabbed her. "Let go, you asshole!"

Bonnie approached her, pistol in each hand. "I have had just about enough of all your shit. Shut up or I shall rearrange your face. You assume that because I am slow of speech, I am unintelligent—how very insulting that is to me."

"*Are you fricking nuts?* She could've shot us."

"The safety was on, and there's no way a woman that size could safely discharge that weapon with one hand. She's scared to death and doesn't know how to use it."

"You might tell me that next time so I don't stroke out." Alex hoisted the petite woman and took her back into the holding room, and secured her face-down on the cot. He then found some duct tape that he placed over her mouth. He put Tomas' bloody, lifeless body on the cot he had occupied. With any luck, no one yet knew what had happened. Someone would eventually notice the camera was off, unless the FBI had played the "dummy" video clip over and over again. He looked at the gun Bonnie had taken from "Cindy."

"Can you show me how to use this?" He had to look directly at her; her processors' lithium-ion batteries were nearly exhausted, and she had to lip-read.

"It's a semiautomatic nine-millimeter pistol, and contains seventeen rounds when full. The safety is here. See, it's on, as I said." She showed him the controls. "Please do not injure yourself."

They headed down the corridor of the wing where they had been detained and came to an exit door that required biometric identification for exit. He then went back to get Cindy from the other room. The gagged woman tried to scream as he removed her restraints and then cuffed her again. "Dammit, I'm not going to hurt you." He looked again at her face, as if he'd seen it before, but he couldn't remember where. She flailed desperately, trying to get loose.

He dragged her to the door and placed her hand on the fingerprint scanner, which opened it. "I'm bringing her with us. We may need her print again."

"You could just cut her finger off," Bonnie said as he stared at her in astonishment. "Kidding!"

"I saw the camera feeds earlier—wireless out here too. I assume the feds turned those off as well. I wouldn't put it past them to have captured dummy signals and re-fed them. But we can't go into the main area."

"We should simply stay hidden. If the FBI are outside, as the Morse coded message would indicate, they will rescue us."

"Yeah, but I'm worried if they bust in, Lewis' guys will destroy most of the data." He paused for a moment. "There should be an auxiliary room around here." They found a computer room off a side corridor with a laptop. Again, it needed biometric identification.

He took her to the laptop, and she continued to struggle.

"Look, lady, the freaking FBI's out there. You either do this, or I let my girlfriend have a piece of you—your choice." She quickly shook her head and allowed him to put her index finger up to the biometric pad.

The computer came on, with a photo of the woman, with lighter hair, but the same person, no question. The name "Cynthia L. Miller" came up on the computer.

"That's it," he said excitedly. "I thought she looked familiar. This is the 'Cindy Miller' from Rensselaer's lab in Iowa City." He logged on to the computer and began downloading information from the server. Ten minutes later, the server had completed the transfer to the 250-gigabyte laptop hard drive. Cindy's fingerprint was necessary to open many of the folders, which saved him the difficulty of decrypting them. "Finished."

He instructed Bonnie to take "Cindy" back to the holding room and secure her again. She returned, and they took their commandeered laptop and walked down the corridor. With any luck, Lewis would have no idea what had happened. They would've only seen Cindy log onto the server.

He then viewed a number of documents and files on the computer. There were tens of thousands, but he found several of interest, as Bonnie returned. "I don't have time to look at many of these, but listen—the Anne Markham arsenic voice recording is on their server, and that pretty much exonerates her from killing her husband. A lot of other bad stuff, too."

As the laptop downloaded files from the server, he began taking apart the electronic flash he had found. He exposed two wires from the capacitor and put the batteries in. The flash whined as the capacitor charged.

"We have two firearms, so what do we need with that stupid contraption?"

"*I don't want to kill people. If you want to kill someone else, be my guest,*" he signed, since her processors were dead, and ASL was more efficient for her than lip-reading.

He would need his modified Mavatar 500 Super Flash in about thirty seconds. Another armed man came down the corridor, and he and Bonnie hid behind a structural support. As the man approached, Alex discharged the device into him. The man let out a scream and fell to the floor.

"*Is he dead?*" she signed.

"*I don't think so. It's like a stun gun.*" They took some duct tape and taped his hands, feet, and ankles. "*I want to see what's down here.*" They went into a large room, where they saw dozens of industrial barrels labeled "Deuterium Oxide." "*This is it. The proof we need.*"

"*There must be thousands of gallons here. My God—it all can't all have been for John Markham.*"

"*I don't think so, either. They could have been planning to build a reactor. But there's something else I saw something when I looked at the video feeds.*" They went into another large room. "*Look at this. It's what I thought.*" The room appeared to be an operating suite, complete with anesthesia equipment.

"*It looks like a surgical suite that hasn't been used very much. Why would this be here?*"

"*Why do you think? They're planning to harvest organs here, and ship them out. No bothering with a regular hospital. They probably have some illegally resident surgeon and anesthesiologist of ill repute working here.*"

"*You cannot be serious. That's ghoulish.*"

"*You don't know what I saw out there. They're planning things on a scale I can't even imagine.*"

She was tired, hungry, and started crying after she put her head on his shoulder. "*Alex, I want to get out of here.*" They went into a storage room, where he removed the 3.5-inch hard drive from the laptop and placed it into a nylon padded case that he had found. They now possessed all the evidence they needed.

Chapter Thirty-five

Terrell Lewis was talking to one of his men in the room and picked up the wristwatch that was lying on the table. "What the hell is this thing, Bruce?"

"It's the watch we took from the *chica*."

"What?" he said as he played with it. "I've never seen anything like it before." He turned the watch on and it looked as if it were searching for something. It had several buttons, like a stopwatch, but a different display. "Shit," he said.

"What's wrong, Lewis?"

"This damn thing's a GPS watch." He fiddled with the buttons and found that the memory had been cleared. "Trace everything that Darkkin sent out. Now." They looked through the cached pages, but didn't find anything that looked suspicious. "Make sure you watch him closely. I don't trust him."

"So the watch had the location. Big deal—it's cleared now. That *chica* doesn't sound real bright, anyway. Probably needs it to keep from getting lost."

"She's much brighter than you think, you dumb ass."

"What? If it's a GPS, it won't work in here. And it doesn't even transmit anything. Look at the cameras—they're right in there, Terrell. Damn, calm down."

He looked at the video monitors and saw his prisoners safely in the holding cell. "All right—just be careful. I need to leave for a few hours to make some connections. Make sure nothing goes wrong here." Lewis retrieved his car keys and left in his car.

• • •

"Look, this one guy's leaving," Thornton said to the other agent in the car, watching the fortyish man leave and drive off through his set of $3,000 image-stabilized binoculars. He then took several digital photos which were stored on a flash card. "One less person to worry about. I guess he has no idea what's going on." He thought about sending someone to get him, but wanted to wait until they had rescued Alex and Bonnie. They would deal with the fleeing man later.

The occupants of the covert FBI van, however, had no idea of their exact location, since they had left the holding room and were not visible on other cameras; Thornton had killed the cameras, anyway, to avoid sending a duplicate signal; Jim's recording was still being transmitted to replace the live video. The reinforcement team was about two minutes out and had orders to storm the complex and seize anyone or anything found inside.

Two minutes later, the FBI helicopter flew overhead as two vehicles pulled up outside the warehouse. One guard was outside with a rifle, and immediately dropped his weapon and put his hands on his head. The third pulled his gun and was immediately cut in half by multiple rounds of FBI assault weapon fire.

"Damn feds," Bruce, Lewis' assistant, said. He didn't have time to escape, and instead poured lighter fluid on the server and ignited it.

The computer servers instantly exploded into flame, making their data impossible to reconstruct. Simply erasing it would be inadequate for the FBI, who had means to recover data from even badly damaged hard drives. Four agents, wearing protective gear, burst through the door. Bruce and another man were restrained by the agents.

"Two men captured, Ken," the leader of the team radioed to him. The team then went through the complex with heat-seeking goggles which would allow them to detect human forms by the difference between body temperature and the ambient environment. They found two other armed men shortly outside the computer room.

They came to the room where Alex and Bonnie had been held.

Cindy was face down, mouth still taped shut, struggling on the bed frame. The man, Tomas, was unconscious, with his face a bloody mess. "Two in here, boss. One's a woman's who's tied up but seems okay. The other is a dead guy whose face is like hamburger. Somebody really beat the shit out of him." Another agent released Cindy, took the tape off her mouth, but then re-cuffed her. It was the FBI policy to take everyone into custody, no matter what their appearance, until things could get sorted out.

"Yeah, we know," Thornton said. "We watched the scientist lady kick his ass before we shut the camera off."

"Woman's about five–three, maybe, 110 pounds, dark hair, Caucasian. Male corpse looks Hispanic, about five–nine, I guess."

"Okay, bring the woman and get the man's body later." One agent took Cindy out to the others as she pleaded with him.

"I'm a hostage, damn you! Let go of me! They killed my friend, don't you see?"

"Yes, Ma'am, that may be, but our policy is to take everyone we see into custody. You'll be safe and released once we confirm your identity."

• • •

Fifteen minutes later, the agents found the tied-up man that Alex had shocked with his modified stun gun. He was groggy but appeared to be breathing normally. They then spotted two human shapes down the storage corridor with the heat sensor and burst inside. They found Alex with his electronic flash and Bonnie wielding dual autoloading pistols.

"Get down and put your hands on your head," the leader said.

He protested. "We're not the bad guys here."

"Dammit, Alex, do as they say and get down. They don't know who's who in the confusion." The agents put plastic restraints on Bonnie and cuffed his dangling broken cuff to the other wrist. They then took them outside, sitting them down with the other people found. He looked angrily at Lewis' assistant.

"Goddamn you, Darkkin," Bruce said, spitting at him on the ground. "You're dead when Lewis finds you."

"Actually, he's the one that's dead," he said as agents removed

Tomas' lifeless body from the building. "You know, I don't get it. If you had left us alone, you might have still been in business, but you just had to be so arrogant. I'm going to watch you with the needle in your arm, asshole."

"Alex, shut up. Whatever you are saying, I am sure it is something obnoxious."

Ken Thornton came up and greeted he and Bonnie, who were sitting cross-legged on the dirt. "I think we can release these two terrible ruffians," Thornton told the junior agent. "I have a police ID on you, young lady. And this gentleman must be Alexander Darkkin." The younger agent was about to release Bonnie with a pair of plasticuff cutters.

"That effort is not necessary, Special Agent." She quickly freed herself and removed the right cuff from Alex's wrist. The left one was too damaged to remove with a key.

"I'm FBI Special Agent in Charge Ken Thornton."

He and Bonnie shook hands with him. "We're *very* glad to see you," he said.

"You two are very lucky. It took quite a bit of tracking to find you."

"How did you?"

Carlos came up behind Thornton. "Your friend Krakowski called Wendy, who called me. To be honest, Alex, I thought both of them might be insane."

"Jim received my worm, no doubt. But how did you figure that business out with the wireless camera in our holding cell?"

"He intercepted the signal up on that hill and played back an endless loop of you both still in there. Luckily he remembered about your knowing Morse code. He's safely up on that hill in the surveillance van."

"I guess you never know when something from your past will come in handy."

"I was really impressed how you handled yourself, young lady. I wouldn't want to tangle with you," Thornton said. Alex signed the message to her, as she couldn't understand very well.

"Loose cuffs are a very good weapon," she replied. "The good ones have very sharp teeth. I didn't intend to kill him, but he would not stay down."

"Huh. I'll be damned," Thornton said. "I guess we'd better round up all these folks and sort out who's who."

"We know who the dark-haired woman is," he said. "Cindy Miller, but I doubt that's her real name. Her ID came up when we used her to access the network."

"I see," Thornton said. "That's good. By the way, the team found this case on you when you were captured. What is it?"

"Be careful with it. It contains the files from Lewis' server."

"Sorry, but you should know—somebody set the server on fire. It's extra crispy, Darkkin. Crypto will try to get some data, but I'm not hopeful."

"Cheer up, I'm one step ahead of you—I downloaded it all before he could do that. It's all on the hard drive."

"Is that right?" Thornton said as he slapped him on the back. "I can't believe you were able to do that, but it's probably encrypted."

"It *was*. We used Cindy's fingerprint to decrypt them. A ten-year old could read the files now."

"Anything else back there?"

"Yeah—about a thousand gallons of deuterium oxide, and the beginnings of what appears to be an operating suite. Looks like Lewis was planning to use that later. A kinky little play place, too, for someone's special leisure activities."

"Terrell Lewis. We took his photo when he left, and he's in the database of wanted criminals. We let him go to see where he leads us. Two agents on his tail."

Everyone had lucked out, it seemed. They rounded up their prisoners and headed back to the San Diego field office. Terrell Lewis was still roaming around somewhere, though. Alex hoped this was the end of this mess, but he had been wrong before. Bonnie shimmed the broken cuff from his wrist and he put them into his pocket.

Chapter Thirty-six

Alex and Bonnie were taken to the FBI office in San Diego as guests of Kenneth Thornton. They had no further need to talk to Jim Krakowski, who had helped them immensely; Jim had to get back to Houston, but would keep in close contact.

After cleaning up, recharging Bonnie's lithium-ion batteries, and eating a tasteless microwaved meal, they went to Thornton's office. Bonnie noticed that Alex's right wrist bore a single linear red blistering measuring about 3/8" in width on one part, with dual such markings on the other side. The left wrist had no such welts.

"You must've really irritated that wrist on those cuffs," Bonnie said. "But the other one looks fine, which is odd, since you wore the broken one on that side much longer. It was an unusual model that I do not own."

"It's not an abrasion, but nickel dermatitis. The handcuffs must've contained nickel." He had the most severe type of nickel allergy, and developed a blistering form of eczema if he came in contact with the silvery metal for more than a few minutes.

"Yes, most are constructed from nickel-containing alloys. But the rash should then be worse on the other wrist."

"I don't know why. I just must've just rubbed the right one more."

"It's fortunate I do not share your affliction. I would be one big blister all over."

Thornton came in and talked to them. "Darkkin, Mendoza, you're involved in this, so we have to go all the way here. I need all information you have about these people."

"Not much. We assumed the person on the inside was from the police department. Who else would have known we were looking into the Markham case?"

"We've conferred with Lt. Owens at SDPD to get up to date on the information. Kristin and Anne Markham lead nowhere, Darkkin," Thornton said. "The arsenic case is purely circumstantial, since her attorney got the recording suppressed. The recording also, amazingly, appears to have been fabricated. It's on the hard drive you recovered."

"We know all that, but what about the woman who came forth with it?"

"Pamela Riggins? She apparently was having an affair on her husband. She was sent anonymous photos threatening blackmail unless she told SDPD the recording was real. She doesn't have any names."

"What else?" he said, reclining in his chair and sipping coffee.

"Although this Lewis guy admitted it to you, there's nothing concrete linking Kristin Markham to your supposed heavy water poisoning. Just the bottle of Quattra in Underwood's refrigerator, his secret lab studies which don't match the hospital medical records, and heavy water in Underwood's pen."

"Where did Lewis go?"

"Our guys are on his tail. He's probably headed out of the country. But what was their motive?" Thornton said. "These people may have been professional hackers, but their security wasn't. Most of the guys inside weren't professional criminals."

"Not yet, anyway. I think you need to look for someone who wanted revenge on Markham for having an affair."

"There's no clues. Do you have a suggestion?"

"Yeah. The girl from the warehouse is Markham's daughter, we think. A while back I visited a physiologist who was interested in heavy water poisoning, and he said a young woman had been there asking the same thing. Bonnie earlier analyzed a photo that he gave me, and I'm certain this gal's the same person. Facial analysis is compatible with 'Cindy Miller' being a half-sibling of the Markham daughters."

"You sure?"

"He's correct," Bonnie said. "I performed eigenface analysis myself on the photo and compared them. We found out she was arrested at age nineteen for cannabis possession."

"Right, that's not her real name," Thornton said. "We ran prints. Seems she has a rap sheet, as you said. Real name's Cynthia Gottesmann."

"We know—Gottesmann's the name Bonnie found earlier, but there were no additional data available on her," he said. "If Cindy Gottesmann is Markham's biological daughter, then Markham had an affair with someone."

"So what?" Thornton replied. "Everybody knows Markham had affairs. It's not surprising that he had an illegitimate child around somewhere."

"I briefly looked up some medical records before your men burst in. One was of a 'Corrine Gottesmann' who died of a medication error. She was hospitalized for diabetes, was given injections of a special insulin that's five times more concentrated than normal, and died. The hospital reported it had been entered improperly into the electronic medical record."

"You could check and see if Cindy or any of those people, like Kristin Markham, purchased heavy water," Bonnie said.

"We have, and none of them did. I don't think anyone would be that obvious," Thornton said. "And why kill him slowly with heavy water, anyway? There would've been a hundred better ways."

"That's just it," he said. "It's so bizarre, no one would think of it. After all, it's untraceable—if not for Underwood's hidden lab reports and the frozen water in his refrigerator, we'd never have known. And, from my research, it exactly mimics the pain and suffering of terminal cancer."

"Underwood left the clues for us to find," Bonnie added. "He somehow was aware, and was found out."

"But why such a cryptic clue? And do we know whether or not the note left by him was actually his?" Thornton asked.

"The suicide note was not handwritten," Bonnie said. "I ran an analysis of the ink shortly after I found it. Like Markham, he used vintage fountain pens, and was left-handed. The suicide note, however, appears to have been written by a computer with an ink that looks similar, but is chemically different than the one from the pen. But, the one in the credenza note with the numbers and riddle matched the ink in his pen, and those pen strokes were consistent with a left-hander. The circled lab values on the reports from the safe also were written with a fountain pen, but with a standard, commercially available ink."

"That's what Owens said—you thought Underwood's death had been made to look like a suicide. But there's still no suspect in that, either."

"The other thing was the composition of the ink in the pen itself. The ink spectral pattern did not resemble that of any known commercially available fountain pen ink. Mass spec showed that the solvent, however, was over ninety percent deuterium oxide."

"Why would that be?" Thornton asked.

"Apparently Markham used his drinking water to make his own ink," he said. "He was so obsessive about that that he wouldn't use just any old water. Left-handers sometimes have trouble with fountain pens, but this ink is more viscous and apparently writes better than normal ink. Since Underwood was also a southpaw, Markham gave him some, too."

"But where did they get all that heavy water? There's not enough that's been purchased to be significant," Thornton said.

"The best theory is that it was somehow diverted from an Indian company, Bertaxy, which is, coincidentally, a Clystarr-Pyrco subsidiary," he replied as he stood up.

"Is it possible that Lewis and Underwood were working together? That they were doing illicit studies for Pyrco?" Thornton asked him.

"I don't know. I suppose that's possible. I guess that Underwood couldn't take the disgrace any more and decided to end it all."

"It appears Lewis was just a middleman. Skilled at computer technology, to be sure, but not the main guy," Thornton said.

"What about organ trafficking? Many desperate people are willing to pay tens to hundreds of thousands of dollars or more for an organ, which may cross several continents before it gets to the buyer. It's a horrible ethical nightmare," he said.

"There's some stuff in the computer files, Darkkin, but we're not sure how far they had gotten. But they clearly had designs on organ trafficking in the future."

"Why did they want us? I know some nuclear physics, but don't know that much about quantum computers."

"Maybe to scare you, I don't know. Carlos thinks that maybe they wanted Ms. Mendoza."

"*Me?* Whatever for? What use is a deaf scientist and magician to anyone?" she said, waving her hands.

"The evidence shows that Lewis and the late Dr. Underwood were into cryptography and quantum computing. You appear to possess many skills that could've been useful."

That answered one question—Underwood apparently had secretly left the puzzle book clues in case something happened to him. Without that, the investigation would've gone no further, and Markham's heavy water poisoning would never have been discovered. But he knew Underwood lacked the financial acumen to pull this off by himself.

"One thing puzzles me," Thornton said as he rustled through some papers. "They had a lot of information on you, Darkkin. But Ms. Mendoza here is a superb athlete and a talented escape artist. They appeared to know about your math abilities, but not the other stuff."

"Lewis is British, and I doubt that anyone outside of San Diego knows me. They likely made a common error with Hispanics by searching for information under the name Flores."

"Flores?"

"My second surname. If you look under Bonita Flores, which is how my earlier medical records were all indexed, you'll find that information, since the medical record system at that time would not accept two surnames. But you would never find any recent information under Flores."

"I don't understand," Thornton said.

"Latinos typically are called by the first surname, never the second by itself. Mendoza Flores is my legal name on official documents, but I never use the whole name publicly. And, there was a glitch in my Social Security number as a child, which still persists in the older records under Flores."

"She's right," he said. "Lewis' files revealed a variety of her old medical records from the late 1980s under the name Flores. And they kept calling her Flores when I was with them. This is consistent with the leak being in the medical system and not the police. Do you know what this means?"

"No, Darkkin, but I'm sure you'll tell me," Thornton said with a hint of sarcasm.

"It means a medical record glitch finally did us some good."

• • •

Alex and Bonnie were again at the FBI office in San Diego two days later as Ken Thornton came into the conference room.

"We discovered some other interesting things about Lewis," Thornton said. "In addition to whatever else he was involved with, he's apparently been involved in some nasty Web sites. This was before he got involved in this stuff and was able to cover his tracks. More specifically, child pornography sites. I have enough to get him on the cyber crime and poisoning John Markham at this point, but the FBI also has jurisdiction in child pornography crimes. He'll be off the streets for long time when we pick him up."

"Don't forget that he kidnapped and assaulted two people," he said.

"I'm not, but there's no direct evidence linking anyone else to your abduction at this time."

"I suppose the filed off firearms serial numbers won't be of any use," Bonnie asked.

"Probably not, unless we can recover some."

"What about the numbers of the handcuffs they used to hold us at the warehouse?" Bonnie asked.

"We're looking at those."

He looked at her, puzzled. "Handcuffs have serial numbers?"

"Of course they have them. It is a requirement for equipment certification."

"Why?"

"In case of a defect, the product can be recalled and replaced. Many models haven't changed for years, so it's essential to track manufacture dates," she replied.

"Any other reason?"

"Well, if they were stolen and used for malevolent purposes, it might be possible to trace them back to the criminal who purchased them."

"They're traceable, then, like a gun or car?"

"No, not completely. There's no central database for handcuff serial numbers. However, most reputable vendors will record the number and who they were sold to at the time of purchase. They also will demand to see an ID or badge, verifying law enforcement status. Or some other legitimate reason for owning them. But those were pretty common models. Do not get your hopes up."

"What about illegitimate methods of procurement?" he asked.

"There will always be a black market for things, just like with guns."

"Huh. So, what do we do now?"

"Well, I've got a proposition for you," Thornton said. "You've both been immensely helpful, but we just can't have civilians wandering around here. Ms. Mendoza, I'm authorized to make you a guest scientist here, temporarily. I have cleared that with your boss. And your buddy Darkkin here can be a guest 'medical expert.' I hope that's all right with you."

"Absolutely," Bonnie said.

"Sure," he said, as his temporary position with Parkwood was on the downswing, and he could work as needed. "How's the food here?"

"Crappy," Thornton replied.

• • •

Bonnie and Alex went back to the FBI's laboratory area where she examined the gun, the cuffs, and other items. Alex still had the broken pair of cuffs in his pocket.

"Let me see the broken ones, Alex. I just thought of something." He handed them to her. She ran a simple chemical test by placing dimethylglyoxime on the metal and adding ammonium hydroxide. This mixture would create a complex with ionic nickel, producing a distinct pinkish color. But the area on the broken handcuffs didn't change color upon application of the reagents.

"That is what I thought," she beamed. "Your broken set here is nickel-free. It's a rare-earth metal alloy steel, containing chromium, titanium, iron, and lesser amounts of molybdenum and ruthenium. These others were the ones on your wrist that had the allergic reaction." After three days, the marks were still there but fading.

"I don't understand."

"These stainless alloys won't cause nickel dermatitis for people like you. Most steel alloys use some version of carbon steel with a high nickel content. Other less commonly used hypoallergenic types include: aluminum, which is lightweight but not as strong; gold plate, pretty but not very durable in the long run; and pentrate black oxide, which is durable but rather ugly. A plus for aluminum is that it can be anodized in a number of delightful colors: pink, purple, blue, green—"

"Thanks. That takes care of my Christmas shopping ideas. We can coordinate outfits to match them."

"Remember the big chunky German ones in my apartment? They are made from a similar alloy. You touched those, and did not have a reaction."

"Come on—you're telling me there's a market for these things for people with nickel allergy?"

"Not really. The special alloy is used in corrosion-heavy or salt-water environments. The other is simply a corollary benefit. The interesting thing is, though, is that these are fairly rare, while the others are ubiquitous models like Peerless. They may not yield much information."

Just another inane bit of trivia that would lead nowhere. He put the broken cuffs back in his pocket to keep as a souvenir.

Chapter Thirty-seven

Ken Thornton took "Cindy Miller" to the interrogation room. She was a smallish young woman with dark brown hair, perhaps twenty–five, dressed in orange detention coveralls.

"Look, young lady, you'd better start talking here," the agent said. "You have no idea what kind of trouble you're in. And I'm in a piss-poor mood."

"That's so corny," the young woman said as she leaned back in her metal chair. "Go screw yourself, asshole."

"You've got a real big mouth for such a small gal. You and your friends are looking at least ten to twenty years. Death penalty if we can link you to the death of Markham or anyone else."

"Go to hell. You're full of shit—we haven't done anything like that."

"Well, we have all the information from your computer server, courtesy of our friends you kidnapped," he said. "And kidnapping itself, computer crime, and . . . where do I stop?"

"I doubt you'll get anything off that hard drive."

"You could've been right, but Darkkin used you to decrypt it. Lots of interesting stuff. You may think it'll be hard to prosecute you for the computer crimes, but there are many other files contained on that drive that you're dead on."

Cindy turned her head. "What are you talking about?"

"The child porno, little lady—it's all over the goddamn drive. You were running a server out of that old warehouse."

"Hey, cop, that shit isn't mine. I was just working for those guys at the warehouse."

"Well, maybe you should've looked for a better job—one with a brighter future. But I don't think you worked there for a pay-check." He pulled out a DNA analysis report. "I'm wondering why the DNA homology between you and John Markham is fifty percent."

"*DNA*? That's crazy. I never even met that drug company guy."

"I never said you met him. But he's your father, right, Cindy? Cindy Gottesmann, that's your name, isn't it?"

"No, I told you before—my name's Cynthia Miller."

"We identified you from your record, Cindy. You had some misdemeanor arrests for marijuana possession a few years back. Don't lie to me."

"All right, that's my real name, and I smoked some weed. So what? I didn't know the Markham guy. And he wasn't my dad—are you crazy?"

"He was, and you had something to do with killing him with heavy water."

"Heavy water? What's that?"

"You deny knowing about heavy water? University of Iowa?"

"Okay, I know what it is, sure. But I was just paid to get some information. I don't know about killing him with it."

Cindy Miller was Markham's daughter, Alexander Darkkin had said, but was it possible that Cindy didn't know that? Thornton pondered that question for a few minutes.

"Your DNA is also a half match to someone who was in the transplant bank and needed a kidney transplant for diabetes—Corrine Gottesmann. Died a year ago in Parkwood of hypoglycemia. They administered the wrong type of insulin—it seems that she was one of the victims in Lewis' scheme. Your DNA also matches the Markham daughters by fifty percent. They're your half-sisters."

"Okay, she was my mom, but so what? She died of diabetes. They said it was some 'complication.' But I don't have any half-sisters."

He stood up and crossed his arms. "Are you going to tell us what we want?"

"All right, I'm listening. What info do you want?"

"I want all the information you have regarding anyone behind this. In return, you get the kidnapping and computer crime charges, minimal time."

"Look, man, this whole thing was Lewis' idea. I don't know anything about my mom being killed on purpose, or this drug guy being my dad. If Lewis did that to them, he can burn in hell. All I was told was that we'd screw up the Markhams' finances and blackmail some people with their medical records, but we didn't plan on hurting anyone. They wanted to do something with heavy water, but I didn't know it was to kill Markham."

"The others won't say anything or don't know. And we'll be bringing in your pal Mr. Lewis soon."

"You don't know where he is," she smiled. "You'll never find him. He knew something went down."

"We know exactly where he is, so you better hope your story holds up."

• • •

The Boeing 767 aircraft bound for Buenos Aires, Argentina was beginning to board at San Diego International Airport. Suddenly, two official-looking plainclothes men approached the distinguished-looking man in the first-class line.

"Mr. Terrell Lewis?"

"No, you must be mistaken."

"FBI. You need to come with us."

"My name isn't Lewis, it's Benford. Thomas Benford. What is this about, sir?"

"Terrell Lewis, you are under arrest for suspicion of computer espionage, murder, and trafficking in illegal pornography." He was read his rights.

"I demand to know what's going on. I'll have your job."

The agents removed him from the gate area. "Shut the hell up. You're in enough trouble as it is."

"You have the wrong man. I don't know anything about that. My name's Benford." His passport and identification supported that identity.

"It's a forged passport and ID. I don't know how you got it, but you're Terrell Lewis. Facial recognition confirms you as someone who left a crime scene at a deserted Clystarr warehouse. You'll have the opportunity to explain yourself downtown."

• • •

Ken Thornton was waiting for Lewis back at the San Diego FBI office in the gray interrogation room.

"Lewis. I'm Special Agent Thornton. We're going to talk a long while. Have a seat."

"I don't see that you have any evidence here," Lewis said. "I want an attorney. I know my rights."

He pointed his finger at Lewis angrily. "This is terrorism country here, you shithead. You aren't a US citizen and you don't have any goddamn rights under the Patriot Act—you got that? Your server contained information that implicates you in several counts of computer crime. You were obviously fleeing the country."

"Of course I was leaving the country. I was just going on a vacation. I've planned it for weeks."

"Yeah, right—with a forged passport." He pulled out a bottle of water. "But let's change the subject. Good stuff, this Quattra water. You have a storage warehouse full of it."

"So what? Nothing illegal about hoarding water, is there, fed?"

He stared at the man angrily. "Don't screw with me, Lewis. Homeland Security will fry your ass. You know what this shit is— it killed John Markham."

"It's just a bottle of water. And I don't know anybody named Markham."

"It's a bottle of goddamn heavy water. We just can't figure out how you thought of it. And, we've been following you ever since you left the old Clystarr warehouse where you had Darkkin."

Lewis cleared his throat, took a sip of light water, and paused for a few minutes. "If you think I'm the mastermind behind this, you're wrong. I'm not capable of something of that magnitude."

"Then who is it?" Thornton said menacingly.

Lewis laughed. "You have no fucking idea what you're

dealing with here."

"Yeah, I do. This whole thing is way bigger than killing off Markham with heavy water. There's a big market for a number of things that altered medical records could be good for—organ trafficking, for example. An organ is needed by someone in a foreign country, for example. The database is supposed to be secret, to prevent anyone from doing that, but it gets hacked into. The unfortunate organ donor has a medical 'accident' and dies, leaving our recipient with a new organ." Alex had talked to him about Lewis' grand dream, and at least they had stopped those horrific plans from reaching maturity.

"It seems you have everything figured out, so why are we talking?"

"I can't believe you thought you could get away with it. It's science fiction."

"Believe it, fed," Lewis said. "It's true. And, there's more. Where the hell did you think we got the heavy water?"

"I don't know. Some lab or something. Or deuterium oxide used for medical tracer purposes."

Alex was behind the one-way mirror. "No, that's not it," Alex said to Bonnie and the other agent. "Tell Thornton I need to talk to him," he said to the other agent.

He went outside and talked to Alex. "What is it?"

"To produce nuclear weapons, what do you need?" Alex asked.

"I don't want to play twenty questions, Darkkin. Uranium?" Thornton said loudly.

"Not really. One type of weapon uses enriched uranium, like the 'Little Boy' type used at Hiroshima. But the yield of uranium-grade weapons isn't that great. For really powerful weapons, you need weapons-grade plutonium. More complex, as they use an implosion device, but much more efficient."

"Who cares, and what's that got to do with heavy water?"

"One way of making Pu-239, the fissionable isotope of pluto-nium, is to breed U-238 in a reactor, where the heavy water slows neutrons sufficiently for the natural uranium to capture neutrons. This converts the uranium to neptunium, which then beta decays to Pu-239. You just need a lot of unenriched uranium. It's not terribly efficient, but cheap, and fairly easy to do."

"So you're saying that some terrorist power wants to build nuclear weapons?"

"It's at least a possibility, and you have to consider it. Iran, for example, would surely want to build one. Or North Korea, or Al-Qaida. Take your pick."

"Shit," he said as he went back in to continue his interrogation of Terrell Lewis. Things just seemed to be getting worse and worse.

"So why kill John Markham, Lewis? I guess you could sell off all your shares of Clystarr stock and purchase Pyrco stock before the merger. The ultimate form of insider trading."

"I don't give a shit about Clystarr," Lewis said, shaking his head. "That company was a piece of crap."

"I want to know about the arsenic and Anne Markham," he said as he threw his coffee cup against the wall, spattering hot liquid. "Who made that up?"

"I don't know what you're talking about."

He leaned forward. "Darkkin found wave files of Anne Markham on your server. Pieces of her voice, likely reconstructed to form the voice heard on the digital recording."

"Okay, so we made a recording," Lewis said, rolling his eyes. "That's not illegal. We emulated her voice, that's all."

"Trying to pass something off as evidence and implicate someone is illegal. I want to know how and why."

Lewis gulped his water. "One of my guys overheard Darkkin telling this Dr. Mary Williams in a hospital coffee shop he thought Markham's CT images were altered. Darkkin wanted a crime, we gave him a suspect, okay?"

"Where did you get the technology to do that? It even fooled SDPD's analyst, and she's no chump. God, I really loved seeing her break your lackey's neck, though. Beautiful."

"Shit, he wasn't worth anything, anyway. And I've got a lot of things you've only dreamt about. Maybe I'll share them with you sometime." Lewis laughed and leaned back in his chair.

"You paid that Riggins lady to play the tape for SDPD Lt. Owens."

A long pause. "No, not me directly. The guy who gave me

money had something on her, he said. Was having an affair or something."

"I'll ask you one more time," he said, exponentially growing more impatient. "Fact—you're going to prison for a long, long time. But the time you do can be goddamn miserable, or slightly less miserable. There's no way you could've funded such a stunt, so you name the backer. Darkkin says you confessed it's Kristin Markham."

"Of course—it's all right in front of you. Who else would benefit more?"

"You're a lying son of a bitch. There's evidence that Kristin also drank the water. Why would she poison herself?"

"I don't give a shit if you believe it or not."

"Darkkin found some good stuff on some computers that we are already interested in. Not nearly as glamorous as cyber-terrorism, but still within our jurisdiction. The child pornography sites you were running. The boys you meet at Pelican Bay will love you for that."

Lewis' face turned white as he paused for a minute. "That shit isn't mine. I can tell you whose it is, and who my contacts are. What do I get for that?"

He picked him up and slammed him into the wall. "Sorry, bastard. You'll go into the hole. I'll turn the whole fucking bunch of you over to CTU—they'll hold you indefinitely and will shoot you up with shit that'll make you wish you'd never been born. Neurotoxins will make every nerve ending in your body seem as if it's on fire."

"You want the facts, I'm giving them to you."

"How was this Underwood guy involved?"

"*Underwood?* We needed that moron because he had the most access to Markham. It was all his idea about the heavy water. He was also doing illegal drug trials for money with that company Clystarr merged with. He was a compulsive gambler and needed to come up with some quick cash for the sharks. I shouldn't have trusted his stupid ass."

"His suicide note was one thing that tipped Darkkin off—he found heavy water in some private urine samples he did on Markham."

"Then Underwood must have done those tests for the illegal studies, and he got into that shitty mess all on his own. If he found deuterium oxide in the samples he would have tried to cover it up to avoid messing up the study, and his money. Look at what he did—blew his head off because he might be found out."

"He didn't do it. You or someone else shot him to make it look that way."

"Why would we kill Underwood? He had nothing on us."

"Then give me some names."

Lewis paused for a few seconds. "The money man was this other guy who looked like he was in his late forties. His name was Harter—Frank Harter. It was his kid porno stuff, you have to believe me. I can give you some e-mails and other info I have, but he was my main contact."

"It better be right, Lewis."

Lewis wrote down all the information he could find about the other man he worked with, and Thornton had his people get to work on finding Frank Harter as quickly as possible.

Chapter Thirty-eight

Bonnie decided to take a week off after their ordeal, although she would check in with the SDPD office periodically. Alex was only working as needed, giving him ample time for other pursuits. They were sitting in the kitchen of her condominium.

"The serial number on the Watson alloy cuffs does not correspond to any sold at any police supply store within a three hundred mile radius during the last ten years. I also checked the online retailers where I have accounts. There were very few of that model sold to anyone."

"What about overseas vendors?"

"I suppose that's possible, but handcuffs are illegal for export outside of the US and Canada. Since Watson is an American manufacturer, that's unlikely. Another dead end."

"Maybe not. You're forgetting the great cyber-frontier."

"Huh?"

"Internet auctions, like E-Auction. I'm sure you can buy all kinds of things out there."

He set out, using hacking technology, to determine how many of that particular model had been sold on E-Auction within the last three years, using a server that archived old Web pages. It would be a long shot, but maybe something would turn up.

He found more than he had anticipated. Five of that model had been sold on the Internet over the last six years, probably to collectors, because of their rarity. He looked at the purchaser profiles and focused on one from four years ago. E-Auction alias "Topdoc99."

A photo of the item was even available, which he downloaded it and looked at with his photo editing software. He would need to talk to Jim figure out how to hack into the database and learn who the buyer was.

Later in the day he was, after conferring with his old friend, able to hack into the profile; this search revealed the surprise identity of "Topdoc99." He thought about the alloy cuffs and why anyone would buy those instead of the "standard" ones. He then thought about something he ran across earlier in his investigation and called his personal manacle maven over to the laptop.

"Get this—they belonged to Monte Buechler, and he purchased them on E-Auction four years ago. The alias 'Topdoc99' is him. Somehow, those cuffs got into Lewis' warehouse."

"So what, Alex, if he bought that model on the Internet? I have over two hundred sets myself, and I am not a criminal."

"No, that itself doesn't prove he's involved, but I just *know* that damn bastard's involved with all this."

"*Bastard?*" she said with a puzzled look. "He is the chief of staff, no? And you said he was very helpful when you went to see him about Underwood. Wendy believes he is superb."

"That's just it—he's too smooth a character, and Wendy's almost as gullible as you. He could've done that to throw us off."

"Yes, and someone also could have framed him just like with Anne Markham. Accusing someone of that stature is absurd. You believe everyone is involved or out to get you."

"Maybe." He looked at the photo of the cuffs purchased on the Internet. "There's even a serial number on them. I can barely make it out—301307, I think."

"That is not the number off the ones you wore, it was 801837."

"And I know that can't be the serial number."

"Why not?"

"Because I looked them up in your own manuals." He pulled out one of her inch-thick handcuff reference guides—essential tools for any practicing escapologist. "That model is only up to numbers in the 350,000 range. Someone must've altered it. There must be a connection—something I remembered from before."

• • •

Bonnie went to the SDPD lab and re-examined the alloy cuffs from the warehouse. After the dust had cleared, it did seem that their little adventure had produced quite a bit of information. Computer files implicating Terrell Lewis in the deuterization of John Markham; proof of the digital forgery of Anne Marhkam's conversation with Pamela Riggins; seeds of potential organ trafficking, using Lewis' advanced technology; evidence of Parkwood medical errors being engineered by Lewis. At least they got a child pornography server off the Internet. But he knew there was no way the British hacker could've funded and engineered it all on his own.

"Alex, it appears that there have indeed been subtle manipulations. The two 3's have been altered to resemble 8's, and the 0 altered to look like a 3."

"So they really are Buechler's, after all."

"It would appear so. But it's no big deal to me. Any defense attorney would have that laughed out of court."

"Come on—what's the likelihood of those ending up at that old warehouse by simple coincidence? On second thought, don't answer that." She probably could come up with an exact number.

"But why would he have purchased those anyway? I don't think he was a magician."

"Wrong. He's a magician at keeping his name out of this whole stinking mess."

"Did you remember what you thought of before?"

"Yeah. A way to connect those handcuffs and the former tenants of that abandoned Clystarr warehouse. How would you like to take a trip to San Francisco?"

"I suppose, but what's of interest there?"

"Someone Buechler knows who might need to have something like that. It's just a hunch, but we need a little rest and relaxation, anyway."

"Buechler knows a shore patrol or Coast Guard officer who works in a corrosive or extreme environment?"

"Uh, I think we've had this conversation before. They're for a different kind of 'extreme environment'—like the recreational area I saw on the video cameras at the old Clystarr compound."

Chapter Thirty-nine

Alex and Bonnie flew to his old stomping grounds—San Francisco—and checked into a posh downtown hotel. They then proceeded to go to various clubs, most of which were far different than ones Bonnie had ever experienced. There were similar places in San Diego or Los Angeles, but he had special reasons for going to these.

After a long evening, they finally went into an upscale club in a swank district of San Francisco. The former Stanford student knew most of the clubs, but had not been to this one for a while. The entire place was very dark, with a variety of seemingly upscale clients flashing lots of money. Bonnie gaped in awe at the variety of couples that she saw. Men with women. Men with men. Women with women. Transgendered men and women with each other. Most dressed in leather or rubber. A high-priced fetish club.

"I am most displeased with you," she said as they took a seat at a back table. "I can't believe you brought me to this type of vitiated establishment for entertainment."

"I thought you liked San Francisco. You have to take it all in."

"There are many experiences I enjoy in this wonderful city. Ghirardelli Square, Fisherman's Wharf, Golden Gate Bridge, and Chinatown. And, my favorite place of all."

"What's that, may I ask?"

She looked surprised. "Why, Alcatraz, of course!"

"Right, I should have guessed."

"This place is hideous! Look at these people, if they qualify as that." She began pointing at several individuals.

"Don't be a bigot—they're just people, like you or I. You're the charitable person, or so you say. Have a little tolerance."

Her brown face turned a deep red. "*You* are telling *me* about tolerance? I am not a bigot, and they are not like me in the least! Unlike them, I am not trying to be something that is against the laws of nature."

"You shouldn't judge people on their appearance. Who are you to determine what's right or wrong? Discrimination in any form is a bad thing. Of all people, you should be sensitive to that."

"What's *that* supposed to mean?"

"You're a minority with a disability. Surely you've been the object of prejudice at some point in your life."

"What could you possibly know of prejudice, my fair-skinned boyfriend?"

"Well, I'm from the South—an Appalachian-American. Lots of people stereotype us as dumb hillbillies."

"Oh, yes, make jokes. I cannot help being Latina or deaf—it's who I am. I do not choose to make a spectacle of myself like some ghastly chimera."

One fringe benefit of dating Bonnie was a free membership to the Word-A-Day Club. "*Chimera?* What the hell is that?"

"A chimera is a horrible or frightening fantastic combination of incongruous parts, like that individual over there." She pointed to a person wearing a dog collar and rubber helmet. "I cannot even determine its gender. I suspect this is the type of place you secretly enjoy when I'm not around." She squinted at him.

"This is my first time here, but I'm looking for something." The high-end fetish club catered to high rollers and people from all walks of alternative lifestyles, and it had cost him $2,000 in cash just to get in the door.

Suddenly a curvy strawberry blonde in her mid-thirties came through the club, wearing a skin-tight leather catsuit and smoking a cigarette. There was no smoking in San Francisco bars, but apparently the rules were bent for high rollers. She saw him and stopped. "Alex! Alex Darkkin! I can't believe it," she said as she went up to their table. "It's been years since I saw you. Looking good, lover," the attractive woman said as she kissed him on the cheek.

"Yeah, hi!" he muttered, remembering the face but not the name—a common problem with women from his past.

"Samantha," she said. "You remember me—we came here several times!"

"Oh, yeah. How are you doing, Sammy?"

"So, this is your first time here, eh? The truth is exposed," Bonnie said sternly.

"I'm great. So, whatcha doing now? Still live here? Haven't seen you in, like, forever."

"Uh, no. I moved back to Nashville seven years ago, but I've been living in San Diego for awhile."

"Who's your nice friend here?"

"This is Bonnie. Bonnie . . . Sammy."

"Oh, it's so nice to meet old friends of Alex," Bonnie said sarcastically.

"Likewise," she said, sizing up the scientist. "Anyway, Alex, it was good to see you again. We sure had some good times! Let's get together soon."

"Right—we'll certainly do that. Bye."

Bonnie was visibly displeased. "Who was that girl? Was she one of your girlfriends?"

He sighed. "I lived here for eight years—you have to expect we might run into some of my old girlfriends."

"You slept with her, I'm certain of that," she said, pointing a finger at him. "I know you did."

"So? What's that got to do with anything? You had relationships before, too."

"There is one difference—you will not encounter my old flames in this type of debased place. And you lied to me about not coming here. For that, you will pay."

A transgendered waitress, wearing five–inch latex platform boots, came up to them and stared at Alex. "I think you're in the wrong place, Mister. You *sure* you belong here?"

"I'm sure." He showed a waitress a photo. "Miss, do you know this lady? She's a friend of ours."

"I don't think this is the place for you, tumbleweed. Country-western bar's a couple miles up the road. Yee-haw!"

"I'm more progressive than I look, trust me. I'm a friend of

Sammy's." He pulled the alloy handcuffs from his pocket. "See, we bring our own hardware."

"Any friend of Sammy's is a friend of mine. Say, those are nice ones," the waitress said as she fondled the cuffs. "Maybe I misjudged you. Which kind are you?"

"I'm sorry?"

"You a top or bottom?"

"Do I prefer being on top or bottom? That's a pretty rude question, don't you think?"

"Sheesh—top is the dominant, bottom is the submissive. I guess you really are a greenhorn."

"Oh. I'm the bottom, of course. She's the boss."

"That's what I figured. She probably can whip your butt good. You probably like it, too."

"What did she say? I didn't get that. You are the bottom of what? The human evolutionary chain?"

"You're in charge, I said."

"Oh. At least you are coming to your senses."

"But, anyway, Miss—do you know either of these people?" He showed her two photos.

"I don't think I remember either one."

"Maybe *this* will help you remember." He slipped her five one–hundred dollar bills.

"It's a little familiar, but I don't know for sure." He handed her another five hundred dollars.

"Try a little harder."

She stuffed the cash inside her bra. "Okay—this one girl, I swear I've never seen. The other, I've seen her before—a *lot*. I doubt she's your type, though, cornpone." She turned towards Bonnie and grinned. "Hey, you're pretty hot, do you know that?"

Bonnie was having a hard time understanding conversation in the noisy club. "What did that . . . person say?"

"*She likes you*," he signed to Bonnie in ASL. She suddenly crossed her arms and frowned. "Miss, I don't want to ask the gal in this photo out. But you're sure she comes here?"

"Sure, she's loaded. Comes in here all the time with a lot of different people, but usually with a certain guy. She's a pretty wild rich chick."

"Can you be more specific about the guy she comes with?"

"My memory's fading quick, sweetie." Alex produced another $500 and greased her palm.

He then produced a man's photograph and showed it to the waitress. "You seen this guy before?"

"Oh, yeah. She hangs out with him all the time. They're really into the scene here."

"For how long?"

"I've worked here two and a half years. They come in at least once every couple weeks, sometimes more often."

"Thanks."

"Now, you gonna order something or what, people?"

"Bring us some nachos. Margarita for the lady. I'll have some ginger ale."

"Wow, a big drinker. I'll be back." The waitress, standing about six-seven in boots, walked away.

Bonnie leaned over towards him. "I have studied our waitress in detail. I don't want to alarm you, but my skills and experience indicate that she likely is a man in disguise."

"No, really? Jeez, that's the stupidest thing I've ever heard. Of course it's a man in drag. Haven't you seen that before?"

"I am fortunate you're so experienced at such things."

"Don't be so sarcastic. This stuff is important."

"Anyway, I understand why you brought the photo of Buechler, but why the Markham daughters? Do you truly think they are involved?" Bonnie recognized the photos from her previous facial analyses.

"I have medical records proving this woman has a severe nickel allergy."

"I see. Well, if you have what you need, I would enjoy leaving. And I expect to be fed something better than terrible nachos back at the hotel."

Interesting information he'd found out, although it had cost him a small fortune. Too bad it wasn't tax-deductible. They would spend the night and go to Chinatown, Golden Gate Bridge, and Alcatraz in the morning.

Chapter Forty

Dr. Wendy Williams waited on a sofa in the administrative suite of Parkwood Memorial Hospital at nine AM on the warm November morning, the week before Thanksgiving. Richard Wagner, the CEO, had requested a meeting with her to discuss the bad press the hospital had been receiving for the last year. The ever-grim specter of closure sparked by the astoundingly high medical error rate continued to rear its ugly head. She knew Wagner was originally from the East Coast and had worked in a number of medical management positions before being brought to San Diego five years ago by the board. He was well liked by board members, although he'd been losing some ground with the medical staff of late.

Dr. Monte Buechler, the medical staff president, had been supportive. But Wagner told her he needed some political help outside San Diego, and Buechler wasn't a big help there. Wagner asked her to arrange a meeting with officers of the state medical society in Sacramento. She knew most of those people and was easily the most personable of physicians Wagner had to deal with. Buechler was still more influential with the local staff, but that situation was going down the tubes quickly. His assistant brought her into his large office and offered her a seat at his conference table.

"Thanks for meeting, Wendy. I don't know who else can help," the thin, late-fortyish man said, offering his hand.

"I don't know what I can do, Rick, but I'll do everything I can. I'm sure Monte will, too."

"Monte's a good friend. But I need some help in Sacramento to get us through this."

"You overestimate me. I'm just a newcomer."

"You're great at schmoozing those guys—the best I've ever seen. And you're impeccably honest. There's no one more credible here."

"I appreciate that. I went ahead and talked to Dr. Tom Lewiston, the president of the California Medical Association. He's going to set up at meeting with us in a couple of weeks."

"That's good. In preparation, I think we need to stress that the opening of a new hospital isn't going to solve any of the problems we have. People depend on us. Even though we don't have a lot of indigents out here, they're people that won't get care in the new proposed hospital."

"I know. And medical education is going to suffer. They'll have to close the existing residency programs, and the residents will need to find new programs. We'll lose good faculty to other centers."

"Nobody cares about losing faculty. All anybody around here is concerned about is the money, you know that."

They went over reports for the next ten minutes, until Wagner's phone rang.

"Do you need to get that, Rick?"

"Cathy will get it. I'll call whoever it is back." A few seconds later his assistant opened the door. "Cathy, I'm in a meeting. Tell the person it'll have to wait."

"It's Warren in Security. He has to speak with you now, Mr. Wagner—he's on hold."

Wagner was getting angry, a behavior she had never seen in the normally cool executive. "I don't like repeating myself. Tell him to wait and I'll call him back when I get a chance!"

"He says it can't wait, sir. He needs to talk to you. Now."

"Rick, it's okay. Do you want me to step out?"

He threw his pen against the wall. "No, you don't need to go. I'll be just a minute. Cathy, get Dr. Williams some more coffee, please." He went to the phone at his large cherry desk. "Warren, I'm very busy. What do you need?"

She observed the man's face turn white as he dropped the

phone and fumbled in his desk drawer for something.

"What's wrong, Rick? Was there an accident or something?"

"Please let Kate and the kids know that I love them. But I can't go through this humiliation, Wendy. Goodbye."

"What are you talking about? What are you doing?"

She watched in horror as Richard Wagner pulled a Beretta Bobcat from his desk, placed it next to his right temple, and pulled the trigger. The bullet exited the left side of his head as he slumped over his desk. She let out a shrill scream as the room filled with his assistant and numerous other office personnel.

About ten seconds later two men in suits entered the room and flashed badges. "FBI. We're here to arrest Richard Wagner. What's happened here?"

She was now trembling. "He . . . he just killed himself with that small pistol."

"Oh, my God," the administrative assistant said. "Warren must've tipped him off that you were coming up. It's my fault. If I hadn't told him, he wouldn't have known and killed himself."

"It's not your fault, Ma'am. You couldn't have known that," one agent said, as he escorted everyone out except Wendy, who had witnessed the suicide.

"What did you want with Rick?" she said, crying. "What did he do?"

The first agent looked at her name badge. "You're Dr. Gwendolyn Williams, aren't you?"

"Yes," she sobbed.

"Then you already know quite a bit. We were going to arrest this guy for trafficking in child pornography. He was using the alias of a Franklin Harter. Harter's some dead guy that Wagner stole the identity of as a cover."

"What? That's impossible. I've worked with Mr. Wagner extensively, as have many other physicians."

"I don't think so, Doctor. This has to do with the information your brother retrieved from Terrell Lewis' server when he was kidnapped. This Wagner guy was operating over a dozen child pornography sites. Some pretty sick stuff."

"I can't believe that! Not Rick Wagner."

"I'm sorry, but it's true. The IP addresses from the chat room logs trace back to him. Almost a terabyte of photos and video that we believe he helped create and distribute."

"Why would he do that?"

"I don't know, but what he did here pretty much proves his guilt, doesn't it, Doctor?"

"I suppose." She sat down and drank some water. "He seemed fine . . . a good man."

"I need to get a statement from you, Dr. Williams. Can you tell me what you saw?"

"There isn't much to tell. We were just . . . having a meeting. His assistant told him the chief of security was on the line. After Rick talked to him, he pulled out the gun and shot himself. That's it. It all happened so fast."

"Neither you nor anyone else suspected him of doing anything like pornography?"

"God, no! He was an upstanding family man. Two kids in college. I've done a lot of charity stuff—he was involved in a lot of that."

"You don't always know who the perverts are, Doctor. He probably had been doing it for years."

"I'm sorry," she said as she continued to cry. "I'm going to have to lie down, I think I'm going to vomit. Do you need me for anything else right now? The hospital operator will know how to reach me."

"Not right now. We'll probably need to talk to you later. I'm sorry you had to see that, Dr. Williams."

She called the clinic to cancel her patients for the rest of the day, called Stan, and went to rest in a call room until he arrived. She didn't want to drive home in her current state.

• • •

The headline on the front page of the San Diego Union-Tribune certainly didn't help the beleaguered Parkwood's declining standing in the community. The article with the headline "Parkwood CEO Commits Suicide" wouldn't elicit many donations to the Foundation, especially when the readers learned the reason for the suicide. As the sole witness, Wendy's name was mentioned, of course—not the type of publicity she wanted.

"I still can't believe it," she said at her home that morning. She decided to take the rest of the week off, since she was in no emotional condition to see patients. Stan and Alex were there as well.

"So, it happened just like that?" Alex asked.

"It's just a fog. I can hardly remember what happened yesterday. He went to answer the call from the security chief, and then blew his head off."

"I can't believe the stuff I got off Lewis' server was his."

"Apparently so. I guess Lewis had some information that led the FBI to Wagner."

"No one suspected anything? He was a pretty upstanding guy?"

"He was. No one would've thought in a million years he could've done something like this." The phone rang, and she took the portable unit into the dining room to answer it.

"Some people have their secret addictions," Alex said.

"I guess this is the end of it, Alex," Stan said. "Time to move on."

"What do you mean? He's dead, and you don't know what was in his mind. What if there's someone else?"

"Who else could there be? Don't you think that you've done enough?"

"Great—blame me. I didn't do any of this, Stan. It all existed before I got here. Would you rather it still be going on?"

"No, of course I don't. But it's affecting us all personally— bringing us all into danger."

"So I just forget about it. Somebody else's problem, right?"

"Look who's talking—all you've ever done is worry about yourself, and now you're talking about the 'greater good.' It's the police's responsibility, so let them deal with it once and for all."

He stood up from the sofa and pointed a finger angrily at his brother-in-law. "The police thought I was crazy until I found some concrete evidence. It's Wendy's hospital too, and you should be glad that pervert's gone. Good riddance to dirtbag scum."

"Oh, you think a man dying is good?"

"Don't start in with your liberal, bleeding-heart, anti-capital punishment politics, Stan. I just can't believe this is the end of it. Someone set Wagner up and used his addiction to gain leverage, just like Underwood with his gambling problem."

"Yeah, why don't you just go get your shotgun and gather a posse, like the hillbilly you are?"

Alex pointed at Stan and laughed. "That's a damn good idea. Someone needs to clean up this rotten place."

Wendy hung up the cordless phone and went back into the living room. "Stop bickering, both of you—I'm not up to it. I don't want to hear any more about Parkwood, or John Markham, or anything right now, so shut up."

"Who was that?" Stan asked.

"Monte Buechler. He wanted to see if I was okay, and wants to stop by tomorrow and talk."

"Buechler? You think he's such a good guy, don't you?" Alex asked.

"Of course I do. He's been wonderfully supportive."

"Well, you also thought Wagner was the cat's meow. Not very good judgment there, sis."

"You're just jealous of him and his accomplishments."

Alex laughed. "Hardly. I think he's an asshole."

"Alex, I'm tired and don't want to answer any more questions. I want to forget what I saw today, and I'm going to take a nap. Please leave if you can't be quiet."

Chapter Forty-one

"I still can't believe Wendy saw the hospital CEO do that," Bonnie said at Alex's apartment the next evening.

"Believe it. She watched him blow his head off."

"I guess sufficient evidence exists now to say that you were right. It pains me greatly to say it, however."

"Of course I'm right, but it still doesn't all add up. These guys would've had better plans if they were the real ones behind it."

"What more do you need?"

He was still fixated on "Cindy Miller"—the alias of Cindy Gottesmann, the woman from Lewis' abandoned Clystarr compound who had studied heavy water toxicity at the University of Iowa. Bonnie had earlier deduced she was a Markham daughter and half-sibling of the sisters.

"Cindy Gottesmann—there *has* to be something there. Her mother, Corrine, for example. We believe that she was one of the 'medical errors' at Parkwood? But why?" he asked.

"Cindy? Of all the people at Lewis' warehouse, why her? She hardly seemed threatening."

"Maybe not, but she's our only living link to the heavy water." He busily looked up names in the Internet telephone directory. Gottesmann was not a common name, he learned; there were only about thirty Gottesmanns in California, and eight in the San Diego area. Of those with listed numbers, of course.

"What grandiose scheme are you contemplating now?"

"Medical record says Corrine Gottesmann was divorced and remarried. The husband listed on the face sheet was a Charles

Gottesmann."

"Where is this Mr. Gottesmann's residence? Alaska?"

"Search says he moved somewhere much closer. Fresno. The land of raisins."

• • •

Alex made the several hour trip to Fresno and pulled up to the modest ranch-style home at about noon on the first of December. He walked up the sidewalk and knocked on the door. A man answered the door.

"Mr. Charles Gottesmann?"

"That's me. Who are you?"

"I'm Dr. Alexander Darkkin. We spoke on the phone yesterday."

"Oh, yeah. Come on in." Gottesmann was in his late fifties, a slight man with obvious chronic lung disease, given his barrel chest. From the smell of the house it seemed as if he was still smoking. "You said you were with the Parkwood hospital."

"That's correct. I'm looking into some medical errors, and I was wondering if you could tell me a little bit about your wife."

"What's there to tell? The sons of bitches killed her, it's that simple."

"Insulin error. They administered the wrong kind, from what I understand."

"Damn right—U-500. She was supposed to be on the usual kind, 100 units per cc. But that shit was 500 units per cc, and somehow it showed up on her medicine list. They said it was a computer error. From what I hear, though, it's business as usual at that stinkin' Parkwood hellhole."

"I hate to pry, but I have to ask—would anyone have wanted your wife dead?"

"Why would they want that? She had only a few thousand or so in life insurance—barely enough to bury her. I'm glad I don't have to go to that goddamn Parkwood no more. It'll kill your ass, Doc."

"What about Cindy?"

The man's mouth opened wide. "Jesus Christ. What the hell

do you know about that good-for-nothing kid?"

"She was arrested for kidnapping and computer crime."

"Yeah, I know. That FBI bust was all over the TV news and the papers. Hell, don't surprise me none. Little slut never listened to anything I said. Into drugs, screwing around, you name it. Bad seed."

"You know anything about her going to the University of Iowa to study with a heavy water expert?"

"Iowa? I don't know about no Iowa. She dropped outta college, so I can't believe that—unless it had to do with something crooked."

"Was she good in school when she went?"

"Pretty smart, yeah. Good at science. A lotta good it did her. Didn't listen to old Dad, though."

"About that—I know you're not her biological father."

"Just how do you know that?"

"DNA. Her father was John Markham."

"Who?"

"Markham—the Clystarr chairman."

"That drug guy who died of cancer? You gotta be kidding."

"Why's that?"

"Corrine was a fine lady, a real good-looker when she was younger, but there ain't no way she was involved with a rich guy like that—give me a break. Look at me. I've got a decent place, but come on, I ain't no billionaire."

"I found out she used to work for Clystarr—she was one of Markham's secretaries. Why couldn't it be possible?"

"Doc, a lotta people worked for that place. It don't mean she screwed that guy."

"That was a long time ago. But would Cindy have wanted your wife dead?"

Gottesmann shook his head. "No way. As messed up as she was, she loved her mom dearly. Came to see her in the hospital every day the last time. Corrine had a lot of problems with her diabetes of late. Cindy even offered to donate a kidney, but she wasn't a good enough match."

"Corrine was married before, correct?"

"Yeah, she married some guy in med school who's a big shot

doctor now. Lives in San Diego still, I think. Divorced around '81, '82. We got married in '83. Got a bunch of money in the settlement—future earnings and all."

"Cindy was born in 1982. So the doctor divorced her because she had the affair with Markham?"

"Like I said, I don't know nothing about no Markham. I knew she had an affair and Cindy wasn't the doc's kid, but she always said the dad was some guy she knew from college. Didn't want anything to do with him. But, yeah, that's why they split."

"One last question—who was the doctor she was married to?"

"Arrogant horse's ass—Buechler was his name."

• • •

"It's a brilliant plan, you have to admit," Alex told Bonnie at the SDPD lab. "Buechler must've had Wagner and Underwood create these 'medical errors', including his own ex-wife's death. The error rate of the hospital would skyrocket, and the number of sentinel events would threaten the hospital's accreditation."

"Why would Buechler want to kill his own ex-wife?"

"I assume it had to do with her affair with Markham. It also gives Buechler motive to have engineered his death."

"But we found out about Lewis, and that the medical errors were in fact deliberate attacks on the electronic medical record system. Does this not vindicate the hospital and restore Parkwood's credibility?"

"That's the genius of it, don't you see? If things had continued as planned and no one found out, the hospital would lose its accreditation. And, if it was discovered, it would all be blamed on Underwood, whose 'suicide' prevents him from saying anything. Finally, Buechler leaks Wagner's pornography stuff to the FBI, and he kills himself in disgrace. The hospital's credibility is still shot because of the weakness of the entire electronic medical record system. Buechler gets what he wants either way."

"But why would anyone do it? There is no money can be made from that."

"He has to be someone so narcissistic that he wants the whole world focused around him. He gets the old hospital shut down, all the while pretending to be an advocate as president of the medical staff. No one would suspect him. Buechler becomes the leader of the new hospital, developed to help make more money for the doctors and provide lucrative clinical trials for Pyrco. All for no other reason than he could do it — a tribute to his arrogance."

"I still don't understand about the Anne Markham arsenic thing, though," Bonnie said.

"Someone set that up to throw us off. The recording was engineered so well with Lewis' technology that it fooled even you, and that's not easy. For what? To kill Markham with something as corny as arsenic? I never believed that, anyway. And Buechler refuted it to make it look like he was on our side."

"About Underwood — the ballistics matched the bullet with the gun, which was unregistered. The serial number was traced back to a gun shop that sold it to him ten years ago. Held in his right hand, but he was left-handed, according to your analysis of the pen nib. Wendy learned from conversations with others that he was left-handed as well."

"So someone made it look like he killed himself. Desperate because of gambling debt and such."

"We don't know that someone killed him. There were no poisons or any other causes of death found at his autopsy."

"I assume the scenario with Wagner was similar. Buechler must have dug deep for dirt on everybody. If Underwood's problem was good, Wagner's was striking gold. Buechler exploited his child pornography addiction and threatened to go public if he didn't comply. A sweet plan."

"At least he would've been alive. Living with disgrace would be better than not living at all."

"Not for some people. He thought he would be better off dead. But now . . . it's the beginning of the end for our good friend Monte."

"Alex, what are you going to do now? This evidence that you have uncovered is circumstantial."

"Then I'll make him pay myself." He got up from the table and stared at the wall.

"You're obsessed — what more do you want? They caught Lewis, and Rick Wagner was even involved. Let it go. You can't go confront him like some Old West vigilante."

"I'm not going to confront him—I'm going to play him at his own game. That son of a bitch had Markham killed, did God knows what to others, kidnapped us, and caused Wagner to blow his head off. That prick Monte Buechler's going to wish he'd never been born—and I won't lay a finger on him."

• • •

Alex set out with a vengeance to find out all the personal information he could on Dr. Montgomery Buechler. He knew that Bonnie might have access to some information, but didn't want to ask her. First of all, that would be illegal. Second, it would involve her to an extent that he didn't want. There was something she could help with later that she could do better than anyone.

How simple it was. Buechler's birthdate was available from the California Medical Licensing Board Web site. With that and information from a traffic citation he found online, he could find other information, such as his Social Security number, which was linked to Buechler's own electronic medical record data. He logged in under an alias no one would ever detect.

Jim helped him hack into Buechler's office computer and place onto the boot partition spyware that would keep track of computer keystrokes and report them back to him. Analyzing the keystrokes would allow him to determine computer passwords for various accounts, such as his tax-deferred annuity and credit cards, which he likely paid online.

Pretty soon he had the credit card numbers and a host of other data. He had learned recently that the best way to defeat the pathological narcissist was to get inside his head, to get him angry. Granted, that person didn't give him that information expecting him to act on it, only for his general information. But knowledge was power of a higher order.

He pulled up Buechler's retirement account. He had done pretty well with his stocks and mutual funds, it seemed. He couldn't directly transfer money out of that, but did discover that Buechler paid all his bills online. His checking account balance was about $64,000, with over $250,000 in savings. The rest was in his 401(k), certificates of deposit, bonds, and other investments.

He couldn't directly extract the funds, but he could run up charges on his credit cards and then pay the bills with the bank account. He purchased a lot of big-ticket items for Buechler: computers, digital cameras, antiques, etc. He used "E-Auction" for some of those, since he already had the password for that from his prior investigation. Since that was directly linked to his bank account, money would be sucked out.

It occurred to him he could get into a lot of trouble for this, but Jim assured him they couldn't be tracked. He wasn't taking any money, merely shifting funds around in the accounts and making purchases. He used a generic laptop at a public library with unencrypted Internet access. The MAC (Media Access Control) address could be traced to the laptop, but he would be sure to destroy it later.

Buechler likely wouldn't know about the purchases for several days, until they arrived; he could return the items, but that would consume a lot of time and effort and aggravate him even further. Alex had disabled the "automatic notification" for large purchases and redirected Buechler's e-mail to his own dummy account, in case any confirmation would be necessary. After a day, the charges would be posted to the accounts; Alex would pay the bills with the bank account money. And then he would cancel the cards, after changing the passwords.

Buechler might eventually get these problems straightened out, but it would take him weeks. And his bank account would be severely depleted. He then thought about the handful of physicians he'd seen who didn't like Buechler, and how he could get them to play into his hands. He particularly remembered the large physician who stomped out of the medical staff meeting months ago, and concocted a sure-fire way to get him to blow his stack.

One thing was certain—good old Monte would be one mighty pissed off doctor at the winter Charity Ball. Alex couldn't wait for the fireworks on Saturday night.

Chapter Forty-two

The annual Charity Ball for Parkwood Medical Center took place the week before Christmas, a black-tie gala with most of the medical staff and high rollers in attendance. There would be several items auctioned off for charity, in addition to a ballroom dance and "casino night." California law prohibited actual gambling, but the games weren't for money, only entertainment.

Buechler was in a hurry to get to the event and was not in a very good mood. The last two days hadn't gone so well. Someone had ordered $40,000 of computers on his Visa card. What was even worse, they didn't believe him when he tried to call and rectify the situation. He had also been stopped by the police for several outstanding traffic tickets, which he was sure he had paid months ago.

He sat at his table in the front of the room with the Mayor of San Diego and a state senate representative. Alex and Bonnie were seated at a table in the middle of the room. Wendy and Stan Williams were seated at one of the tables close to the stage, at a table marked "Reserved." He also spied the two Markham daughters, as well as several other high-ranking officials and executives, at another VIP table. He then went up to chat with Stephanie and Kristin, whom he had met several times at other fund-raisers.

After a tasty dinner of filet mignon and shrimp scampi, the charity auction took place. He wanted to keep up his charitable image and bid on several items for sale. Afterwards, there was a brief intermission as he went to the cashier to pay with a credit card. The young woman ran the card through the reader. She tried it again with the same result.

"Is there a problem?" he said.

"I'm sorry, Dr. Buechler, but your American Express card was rejected," she said in a dejected tone.

"That's impossible. It's a platinum card. No limit."

"I can't run it, sir. I can void the bid if you like."

"Dammit. Run this one." He handed her a gold Visa card. The card reader beeped as it was rejected again.

"I'm sorry, sir. I can't take this payment."

"It must be your goddamn machine."

"It has worked fine for the others, Doctor."

"You'd better get it to fucking work."

A distinguished-looking man came over. "Doctor, I'd appreciate your not using that kind of language here."

"Who the hell are you?"

"I'm in charge of the charity auction."

"Do you know who I am?"

"Yes. You are Dr. Buechler, the president of the medical staff. Nevertheless, I still request that you watch your language, sir."

"Shut the hell up. I'll send you a goddamned check." A large figure in a tuxedo blocked his way. "What do *you* want? Get the hell out of my way, Darkkin."

"Chill out, Monte. Have a drink—I know it's your favorite." Alex handed him a White Russian with one distinct difference from the usual libation—the ice cubes were on the bottom of the glass.

He looked at the drink, then threw it Alex's face, while numerous patrons observed the altercation. "*You* did this, Darkkin. You fucked up my credit cards, you son of a bitch. They'll be closing this hospital soon, anyway. You all suck as doctors, and I'm glad I'm getting out."

Alex walked around, as if he were surprised. "What's wrong with him? This guy's nuts! I'm just trying to be sociable."

Buechler was fuming as he sat down for one of his favorite pastimes at "casino night"—poker. He sat down with several physicians he knew and hoped to get his mind off his troubles.

Alex walked in with Bonnie, who was sporting a black strapless gown. "Hey, Monte," Alex said in an irritating voice. "Going to have a good game?"

"Get the hell out of my face, Darkkin."

"You big enough to make me, little man? Come on, go for it—you don't have the guts."

Buechler stood up, looked up at the taller and heavier Alex, and clenched his fists. About twenty people were watching.

"Alex, he's not worth it. I would like to play, though."

"You're right, he's just a loser. But you don't know anything about poker."

"I know, but it's for fun. You can go talk to Wendy and Stan while I play."

"It's your funeral," Alex said as he walked off. "I don't want to be responsible. At least there's no money involved."

The crowd dispersed as she sat down at the table to play five–card draw poker. Buechler was an excellent poker player, unlike his late colleague Bill Underwood. He attempted to relax, since he had a half hour or so before his speech to the assembly. After a few hands, he was doing well, even though it was just for fun and not money. The latter wasn't especially important to the ultra-competitive medical staff president; winning the contest itself was, as always, the first priority.

"I still don't understand the rules. A pair of threes—is that good?" Bonnie said as she turned her hand over.

"Ha, that's pretty bad, little lady," an older physician said as he gaped at her muscular arms and shoulders. "You need some practice."

She pouted. "I am hopeless and almost out of chips. Perhaps you can give me some tips later."

"You just ask all the questions you want, Miss. Could I . . . touch your arm? I've never touched ones like those before. They seem so nice and solid."

She rolled her eyes and sighed. "All right, you may touch it once, but no more."

The next hand was dealt. Buechler couldn't believe his good luck as he was dealt a full house, three fours and two jacks. He raised the bet to $1000 in faux chips.

"I have no idea what I am doing, but I will take two cards, please." The dealer gave Bonnie two cards.

"Full house," Buechler said.

"Three kings, shoot," the older physician said.

"Two fives and two tens," Dr. Steve Kahana, the large physician to her right, said.

"I have four of this kind. Is this good?" Bonnie said as she turned over four eights.

"Four of a kind beats a full house, Buechler," Kahana said. "The lady wins."

"Shit," he said.

"I win, finally. Yay!"

He next was dealt four-fifths of a straight: four, five, six, and seven, with the fifth card being a queen of diamonds. He couldn't believe his luck as he drew an eight to replace the queen. He then raised the bet again.

"Straight," Buechler said as he lay down a seven, eight, nine, ten, and jack. "Beat that."

"Is his a good hand?" she asked the heavily-built Hawaiian-American doctor to her right.

"That's a great hand. He's a good player, that's for sure," Kahana said.

She called the bet. "Oh, I am foolish—none of my numbers are the same or in a row. I have *cinco* clover cards, so I guess I lose." She lay down five clubs.

"Hey, you win! That's a flush. Flush beats a straight," Kahana said, pointing at the cards.

"*¿Escalera?* I must be very lucky."

Buechler blew up and threw his cards at Bonnie. "*You lousy cheating spick!* There's no goddamn way. You're using marked cards or something." Bonnie started crying.

"Aw, come on, Monte. No call for that, insulting the lady. There's no real money," the older physician said. "She wasn't even dealing the cards."

"Yeah, well, you can bet it was a trick of some kind. Come on, you know who she is—Williams' magician pal."

"That's it, you racist son of a bitch!" Kahana yelled as he turned over the table in rage. The 250-pound bulk moved towards him angrily. "I never liked you, and I'm going to take you outside myself. Apologize to her—now."

"I won't, Steve—she cheated me on purpose."

"That's all right. I am not wanted here, Doctor, so good day to you." She got up and left, still in tears.

The intimidating Kahana stormed off. "Get the hell out of my sight, Buechler, before I smash your sorry white ass. Next time you won't be so lucky."

"You're paranoid, Monte," the older physician said. "Get it together, man! You're the leader, making a fool of yourself."

Alex wandered back to the table. "Bad luck, eh?" he said sarcastically.

"Go to hell, Darkkin." He was angrier than ever by now. His credit cards and bank account were screwed up, he was embarrassed at the auction, and he lost at poker in front of colleagues. Now he had to get up and talk to the assembly. His mental state wasn't the clearest it could be.

• • •

Buechler was announced by the interim hospital CEO and took the podium, drank a sip of water, and cleared his throat. "I want to again acknowledge how happy we all are about the vindication of our medical staff in the sentinel events at our hospital. The criminal investigation regarding our medical records has revealed horrific events. The role our late CEO, Mr. Wagner, played, is shocking. Of course, the problems in transparency of our medical records system can't be ignored. Plans on the new Doctors' Memorial will provide much greater security for medical records than what we have at Parkwood. It is my regret that our fine institution will close within the year, but it's for the best."

About two hundred people were having coffee and dessert in the banquet hall. They turned around and watched Dr. Alexander Darkkin make his way towards the podium. Alex stopped about six feet from the table where Wendy was sitting.

"Yeah, I really bet you're glad your great shrine will finally be built, Buechler."

Wendy grabbed him by the arm, not knowing what was going on. "What are you doing, Alex? You're making a scene."

"The good Dr. Williams suggests this isn't the optimal venue for my discussion, but I disagree. It's exactly the place."

"You're interrupting my important presentation, Darkkin," he said in a shaky voice. "You've been very disruptive to this whole affair. I'd like you to leave now."

"Why don't you make me, Buechler? You're the one who accused one of this hospital's biggest charity benefactors of cheating at a poker game—for tokens." Alex walked up a few more feet. "Better yet, why don't you tell everyone what you've done? Look," he said, gesturing to the audience. "This slimebag's duped you all—he's the one that set up the medical errors. He wanted to build his own for-profit hospital so he and his rich girlfriend over there could murder her father and set up a center for doing clinical trials. You don't believe me? I have proof he helped kill John Markham."

"You're an insane man, Darkkin," he said, shaking his head. "Do we have a psychiatrist with some antipsychotic drugs on hand, please?"

The 200 people gathered in the room gasped as Alex continued. "It's true! He's engineered the deaths of dozens of people, just to get Parkwood closed and give you . . . Doctors' Memorial. A memorial to his colossal ego and greed, that's what it is. You may want to take this bullshit from him, but I'm tired of it."

Dr. Steve Kahana, one of the poker players at the table earlier, rose up angrily from his seat. "Darkkin's right—Buechler's full of crap. He needs to step down." Three others got up and agreed.

Buechler got off the podium, wireless mike still live, and pointed at Alex. "I think you'd better take a seat, before I have you arrested. Your accusations are absurd and ridiculous." He was now sweating profusely and shaking.

"You want to call the police? News flash—they're on their way—for you."

Wendy got up and stared at Alex. "Those accusations are strong. You'd better be able to back them up."

"Look me straight in the eye. Haven't I been right on the money with everything that's happened since I arrived in San Diego? I've been wrong in the past, but not about this."

She turned away from Alex and towards the stage. "Is any of this true, Monte? I want to hear it from you." She approached him as he stepped off the stage.

"Get the hell out of my way, Williams. It's really all your fault, you stupid bitch! You're the one who brought *him* here. Everything's ruined."

He shoved the larger Wendy out of the way, leading to more gasping from the audience. The crimson-gowned woman stumbled back—not due to the force, which hardly fazed her, but because she wasn't used to wearing three-inch pumps. Before anyone could stop her, the puissant pediatrician had generated sufficient momentum to tackle him and propel him into the podium, shattering it into a dozen pieces.

"*Get up, you corrupt piece of crap!* You made fools out of me and the whole medical staff. To think I stood up for you."

Three police officers had now flanked the exits. At the start of the presentation, he hadn't done anything, but now he'd all but admitted his wrongdoing, and had assaulted Wendy Williams in front of the entire assembly. His left arm was numb, but didn't seem to be broken, and he felt fortunate to still be in one piece.

One of the officers called for him to surrender. He instead ran out the back of the stage and out a back door into an alley, where he planned to retrieve an old car he had hidden, just in case. He had been in that auditorium dozens of times, and knew the layout better than anyone.

The distance was about a hundred meters to a fence that he could scale to freedom. He knew the officers, Alex Darkkin, or slow-moving Wendy Williams wouldn't be able to catch him, and he continued sprinting down the back alley. He was a superb runner, and there couldn't be anyone in the building who could run one hundred meters in twelve seconds, which was approximately what would be necessary to catch him.

He apparently was mistaken, as he felt strong hands halt his ascent up the chain-link fence and throw him to the ground.

"You!" he said, suddenly recognizing the athletic companion of his new-found nemesis. "I'll kill you!"

"When I saw you today, I knew you were the most evil person I've ever met in my life. Now you're going to pay, you serpentine outlaw." He threw several punches at Bonnie, which she easily dodged. She slammed a powerful right into his left rib cage—that hurt like hell. God—he had two, maybe three broken ribs. Bonnie Mendoza wasn't as strong as Wendy Williams, but she was a hell of a lot faster. But he had to try and get away.

He found another exit down a stairwell, where he went into the laundry room. It was empty except for a middle-aged female laundry worker whom he grabbed by the neck.

Sgt. Mike Mendoza was running up the hall, about fifty yards behind Alex, who was nearing Bonnie. She quickly grabbed the laundry woman from his grasp and pushed her out of the way.

But the dangerously overconfident scientist apparently didn't notice the small puddle of oil in front of her as she slipped and tumbled headfirst into a wall. He was also covertly carrying a screwdriver he'd found in one of the stairwells. He then lunged towards her and thrust the rusty implement into the right side of her chest. She immediately slumped to the floor and gasped for air, while he pulled out the screwdriver and lunged towards the officers.

Mike immediately pulled his firearm and fired at him, barely missing him. Buechler got out a back exit with Alex right behind, as Mike attended to Bonnie.

"Bonnie, are you okay?" Mike asked, as she was now unable to speak and gasping for air. He reached for his radio. "This is SDPD. I need paramedics at the Convention Center now."

Alex caught him about twenty yards from the back exit and rammed him into the wall. "You son of a bitch—you stabbed her. I'll take it out of your ass."

"You don't have proof of any of this, Darkkin."

"I don't need it, Buechler. What's to stop me from breaking your goddamned neck, huh?" Alex had lifted him up and was choking him with both hands. "I'll finish what she started."

He saw the crazed look in the radiation oncologist's face. "Don't . . . do it . . . please," he begged.

"No stinking trial . . . why not?" Alex peered into his eyes, and finally relaxed his grip. "But, no—I'm going to watch you die, Buechler. The legal way."

Chapter Forty-three

Alex ran towards Bonnie, who was now barely able to make eye contact, and noticed only the left side of her chest was rising with inspiration. "Is she all right?" he asked Mike. Wendy and Stan had just arrived.

"Buechler stabbed her in the chest with that screwdriver." Buechler likely had been aiming for her heart, but fortunately she had turned just enough for him to miss that. But the jagged wound was sucking air. He ripped her gown open and put his ear down to her chest, and noticed no breath sounds on the right.

"She's got a tension pneumothorax. Stan—go back and find a trauma or thoracic surgeon." He'd worked in emergency rooms enough as a resident to recognize the deadly condition in which trauma to the chest cavity resulted in collapse of a lung. The sucking chest wound acted as a one-way valve in which air would accumulate with each breath, but couldn't escape. The resulting air pressure compressed the heart and great vessels, resulting in circulatory compromise and death without immediate intervention. The first thing he needed to do was cover the sucking wound so no more air would enter. He took out his handkerchief. "Mike, hold this over the wound." As he did so, the sucking stopped.

Stan was taking far too long; perhaps the building had been evacuated and no one was still there. He panicked as he found her pulse was down to thirty beats per minute.

"First aid kit. Surely they have something here in the laundry," he said. But the Hispanic laundry woman spoke no English.

"*Primeros auxilios,*" Mike told the woman. She shook her head, indicating that she didn't know where one was.

"Dammit, where are the paramedics?" he said.

"Shouldn't we start CPR?" Mike said.

"That won't help. The great vessels are compressed so much that she's not getting any blood flow to the brain. I need something hollow bore, to do a needle thoracostomy." A hollow needle placed into the chest cavity would temporarily decompress the air, allowing the lung to re-expand slightly. This would relieve the ever-expanding pressure that the sucking chest wound was creating on the heart and great vessels.

"Can't she breathe with just one lung?" Mike asked.

"The collapsed lung isn't the issue. It's the pressure that's being created."

Wendy looked at Mike's shirt pocket. "Give me your Hama tool."

"Hama tool? What the hell for?"

"Give it to me." He handed the escapologist's assistant what appeared to be a brushed aluminum pen, but was in reality a handcuff key with removable ball point pen. It was about five inches long and had a pen clip.

"What the hell good is that?" Alex asked.

Wendy broke the flag, or protruding part, off the key. She then disassembled the device, revealing a four-inch cylindrical barrel which was part of the key. The resulting cylinder measured about one–sixteenth inch in diameter.

"It's a cylinder, larger in diameter than a needle, but it should work. She uses this often to hide smaller keys inside. It's probably sharp enough to penetrate the pleura."

He took Mike's small knife and made a small incision in the area between the second and third ribs, and then inserted the modified tool into it. He pressed down until it went in and immediately heard a whooshing sound as the key entered the pleural cavity. "I think the pressure's being relieved. But she's not breathing."

Wendy immediately started administering mouth-to-mouth resuscitation. Alex watched as both sides of the chest rose now. Her pulse was now weak but palpable at fifty–two beats per minute. The paramedics finally arrived with Stan Williams and a general surgeon he'd found.

"Tension pneumothorax," Alex said.

"That was the right thing to do," the surgeon said. "We need to get her intubated." One of the paramedics used the laryngoscope to insert a number seven endotracheal tube. After it was inflated, the paramedic breathed for her with a hand ventilator. They then needed to get her to the hospital for stabilization. San Diego Community was the closest.

• • •

The officers took Buechler back to the banquet hall. His voice was a little raspy and his arm only badly sprained after his flight into the podium. But he was spitting blood from the broken ribs.

"You know what you've done, punk?" Lt. Marcus Owens, who had just arrived, said to him angrily.

"What's that?"

"You've just seriously injured a police department employee. The boys at the jail are going to love you—they'll make your life a living hell, asshole. We're also going to get your girlfriend now."

"I have no idea what you mean."

He pulled out a pair of the Watson alloy steel handcuffs. "Do you recognize these? You should. You bought an identical pair on an Internet auction a while back."

"So what, dick? That's not illegal."

"It is if they were used for terrorism or other illicit purpose. We found them at your associates' warehouse."

"They were stolen."

"Yeah, and you reported them stolen, I'm sure."

"Do you know how busy I am? It wasn't worth the hassle. And it's none of your business."

"Only two reasons people would own this model. Those working in a high corrosion environment. Don't think that's you, Doc—your hands are pretty soft. Other use is for people with a nickel allergy. Guess you moved on to gold. That's what the affluent people use these days, I hear."

"I don't have a nickel allergy."

"No, but your rich girlfriend does. Darkkin found that out

from medical records. You had to get her a gift for those special moments."

"That's crazy. I don't know anyone with a nickel allergy."

"But we do—somebody important, with enough money to make all this happen."

An officer took Buechler away, and Owens had one more person to apprehend. He went up to the VIP table, where Kristin Markham and Stephanie Farren were still seated.

"What can we do for you, Lt. Owens?" Kristin asked.

"I'm SDPD Lt. Owens. I think you need to come with us, Ms. Farren."

"What for? What's this about?" Stephanie asked.

"Well, we already know the good doctor over there provides his patients with the healthiest of drinking water," he said as he produced a bottle of Quattra water Alex had given him. "Even has a warehouse of the stuff. Ms. Farren, would you like some?"

"I don't want any of your water."

"Right, you really don't want to drink this—but it's *your* water, actually. I'm just giving it back to you."

"I don't know what the hell you're talking about."

"I think you do. You're under arrest for conspiracy in the murder of John Markham, kidnapping, and multiple other atrocities. Seems you and Buechler here went on a lot of trips together. Lots of special interest clubs. Hard to track, but it's amazing what Darkkin was able to find out about you two."

"I'm only an acquaintance with Dr. Buechler. He's the chief of staff, so we attended several functions together. I didn't go on any trips with him."

"Come on—there are dozens of airline tickets, hotel reservations, and other things for both of you in the same place at the same time."

"What if I did, then? It's a free country."

"That can't be true," Kristin said. "Is it? Steph?"

Stephanie turned to her sister. "You think about it, Kris. You ignored it because you could, but I had no choice. You and Mom disgust me. All these years . . . you're both lying pieces of shit. Whatever happens to me, I don't care. I did what I had to do to make peace with myself. Can you say the same?"

Chapter Forty-four

The paramedics wheeled Bonnie into the emergency department at Community Hospital. Dr. Takayashi, the ER attending on duty, took over.

"What do we have here?" the short, thin, fortyish physician asked.

The surgeon from the convention center told him. "I'm Rob Benson. General surgeon at Parkwood. Thirty-year old woman stabbed with a screwdriver at the charity ball. Tension pneumothorax. Other doctor here decompressed it."

"What the hell is that?" the attending asked, seeing the protruding part of Mike Mendoza's police tool.

"Hollow key barrel," Alex said. "Nothing else to use. Not very pretty."

"Looks like it's working, though," Takayashi said. "What's your specialty?"

"Radiation oncology."

"Damn, that's not bad. Get her on the table. Doctor . . . what's your name?"

"Darkkin. Alex Darkkin."

"You on staff here? Either of you?"

"No," they both answered.

"I appreciate your help, but we'll take it from here. Thanks."

"I want to stay. She's my girlfriend."

"All right—you can come back with us, as a courtesy. But the rest of you need to go to the waiting room."

Dr. Takayashi prepared a thoracostomy or chest tube, which

was a device designed to inflate a collapsed lung. As Alex had said, the issue wasn't the collapsed lung, as Bonnie could easily survive with one, but rather the pressure the expanding air had created. Once decompressed, her heart began pumping again.

But she still wasn't breathing on her own. They had attached her endotracheal tube to the ventilator, and the pulse oximeter showed ninety–five percent oxygen saturation. Alex had saved her life with the modified needle, but her brain had been without oxygen for several minutes.

The large chest tube was inserted and sutured into place, and the original wound Buechler had inflicted was also closed and dressed with sterile gauze. The portable chest x-ray would verify correct placement of the endotracheal tube as well as full inflation of the right lung after the tube was connected to suction.

"Dr. Darkkin, her lung has fully inflated and she's oxygenating well, but she's still unconscious. How long was she down?"

"Probably four or five minutes, until I found something to decompress her with."

"Any special health issues? Allergies, medications, surgeries?"

"No, she's in phenomenal health, aside from being deaf. No surgeries other than the implants, no allergies. She takes an oral contraceptive, a calcium supplement, occasional ibuprofen, some vitamins."

"Okay, we're going to get her a bed in the ICU. We're doing all we can for now, and we'll have to watch her mental status minute by minute."

He took a seat in the waiting room, still dazed about what had happened, and waited for Wendy and family members.

• • •

Several hours later, Special Agent Ken Thornton was beginning the interrogation of Stephanie Farren at the FBI San Diego field office. SDPD Detective Lt. Marcus Owens was also there, as he had been there during the apprehension and turned her over to the FBI. The case would predominantly involve federal charges, but there would likely be local charges also. Alex had given them an interesting theory about using heavy water to develop breeder reactors for foreign countries. If any of that were true, that and the organ trafficking crimes would be cause for CTU (Counter-Terrorism Unit) to become involved. Stephanie's attorney, Brad Langford, a portly man in his late fifties, was also present.

"Anything you want to say, Ms. Farren? I'm all ears," he said as they sat on metal chairs in the dingy gray room. He was an agent who most knew could get close to the edge.

"You have no real case against her," Langford, a fiftyish, medium-built man, said.

He laughed. "Come on. We have both Lewis' and Buechler's testimony, as well as records of millions of dollars being deposited in offshore accounts under your name. The files recovered from your base of operations implicates you."

"Base of operations? I can't believe Buechler would've said anything," Stephanie said. Langford motioned for her to stay silent. "And I'm already rich. Why would I do that?"

"Don't know, but Buechler's dog meat. It's good you and your boyfriend went to those kinky clubs, as he'll soon find that experience useful with his new pals. But, what I need to know is, were any other family members involved?"

Her attorney again asked her to stop talking. "Why the hell should I stay quiet, Brad?" she yelled, moving her arms around. "There's nothing to live for, anyway. Hell no, nobody else was involved. Mom was too dumb and sentimental. Put up with the rotten asshole all those years. And Kris had nothing to do with this. She was a cold bitch, but she didn't hate the bastard's guts that much. I did."

"But she benefited from the money and the merger."

"She got money out of it, and power . . . of course—can't you see now why it was done this way? Why would anyone suspect me, not even living in town, with two other people to blame his death on? My mother, who wanted to poison him, and greedy Kris."

"Why did you hate him so?"

"Everyone thought he was so wonderful—the great corporate philanthropist, the generous captain of industry. What they didn't know is that he sexually abused me."

"Come on. You expect us to believe that, after all these years?"

"Ask Mom or Kris, if you want—those lying bitches know. For some reason, he left Kris alone. She was Daddy's girl, if you can believe that—the one that followed him to the corporate suite."

"You're one screwed up family, that's for sure."

She sat silently and looked down blankly at the table. "I'm done answering questions." They concluded their meeting and guards took her away.

"What are they going to get, Thornton?" Owens asked, his spindly six–four frame towering over the much shorter and stockier Thornton.

"Farren could be looking at a minimum of life in federal prison without the possibility of parole. It's also possible she'll get the death penalty for what she's done. There's also the business about the diverted heavy water from India, which could be part of a larger plot to set up a foreign power with a breeder reactor. Darkkin tipped us off to that."

"Lewis and Buechler?"

"Buechler could get life or death penalty, too, if convicted. Lewis will probably get life. Cindy Gottesmann probably will get a break due to extenuating circumstances, but she still unwittingly helped plan her biological dad's death. Probably eight to ten years for her. And various long sentences for the lackeys, too."

"We still don't know for sure why she did it. Did she hate her father that badly?"

"Hate and greed, I've seen it too many times before."

"What about Underwood? I'm still puzzled about that one, Thornton."

"According to Farren, Underwood had gone to Buechler raving about being investigated by the IRS and being seriously in debt. He apparently was involved in an illegal clinical trial with the experimental drug moxplatin, through a Pyrco Indian subsidiary—but that's just coincidence. Buechler didn't know about that and the in-house lab files in Underwood's safe. Underwood must've put them there for safekeeping. Mendoza suspected someone killed him, but everything still points to suicide. It looks like Underwood wanted someone to think he was killed."

"So Underwood was just a poor sap with gambling debt who was in the wrong place at the wrong time. The fingers pointed at so many others. Anne Markham and the arsenic, Kristin, and Underwood. We never would've suspected Farren. Damn."

"Not without Darkkin's strange 'link' between Farren and Buechler. 'Link' — that's kind of funny, come to think of it, friend." He slapped Owens on the back.

The larger man grabbed his arm and looked at him with a steely gaze. "There's nothing funny about this, Thornton. And get one thing straight — Carlos may be your old buddy, but I'm sure as hell not. I only care about one thing right now, and she's going to an intensive care unit right now."

Chapter Forty-five

Alex waited sleepily in the Community intensive care waiting area with Bonnie's parents at three AM. He thought about going home, but knew he wouldn't be able to sleep. The sadness was worse than it had ever been, and the guilt was overwhelming. He remembered his brother-in-law's prior admonition about bringing others into danger. Had he truly been responsible for all this?

"Carlos, Elisa . . . I'm sorry. None of this would've happened if I hadn't kept pushing this case. You warned me."

"You don't have to keep saying that," Carlos said. "A criminal will be brought to justice, and you did what you thought was right. I know how it feels. You can't second-guess yourself."

"But why did she go after him? Buechler might have gotten out of the convention center, but they would've caught him."

"Bonnie can be very reckless. She's a genius—but incompetent in many ways. She sees the people applauding her at the magic shows and the Olympics, and it inflates her ego. I don't ever want that to go away—she deserves that after what she's been through. But police work is neither a show nor a game. For all those reasons, I made sure she would never be an officer."

"She wanted to be in the FBI. She could've done that?"

"Not the Bureau—federal law enforcement branches have very strict hearing standards. But, with the Americans with Disabilities Act, she could've been on the SDPD force as a reserve officer. I told her it wasn't an option, though."

"She could've easily passed the physical exams and the testing, though."

"The physical tests, sure. She's done the academy fitness tests and obstacle course—there are no women and only a handful of guys who could beat her times. She's a damn good fighter and can handle most anyone in a scuffle. But she did terribly on the written tests I gave her."

"No way. How is that possible?"

"Lots of the questions involve a case and having to recall the details. Oh, she could recall numbers, addresses, things like that. But which leg was injured, right or left, or which direction you go to get the suspect, forget it. Or four different things are happening, and you decide which one to take care of first. She can read and write six languages and perform calculus in her head, but she gets lost going to the supermarket."

"How much of that is from her illness as a child?"

"None. Always like that, without a lick of common sense. If anything, her deafness has helped her sort things out and focus."

"She seems so efficient and organized at the lab."

"Well, you've seen what her house looks like—it's a disaster. Her assistant keeps her on schedule and her office organized. Stan invests her money and sets up automatic bill payments. She can be amazingly productive with the help we all provide."

"I guess I've seen those tendencies." He finished eating a stale doughnut from the vending machine as Lt. Marcus Owens came into the waiting room.

"Darkkin, Carlos, Elisa, I'm so sorry. How's Bonnie doing?" Owens asked.

"Stable, but still unconscious. Her lung has inflated fully. It's just wait and see for now," he said. "What about Buechler?"

"I suspect he's going to have a mighty unpleasant time at the jail when he gets there."

"They won't let him out on bail, will they?"

"I doubt it. They haven't quite sorted out everything, and the federal stuff will take a while to figure out."

"What about Farren?"

"We picked her up too. She blew up and spilled a whole bunch of stuff until she realized she was in deep shit."

He realized his plan to get Buechler angry had probably translated over to Farren. Was it worth it, or just another stupid idea? If Bonnie hadn't been involved, she wouldn't be in a coma on a ventilator. Was he as reckless as she was?

"Thanks, Owens. I appreciate it. All you've done."

"Okay, I'll talk to you tomorrow. Again, I'm sorry. She's a strong gal—she'll make it."

He went in her room briefly. She was intubated and attached to a mechanical ventilator. A chest tube had been placed into her right pleural cavity to re-inflate the right lung and was attached to a suction device. Various intravenous lines were attached, including the milky white parenteral nutrition mixture. The neurologist said her electroencephalogram showed higher brain function, although it wasn't known when or if she would wake up.

He went outside in the moonlight. It had been seven months since he'd smoked a cigarette and he thought about it, but decided not to. Abstinence from alcohol was also torturing him. He saw a tavern down the street a few blocks and thought briefly about going, but again changed his mind.

He looked at the full moon and thought about what his life had become and how much better it was with someone he cared deeply about. He had to contemplate that she still could deteriorate, might never come out of her coma, or would be left severely disabled. He couldn't remember the last time he cried. He was sad when Jenny left, but nothing like this, and he didn't know how he was going to make it.

Nothing changed for the next week as her condition remained the same; he continued his routine of coming and staying most of the day and night. He wasn't working in the practice but was living off his savings and income from software royalties. His mother had come up to see him and was staying with Wendy and Stan. He did talk to his father but declined his offer to come up; he didn't need that right now. Maybe it was a mistake to have talked to him at all.

• • •

The next morning, Stan Williams came by to visit Bonnie. Elisa had been spending the night in the room, just to be there if something happened. Alex had gone downstairs to get coffee while the nurses bathed her.

"Hi, Elisa."

"Hello, Stan," Elisa said sleepily. "Is Wendy here with you?"

"No, she's home with Jake. Alex here?"

"He went downstairs to get some coffee, I think."

"Thanks. I wanted to talk to him. I'll be back in a little bit." Stan went downstairs and found him by the hospital coffee shop.

"Alex, how are you doing?"

"Day by day. Wendy up visiting Bonnie?"

"No, I'm here by myself. She's got a cold and didn't want to come today. She doesn't know I'm here."

He was puzzled. "Why *are* you here, then?"

"To talk to you."

"What is it you want to talk about, Stan?" They went to a booth and sat down.

"I want to tell you how sorry I am about Bonnie. And to . . . apologize for some things."

He wasn't sure what was going on as he stared at his brother-in-law intently. "Wendy sent you up here, didn't she? Bonnie wouldn't be in there if not for me and my obsession with John Markham."

"Like I said—she doesn't know that I came. And you can't be someone else's keeper. We all saw her take off after Buechler. You didn't make her do that."

"What is it you want to apologize for, Stan? I'm not mad at you about anything."

"I guess for the years of not liking you very much. That was unfair. I suppose, in some ways, I was jealous of you. It's hard for me to say, but it's true."

"I can be an ass sometimes, and you don't need to apologize for being critical of me. I'm sure I haven't treated you the best. A lot of times I was jealous of you, too."

"Really? Why?"

"You and Wendy always seem happy. I thought I could never have that. Maybe I still won't."

"We have our disagreements, believe me. A marriage is a lot of work and problems. But if you want it, you can find a way."

"I guess I use my parents as a reference point. Not a stellar example of a good relationship." They got up and walked outside in the cool air.

"I never liked your dad, either. He and Wendy never really got along."

"My dad can be a jerk, but I basically think he means well. He wanted to come up, but I declined the offer. More trouble than it's worth."

"It's possible I channeled my dislike for him into you."

"That's natural, since we're very much alike. More than you know, unfortunately."

"I don't believe that, Alex. But have you been happy the last few months?"

He thought a few seconds as he sipped his coffee. "Yeah, more than I've ever been. It's like my life has some type of purpose now. Most of it's Bonnie, but not all of it. A sense of accomplishment for a greater good, I don't know."

"I've been around you more in the last few months than in the whole time we've been married. I guess I really never got to know you."

"Is that good or bad?"

"You're not the jerk I thought you were. You're a good person, underneath it all."

"I'm still the same in a lot of ways. I've tried to grow up and be responsible—and look what happened."

"I know I gave you a hard time about your investigation before, but I maybe I was wrong. You stopped a lot of bad stuff. I wouldn't have had the balls."

"If you say so," he said as he looked down in sadness.

"I just want us to get along. Wendy's lived in this town since she was eighteen, and the Mendozas are like family to her. If you're part of her life, then you have to be part of mine too."

"I appreciate it, Stan. I guess we'll never be best buddies, but we can at least be social."

"Who knows? At least we won't be arguing all the time."

They shook hands and walked back to the hospital entrance. He truly appreciated his brother-in-law's gesture, as he'd felt uncomfortable for years about their unresolved conflicts. They wouldn't all be straightened out today, but at least it was a start.

Chapter Forty-six

Detective Lt. Marcus Owens was usually right, but this once he was dead wrong. Somehow, Buechler made bail. His high-priced attorney charged he'd been goaded into threatening people by Alex Darkkin and others. He would still be charged with battery on Wendy Williams and aggravated assault on Bonnie Mendoza. His attorney also argued Bonnie wasn't a sworn officer and had no right to detain him. There would, of course, be the numerous federal charges that would be brought when the FBI sorted out all of Alex's information, but that might take weeks. It also might take some time to link Farren to the crimes. But they both had done an exemplary job of covering their tracks.

The concept of fleeing the country entered his mind, although he had surrendered his passport. He had the means to engineer false ones, though. He also had the defense that someone had hacked into his bank and credit card accounts. But he would undoubtedly lose his medical license, as well as all credibility with the medical community.

He'd plummeted to rock bottom and was looking at real jail time, with his grandiose scheme at its gruesome end. The broken ribs still hurt like hell, too. What else could he possibly lose?

The medical staff president was about to find out.

He had gone out to get something to eat and was on his way home when his green Porsche Carrera GT suddenly lost power and came to a grinding halt with a loud *whoomph*. No radio, lights, or horn—dead as a doornail. He got out of the car on the eerily quiet deserted highway and walked around, wondering what had happened to his vehicle. His cell phone and analog quartz watch were also inoperative. He wasn't used to being scared, but he was today. More than he ever had been before.

His preoccupation with his predicament caused him to barely notice the ursine figure quietly coming up behind him. Despite his bulk, the hulking man moved fluidly and silently. He suddenly felt a massive hand grab him by the neck.

"Who's there?" he yelled. "What do you want?"

The huge man turned him around. He looked about sixty–five years old, about six–five in height, and he weighed at least three hundred twenty pounds. He had neck-length scraggly silver hair with a beard to match, and wasn't really *obese*, just one gargantuan fellow. And the bizarre figure scared the hell out of him.

"Heh—you don't know me, but let me introduce myself," he said with a raspy bass Southern voice that had smoked far too many unfiltered cigarettes in the past. "I'm about to become your worst nightmare."

He tried to run away and was stopped by the larger man's single hand. "Listen, shitass—I'm probably at least fifteen years older than you. But, heh—I can still bench press over three hundred fifty pounds, and can pulverize your puny little skeleton into primordial dust."

"What the . . . hell did you do to my car?"

"Portable focused EMP. Electromagnetic pulse. Your car's toast, like you're gonna be soon."

"Nobody has a weapon like that. Who are you with?"

"This weapon, heh, doesn't exist—not to anyone you ever heard of, anyway. And we're not with any 'agency,' just here to see you. For fun—ours, not yours."

What type of hell had he stumbled into? Just then, a second man, as tall as the first man but weighing about half as much, got out of a white panel truck, laughing hysterically.

"This is my cousin, Smiley. Real name's Zack, but all he basically does now is smile and laugh. We go way back, Smiley and I. Not much meat on him, he's from the skinny side of the family. Now we're going for a little ride. Get in the car." The thin man held a semiautomatic weapon on him in the back seat of the van while the larger one drove the car. "Goddamn—I always wanted to say that."

"I've got friends. You don't know who you're messing with."

They both burst out in crazed laughter. "Where? You see any, heh, 'friends', Smiley?"

"Don't see no friends, Rad! We ain't his friends, are we?"

"No, we don't befriend his kind. I don't believe we've formally met, but we have a common acquaintance. And we'll disappear just as quickly as we came—after you've gone to hell."

"Again, who *are* you?" He thought he had seen that crazed look twice at the charity ball, if only for a few seconds.

"I'm retired. Some people don't think I exist anymore. But, unfortunately for you, I do. I'm the guy whose family you decided to screw with."

He noticed the uncanny resemblance in the face and body type to a pediatrician he knew and, to a lesser extent, her brother. "You *have* to be . . . Williams' and Darkkin's father."

The large man lit a giant cigar, looked out the driver's window at the moon, and exhaled a blue cloud of various carcinogens into the air. "Yes, I am Dr. Rad Darkkin, prominent nuclear physicist. It is now time for us to contemplate how you have lived."

"*Contemplate how I've lived*? Are you supposed to be the Ghost of Christmas Past or something?"

"Silence! I hate Christmas." He did say months earlier this would be his last one, after all. "You took something from my son. And that means, in my family, you took it from me. Albert Einstein once said, 'the world is a dangerous place, not just because of those who do evil, but because of those who look on and do nothing.' I've chosen to heed Al's advice and do something."

"Hey, I didn't do anything to your son. That kidnapping thing wasn't my idea—I didn't know anything about it, or about the organ trafficking stuff they were planning. Wagner and Lewis did that on their own."

"You stabbed his woman and damn near killed her. She was like a little sister to my daughter, too. Get ready to visit your friend Mr. Wagner. I hear it's nice and warm where he's at."

"I didn't mean it, but that Mendoza woman's crazy. I thought she was going to kill me."

"*Crazy*? I hereby proclaim you've never met *anyone* as crazy as me. And, make no mistake, I *am* going to kill you."

He started shivering, as he realized he probably couldn't talk his way out of this one. He held out the faint hope that maybe they were just going to scare him.

They drove about thirty miles out to an old warehouse. It was about midnight by then, and the light of a full moon illuminated the field. They got out and went inside the small abandoned structure. Inside the musty building sat a table, a few chairs, and a variety of tools. He didn't guess they were going to work on old cars or build furniture in there.

Dr. Rad Darkkin pointed to many gallon jugs of water on the floor. "Take a look, that's what you're going to drink. And then I'm going to pump it into you."

"What is it?"

"You don't know? You should. Take a sip." Buechler took a jug and drank a sip of the clear liquid.

"It tastes like water."

"Damn, you're smart. Think about what you put John Markham through. I wish I would've thought of it, though—I commend you on your ingenuity."

"Heavy water? Where did you get it? There must be over fifty liters here."

"Trust me—I have connections. You really don't, heh, want to know about it," the long-haired man said, shaking his head.

"I didn't do it. That was Underwood's idea."

The massive Rad threw him against the wall. "Don't you even have the balls to take ownership for anything you've done, you fucking coward? You helped engineer the idea, and your little rich girl helped you get it. I just want you to experience it fully."

"Start drinking, buddy," the laughing thin man said as he took a swig of whiskey.

Rad lit another cigar and blew large clouds of smoke as he took the flask of Jack Daniels from his cousin. "Big man, you are. President of the hospital medical staff. People looked up to you. Greed at the highest level of the medical profession, you piece of crap."

"You can't prove any of that."

"*Prove it*? What am I, a goddamn scientist or something?

Whoops, heh, I am, I forgot! He wants me to prove it. What's your opinion, Professor Emeritus Smiley?"

"I don't think we need no proof, Rad. You got all the proof you need in your hand. Eighty proof!"

The large man took another swig of the pungent amber liquid. "Well, since you want the scientific method, I'll, heh, oblige you. My hypothesis is—you're going to die. 99.99% confidence interval." He pulled out a box, within which appeared to be some type of weapon.

"What's that? A bomb?"

"What the hell you think it is, moron? Smiley, can you believe this guy's never seen a goddamn nuke before? You want to play with the big boys so badly—here you go! I'm going to, heh, blast us all to Kingdom Come!" Rad started a timer for five minutes and set it counting down.

"You're bluffing. You'll die, too—there's no way you can get far enough from it. You don't scare me." Actually, he was terrified beyond comprehension.

The larger man started laughing like his cousin and consumed the rest of his whiskey. "I don't give a shit. We'll die together—see you in hell! I know that's where I'm going."

Rad pulled out an old mandolin and started playing and singing some horribly off-key bluegrass song with Smiley, who was dancing around. "You don't think it's real?" He pulled out a portable Geiger counter and switched it on. "35,000 counts per minute, and that's with the shielding. Think I'm faking now? It's the radiation signature of plutonium-239."

He finally realized that he was dealing with two men who were totally insane and had no regard for the consequences. One had a Ph.D. in nuclear physics.

Smiley was now singing some type of crazy gospel song. "Satan is within Ye, Ye'd better get him out! He's awake and he's infested Ye, he's in there without a doubt!"

"As you can see, Smiley has, heh, found religion. Not my cup of tea, but to each his own."

He felt like he was living a scene from some cheap old horror movie and doubted he was going to get out alive. He'd never seen a real nuclear weapon, but it looked genuine to him. As the timer continued going down, he was sweating profusely. "I'll give you anything you want. Just stop this, please! Money, anything— you'll get it."

"I don't need any goddamn money, or anything from you, except to see your sorry ass dead."

Smiley continued his demented, off-key singing. "Oh, we'll all be dead soon, and the judgment day will be upon us, we'll burn, burn, burn in the fiery hell—"

The timer went down to zero. Nothing happened. The two men continued laughing and drinking whiskey.

"It's—it's a fake. What are you trying to do?"

"Of course it's a fake! I don't have any goddamn live nukes any more, you an idiot or something? Used to have a bunch, though." He inhaled on his cigar and closed his eyes. "Yessir, there's nothing more relaxing than watching a twenty–megaton thermonuclear weapon detonate from a safe distance. But that's too easy a demise for you. Just thought I'd have a little fun."

"It's radioactive!"

"That? Hell, just a little plutonium oxide powder inside to set off the counter. Mostly alpha radiation—pretty harmless in small amounts unless you eat or inhale it. Anyway, keep drinking, buddy. A toast to you and your very shitty future."

The large man and his skinny cousin consumed the remainder of their Tennessee bourbon and continued to sing and dance to bizarre country melodies that certainly couldn't be found in the usual music stores.

● ● ●

After consuming about two gallons of heavy water, Buechler was visibly ill and shaking. After three gallons, he was shivering on the floor.

"Looks like you need some IV fluids to pep you up. Help me get him up here, Smiley." The two men lifted him up to and strapped him to a table. The larger man started an intravenous line in his right brachial vein, while his spindly cousin laughed maniacally.

"Have some, heh, special fluids." Rad lit another Cuban cigar and blew a cloud of smoke in his face. "I really should quit smoking these. Damn commie cigars will kill me!"

Buechler's body continued shivering as the small remaining natural water in his body was replaced by deuterium oxide.

"How does it feel, Doctor? Each hydrogen atom in your body now replaced by a deuterium atom? Your proteins and enzymes don't, heh, function so well anymore, do they? Just think what you put Markham through." The pain, like dying of metastatic cancer, was multiplied several times because of the acute nature of the toxicity.

"You . . . need to know. Your son could've killed me. He didn't."

"Like I care," Rad chortled. "He's too noble to do what needs to be done, but I'm not. I'm glad you made bail, because it made this a whole lot easier. But you won't, heh, do anything to anyone else."

"You'll . . . go down for this."

"Go down? How? And what the hell makes you think I care? You think Smiley over there cares? He can't spare any brain cells to worry about such things—he does well just to maintain basic brainstem functions. Smiley was once a genius with a very bright future, but the sixties were not kind to him."

He was now screaming in pain. "Just let me die, please!"

"I want you to think about Markham and all the other people you killed with your medical record alterations. And I want you to remember my face as the last thing you ever saw, scumbag."

Even Rad Darkkin couldn't stand it any longer, and he picked up the seizing physician and threw him against the wall of the old warehouse. The impact broke his neck, killing him instantly.

"Well, that was fun," Rad said, showing no remorse. "It's been a while since we did this. Might as well get this shit cleaned up, it's time to get back. Smiley, don't forget my damn mandolin."

Rad carefully arranged several charges of C-4 and set the timer for fifteen minutes while he and his laughing friend cleaned up all traces of their existence. Fifteen minutes later the old warehouse exploded, disintegrating the cachectic remains of Buechler into nothingness. The bulky nuclear physicist and his demented stick of a cousin disappeared into the night as quickly as they came.

Chapter Forty-seven

The blue-uniformed adventurer hurtled through the air at 120 miles per hour towards Earth. Flying, free as a bird, at terminal velocity—the speed where gravitational pull equaled atmospheric drag. The supple twenty–seven-year old could increase her speed to almost 150 miles per hour by drawing in her limbs.

It was always exhilarating to leap from a plane at 6,000 feet—especially while hundreds of people below were cheering. She had already removed the trick handcuffs, although she had wanted to use real ones for the charity stunt; her assistant had wisely confiscated those, however. The whole stunt only seemed dangerous, as she was an excellent skydiver, after all; this activity was actually safer for her than driving her car.

She deployed her parachute at 2,500 feet and drifted down to the landing point, where she would be met by the screaming crowd and photographers. Floating, floating down, like in a dream . . .

The dreamy memory ended as she saw images—unfamiliar, blurry shapes that gradually came into focus. She saw the dimly lit room with the nurses' station outside, then turned her head and saw the monitors and IV poles. She spied the beautiful glow of the lamps from the small Christmas tree in the corner of her room. But it was summer, not December—had she been in a coma for six months?

She tried to speak but realized she couldn't, because she was intubated and attached to a ventilator. She recalled that memory from childhood. She wanted to bring her arms up, but couldn't—

was she paralyzed? Had she crashed from the jump? No, some-thing was holding them down. She looked and saw her wrists in soft Velcro restraints. She almost instinctively found that, with a little effort, she was flexible enough to unbuckle each one.

She sleepily moved her legs and deduced she had not broken anything seriously. The nurses had reattached her aural proces-sors after a few days to try to provide as much stimulation as possible. She then remembered that she was deaf, and she couldn't make out any familiar "sounds." She finally made out a regular "whooshing" sound that seemed like a ventilator.

She saw the clock on the wall—two o'clock. The window was dark, so she guessed it was two AM. She spied the magenta-colored, banana-scented woman sleeping in a chair next to her bed. She could just reach the plastic water glass sitting on the bedside table; she began banging it loudly, as she couldn't locate the nurse call button.

Elisabeth Flores woke up to see alert dark brown eyes staring at her. "Oh, my God—you're awake!" She ran out to get the nurse.

She remembered how to relax while on the ventilator and let it breathe for her; she could take additional breaths if she wanted to.

"What happened?" the nurse asked as they walked back in.

"I was asleep, and I heard the sound of her banging the glass on the table. She must've removed her own restraints. She'd shown some erratic motor movement the last few days, and they were worried she might pull her ventilator tube or IV lines out. Bonnie's pretty strong."

"I need to get the resident." The nurse paged the medical resident, who came in about five minutes later.

The third-year medical resident spoke to Bonnie. Her vision was still a little blurry, and she couldn't lip-read well enough to make out what he was saying; she also couldn't "hear" him with the noise of the ventilator. She signed to her mother, who re-sponded in kind.

"Ask her some simple questions. Name, date of birth, who you are, what the approximate date is—things like that," the young doctor said to Elisa.

Bonnie correctly wrote on a tablet the first three, but was unsure of the date. She thought it was June 2004. But it was

January 2007.

The resident had the respiratory therapist come up to determine her breathing capacity and if she could be safely taken off the ventilator. Her chest suction tube had been removed the day before, since the pneumothorax had resolved. The respiratory therapist hooked up a measuring device in line with her ventilator tube and turned the ventilatory rate to zero, meaning that she had to breathe on her own. If she couldn't, the rate would immediately be increased again. But she easily ventilated herself, as the oxygen monitor showed ninety–nine percent saturation.

The resident called his attending physician, who agreed she could be extubated. He came back in and disconnected the ventilator from the endotracheal tube, and then deflated the tube so it could be removed.

"Don't try to talk. You've been on a ventilator for a week." She nodded her head.

Elisa made several telephone calls from Bonnie's room, even though it was 3 AM. To her husband, to her sons, to Wendy, and to Alex.

"Hello?" Alex answered sleepily.

"Alex, it's Elisa. Bonnie woke up about an hour ago. They have her off the ventilator and everything."

"Is she all right?"

"She's still a little confused. She recognizes me and can recall some things. It's hard to tell. I was asleep and she woke me up."

"I'll be right down there."

• • •

Alex arrived at San Diego Community Hospital about ten minutes later and went straight to the ICU. He went into the room, where she was still awake. Carlos was also there. She was still unable to talk, as her throat was still sore from the endotracheal tube.

He walked in and kissed her on the cheek. Bonnie looked at him and stared. "Thank God you're all right. We were really worried about you." Elisa said she could now discern some speech with the ventilator off.

"Bonnie, Alex is here. You know who this is, don't you? Alex."

"*Mother—is that Wendy's brother?*" she signed back.

"*What?*" he signed. "*Of course I'm her brother. You know that.*"

"*Why are you here?*"

"*I'm here for you, of course.*"

That puzzled look, so familiar to him, appeared on her face. He knew what that meant—she couldn't remember anything about what had happened between them. His presence there was a complete mystery to her.

"Alex, I—," Elisa said.

"You don't have to say anything. I'm a doctor. I understand."

• • •

The neurologist came out to talk to Alex, Wendy, and her parents in the waiting room the next day.

"As you know, Bonita has suffered moderately severe anoxic encephalopathy, or a period when her brain didn't receive oxygen. Were it not for her outstanding physical condition, she likely wouldn't have survived."

"What's her status? Have you completed the tests?" Carlos asked.

"Physically, she seems quite good. She seems to have extraordinary language and mathematical skills, despite her speech difficulties. Long-term memory appears intact. She has some definite deficiencies with direction sense and right-left orientation, although it's my understanding that those problems have been present since birth and are related to her synesthesia. Her motor strength and coordination are far above normal. That's remarkable given her injury."

"What about her memory?" Elisa asked.

"That's tougher to assess. She has some significant retrograde amnesia. Her memory before about thirty months ago seems intact. But after that, it's just small pieces. She seems to think she's here because of crashing after a parachute jump in 2004. It sounds odd, but she recalls the events until just after parachute deployment. Is that possible, or just a hallucination? I know she was a local TV personality who sometimes did things like that."

Wendy thought for a moment. "Yeah, she did a jump in summer of 2004 as a stunt for charity. But she's an excellent diver, and landed fine. Absolutely nothing went wrong."

"That's really odd, then, why her memory stops there," the neurologist said.

"Will she get the rest of her memory back?" Alex asked.

"I don't know. The fact that this is her second serious neurological event makes it less likely. It's only been a little over a week, but I'd say the chances of that are very poor."

"Can she go back to work? Lead a normal life?" he asked.

"I think so, in time. Her scientific skills, at least on a rudimentary level, seem intact, and she could probably resume some duties in a few weeks or so. I'm sure her employer will need to assess her cognitive abilities in detail, however. She's going to need a lot of help filling in the gaps."

He questioned if he was the person to do that. Would she even want him around? She didn't even know him any longer. He walked outside, alone, as an unnerving sense of panic gripped him.

Chapter Forty-eight

"I know this is hard on you, Alex. It's hard on all of us," Wendy said to him in the hospital cafeteria the next morning. "I'm so sorry for both of you."

"It's all my fault. If I hadn't come here, none of this would've happened." He nibbled on his blueberry muffin.

"If you hadn't come here, Buechler, Underwood, Wagner, and everyone else would still be around killing people, and those other guys might be trafficking in stolen organs. I thought those guys were the leaders. How could I have been so blind?"

"It was so hard to figure out—they did a good job of fooling everyone. But *you* didn't endanger anybody."

"Yeah, I did—indirectly. Her family, I, some others—we wanted her to be happy. We made her into a kids' superhero—a genius of almost limitless potential, a star athlete who overcame a disability. You don't think I feel guilty for what I've done? That stuff was to benefit me too."

"Thanks for trying to make me feel better. But it doesn't change anything."

"Parkwood would be shut down now if not for you. You've done much good, you've got to remember that. Bonnie made the choice to go running after Buechler."

"Whatever. It's all gone, Wendy. Everything we had."

"You don't know that for sure."

"The neurologist said the chances for her remembering are remote."

"Okay, then, suppose the memories are gone. She's still the

same person that you fell in love with. You can again."

"Maybe I should just go back to Nashville. I have things to attend to there."

"You have things to attend to *here*. An obligation."

"Bonnie has all she needs—a family and you for a friend. She doesn't even remember me."

"I see. So, you're really thinking of going back to Nashville?"

"Maybe. I have a few things to take care of here first."

Wendy perked up as her eyes brightened. "It just occurred to me. This is a perfect situation for you, isn't it? Why didn't I see it earlier?"

"I'm sorry?"

She grinned. "It's tailor-made for you. You got to come here, have a ball with my best friend, and now it's time to leave. Just like always, isn't it? Before, someone always got hurt—like Jenny, or the countless others I don't even know about. But this time, you think you won't be hurting Bonnie, because she'll never remember any of it. How could it have been better for you?"

"It's not like that, dammit."

"What *is* it like then, Alex? Because it's all about you and how you feel, as usual. Even though she doesn't remember what you shared, she still needs you. Put aside your selfish feelings for awhile and reflect on that."

"Things won't be the same."

"What—you want a written guarantee that you always get what you want in life? Whatever got scrambled in her brain, she's still the same woman that used to love you. How do you know if you don't try? You haven't said twenty words to her since she came out of the coma. But, if you want to leave, that's up to you. It's exactly what Dad would do."

"I want to, Wendy. It's just hard."

"Of course it's hard. Maybe you've never done anything that was hard before or lost something really important to you. She asks about you, but we keep avoiding the subject. The doctors say she doesn't remember, but she can sense things that you or I don't. I'd like to sock you in the face, but I don't hit weaklings. You're less of a man than I am, you ass."

He watched as she got up and stormed off. It wasn't entirely as she had suggested—he knew she was angry and probably displacing her feelings towards him. But the thought of leaving had definitely entered his mind. Would Bonnie even care? And what would it matter? She had a life, a family, and friends. Why would she want to get involved with him all over again?

He went somewhere he had never been before—the hospital chapel. To pray he would do the right thing.

• • •

"Hi, Alex," Bonnie said, sitting in a chair in her private room at the hospital in late January. She had been transferred to the rehabilitation section the day before.

"Hello," he said as he brought in a dozen roses. It was only the third time he had seen her since she awoke.

"These are beautiful. Thank you." She sat them in a vase.

"How are you doing?"

"I'm okay, but it's all very overwhelming. When I woke up, I was terrified, and can't remember what happened. They said you saved my life. I haven't asked about the details of why I was fighting someone."

"We'll talk about it later. Here, I brought you something—a Christmas present. Sorry I couldn't give it to you earlier." She opened it and discovered one of her favorite things—a small music box with a dancing ballerina. Although she couldn't hear it, she loved them because she collected them as a little girl before she lost her hearing. She burst into tears.

"You don't know how much this means to me," she cried. "I faintly remember listening to them as a small girl and can still remember the music. One of the few remaining memories from my childhood." She turned it on and felt some of the vibrations, although the sounds were too complex for her to "hear."

"It's a simple thing, but I thought you'd like it."

"Thank you." She paused for a couple of minutes, staring at him. "But it is time for complete honesty. My mother tells me little about you. In addition, Wendy avoids the subject. Why's that?"

"Wendy doesn't want to confuse you. You need time to recover."

"I know you wouldn't have been here when I woke up unless something was between us. I can't put my finger on it, but I know it's true."

"Do you remember anything?"

"I remember nothing after about two and a half years ago. Wendy tells me about the Melbourne games in 2005, but I have no recollection of that. She showed me photos as proof I set the world record."

"Right. I've seen them, too."

"This may seem odd to you, but people have colors, sounds, or scents to me. People, scents or colors mostly. Numbers, mostly colors. Words have all three."

"I know all about that and how those abilities help you manipulate numbers and words."

"But you have two colors that conflict. One is kind of a faint burgundy. It's faint, accompanied by a smell of garlic. The other is a bright aquamarine. When I see you, I hear a complex sound, like a dominant seventh chord, and smell burnt cinnamon."

"Does that mean anything?"

"They don't necessarily mean anything like good or bad. But it means I had met you a long time ago, and a second time, past when I can remember. The way I feel about you has become different than before. A warm feeling."

"Does anyone else have two colors?"

"No. For example, Wendy is one color, a bright green, and reminds me of citrus. She must be the same to me as before. Mother is magenta and smells of bananas and caramel."

"While we're on that subject, I have another present for you. It's an experiment, so bear with me. It may take some tweaking."

"What is it?"

He pulled out a bulky visor from a box. "Put this on. It's just a prototype."

"I will look silly, like that character in the space show." She put it on. "What is this supposed to do? I can't see anything."

"Just wait." He turned on a switch and moved a small microphone to the music box and started it playing. The sounds were digitally converted into a stream of numbers and letters that appeared on her visor. "Concentrate on the visual data flow and tell me what you hear."

She concentrated for half a minute. "Strange—there's a sort of melody that is unfamiliar. What does the music box play?"

"Tchaikovsky's Nutcracker Suite." He handed her a piano music score. She pulled up the visor and studied it for a couple of minutes, then put it back on.

"Nutcracker?" He knew that, although she wasn't particularly musically talented, she possessed the amazing synesthetic power of "perfect pitch"—the ability to recognize and reproduce exact frequencies. "Well, it doesn't sound like that, pitch-wise, although the note frequency and cadence seem to be correct. Nevertheless, this is quite unique. How did you do it?"

"It's a work in progress. A couple of months ago, I contacted a world expert in synesthesia. She thought if I could reduce an audio stream to words and numbers quickly enough, your brain might interpret them as actual sounds. Jim helped me with the hardware and software. It's actually quite sophisticated—that visor contains two 3-GHz processors and four gigabytes of memory. If we can tweak it, it may allow you to experience the fullness of music again."

"That's amazing, Alex. Thank you." She removed the visor.

He sat on the edge of the bed next to her. "I'm sorry I haven't talked to you a lot. I've been around but didn't want to overwhelm you."

"I understand your concern for my welfare. But I need to know what our relationship was. I'm sure I know, but I have to hear it from you."

"I'd like to think we still have one. We were very close and had many adventures together. Some fun ones, and others I would like to forget."

"I wish I remembered more. What types of things did we like to do?"

"We rented a cabin in the mountains several times. You liked to go there and do lots of outdoor things. You enjoyed looking at your element collection. Best of all, you liked to go eat burritos and tacos late at night."

She paused for a moment. "The last statement is a lie—I did not like to eat burritos and tacos," she said with a smile. "Mexican food is horrific."

"Just seeing if you're paying attention."

She looked into space for several seconds. "I have to ask you something serious. I assume we . . . had a strong physical relationship?"

"Yes, we did. I'm sorry—is that uncomfortable for you?"

She chewed on her lip for a moment. "No, I'm glad. I know it seems as if it would be awkward for me, but it's not. I'm just trying to piece together the puzzle."

"It was wonderful for both of us. Every time."

"That is comforting." She paused for a moment. "I know that I wouldn't have engaged in that were you not a very special person to me."

"I don't want to push you."

"I'm going home tomorrow. Are you going to be here?"

"Of course I will be. I'll stay with you if you want, in the other room, of course. Unless you want to go and stay with your parents."

"As much as I care for them, I need to get on with my life, and my mother's cooking will give me ulcers. But staying in the guest room doesn't sound very fair to you."

"What I want is to give you what you need. To be with you. It's not about me." The last four words were ones he had seldom uttered before.

She pulled out the diamond bracelet he had given her last August. "I know that this must have been special. When did you give this to me?"

"Last August—your thirtieth birthday."

"It seems like I should only be twenty–seven. I don't remember it at all. Was it a special day?"

"Yes, for both of us. It was our first time."

"That's good." She stared at him for several seconds. "It's peculiar, looking at you . . . like looking at a stranger, but oddly familiar. Sometimes, when I'm in here, I feel so alone. I have been completely alone before."

"We've all felt alone."

"Not like me. When I woke up in the hospital in 1987, I was deaf, almost completely mute and hardly even recognized my parents. I was terrified beyond anything you can possibly imagine. I felt some of that again this time. But those things made me stronger. There's not much that I fear, as I have faced the worst and came through it." She stared out the window at the mid-morning sky and spread her arms wide. "Do you know how I got the name *Mendoza the Miraculous*?"

"I always assumed it was a magician's stage name."

"No—Wendy named me that when I was thirteen, because the doctors said I was a 'living miracle.' Some thought I would die, the rest said I would be institutionalized for life. They were wrong—I came through the darkness. I will again."

"You'll never be alone again. Not as long as I'm here." He knew even though most of her memories of him were gone, she was still the same person he fell in love with. She woke up nineteen years ago in a coma, with no memory. Now she woke up from a second coma. He would never let her be alone, to face this by herself. Things were going to be all right.

Chapter Forty-nine

Bonnie traveled with Alex to the San Diego FBI office to talk to Thornton one last time. She had been there a few years ago to talk to a consultant, but remembered nothing about their recent visits concerning the Markham case.

"Hello, Ms. Mendoza. We've met before. Ken Thornton."

"I'm sorry that I can't remember you. Many things are new to me."

"That's okay, I know you've been through a lot. I just wanted to talk about some things."

"I understand this was a fascinating case for all of us."

"That's an understatement. This is the damndest case I've ever been associated with."

"So, I guess this is our last visit at the FBI, Thornton."

"I hope so, Darkkin. Anyway, we found some information that might shed some light on Buechler's disappearance. They thought he skipped bail."

"I know—I was really worried about it. They find him?"

"Yeah. Thought you should know. Agents found some old warehouse about thirty miles out of town that had basically been disintegrated with C-4 explosive a week or so ago. Nothing left, except some human bones, including a partial mandible."

"Buechler's?"

"Looks that way, after comparing the dental records."

"Who killed him? Someone he crossed do him in?"

"Can't say for sure. Looks like some guys took him out there, roughed him up, then blew him to smithereens. And not punks

292   *J. Matthew Neal*

like the ones that kidnapped you."

"What do you mean?"

"Lewis and those guys maybe knew computer stuff, but were amateurs at other details of espionage. These guys were pros. No trace of anything—except what they wanted us to find."

"Damn. I wanted to see him go down in court," he said, stomping his foot on the ground.

"There's something else you should know about, Darkkin. The samples of the debris were tested, of course, for explosives and other things. Along the way, we found some samples that had trace concentrations of deuterium. Would you know anything about that?"

"I have no idea. What—you think *I* did it? If I wanted to kill him, I would've done it at the charity ball. And I've had enough of heavy water, thanks."

"Just asking—I'm not accusing you."

"I've been at the hospital most of the time, anyway. You think someone—"

"Killed him like they killed John Markham. You have any idea who did it?"

"Of course not. Must've been someone he worked with—the mob or somebody."

Thornton chuckled. "Don't know any mobsters who use heavy water in a rubout. And something else that we can't explain—minute traces of radioactivity. Not enough to be harmful, but there were femtocurie amounts of plutonium found there."

"I don't know anything about that. Why would I?"

"You might know someone who has plutonium oxide sitting around. I did some investigating into the past of one Conrad Darkkin, but didn't find much information. What I did find out was damn interesting, though."

"You're crazy. My dad's retired."

"Here's some reading material about your old man, when you get a chance." Thornton handed him a manila envelope. "But you better be straight with me."

"I swear this is the first I've heard about it."

"Anyway, this is probably our last meeting, but . . . Ms. Mendoza, would you consider a different kind of career? Working for the FBI?"

She was clearly surprised. "It's premature to make any decisions right now about what I want. I need to get my feet back on the ground first. I thought about being a Special Agent at one time, but I can't be considered because of my deafness."

"That's not a problem with Professional Support. But don't entirely rule out the possibility of being an agent in the future. People with myopia who underwent refractive eye surgery were at first excluded, but now are being accepted, contingent on maintaining good vision."

"That's vastly different and you know it," she said.

"Technology improves all the time. In a couple of years, who knows? But, for now, there's a Forensic Chemist administrative position at GS-15 available. For an extraordinary person."

Her eyes brightened. "That's tempting. I always wanted to be in the FBI."

"Only drawback is, it's at Los Angeles. San Diego office isn't that big. After a training period, you'd actually be in a supervisory position."

"GS-15 is far above the starting grade. GS-9 is the typical starting position."

"But you have excellent qualifications and experience. Have you ever considered how your word and number abilities could help the Bureau?"

"I'm sure the San Diego Police still need me. And, it's only fair to tell you, I have had other job offers. I'll have to think it over."

"You need to do what's right for you. We all feel that way. You know your dad does."

Thornton approached and looked up at him. "And *you*. I don't know what to say about you, Darkkin. You pulled some crazy shit and should be dead. You probably would be if not for this lady and your friend Krakowski."

"I'm done with detective work. Right now I've got some urgent family business to attend to."

That he did. He studied the manila envelope Thornton had given him, and decided it was time to resolve some old conflicts and settle a score or two. Now he knew there was only one person who could have been able to obtain that much heavy water and do that to Buechler without anyone knowing about it. A killer brought to justice by the very mechanism that killed his victim. The irony made him feel a lump in his throat.

He logged onto his laptop and booked the first flight to Knoxville, Tennessee. He wouldn't be spending the night.

• • •

The doorbell at 504 Vista Drive in Oak Ridge, Tennessee rang several times before the large man answered the door at eight PM on the cool late January evening. The massive gray-haired man opened the door of the two-story Tudor-style home to find a familiar figure standing on the porch.

"What are you doing here? You didn't say you were coming. I thought about—"

Dr. Conrad Darkkin's words were silenced by his son's right fist smashing into his jaw, knocking him down. "What the hell?"

"Why, Dad? Why did you do it, you asshole? Get up!"

"Why did I do what? Don't ever hit me again."

"Look in my eyes. You see that crazy look? You see it in the mirror every day. I'll take your head off, Dad. I'm stronger than you, and a hell of a lot faster. Tell me why I shouldn't."

"I don't know what you're talking about, Dirk. You're, heh, crazy."

"*I'm crazy*? I'm not stupid—I know you did it. You killed Buechler with heavy water, and you had a live nuke out there, too. You're insane."

"The nuke wasn't live, it was just a replica, to scare him. Heavy water was, heh, simple, yet so cool. Always wondered about that, and now I know."

"You killed him! What have you done?"

"I did what, heh, needed to be done. Things that you couldn't do. You could've killed him, I heard. Wouldn't go through with it, though."

"Because I'm a pussy? Is *that* what you think? I should've gotten rid of Buechler myself, like a hit man?"

Rad rubbed his sore jaw and paused for a moment. "No, I guess not. You couldn't have done that because you're too, heh, good a man. I guess I don't want you to be like me—a goddamned fossil, a dinosaur. A remnant of bygone days."

"Why didn't you tell me about it?"

"What, and involve you? What the hell would you have done? Tried to stop me? Help me? You would've just gotten in the way. I tried to do you a favor, Dirk."

"You can't take the law into your own hands!"

"Look at the way you handled it. Were you successful? Playing around with his bank accounts and credit cards—what kind of amateur bullshit was that?"

"Anything I did was reversible and meant to get him buzzed up, to rattle him. Not to execute him, for God's sake. Buechler would've been tried and convicted."

"Yeah—in two or three years. Wake up and smell the roses, boy. This isn't a fairy tale. Trust me—what I've done can't be, heh, traced back to me. And certainly not to you, since you didn't know anything about it."

"I don't see how you could've done something like that."

"There's a lot you, Wendy, and your mom don't know about me. Things I can't ever speak of. I did some pretty bad shit in the seventies and eighties."

"I know about some of it now. Why didn't you tell us?"

"Because I wanted you and Wendy to be more than what I could be—a goddamn spook. I designed weapons for the, heh, government. Are you so naïve not to know? Lots of the nukes on current missiles were designed by my staff. You don't want to know what the hell we did, the experiments, the shit prototypes we tested that didn't work. You think I wanted that kind of life for you? I did that to protect both of you, son. Your mom's better off, too."

"I can't live that way, Dad. I couldn't kill someone in cold blood."

"He damn near killed your girl. No one screws with my family. I only kill things that, heh . . . deserve to be killed."

"I didn't ask for your help. And who made you God—judge, jury, and executioner?"

"Done it before. Don't be so fucking principled. It makes me sick to my stomach."

"*You* make me sick, Dad. Mom always feared I would turn out to be like you. I'm finally seeing what she was talking about."

Rad stared out into space blankly. "Ah, yes, your principled mother—so insightful. But you've been doing a fairly good job emulating me."

"I'm *nothing* like you. I have a new career and new direction. I want to try and make the world a better place. And I took a sacred oath to help people. I'm sorry that you don't have the same moral fiber."

"You stand there and judge me? A 'sacred oath', like you're a goddamn priest or something. What about my obligation to make the world a safer place? You don't know the bad shit that's out there."

"This is the twenty–first century, Dad. Get real."

"If you've seen what I have . . . you try your 'new direction' for awhile, especially after the novelty wears off. Then you'll see."

"I have to take my own road, Dad. I don't have to prove myself to you any more. I'm twice the man you'll ever be, you bastard. Making weapons to kill people, for God's sake."

"And I didn't want you to know, but I did what I thought was best for my country. I didn't want you or Wendy to live your life like I did and end up some goddamned crazy drunk. She's become damn respectable and I'm proud of both of you."

"I wanted us to have a better relationship, Dad. But now—"

"You do what you have to, Dirk. Don't, heh, do me any favors. I'm always here for you. If you don't want me, that's okay, too. I don't need anybody. Never did."

"I wanted to tell you in person—Bonnie and I are getting married. After that, she's going into the Ph.D. program in theoretical physics at Caltech."

"Shit, that's impressive. I'm happy for you, you have to believe that. She's a great girl. Gonna invite me to the wedding?"

"You can go burn in hell. If you ever come around Bonnie, there'll be a quick funeral—yours. And I dare you to see if I'm kidding about *that*." He stomped off the porch.

"At least you've got some goddamn guts now. But you came all that way to punch me in the mouth, and you just leave? Drinks are on me, for old times' sake."

"I just can't deal with you right now. I don't think I can ever forgive you for this."

"That's your choice, I guess. You going to say anything about this to anyone? Not that I give a shit."

"Don't know right now, Dad—I'll have to think about it. Once again, you've made yourself the center of attention. But I have more important things to take care of now than you."

"The world's a tough place, son. You'll learn that," Rad yelled at his son, who was now halfway down the driveway. "Someday, you'll know I'm right."

"And when that day comes, it'll be a really sad one. Because I know then that I've hit rock bottom."

He'd finally accomplished what his mother hoped he would do someday—conquer the demon that was his father's legacy. He was thoroughly disgusted and shocked by what his deranged parent had done. Marianne Darkkin always told him there was a sinister side to his father. And he often felt the same tendencies inside himself, and could decide to go down the same path, to ruination. He would instead choose to channel that energy into something constructive, a concept that had been foreign to him until the last several months. He just happened to have a special person to show him the way. Even if a few more of her marbles were gone, she was still the most positive influence he could have in his life.

Chapter Fifty

Two months after the injury, Bonnie had moved back to her condominium and had asked Alex to stay with her. For the first week he stayed in the guest room, but after that she wanted him in the master bedroom with her; he noticed his previous "problem" was much less evident.

She had started exercising a bit, some light running and weight training. He noticed that she was thinner, down from 165 to 148 pounds. Her appearance was softer than before, and many of her clothes were loose.

"You know what? I may cut back on the weights a bit," she said, looking at her figure in the mirror.

"Why do you want to do that?"

"I'm getting older and must take care of my joints. No sense in wearing myself out. Time to enjoy life a little bit."

"You're thirty years old—hardly over the hill. I think it's just an excuse to buy new clothes."

"Ha. Many of my personal things are new to me each day. At any rate, I need to go to the lab office tomorrow. They want me to come in and sign some papers that are overdue."

"That sounds good. Just take it easy—I know how stubborn you can be."

She paused for a moment. "Alex, I have been reconsidering SDPD. Maybe I don't want to go back there for the rest of my life."

"What do you mean? You liked that job."

"I know, but is it the best destiny for me? Maybe this is an opportunity for me to re-evaluate my life, my priorities."

"You help a lot of people in your job. Children look up to you. The things you do for charity, for example."

"I know, I can still do those things, but . . . maybe there's something more. Did you ever wish that you could do something more? Something just for you?"

He had been thinking a lot about that lately. How his life had changed, and how he could make a difference in people's lives. "I guess so. Your dad and I talked a lot when you were in a coma. He said that of the three children, that you were special, the one destined for true greatness."

"He's my father, of course he would say that."

"But it's true. You have to follow your dreams."

"I know—I'm just confused right now."

"Does it bother you that you don't remember about us?"

"No, not really. Oh, I certainly wish I had those memories, Alex—but you must remember, this is my second time around with memory loss. It's fruitless to worry about what can't be changed. I can only go forward."

"Is it awkward for you?"

"No, the memories aren't lost, because you have them and can share them with me. Little things to tell me about each day. Do you remember the excitement when you first fell in love with me?"

"Sure I do."

"You can't ever experience that again—the thrill of discovering love again. But I can. In that way, I'm lucky."

"I know that you want commitment. And I need for you to know that I'm committed to you."

"I believe you."

"I know you do. Tomorrow I have something to give you."

"What is it?"

"You'll see."

• • •

Alex, Bonnie, Wendy and Stan were having dinner at a outdoor restaurant on the cool early March day. The police and FBI were finished with them, at least for now. Bonnie had received a letter of commendation from the chief of police and a phone call from the Governor of California, whom she had met once at a charity event.

"I still don't know how you knew it was Farren," Wendy said as she chomped on a cheeseburger.

"I remembered from examining Kristin's medical records that she had a visit to the dermatologist for a rash."

"But, wasn't it Kristin who had the nickel allergy?" Wendy asked.

"No, she was tested, and she had an allergy to something else. However, the very complete history taken by the dermatologist indicated Stephanie has severe nickel dermatitis, like yours truly.

"I was also able to trace the purchase of the alloy cuffs to Buechler. After that, it was just a matter of time until we were able to link up travel arrangements to place the two together. She would have benefited from Markham's death, and certainly had the resources to back it up."

"What about Bill Underwood?" Wendy asked.

"Underwood was involved too, from what we could tell, albeit reluctantly. He had found out about it, but was blackmailed by Buechler, who knew all about his gambling problems. Buechler threatened to expose him to the public if he didn't help. Kristin had earlier mentioned how eager he was to dispose of Markham's urine after he died."

"But why would he leave such a cryptic message in a word puzzle book?"

"Apparently he was obsessed by numbers and secret messages. So was Lewis, obviously. I think Underwood figured out whoever could solve that puzzle might be able to bring down Lewis and Buechler. I guess he was right. He killed Markham, but indirectly brought us the real mastermind, so he didn't die in vain."

"I know you thought someone else killed him and made it look like a suicide," Wendy said.

"That's what we thought, but all evidence points to a simple suicide. They found a computer printer cartridge in his trash with the same ink as the computer note. It looks like he shot himself with his right hand and engineered the other clues to make it look like a murder, so that people would be suspicious," he said.

"What about the heavy water? Did they ever figure out the origin?" Wendy asked.

"It appears Farren was involved in heavy water being shipped from India to Iran, where they were planning on building a heavy water reactor for medical purposes," he replied. "But, I suspect the ultimate plan was to eventually make weapons-grade plutonium. She used a Clystarr subsidiary—Bertaxy—and Kristin's name to accomplish that. Buechler's main goal was to get Parkwood shut down and build the new hospital, which would line his pockets with research bucks from Pyrco."

"What became of the organ trafficking thing?"

"As far as the FBI can tell, it never got under way. If Lewis had continued on that track, perhaps. It appears Buechler got what he wanted out of the deal, with the medical error stuff and all. Underwood was in on it too, until he killed himself. By that point, Lewis was on his own. Buechler didn't want to involve us any more, but Lewis had bigger ideas beyond ruining Parkwood and killing Markham. "

"What about Buechler, Alex?" Wendy asked. "They said his body was found somewhere. Do you know anything about it?"

"I know he was killed with heavy water, like Markham," he said with a solemn expression on his face. "But that's all I know." Which was a lie—he knew exactly what had happened to the medical staff president. But telling Wendy about their father's evil misdeeds wouldn't help anything now.

"So, anyway, what are you going to do, Alex?" Wendy asked. "Bhavin Agarwal is back, but they said they'd keep you on as a partner if you want to stay."

"I've decided to leave the Parkwood radiation oncology practice."

"What? I'm confused. You aren't going back to Nashville," Wendy said. "Bonnie *is* taking the job with the FBI, right?"

"I don't think so. She has some things to do first. I do, too. I have to get signed up for catechism classes at St. Lawrence's church."

"Since when did you get an interest in religion, Alex? You never cared much for it."

"Trust me, I have my reasons."

Wendy paused. "Oh, no—It can't be."

"I forgot to wear this today." Bonnie reached behind Wendy's left ear, produced a two-carat diamond ring, and put it on.

"Look at that rock! I don't believe it. When did this happen?"

"Last night," he said.

Wendy started crying and hugged her friend. "I'm . . . speechless. I was worried you two might drift apart."

"That would never happen. I would never let her go."

"I always thought of you as my little sister. Now it'll really be true," Wendy said. "But it's only been three months since your injury. Are you guys sure?"

"Alex remembers things for both of us. I have learned to trust in people, especially all of you."

"So, since that's decided—what kind of a wedding ceremony does an escape artist get?" Wendy asked. "A ball and chain?"

"It could be magical, like O-Tar and Tara of Helium's wedding," Bonnie said, with a misty look in her eyes.

"What's an otar? That's one of those Indian guitars, isn't it?" Wendy asked in a half-kidding way.

"*O-Tar*, not sitar. He is Jeddak of Manator, for crying out loud."

"A minotaur is one of those mythological creatures, half-man and half-bull, right? Will there be a 'best minotaur' at the wedding?" she chortled in her best Falstaffian tone.

"Manator is a city on *Mars*, Wendy. You're really dense, you know that?"

"Sorry. Got it now."

"You show your ignorance by making fun. Edgar Rice Burroughs' *The Chessmen of Mars*. You know—the golden handcuffs on the silken pillow signifying the unbreakable bond of wedlock."

"Some things never change," Stan said.

"But, about the FBI, that's a definitive no. We're moving to Los Angeles. Pasadena," he proclaimed.

"Pasadena? What's there that's not here?" Wendy asked.

Bonnie gave Wendy the envelope. Inside was a letter addressed to her from the Caltech—California Institute of Technology. One of the most prestigious scientific institutions in the world.

"What's this?"

"Read it."

Wendy opened it and read it out loud. "Dear Ms. Mendoza Flores—I am happy to announce your acceptance into the Ph.D. program in the Department of Theoretical Physics beginning Summer Semester."

"I've thought about things at length and this is what I really want."

"Theoretical physics—wow," Wendy said. "What about the police lab?"

"Although I enjoy the work and the people, I discovered I was really doing that because I thought my family wanted it. In reality, they want me to do what I'm best at. Perhaps I can meet others who are more . . . like me. You understand that, don't you?"

"Rest assured, there's *nobody* like you," he said.

"Yeah, but . . . Caltech, wow. That's one of the most difficult schools of all to get into," Wendy said. "But I guess I shouldn't be surprised. I wouldn't have made it into med school without your tutoring. What will you do with it when you're done?"

"Perhaps research, or working for the government, or as a consultant."

"What about you, Alex?" Stan asked.

"I've considered the practice, and I'm leaving."

"Is there a problem with it? I'm sure that there are some other good places available," Wendy said. "I guess you can't do it and live in LA."

"It's too crazy of a health care system for me, you know that? Seriously, though, I've decided to embark on a new career. You of all people should be happy with it."

"What?" Wendy asked.

"My experiences over the last few months have enlightened me to the number of medical errors that have the potential to do serious harm to people. I know the ones I encountered were due to malicious intent, but there are thousands of errors each day simply due to mistakes. How can we continue to function in this type of environment?"

"It appears that Dr. Darkkin here is planning to help his fellow man and woman. What a revelation," Bonnie exclaimed.

"I still don't understand what it is you're doing, Alex," Wendy asked. "Don't let sudden celebrity go to your head."

"I'm taking some medical policy courses, and will do some work at the hospital, serving on committees and such. I know that I won't get paid a lot, but, I have a good income from the software royalties, at least for now. I'll still work radiation oncology a few hours a week, to fill in."

"Do you really know what's involved with that?" Wendy asked. "There's not a lot of glamour in being a consultant."

"I think so. Hospitals and medicine in general have an extremely high error rate. If any corporation had that level of error rate, they'd be out of business."

"I don't think anyone will be hacking into databases giving people heavy water anytime soon," Bonnie said. "I hope that you will be focusing on more mainstream cases."

The politically astute pediatrician was excited. "That's great, Alex—but you're going to have to cut down on your style of living."

"That's okay. I gave those up a long time ago. There are more important things than money. Not too many, but a couple."

"You continue to astound me," Wendy said.

"What about the void in the hospital leadership?" he asked.

"They're looking for a new CEO. It may be hard to recruit someone good, given our history, but I'm on the search committee. Looks like they'll elect me president of the medical staff soon. You usually have to be on staff for five years, but they'll make an exception for me."

"I hope you'll be a better officer than good old Monte."

"I have one more question for you, Bonnie," Wendy asked.

"Yes?"

"How many names will you have after you get married?"

"Hmmm. Well, my full name will be Mendoza de Darkkin, but I will always casually go by Mendoza."

"So it really won't change for you, in most settings."

"No, but it will be important to our *niños*, of course, when they get older."

He turned blue as he choked on his coffee and almost required CPR from his sister.

• • •

Alex and Bonnie were packing up her things in late March for the move to Pasadena. He was grateful that the news media were no longer calling or knocking at his door on a daily basis. Wendy had enjoyed the CNN interview they did, but he didn't really care for the limelight. He still had no takers from pen companies about his marketing idea for heavy water-based fountain pen ink. And he was ready to forget about John Markham and start planning their wedding.

He knew Bonnie liked familiarity and had lived in San Diego her whole life. Moving away even a short distance would be challenging for her. But he would be there to help.

"You still don't speak of your recent visit with Conrad. I'm sorry if my prior impression of him was true."

"They were right on the money, as usual."

"I thought you used to think highly of him."

"Things change. I found out a lot of stuff I didn't know before. Some of the things he's done—I just can't deal with it."

"Sorry. Do you wish to share them with me?"

"No—I can't turn back time. I want to just forget about him for awhile. Maybe forever."

"I wish I could help. I seem to be good at forgetting things."

They continued packing boxes for the next half hour before stopping for a snack.

"I've never moved away before."

"It's only 110 miles, less than a two hour drive. You can come back whenever you want."

"I know you've lived a lot of different places."

"Not that many. It's the people you're with that are the most important, anyway."

"I guess so. I have some buyers for the condo, but it'll be sad to leave it. I guess I could rent it out."

"Why worry about that? It's just a place. The next one will be one that we pick out—ours."

"I know, it's just sentimental for me. I know that we probably had some special moments there. I wish I could remember." She started crying.

"You said they're with both of us since I remember. And we'll have lots of special moments again." He held her in his arms for a few minutes. "I'll always be here for you."

"Do you promise that?"

"Of course." They sat and cuddled for a half hour or so.

Afterwards he got up. "We need to get rid of some of this stuff. Do you need to take all of your magic equipment?" The entire collection of equipment weighed well over two hundred pounds.

"I will have little time for it at my new destination. Time to grow up. I am *Mendoza Milagroso* no more."

"Don't say that after all you've done for people. You need to keep in practice, and you can still help teach kids."

"I suppose so, and we will make new friends. I can always come back and do some charity events so Wendy can continue to raise money. What about the troubled hospital, though? What will become of it?"

"The Joint Commission gave Parkwood provisional accreditation, contingent on cleaning up their act. They wanted me to help them redesign their medical record system to help prevent intrusion. I did suggest some new mechanisms, but declined to be their official consultant. I enthusiastically recommended an expert who could probably do a better job than me."

"Crazy Jim?"

"Yeah. At least he'll be close by for the wedding." He had sold his condominium in Nashville and would use that money to purchase a similar place in Pasadena. Jim would help him run DarTech in addition to doing private consulting in San Diego. Alex planned on enrolling in a medical management program at UCLA while Bonnie was at Caltech.

He walked outside in the cool spring air. He would miss San Diego, as he reflected on how fortunate he was to have found things he didn't think were possible. Adversity served to make him a more compassionate and humble person.

Was he doing the right thing? Devoting his resources to helping make the medical world a better place? He always criticized his sister for doing that. But he had seen first-hand the devastating consequences of medical errors. The ones he had seen had been criminally engineered, but many others occurred throughout the country simply from human error. If a manufacturer operated with the same error rate as the medical profession, it would be bankrupt. Hospitals should be the safest places in the world, but why weren't they?

He also saw the folly of a single person becoming God. Dr. Montgomery Buechler, the penultimate narcissist, was one. His father was another. Did he really have such wickedness inside of him? He had his own destiny, one only he could control. But it was not until just then that he fully believed it.

His fiancé would also discover new things each day. There were others who could run the police laboratory as she embarked on a new career. But there wasn't anyone else with the unique gifts she possessed, or the oddities that could be very charming at times. What would she do without someone to watch over her?

Epilogue

Rain poured down mercilessly on the roof of Concata Community Hospital as Dr. Laura Baxter took the emergency call from the paramedics. Concata, a quiet town of 16,000 along the northern California coast, was a community typically devoid of excitement. That was about to change this foul-weathered June day.

"What's going on, Dr. Baxter?" the emergency room charge nurse asked.

"God, some prison van going to Pelican Bay slid off the road and crashed into the median. Carrying five prisoners. Four just banged up, but one's unresponsive. Guards are okay. Don't need this today. I wanted to watch the NBA Finals."

"Wow," the nurse said. "Not that much excitement around here in years."

Ten minutes later the ambulance pulled up to the emergency vehicle entry as the rain poured outside. The paramedics wheeled the patient into the small, 5-bed emergency department.

"What happened?" Dr. Baxter, in her late thirties, asked.

"Prisoner en route to the Bay. Slid off the road. Smashed into the cement divider, and he's out cold," the prison guard said.

"I guess he needs a CT, Doc," the paramedic said.

"We used to do that, but there's evidence that MRI can pick up diffuse axonal injury that is typical in the motor vehicle whiplash type accidents."

"You're gonna spend money on an MRI for this piece of dung? Don't want to tell you your business, but he's a lifer, they said. Going to Supermax."

"Well, I don't care what he's in for. He's a human being who deserves our best medical care. Don't *ever* let me hear you say that again, Knapp."

"I got a right to my opinion. But you're the doctor, so, whatever. He's your problem now."

The prisoner was unconscious, with several facial lacerations, but breathing on his own. "What's his name?" she asked.

The officer gave the technician his file; the tech then pulled up the prisoner's medical record after linking to the correctional system's database. "Terrell Lewis. Forty—one years old, born in England. Life sentence for cyber crime terrorism. No medical problems, no surgeries."

"Okay. Get an EKG, blood gas, basic metabolic panel, drug screen. Start an IV—D5 lactated ringers' at 200 ml/hr." The technicians performed the electrocardiogram and drew blood while the nurse started an IV line. "Get a pulse ox too, so we can see what his oxygen saturation is."

The nurse attached the finger monitoring device. "Normal. Ninety—four percent."

"Okay. Hook him up to three liters of oxygen," she said. The nurse attached a plastic nasal cannula and dialed the oxygen to supply three liters per minute. "Get him to MRI stat. And get all those handcuffs and things off before you go in the suite. Magnet will lift him clean off the table."

They wheeled him into the radiology suite of the small community hospital. The unconscious Lewis lay on the table as he was placed into the MRI machine. As the technicians fired up the magnets, he began seizing.

"What the hell? Call a code." The radiology technician pressed the blue "code blue" button which brought Dr. Baxter and a number of other medical personnel into the room.

"What's going on?" she asked.

"Fired up the magnet, and he started seizing."

He wasn't breathing. Baxter pulled the laryngoscope from the crash cart and inserted an endotracheal tube while the respiratory therapist bagged him. She then began chest compressions.

"The rhythm's ventricular fibrillation. Defibrillate with 200 joules, and give epi stat."

The physician's assistant discharged the electrical energy through Lewis' lifeless body while the nurses gave the intravenous epinephrine. "300 joules." He defibrillated again, and finally a third time at 360 joules.

"Agonal rhythm, Dr. Baxter."

"Give another round of meds. Now."

Six minutes later she ended the futile resuscitation effort. "He's dead. Tell me again what happened exactly."

"He was unconscious but stable until we started the scan, then this happened."

She pondered for a few minutes. "This is a dumb question, but does he have metal in his head?"

"Of course not, Doc Baxter. We looked up his records. He even had a CT scan a couple of months ago, for headaches." He showed her the CT on the monitor. "Do you think we're that careless?"

"Did you do a scout film?" Scout films were done to survey for metallic objects before MRI was started.

"No, since we had the recent electronic films. You said you wanted it stat, and that would've taken ten more minutes."

"Shit, he's dead now."

"Don't mean to be callous, but who gives a shit? No one will miss this worthless piece of crap."

"I care, dammit. He was a human being," she said, throwing a Clystarr antibiotic pen across the room. "Can we at least see what the scans showed? Not that it changes anything, but I need it for my report."

The technician put the prisoner back into the MRI unit long enough to procure several basic images.

"Damn," he said as he showed her a brain full of blood. "Look at that. He must've gotten that bleed in the accident."

She pondered for a few seconds. "No way—it looks too fresh, and there's no way he'd still be alive with that big hemorrhage. He'd have been toast at the wreck site."

"I'll look at some other views, Doc."

Dr. Baxter stared at the image on the screen and turned white. "Look—a metallic artifact. This guy's got an aneurysm clip, and you missed it. Magnet pulled it and tore the artery. You killed him, you dumb ass!"

"Hold on. It's not in the medical record, so don't blame me. You saw the CT, too."

She was going to have to fill out a lot of paperwork for this one. "I don't get it. Those electronic scans have to be right, don't they?"

"Yeah. Complete Data Systems went bankrupt and we just started using this new imaging software from DarTech—it's supposed to be state of the art. The prison system must've screwed up the records. Not the first time *that's* happened."

THE END

About The Author

J. Matthew Neal is a native of Indiana and has been a practicing endocrinologist since 1993. He earned undergraduate and medical degrees from Indiana University and a Master of Business Administration degree from the University of Massachusetts. He is currently Director of the Internal Medicine Residency at Ball Memorial Hospital (Muncie, IN) and Clinical Professor of Medicine at the Indiana University School of Medicine. He has over ten years' experience in medical administration and has served in various governance roles in regional medical societies.

Dr. Neal is the author of three medical textbooks: Case Studies in Endocrinology, Diabetes, and Metabolism (Lippincott Williams & Wilkins), Basic Endocrinology (Blackwell Science), and How The Endocrine System Works (Blackwell Science). He has also authored numerous peer-reviewed medical articles relating to endocrinology. This is his first novel.

Printed in the United States
95304LV00002B/578/A